A PHOENIX
IS
FOREVER

ASHLYN CHASE

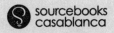
sourcebooks
casablanca

Published by Sourcebooks Casablanca, an imprint of Sourcebooks, Inc.
P.O. Box 4410, Naperville, Illinois 60567-4410
(630) 961-3900
Fax: (630) 961-2168
sourcebooks.com

Printed and bound in the United States of America.
OPM 10 9 8 7 6 5 4 3 2 1

Readers Love Ashlyn Chase's Dragon and Phoenix Shifters!

"Shapeshifting done right! This fast-paced romance is a must-read."

—*RT Book Reviews*, 4 Stars, for *Hooked on a Phoenix*

"This fantastic story will enliven your day and keep you smiling."

—*Night Owl Reviews* TOP PICK, 4½ Stars, for *Hooked on a Phoenix*

"What could be better than hot firefighters who shift into dragons and phoenixes? Another great story from the talented Chase."

—*RT Book Reviews*, 4 Stars, for *Never Dare a Dragon*

"Hot and hilarious. This one is a must-read."

—*Night Owl Reviews* TOP PICK, 5 Stars, for *Never Dare a Dragon*

"Readers will enjoy the banter as well as the steamy encounters that set them aflame."

—*RT Book Reviews*, 4 Stars, for *My Wild Irish Dragon*

"Fantastic. How can you not fall in love with this book, sexy firefighters, both male and female, magical creatures that use their powers for good, a snarky Mother Nature, interfering family members, and some charming Irish accents? Seriously, if you haven't read this one yet, I highly suggest you get it as soon as possible."

—*Night Owl Reviews* TOP PICK, 5 Stars, for *My Wild Irish Dragon*

Also by Ashlyn Chase

This book is dedicated to all the police officers who let me go with a warning, investigated a strange noise outside my window, or had a little chat with a troublesome neighbor…

But especially, this book is dedicated to the officer (who does not want to be named because he was technically outside his job description) who went above and beyond to rescue my fur baby.

Thank you, gentlemen and ladies! You aren't appreciated enough.

Chapter 1

HE WAS ACTUALLY A COP. A REAL, BONA FIDE POLICE OFFICER.

Luca Fierro walked out of the precinct wearing his new BPD uniform as a Boston patrolman trainee. As the new guy, he would be on the graveyard shift for a while with his more experienced field training officer, Joe.

Luca had already taken plenty of ribbing from the guys during roll call. They all knew the Fierro name because his family were legendary firefighters.

"Hey, Fierro, aren't you wearing the wrong uniform?"

He just smiled or said, "Very funny, guys."

"So how does it feel to be a genuine cop, not a cadet?" Joe asked.

"You don't remember? How long have you been on the job?"

Joe laughed. "Fifteen fun-filled years." They paused a moment to get into their cruiser. Joe took the driver's seat. He may have carried an extra twenty or thirty pounds, but he seemed agile enough.

"Did you have a difficult adjustment?" Luca asked as he buckled his seat belt.

"Not really. My dad was a cop, so that may have helped me ease into the job."

Luca couldn't help being uncomfortable. Some cops had real problems with firefighters. They called them "hose draggers" and didn't like being accused of "pillow envy," because firefighters were allowed to sleep on the night shift.

Similarly, the firefighters weren't always fond of cops. His own family called him the "blue sheep."

Luca answered the original question. "I feel good about finally getting started on the job. I've trained long and hard for this."

Joe was quiet as he pulled out of the station's parking lot, so Luca continued. "My folks weren't in favor of my going into law enforcement, but they were okay with my studying criminal justice at Northeastern University. They thought I'd change my mind after learning what was involved. If anything, studying the subject made me want it even more."

"Oh, shit," Joe said. "You're a college grad? You know why it's called a BS degree, right? You know too much to be clueless but not enough to deal with those weird situations they didn't prepare you for." He smirked.

"In other words, you think I know just enough to be dangerous?"

"Maybe. What did they teach you there?"

"All kinds of things. Ethics, courtroom procedures, criminal law, corrections, crime scene management, computer investigation, domestic and international terrorism... I want to be a detective someday."

Joe nodded.

Luca had to get used to one of the aspects of being a cop, and that was not giving too much away. Just answer the questions you're asked and no more. Sometimes volunteering information got you into hot water.

He'd have to guard his family's secrets even more carefully.

Joe turned onto a busy street. Luca wondered how long it would be before Joe felt comfortable trading off driving duties.

"So, fifteen years… You must've seen it all."

"You've never seen it all, kid. You might hear about some crazy stuff at the bar though. If it doesn't happen to you, it's happened to someone else."

Patrolling the city was sometimes tedious and sometimes terrifying. It was that on-and-off pace and the fact of never knowing what was around the corner that both intrigued and made most first-years anxious, to say the least.

It wasn't long before they came across a car speeding and driving erratically. "Shit," Joe said. "I might chalk that up to a typical Boston driver, but the damn car almost sideswiped us."

Luca made a quick call to dispatch, notifying them of the ten code, the vehicle's description, and their approximate location. They turned on the lights and took off after it, spotting the car climbing the ramp onto the Southeast Expressway.

"Dammit," Joe swore. "I hate stopping drivers on the expressway."

"Can't you get them to pull off at the next exit?"

"We can hope." Joe went in pursuit of the black Mercedes sedan. Instead of taking the next off-ramp, the driver pulled over and stopped right on the bridge.

"Fuck. This is going to slow traffic to a crawl."

"Can I approach the driver?" Luca asked.

Joe opened his door. "Be my guest."

Luca, noting only one person in the vehicle, knocked on the passenger-side window, and she rolled it down.

Yep, he smelled alcohol. And this woman looked almost clown-like with the amount of heavy makeup she was wearing. "License and registration, please."

The woman heaved a vodka-laced sigh, dug through her purse, and produced a wallet. She removed and handed over a current Massachusetts driver's license. Then she opened the glove compartment, found her registration, and handed that to him also.

He scanned the information and said, "Do you know why we stopped you, Priscilla?"

"I have no idea."

"You've been driving erratically. Have you been drinking?"

"I am not drunk."

"Step out of the car, please."

The woman sat right where she was and folded her arms.

"You can prove you're sober with a field sobriety test, ma'am. Please step out of the car."

"I don't have to. I don't have to take a Breathalyzer, and I don't have to walk a straight line. I know my rights."

"I'm sure you do, ma'am, but we'll have to take you in to the station if we suspect you're drunk. I smell alcohol, and you've been speeding and weaving all over the road, so you're giving me no other choice. The public's safety is at stake."

"You'll have to drag me out of this car."

"Ma'am, at this point, you're forcing me to place you under arrest. If you don't exit the car, you'll be adding a charge of resisting arrest. Is that really what you want to do?"

She blew out another deep, vodka-heavy breath. The door flew open, and Luca met her in front of the vehicle while Joe ran the plate.

Luca was almost six feet tall. This woman had to be six two *without* the stilettos. That made her about six and a half feet…and wobbling.

"Turn around and put your hands on the car, please."

The woman placed her hands on her hips and looked at him defiantly.

Luca raised his voice. "Turn around and place your hands on the hood of your car. Now."

"Why? Are you going to pat me down?"

"At some point, yes. We need to know you're not carrying any concealed weapons."

By this time, Joe was rolling his eyes and came over to join him. "Lady, you're going to be frisked, but that can happen later." He gave Luca a pointed look. "Cuff her up."

"You're not touching me!"

"Jesus," Luca muttered. He gazed at Joe, hoping he would have the right words to gain her cooperation, but it didn't look like Joe had any such magic. Instead, he reached out, grabbed her arm, and spun her so her torso was leaning against the car. Meanwhile, he had her arm in a viselike grip behind her back.

"Owww. You're hurting me."

"Cuff her, Fierro," Joe said.

Luca took her other wrist and folded it behind her back. He had his cuffs out, but she struggled as soon as he tried to put them on her.

"Don't resist."

She struggled harder. "Leave me alone. You guys are brutalizing me. I'm going to file a complaint."

"Please do. Our dash cam will show you've been given several chances to cooperate."

At that point, she flipped around and ran across the highway, causing cars to stop and blow their horns. Luca gave chase. He eventually had to tackle her to keep her from crossing the line into oncoming traffic. Once he had her on the ground, he was able to cuff the other wrist.

Shit. I have to learn to get the handcuffs out faster— but not too fast. There were a lot of things he could do quicker and better than a human, but he couldn't give away his paranormal abilities. He had superhuman strength and speed, but a cop wouldn't let it go if they witnessed something out of the ordinary. And he'd be in *so* much trouble with the paranormal community if he let humans know what he really was.

Joe joined him and the two of them lifted her to her feet. She immediately started kicking and screaming. They had to half lead and half drag her across the road, back to their cruiser.

"You see?" She was yelling at the cars that had stopped. "You see the brutality? I want witness statements. I want you all to call the Boston police commissioner and tell him what you've seen."

Luca and Joe were beyond reasoning with her at this point. Joe just opened the back door of the cruiser and told her to get in.

"I don't want to. Make me."

Luca shook his head. *What the fuck do we do now? Fold her in half and put her in there like a quesadilla?*

Apparently, pushing on her head and shoving her

into the back seat, then grappling with those long legs and spiky heels was the only option.

"Knock it off, lady. Kicking a police officer with shoes like that is a felony in the Commonwealth of Massachusetts," Joe shouted.

"Ha! I don't believe you."

"We can add it to the charges if that will convince you."

As soon as she had been stuffed into the seat and seatbelted securely, Luca slammed the door shut and joined Joe in the front seat. "Holy shit. That is one determined woman," he muttered.

"Yup. This one's feisty."

As a car pulled around them, the passenger rolled down his window and yelled out, "It took two of you to arrest a girl. Pussies!" Then he and the driver laughed and drove off.

Wonderful. Adolescent humor. Just what we needed.

"I have to pee," said Priscilla from the back seat.

"We'll be at the station in a few minutes," Joe replied, glancing up at the rearview mirror, then he turned to Luca. "Officer Fierro, would you be good enough to read our collar her rights?"

"Crap," he muttered. With all the distractions, he'd forgotten about the damn Miranda rights. What a rookie mistake. "You have the right to remain silent."

Priscilla began singing. "Silent night, holy night…"

Luca tried raising his voice to be heard over her, but that only made her sing louder.

"Oh, for fuck's sake." Then he joined in and sang her her rights to the tune of the famous Christmas carol. "*You have the right to an attorney. If you can't afford one, one will be appointed. If you decide to answer questions now, you have the right to stop until you talk to an attorney...*"

"All right! All right!" she yelled. "Just stop. Your voice is worse than mine."

"Great." He finished the speech in a normal voice. "So, do you understand your rights as I've explained them to you?"

"Yes."

"Are you willing to answer my questions without an attorney present?"

"No. Not until I pee first. I'm apt to wet your back seat if I don't get to a bathroom soon."

"It wouldn't be the first time," Joe muttered. He had Luca call the station and inform them of the arrest and where the tow truck could find her car.

Their passenger was singing again. She certainly wasn't a lounge singer, but now she was crying too. Her voice wobbled and cracked as she belted out a loud rendition of "Rudolph the Red-Nosed Reindeer."

Luca glanced over at Joe and raised his eyebrows. It wasn't Christmas. It wasn't even Halloween yet. He couldn't wait to get to the station they had left only forty minutes ago.

"So, is this normal for a Monday night?" Luca asked.

"Normal?" Joe chuckled. "Fridays are usually heavy OUI nights, but nothing is 'normal.'"

"Okay. Let me rephrase. Do you deal with this often? Including this level of uncooperativeness?"

"Her? This is nothing. Just wait until you have to arrest a suspect wearing green in a rowdy crowd on St. Patrick's Day."

After his first shift, Luca was exhausted, but the adrenaline that surged through his veins would keep him awake for quite a while. He decided to call his girlfriend, Lisa, hoping she was awake. All he wanted was to curl up with her. Unfortunately, they rarely had a place where they could get horizontal.

Neither her parents nor his knew they were dating. Hers because her father was a hard-ass cop and hated firefighters, and his because his mother would have them walking down the aisle in a month. They'd started dating in college, and both of them commuted from home. Their living situations had led them to have sex in some pretty unusual places—including once in a church!

Lisa's father was a police sergeant, and if Luca had to admit it, hoping to gain his approval was one of the reasons why he had chosen to become a cop instead of a firefighter. He'd already been ninety-five percent there in his decision, but his feelings for Lisa tipped his decision to one hundred percent.

Luca had also hoped that he could remove the "fear of the unknown" factor if he was known to her father through the police department.

At first, it was fun to keep their relationship a secret from their families. He fancied himself the bad boy, sneaking around for a couple of years, but it had begun to grate on Luca. He hated keeping secrets from loved ones, but his entire life was a secret, so he could do it. Lisa had no idea what he truly was and what he could actually do. But he'd cross that bridge later.

On his way home, he called Lisa with his car's
Bluetooth technology.

A sleepy hello greeted him.

"Hi, beautiful. It's Luca."

"I know. Your ringtone is 'secret lover.'"

He groaned. "Aren't you afraid that will tip off
your father?"

"No. The only radio he listens to is the police
scanner."

"Well, speaking of that, I just worked my first shift."

She yawned. "How did it go?"

"Terrible. I was hoping you could meet me somewhere. I think I need a hug."

She laughed. "Buck up. I can't always be there to
give you a hug after a tough shift."

Luca wasn't thrilled with that answer. Sure, he didn't
expect her to drop everything and run to him every time
he had a bad day. He wasn't a baby—despite being
the youngest, and all his older brothers accusing him
of being coddled. That was another reason he'd chosen
to be a cop instead of a firefighter. He wanted to show
them he was as brave and tough as they were—if not
more so.

"I know that, but this was my very first shift, and it
makes me wonder if they're all this rough. Do you want
to hear about my bruises?"

"Not particularly."

What the hell? She wasn't usually so cranky. Well,
she could be, but not when he was vulnerable. "What
gives? Are you having a bad day already? It sounds like
you just woke up."

"No. I'm not having a bad day. I'm having a bad

several months. I thought you becoming a cop would be okay since you were aiming for detective someday. They make decent money—not the crap salary they're paying you to get beat up now. But it's not just the money. I'm afraid you'll become hardened like my dad."

"I'm not your dad. Not even close."

"Did you meet him?"

"Yeah. He was in on a practical joke that just topped off my night."

"Oh, come on. You had to expect them to prank the rookie." After a long sigh, she said, "Okay. What did they do?"

"Someone broke into my locker, stole my car keys, moved my car, and put the keys back. I thought my car had been stolen."

She laughed. "That's a good one."

Good? Luca could barely believe what he was hearing. "Lisa. It wasn't just that. They tried to make me think I'd forgotten where I'd parked it. That maybe I was crazy and didn't even own a car. They were trying to *humiliate* me."

"And what did you do?"

"I was about to put out a BOLO when they finally told me where they'd put it—and laughed like hyenas."

"In other words, you played right into their hands."

"Huh? No! What the hell is going on with you, hon? I called to get a little sympathy, and you're being…well, very unsympathetic." He would never call her a bitch— even though she was acting like one.

"Look, Luca. I've been having second thoughts… about us. I've been wanting to tell you this for a while, and this might not be the best timing, but it's got to be said. I don't think you're cut out for police work. Nobody knows you better than I do, right? By the time you make detective, they'll have broken you. I don't want to be shackled to a broken man."

After a shocked pause, he sputtered, "Why are you telling me this now? I've committed to being a cop. Hell, I've just had my first shift and it beat the crap out of me."

"That was your choice. I thought you were just trying to say 'Up yours' to your family. I still do."

"Why would I do that? I have a good relationship with my family, or I did before I said I wanted to be a cop."

"Okay, okay. Look, it doesn't matter what your reasons were. I want to see other people."

And there it was. The bottom had just dropped out of his world.

Instead of going straight home, Luca parked nearby and started to walk off his hurt and frustration. He wasn't in the best part of town, but he didn't care. He wasn't in the best mood either. How the heck had he gotten to this point in his life? Up until a short while ago, he had been hopeful about his future. Now, he wasn't so sure. Still wearing his police uniform, he stuffed his hands in his jacket pockets and walked aimlessly with his head down.

Half an hour later, nearing the fountain of the Christian Science Center, a popular destination for tourists and locals alike, he barely noticed the regal elegance of the domed structure overlooking the calm reflecting pool. But in the quiet of the early morning, his ears perked up in sudden alert when he heard a woman's strained gasp.

He glanced up and saw a young woman standing near the fountain. She was about five six with short, spiky brown hair, wearing a black leather jacket. Neck tattoos and a lot of piercings gave her a bad-girl vibe, but what was even odder was that she was staring right at him, wide-eyed. Then she passed out.

"Shit," he muttered and ran over—faster than a human could. Worried she could wind up with a concussion, he cradled her head before she hit the pavement. He shook her shoulder and shouted, "Hey! Are you all right?"

Eventually, she opened her eyes. Big gray-green eyes. Unusual. Supporting her back, he helped her sit up.

"What's the matter?" He was tempted to ask if she'd ever seen a cop before, but that was because he was in a crappy mood. Sarcasm aside, he was trained not to assume what was going on in a person's brain. Asking open-ended questions would gain more information.

"I...saw blood." She paused and closed those big green eyes again, taking a deep breath. "I always faint at the sight of blood."

"What do you mean? You saw an accident or someone get hurt?" Luca gentled his voice in concern. Perhaps she'd witnessed a murder and had a delayed reaction.

She shook her head and reached out to grasp his hand. "Look, this may sound crazy," she said, "but I'm a psychic. I saw you walking this way, and I got a dreadful feeling. Did something just happen to you? I see auras and have premonitions. Your aura is just…well, terrible. Then I had a vision. I saw you covered in blood."

Blood? Luca helped her to stand. He believed in psychics—the genuine kind. After all, he was a shape-shifter, and he came from a family of shifters. But there were a lot of charlatans out there.

Given where his head was at after just being dumped by Lisa, he could only imagine what kind of energy he was giving off, let alone his aura…but blood? This chick could just be some wacko.

He folded his arms. "Do you want money to tell me more?"

"No! I'm not like that. I help people. Maybe the accident I just saw is something you can prevent from happening."

He cocked his head. "You saw an accident? Where?"

"On a side street. It looked like an older part of town. They were just kids. Maybe sixteen or seventeen at the most. It looked like they were drag racing. A little kid rode his bike into the street and he was struck by one of the cars."

"What does that have to do with me?"

"I don't know. Sometimes I see through other people's eyes. I think I was looking through yours."

Luca wanted to stay open-minded in case she was the real deal.

"Some more weird energy is clinging to you," she went on, her expression seeming earnest. "I think it has to do with other people in your life. Your aura is red. Angry. But it feels justified—and not just that. I-I feel as if someone is out to get you."

Who could be out to get him? Was it just his fellow

cops, taking advantage of the rookie? Doubtful. That was just for their own chuckles and part of the usual hazing. Something all newbies went through.

No, his dark mood was due to getting dumped. Lisa had acted strange that morning, but he didn't see her as a danger. Did she have someone else already, and maybe that someone considered him a threat?

He was still mulling over the possibilities when the spiky-haired girl pulled out a card and wrote her name and number on the back.

"I'm sorry if you think I'm trying to take advantage of you. I'm not. Knowing that cops are usually close-minded about psychics, I wouldn't have even bothered, except I think you're in danger. And those kids certainly are."

Glancing at the card, he saw the name she'd written. *Dawn Forest.* He flipped the card over. It read *ScholarTech: Academic Software for Brilliant Minds.*

"Is that your real name?"

"Yeah. If I were going to come up with a fake name, it would be better than that."

"You mean something exotic, like *Zelda the Magnificent*?"

She laughed. "No. Something like Susan Jones. I don't think my mom realized how many times people would ask me if my name was fake or if my middle name was 'in-the.'"

"So you work at this software company?" He wondered why someone who looked like her, with her tats and piercings, would be working for a company that created academic software.

"Yes, I just started there last month. Someday,

I'll get my own business cards instead of the generic ones."

"Your look doesn't exactly scream 'corporate head office.'"

"Well, your assumption is outdated," she retorted, hands firmly on her hips. "I have a college degree and was top in my class. Not to mention, I'm the only person at ScholarTech, including the engineers, who can recite the entire software manual by heart."

"Wow. And you've only been there a month? How did you learn everything in so short a time?"

"I have a photographic memory."

"You're a psychic and you have a photographic memory? Shouldn't you be raking in the big bucks on Wall Street?" Luca flashed her his trademark grin. It usually got him out of hot water. She smiled back and visibly relaxed.

He took a good look at her, past the tats and piercings and spiky hair, and noticed how pretty she was. Her nose was slightly turned up and covered with cute freckles. The tiny diamond stud in her left nostril almost got lost among them. Her hair made her look like a pixie. Maybe the badass tattoos and piercings were a way to counter-act all that cuteness and be taken seriously.

"So do you do anything with your psychic talent, professionally?"

"Like working at a tea room? Or doing parties? No."

"Anything other than stopping strangers on the street?"

She looked at her feet and kicked at the pavement with the end of her leather-booted toe. "Sometimes. If friends ask me for help, I do what I can for them."

There was something about her body language that had him questioning that statement.

He tucked her business card into his jacket pocket. "It was nice to meet you, Dawn Forest. I should be getting home though. I worked the night shift, and I need to get some sleep."

"Okay. Watch your back," she said and returned to her spot by the fountain to retrieve her backpack.

When he finally reached his family's brownstone, he jogged up the steps and tried to change his facial expression. His mother would pick up on any tension or anger he might still be feeling. He and his brothers teased their mom about being psychic, but she was just intuitive and knew her sons well.

He wondered about what Dawn Forest had said to him. Had she seen something real in his future—some kind of danger to an unsuspecting child that he could actually prevent? Could she have a genuine gift? He certainly didn't rule it out, based on his own abilities and the abilities of his family. Plus she seemed so earnest and not high or strung out, something his cop training had made him all too aware of when moving around the city streets.

After taking a few deep breaths and straightening his posture, he opened the door and strode in confidently.

Gabriella Fierro came out of the kitchen with a platter of scrambled eggs that she placed on the enormous dining table. "Luca! You're just in time for breakfast. I want to hear all about your first day on the job."

"First night, you mean. I'm exhausted, Ma. I just want to fall into bed." He warred with himself. He wanted those scrambled eggs almost as much as he wanted his pillow.

"I'll bet. But you'll sleep better if you have something in your stomach."

"Unless you just ate a bunch of doughnuts." His
father, always the joker, came from the kitchen carrying
a plate piled high with slices of toast in one hand and the
butter dish in the other.

Ah, the hell with it. "Would you mind if I just made a
breakfast sandwich and took it to my room?"

Gabriella was moving toward the silverware drawer
but stopped and turned around. "Did something happen
that you don't want to talk about?"

"Damn," he muttered.

"Please, Son. Sit," Antonio Fierro said. As much as
his father loved to joke around, he also knew when to
be serious.

Luca's posture sagged, and he slumped into a dining
chair.

"So, tell us what happened." Gabriella finished
gathering the silverware and distributed it to the three
of them.

Luca let out a long sigh. "I don't know what to
say. I guess it was a normal shift, but I got the rookie
treatment at the end. They hid my car. I thought it had
been stolen."

"Oh, honey. That's mean. I'm sorry to hear they did
that."

"Cops." His father practically spat the word and
shook his head.

"It's okay. I figured they'd do something. I'm considering it a rite of passage."

Luca took two pieces of toast and scooped some
scrambled eggs between them. His mother always

seasoned them with salt, pepper, and a few hot spices. They were always delicious, and this morning, the comfort food hit the spot.

He was suddenly glad he hadn't moved in with Lisa. He could only imagine how he would have felt going home to his apartment after a bad first day at work, only to be dumped by his girlfriend in bed.

They dug into their food and didn't speak while they ate. Luca figured he'd dodged a bullet...figuratively, so far.

"Did something else happen? You seemed to take the prank in stride." Gabriella's sharp mind picked up on the rest of his crap. What could he tell her that would satisfy her curiosity but not alarm her? He didn't want to tell them he'd had a secret girlfriend since his junior year and all those trips to the library were a ruse. But Dawn wasn't Lisa.

"There was this weird girl. She stopped me and said something about being a psychic and picking up some strange energy. I doubt it was anything."

"Did she want money?" his father asked with eyes narrowed. His dad was shrewd, and his mind usually went to scammers.

"No. If she had, I would've kept walking. But there was something real about her... I don't know how to describe it. Her concern seemed genuine."

"Did you ask what she meant by strange energy?" Gabriella asked.

"Yeah. We talked for a couple of minutes. I think it was just the long shift, my being tired, and maybe the prank on top of everything else."

"Everything else? What does that mean?"

Damn. His mother had the instincts of a seasoned police detective. She picked up on the smallest things.

"Forget it, Mom. Nothing much happened. Just a drunk driving arrest, a bar fight with a few mouthy spectators, and a lot of driving around."

"So you kept the public safe and had a successful shift?" she asked.

"Yeah. I guess so." He gulped down the rest of his sandwich, yawned, and said, "I really need to hit the sack. Thanks for breakfast. Just put the leftovers in the fridge and I'll microwave them later."

Gabriella glanced at her husband.

"Good night, Son. Or should I say good sleep?" Antonio smiled.

"Thanks, Dad." Luca escaped to his bedroom in the finished basement, determined to turn off his brain and indeed get some sleep—if he could.

Chapter 2

DAWN HAD WORRIED SO MUCH ABOUT THE COP THAT morning that she'd handed him her new work phone number at ScholarTech. What an idiotic thing to do! She knew better. *Always keep a low profile, Dawn!* With her past, she shouldn't even be seen talking to a cop.

At least she wasn't in her neighborhood when she'd met him. She had stopped off at the Christian Science Center before work. It was something she'd started doing to help "center" herself. She loved the fountain and the massive pool. She would sit on a bench and gaze at it for a while before heading to her job.

Unfortunately, Dawn had to be careful about how and when she moved around town because of the gang she'd gotten mixed up in from the age of fifteen. Dawn had been involved with the gang for three years until she had decided it was time to turn her life around. One of her girlfriends, who'd been with Mick, one of the leaders of Keene Street Gang, had overdosed. That was Dawn's wake-up call to get out.

They still managed to track Dawn down whenever they needed her "advance warning system," aka her psychic abilities. Especially when an illegal deal was about to go down. Dawn wasn't happy about still being on their radar, but she had no choice. Once you were in, they felt like they owned you until you died or managed to go off the grid.

The problem was that she couldn't afford to go into hiding or even leave town, for that matter. She had her grandma to look after, and she needed to save up before they could even think of heading somewhere warm and cheap, where she could take care of the one person who had never given up on her. She'd been working at ScholarTech for the past month and had started to save toward a little nest egg, but she was a long way from making her dream come true.

Stepping off the subway train two blocks from her house, Dawn made sure her "don't mess with me" attitude was firmly in place. She carried her keys attached to a steel baton that she had made good use of when walking through the streets after dark. Her neighborhood wasn't the best place to live and certainly not the safest. One day, she vowed, she and her grandma would get the hell out of Boston. The crime rate was high and the sense of security was low.

Home not-so-sweet home.

Dawn and her grandmother, Annette, lived in a small, two-story duplex house. It was spotless and uncluttered, unlike some of the other houses in the neighborhood where people tended to accumulate junk like it would magically turn into mountains of gold. Annette always said, "No sense buying something you don't need or needing something you can't buy." Dawn didn't mind that the house was small. What she did mind was the crime-filled location. Dawn threw a quick glance over her shoulder before taking her key out of her pocket. Just as she opened her front door, a male figure stepped out from the dark side yard of the old, battered colonial next door.

Crap.

It was Ice Spider, her one-time boyfriend and a member of the Keene Street Gang.

"Hey, what's up?" she asked, trying to remain non-chalant as she gripped her keys.

"You tell me." He waltzed up the steps and leaned on the railing. "Anything tripping your wires lately?"

She wasn't going to tell him about the cute young cop from that morning, so she just shrugged. "Why? You got something to worry about?"

He snorted. "You know better than to ask that. If you're in, you're in. If you're out, you're out."

"I'm out, so why do you keep coming back?"

He sidled up next to her. "I hope you'll change your mind."

Trying to hide her anxiety, Dawn stood her ground. "I know you want a psychic heads-up to 'conduct business' when the cops aren't around, but I don't like being used. I really do want to move on."

"I wasn't using you. How many times do I have to tell you, she didn't mean anything to me, baby. We can go back to the way things were."

Dawn suppressed the urge to roll her eyes. "I wasn't even talking about that. Look, Ice, I'm really sorry, but it's not gonna happen. I've got things to do."

She opened the door, stepped inside, and was ready to close it in his face if she had to. Her grandmother was home, and she never wanted them to meet.

"So where are you working now?"

What could she say? There was no way she was going to tell him she was working at ScholarTech. "Nowhere."

"Why don't you go back to the convenience store? Carla could use your help."

She liked Carla, the owner, a no-nonsense woman who stood up to everyone, including the gang members. Carla had run the convenience store since before Dawn was born. A chain smoker whose idea of a breakfast drink was a vodka tonic, Carla was the unofficial den mother for the street kids who called Keene Street home.

Dawn had worked at the store for four years while she was going to school part-time to get her associates degree. But she had quit six months ago. Three hold-ups was her limit, thank you very much. The store was where many drug deals were made, and every so often, a rival gang would rob the place when they wanted to send Keene Street a message. *Stupid gang wars.* Besides, she'd been ready to leave and look for a career-oriented job anyway. "No. I'm still looking for work," she lied smoothly. She wasn't about to tell him her business.

He smiled and crossed his arms. "Well, isn't that something. I might have a job for you."

"I'm not interested. That part of my life is over." She began to close the door until he stuck his foot in the doorway.

The smile disappeared. "Fine. But say there is something big about to go down. Are you getting vibes? Any reason to think we could have problems?"

She paused for a moment. "No. I'm not getting any vibes."

"You sure? Because the cops have been spending more time in the hood lately."

"I'm sure."

He shrugged. "Okay. Good to know." He knocked on the railing and said, "Take care of yourself." Then he sauntered down the walk and turned into her neighbor's driveway. She didn't relax until she heard a clang as he vaulted over the chain-link fence behind the houses.

Dawn blew out a breath of relief as soon as she shut the door, locked it, and slid the dead bolt into place. She closed her eyes and leaned against it, composing herself before she had to see her grandmother.

"Dawnie, is that you?"

"Yeah, Gran."

Her grandmother met her in the tiny hallway. She looked about twenty years older than her fifty-six years. She'd been a young single mother, and Dawn's mother was also very young when she got pregnant. It was part of the cycle when you were poor and didn't have many options. Dawn was determined to break that cycle. She had succeeded so far. She just needed to keep saving and steer clear of the lowlifes she used to hang with.

"Is everything all right?" Annette eyed her with suspicion.

"It's nothing to worry about, Grandma. You always say I have a good head on my shoulders, and you're right. I'm taking care of myself."

Her grandmother's posture relaxed and she smiled. "I know, honey. I'm very proud of you. How did work go today?"

"Good. Nancy, my assistant manager, thinks I'm a whiz with the software."

"I knew your going to college was a good idea. You're the first college graduate in our family. I'm so proud of you. Even better things are coming. I can feel it."

"It's only an associate's degree."

"Never say 'it's only' about your accomplishments.

You've really turned your life around. It's more than anyone else in this family has done."

"I guess. Thanks, Gran." Dawn didn't want her grandmother to know the gang was still keeping tabs on her. It would just worry the older woman, and she worried enough. At least Dawn hadn't repeated the pattern of teenage pregnancy. She may have gone through a rebellious phase, but that wasn't part of it. *Thank goodness for Planned Parenthood!*

Dawn smiled at her grandmother and then jogged up the stairs to her small room. She fell on her bed and took a few deep breaths. Something about that cop kept flitting through her mind. She didn't think it was just the fact that he was about six feet tall and drop-dead gorgeous. Or that his dark hair and cobalt-blue eyes captivated her like no one had in...well, ever.

Even if she hadn't sensed some disturbing energy around him, she may have wanted to stop and talk to him anyway. She had noticed the name on his uniform. Fierro. He was probably Italian, but maybe his family came from the northern part of Italy. She had heard there were blue-eyed people in the Italian Alps.

She daydreamed about other countries sometimes. She was barely getting a fresh start in this one. If she had the money, she'd want to go somewhere warm, where it was sunny all year. Unfortunately, she didn't have the money, and her incarcerated mother needed her close for the time being.

Her grandmother had done her best, but her mother had landed in jail anyway. Drugs were rampant all over the city but more so in poor areas like theirs. Her mom had latched onto dealing as a way to make enough money to get them out of there. At least that was the excuse she gave. By now, Dawn had realized her mom was feeding her own habit as well.

"The road to hell is paved with good intentions," her grandmother always said. Back when Dawn was little, she didn't know what that meant. Now, she did. Her mother described jail as hell.

She sensed someone in the doorway of her room and knew it was her grandma.

"May I come in?"

"Sure, Gran."

Annette perched on the edge of her bed. "I've been thinking…"

"Uh-oh."

She grinned, but only for a second. "I know we've talked about it before, but I really do think you need to move out of the city."

Dawn sighed. "And what are you going to do without me?"

"Same old, same old. I'll be here if you need me, but what I really want is for you to be safe and happy. I don't think you can do that here."

Dawn scooted to the edge of her bed next to her grandmother and laid her head on her shoulder. "I'm not going anywhere unless I can take you with me."

Annette chuckled. "That's sweet, child. But I don't drive and I don't want to be a burden. I'm too old to start over somewhere else. You're not. You have your whole life ahead of you."

Dawn hardly knew what to say. Her grandmother wasn't old, and she *could* start over, but convincing her to try seemed like more of a struggle than it was worth, at least for the time being. Once she'd saved enough, then she would think about it. Her mother would be in jail for another five years, but Dawn couldn't wait that long. She would have enough money saved up in a year, and she and her grandma could move to Florida, Texas, or Arizona, and then when her mom got out of jail, they would have a nice home set up for her to come to.

"I'll think about it, Grandma."

Annette smirked. "I've heard that before. It usually means 'I just want you to stop talking about it.'"

The woman was insightful. She might be psychic but had never explained it much. If the sight was inherited, it must've skipped a generation. Her mother wouldn't have landed in jail if she had known the SWAT team was about to jump out of a nearby van while she was being used as a mule carrying heroin and meth.

"Grandma? Do you have more than just a psychic sense?" she asked abruptly.

Annette's eyes grew wide. "What makes you ask that, child?"

"I...I can sometimes feel things. Sometimes even see things in my mind—as if I'm looking out of someone else's eyes. And I can sense when something is going to happen ahead of time. And I dream...about things that happen."

Her grandmother heaved a deep sigh as though she were carrying a secret burden. "Well, I've never told you this, and I have no proof if it's true or not, but I was told that my grandmother was some kind of powerful witch."

Dawn's mouth dropped. Why had Annette never shared this with her before? "As in casting spells and all that?"

"I don't know. I was told my grandmother learned magic from a voodoo priestess. My mother refused to follow her ways. She left New Orleans when she was sixteen and traveled up north with a salesman. By the time she got to Boston, she was expecting me."

Dawn knew the rest of the story, how Annette's mother, Fleur, had run off with the salesman with the dimples, gotten pregnant, and then was left to fend for herself. Fleur had worked hard her entire life but could never make ends meet. She died before the age of fifty of a stroke while she was mopping the steps. Annette had been thirty-three at the time with her own daughter, Elise, or Lissie as they called her. Lissie got pregnant at a young age and had Dawn.

It seemed the women of their family all had babies when they were little more than children themselves, and all had terrible luck with men. Dawn vowed not to let that happen to her. She'd made it to the age of twenty-two without any pregnancies and had managed to extricate herself from the gang she'd run around with when she was a teenager.

"What happened to your grandmother?"

"My mother wrote to her a few times. The old woman made a living telling fortunes in New Orleans' tourist trap—Jackson Square. I don't know what happened to her. They drifted apart. My mother didn't approve of 'hocus-pocus' as she called it."

Annette's eyes teared up as Dawn put her arms around her and hugged her close. There was more to the story than Annette had shared. Dawn could feel it in her gut. Her grandmother had had a rough childhood, and she'd sacrificed her future to help Dawn. Her own daughter, Lissie, seemed to be a lost cause, but at least being in jail gave her access to a drug treatment plan and she was working on getting clean.

"So what do you mean by sometimes you can feel things and see things?"

"I don't really understand it. I've never told anyone much. Once in a while, I'll just mention something to a friend if I think they're going to make a mistake. They don't always appreciate it."

Her grandmother smiled. "Welcome to my world."

———

As Luca walked out of the briefing room for his next shift, the sergeant smirked directly at him, as if he knew something Luca didn't. His thoughts traveled back to the strange girl he'd met by the Christian Science Plaza—and her prediction.

Could the sergeant, aka Lisa's father, have found out about their relationship and talked Lisa into breaking up with him? He still couldn't really make sense of it. Two years down the drain.

He didn't have time to ruminate. He and Joe had barely started patrolling when the radio dispatcher had an assignment for them. Screams had been reported at a nearby apartment building, and the ten code signaled a possible domestic dispute.

"Shit. I hate those," Joe said. "I'll go in first."

"Only if you want to. I'm perfectly willing to give it a try. Might as well get some experience, and it would be a chance to practice some of the techniques I was taught to de-escalate these situations."

Joe laughed. "You sure? I'd hate for you to be killed

your second day on the job. It wouldn't look good for either of us."

Luca smiled. "I won't get killed. I promise."

"Don't make promises you can't keep, kid."

Luca radioed the dispatcher and asked if she still had the neighbor on the phone.

"Yes. He's waiting by the front door to let you in."

"Did he say if the screams belonged to a man or a woman?" Luca asked.

Joe glanced over at him curiously.

The dispatcher relayed the question and answered back, "It sounds like a man."

"Any response from another person? And if so, male or female?"

After a brief pause, she came back and said the neighbor reported only one person was doing the screaming.

Luca thanked her and said, "Over and out."

They arrived at the building quickly. On the way to the door, Joe asked, "What difference does it make if the screams are male or female?"

"I just want as much information as I can get before entering the situation."

Joe shrugged. "Must be something they taught you in college. I usually just knock loudly, announce it's the police, and wait with my hand on my weapon. The screaming usually stops before they let me in."

When the concerned neighbor opened the outer door, he said, "Upstairs. First door on the right."

Luca didn't hear any screaming, but as they got closer, he heard crying and begging.

Oh, crap. I hope we're not too late.

He banged on the door and announced, "Boston Police."

The door opened cautiously, and a thin, unkempt man peeked over the chain through red-rimmed eyes. A moment later, he closed the door to undo the chain lock and then opened it fully and stood aside.

Luca glanced past the man but didn't see anyone in the living room or kitchen. "Is there anyone else here?"

"N…no. Well, not really. I'll explain."

The two of them entered the apartment cautiously. "Mind if we take a look around?" Joe asked.

"You won't find anyone. He's inside me."

Luca and Joe glanced at each other. Joe's face remained stony. "I'll be back in a minute."

The man sounded like he was suffering from a mental illness. In a way, Luca was glad Joe was out of the way. He knew veteran cops often dismissed the "crazies" as he'd heard them called.

"What's your name?"

"George."

"George, I'm Officer Fierro. Tell me what's upsetting you," he said gently.

"I have a demon inside me. I need an exorcism, and my priest won't do it. He won't even come to my home anymore."

"I see. It sounds like this has been going on for a while."

"A few years. I'm praying and taking my medication, like my priest told me to. But it's not working anymore. The demon is too strong." He began to cry again.

"Are you Catholic, sir?"

"Yes. A practicing Catholic. And my priest won't do an exorcism!"

"I might know what to do, if you'll trust me."

Cautious hope entered the man's eyes. "You know how to perform an exorcism?"

"Yes, one version," Luca answered. "Do I have your permission to proceed?"

The man nodded fervently.

Luca placed the palm of his hand on the man's forehead. He caught sight of Joe pausing in the hallway but ignored him. In an authoritative voice, he declared, "In the name of Jesus Christ, evil be gone!" He repeated it twice more. At the end of the third time, he thought he'd add a little Latin and used the only phrase he could remember off the top of his head. "E pluribus unum!"

The man collapsed on the floor. Joe rushed in, and Luca kneeled beside George, placing his fingers against the man's carotid artery. His heartbeat was fast, but at least he wasn't in cardiac arrest.

Joe, to his credit, didn't make a sound. Luca half expected some kind of outburst, like, *What the hell are you doing?* Instead, he just asked, "Is he okay?"

Luca shook the man's shoulder. "Hey, George. Are you all right?"

George's eyes fluttered open. "I—I think so." He tried to sit up. "I'm dizzy."

"Lie back down. Take a few slow breaths first. We'll help you up in a minute."

A short while later, George said he felt better than he had in weeks. They left him resting in a comfortable chair, sipping some water.

As soon as the two cops were safely ensconced in their cruiser, Joe grinned. "Is that what they taught you to do in college? Do you have 'performs exorcisms' on your résumé?"

"No, but maybe I should add it. I was hoping the power of suggestion might help."

Joe burst out laughing. His reaction suddenly had Luca wondering if the call was a ruse. Did the cops set up this whole thing? If so, they found the most convincing actor on the planet. *Nah. I'm just being paranoid. Thanks a bunch, Dawn Forest.*

"Hey, you won't tell the guys at the station about this, will you?"

"Why not? It's hilarious! You're nothing if not creative, kid."

"I'm afraid they'll use it to make fun of the rookie."

Joe piped down to a chuckle. "Okay. I can't wait to see what you write in your report. And I hope you'll share the story over a beer at our favorite bar sometime. I'll take you there to celebrate the end of your first week."

"Sure. If I make it that far. Let me think about it."

Joe just grinned and drove down the street, ready to resume their patrol.

As they drove down a side street on a hill, Luca's eyes went on alert. That girl, Dawn, had told him about an older neighborhood that looked just like the one they were driving through. Homes with front doors close to the street. He recalled she said that there was a drag race, and a kid on a bike was heading into the street…she could see it unfold through his eyes. For some reason, he knew she was telling the truth. She wasn't just another troubled soul like George.

He sat up and unfastened his seat belt. Joe either didn't notice or care. Then he saw them—two cars at the top of the hill, facing the same direction. "Hold it!" Luca called out. The cars' engines revved. "These assholes are getting ready to race."

Joe pulled over. Luca hit the roof's lightbar and jumped out of the vehicle. He saw the kid on the bike, and one of the cars screeched as it took off. The other one may have seen the flashing blue lights and decided it wasn't worth it. *Good decision.*

Luca kicked up his speed as the car zoomed forward. Apparently, the driver was an idiot and wanted to win by default. Luca leapt to the sidewalk and grabbed the kid off the bike a split second before the speeding car whizzed by.

When the car reached the bottom of the hill and turned the corner, Joe hit the siren and made a U-turn, following the drag racer.

"Are you okay, kid?" Luca asked.

"Yeah."

"It's dark. Do your parents know you're out riding your bike?"

The boy shrugged. "They don't care."

Luca was tempted to take the kid by the shirtsleeve up to the house and ring the bell. But something told him not to. The resigned look on the kid's face maybe.

"Look. It's not safe to ride your bike after dark. Promise you won't do it again, and I won't tell your parents."

The boy's eyes widened, like he was being given a surprise gift. "Yeah. Okay. I promise."

"Good. This is my area, and I'll hold you to that."

The boy smiled for the first time. "Thanks, Officer."

Luca wondered if it might be the first time anyone had cared what happened to this kid. It certainly seemed like it. He would keep an eye out for him in the future.

This was what being a cop was about. He wanted to make a difference in as many lives as he could. And thanks to a cute, spiky-haired, tattooed young woman, he'd been able to save a kid's life.

~~~

Nurse Patricia Richardson was looking forward to the next few days. She'd just finished a grueling week of night shifts at the hospital and had four glorious days off before going back. She scooped her little girl from the Sunshine Day Care Center and was ready to hit the road. Her husband, Jack, had dropped off their daughter, Mandy, on his way to work so Patricia could grab a few hours of sleep before picking her up and heading out to her mom's in Rockland for a long weekend. Jack was planning on seeing the Patriots with his buddies, so they were both happy to have their weekend plans all set. Patricia learned early on from her mom that men needed their "bro" time. And while her wonderful mom took care of Mandy, she could scoot over to the day spa and enjoy a couple of hours of R&R herself.

"We're going to Grandma's house, pumpkin."

The four-year-old girl clapped and giggled as Patricia nuzzled her neck and inhaled her soft-sweet scent. Snapping her into the car seat, Patricia kissed her on the nose, making her giggle.

No sooner had they gotten on the highway than Patricia realized she'd forgotten to get some lactose-free milk. Sometimes her mom had some on hand but usually not. Rather than have her make a special trip, Patricia would just pick some up on her way.

"Honey, Mama has to stop off at a store to get some milk, okay?"

"Can I have a treat too?"

"Hmm…what kind of treat?" Patricia knew what Mandy was going to say.

"Gummies!"

"We'll see." Her daughter had been obsessed with gummy bears ever since their neighbor's daughter had come over and shared some with her. Patricia didn't like the amount of sugar and had been trying to wean her daughter off sweets ever since.

She got off the highway and promptly hit a detour. Before she knew it, she was turned around.

Driving along Dorset Avenue, Patricia spied a convenience store on the corner. *Keene Street Convenience*. She wasn't very familiar with the area and knew it was the rough part of town, but she didn't want to backtrack, since the drive would take two hours, and her mom would have dinner waiting on them.

Street parking was nowhere to be found, so she doubled back and drove down a side street where she found a spot at the end of an alley behind the store. She wasn't thrilled about the neighborhood, but it was two in the afternoon, and there was plenty of traffic whizzing by on the main road. She tucked her Ford Fusion in behind an old red pickup and noticed a white van blocking the truck. Hoisting her daughter on her hip, she made her way down the street and around the corner to the convenience store. Luckily, the store didn't carry gummy bears, but she managed to put a smile on Mandy's face with a small box of animal crackers.

"Hooray!" Patricia sang to her daughter on the way

back to the car. "We've got some yummy jungle animals to munch on."

"Mommy, I like the lion the best."

"I'm sure there's at least one lion in there."

Reaching the Ford Fusion once more, Patricia strapped Mandy back into the car seat and then filled a sippy cup with milk. After handing it to her daughter, Patricia opened the box of animal crackers and fished around for the lion.

"*You said we'd get the payment tonight!*"

Patricia, who was standing on the passenger side with the back door open, looked over and spied three pairs of feet on the other side of the van.

"You'll get it next week," a gruff voice replied.

"If we don't get the money, you know what's gonna happen."

"You can't threaten me."

"Oh yeah, Sergeant? I'm sure your fellow cops would love to know all the arrangements you've made for us."

"I told you not to call me that. Use my code name, Blue Wolf."

"You better take care of that pretty daughter of yours," growled a second voice. "You wouldn't want that red Corvette she drives to get into an accident."

"Yeah, nice car. I'm wonderin' how the brass never got wind that you're a dirty cop when your little girl drives around in a new red Corvette."

"You better shut your fucking mouth, or I'll make sure you end up in Walpole with a bunkmate named Rage." Three men rounded the van.

Patricia froze. The box slipped from her hands. She

glanced down and watched the animal cookies topple to the ground as though in slow motion.

"Mummy! My lion!"

She looked at her daughter. Her beautiful baby girl. She had to get them out of there fast. She knew the voice. She knew who that was.

"I'll get you more later, honey."

She jumped into the front seat—no time to fasten her seat belt—and hightailed it out of there.

"Get her!" the man she knew yelled.

In the rearview mirror, she could see the man now standing on the street, staring at her vehicle. The other two were jumping into the pick-up truck.

"Oh God!"

She had to get out of town, and fast.

Chapter 3

THE SQUAD ROOM WAS SOLEMN.

A woman had been found dead, and her little girl had apparently gone missing.

Everyone on the incoming day and departing night shift had gathered in the briefing room. Luca and Joe slipped in quietly while the captain was speaking.

"We typically see the estranged father kidnapping his own kid in cases like this. We're ruling it out since the father was at work at the time of the incident and was not estranged from his wife. He's here, cooperating and crying his eyes out.

"He told us he dropped his daughter off at the Sunshine Day Care yesterday morning at eight. His wife, a nurse, finished her shift at seven a.m. and went home to sleep for a few hours, then she picked up her daughter at one in the afternoon with the intention of driving to her mother's place in Rockland for a few days.

"She checked in with her husband at the day care, and then told him she would check in when they arrived in Rockland. But they never got there." The captain paused and cleared her throat as she regarded her notes. "Her vehicle hit a utility pole on Stilvan Street. The woman wasn't wearing a seat belt and went clear through the windshield. Because the power went out, we can pinpoint the exact time of death to 2:05 p.m., and that means the father's alibi holds up.

"We believe the girl had been strapped into the back seat but was not found in the vehicle. She is now presumed missing. We have reason to believe the woman had been chased down and lost control of the vehicle because of tire marks on the side of the road. At this point, we do not know if the child is alive, injured, or deceased."

Luca dug into his pocket and retrieved the business card Dawn had given him yesterday. Maybe she could help. Maybe she could sense something like she did about the boy on the bike?

On the large screen TV, a picture of a four-year-old girl with blonde pigtails smiled back at them. Luca's heart seemed to block his throat. These were the kinds of cases that everyone dreaded.

His eyes met Sergeant Craig Butts', standing ramrod tall beside the captain, his arms crossed over his chest. Lisa's father. If looks could kill, Luca would be a pile of ashes right now. Luca had a feeling Sergeant Butts had it in for him, and the only reason he could think of was that he had somehow found out about his relationship with Lisa. Had she told him? Was that the reason she'd broken up with him so abruptly? Damn! How in the hell was he going to function on the force if his own sergeant hated his guts?

"We'll be sending this picture to the news outlets," the captain continued. "I don't need to tell you the first seventy-two hours are critical. Keep your eyes open. If you get any leads, you know what to do: call me or Sergeant Butts immediately."

While the force had elite detectives who would do their utmost to find the girl, Luca had a special weapon in his arsenal. He could shift into his phoenix form and fly above the city, searching for her.

As soon as the squad was turned loose, he hopped in his car and drove to an old train station that looked more like a train graveyard. There, he could stash his uniform and shape-shift without being seen. Thankfully, his parents didn't bug him about what time he got home anymore, so he didn't have to check in with them.

He left his car in the parking area and jogged behind a rusting caboose. There was plenty of grime to cover his red and orange tail feathers and plenty of abandoned train cars in which to stash his uniform. About thirty seconds later, he simply looked like a gray and brown bird that flew out of the caboose's broken back window.

An hour of flying over the city streets hadn't turned up anything—except he'd spotted Dawn Forest walking toward the T station. She glanced around nervously and then upward. Could she sense him watching her? He landed on a high branch of an oak tree as she waited on the platform.

She carried a large baton with her keys, like she was ready to do battle if she had to. He wondered if she had already found out about the little girl. Did she sense something?

He decided to follow her. She got on a train marked "Prudential Center." She must be going to work. He flew above the train and hovered at each stop. Finally, she got off. She was definitely heading to work, since ScholarTech was just a couple of blocks away in the Prudential Building.

Realizing it would take him forever to search every street in the city, he flew back to the train graveyard, shifted, dressed, and hopped into his car. He didn't want to spook her by just jumping out naked. He would phone her and set up a meeting. Dawn had predicted the drag racing and the accident with the boy on the bike. Because Luca was ready for it, he had managed to get the kid out of the way before disaster struck. Luckily, Joe had caught up with the reckless driver and issued a citation and hefty fine. No one was hurt, thanks to Dawn.

She might just be their only hope of finding this missing girl. Luca knew enough not to say anything to Joe or anyone else about Dawn. He knew what it was like to be different and how that affected every part of your life.

After two years of being with Lisa, he'd never told her about his shape-shifting ability. Maybe on some level, he had known he couldn't trust her with that part of himself. That still didn't make her rejection hurt any less than it already did. He would have to reach out to her soon and talk about what was really behind it. Her breakup phone call had been a sucker punch to his gut, but he didn't have time to wallow in his romantic feelings nor know how he was going to diffuse his sergeant's hate-on for him. He had to find that little girl, and he needed Dawn's help.

<center>~~~</center>

Dawn glanced around her as she stepped off the subway and walked up the stairs. She wouldn't have been quite so paranoid if it wasn't for the weird dream she had had last night. Like she was being watched from above. Had the gang bought a drone? If so, that might be a good thing, at least for her. She was sick of giving them a heads-up when the cops were around.

She replayed the dream in her mind as she hustled

down the street toward her office building. She looked up at the sky. Bright and blue. So why did she feel like a heavy black cloud was hovering over her? When she got to her building, she took one more peek over her shoulder as she scooted into the lobby and slipped into the elevator just as the doors were closing. *Deep breath*. She punched the tenth-floor button and, like everyone else on the elevator, she watched the numbers of each floor light up and ping as the elevator made its stops.

She got off the elevator and then walked briskly to Suite 1005, ScholarTech, a company that created educational software for academia. The suite took up one entire side of the building, with large windows and an open concept space with sleek Swedish workstations. One or two coworkers were already at their desks, heads down, either checking email or getting a leg up on the day. Good. She didn't feel like making chitchat this morning. She was still feeling weird about her dream.

Arriving at her cubicle, Dawn dropped her backpack on the floor and kicked it under her desk.

"I guess that's not a Birkin bag by the way you just treated it." Nancy, the office assistant manager and her immediate boss, stood with one hand on the front wall that defined Dawn's workstation. Dawn worked the phones at the help desk, and the wall was supposed to give her a sense of privacy.

She didn't like engaging in the everyday office chitchat and gossip that floated around her, but she did enjoy her job. She liked helping people; most of her calls were from frantic students who were having issues with the software and were desperate to get their term papers or theses in. Dawn had a photographic memory, so she was always able to walk them through whatever glitch they had. She felt good about that. It was just one more positive change in her crazy, mixed-up life. Well, formerly mixed-up life.

Dawn gave Nancy a smile. "Yeah, I don't go for expensive designer things. I'd just wreck whatever it is eventually." That and she couldn't afford them. She bought most of her clothes at thrift stores and had her own unique style. Today, she'd paired a long red retro sweater from the '80s with black leggings and ballet flats. She got a lot of compliments on her outfits, which boggled her mind. Most of the women who worked in her office spent a ton of money on clothes, and Dawn couldn't wrap her head around why. Saving money was her top priority. She was determined to make enough to buy a little place for her and her grandmother. The Arizona desert was cheaper and warm. That was her dream. No more Boston winters. No more crazy gang members chasing her down and using her psychic abilities for their nefarious purposes. No way would she give up her dream for a Birkin bag or a Chanel outfit.

The older woman nodded. She was dressed in a smart navy-blue jacket and matching pencil skirt, a bright coral shirt adding a splash of color. It almost matched the color of her bright asymmetrical bob. Inwardly, Dawn rolled her eyes. What was it with middle-aged women and *that* hair cut? It screamed: *I'm a professional woman but I'm also a fashionista. Ready for anything.*

"Can you get that list of office supply orders to me by tomorrow morning?"

"Sure thing," Dawn replied, booting up her computer. It was her job to check the supply closet and order what they needed for the week. Ironically, the march of technology hadn't seemed to stop the demand for Sharpies and paper clips.

Nancy gave her a little wave and marched off to her office. It was still quiet, and many of her coworkers hadn't arrived yet. This was the best part of her day. Dawn slipped into the break room and filled her travel mug with freshly brewed coffee, adding a healthy dose of cream and two sugars. She liked her coffee strong, sweet, and creamy. She poked around the various open boxes on the counter to see what baked goodies were on the menu. Score! A strawberry cheese Danish. Dawn plucked it out of the box and laid it on a small plate, then scrambled back to her desk like a jewel thief who'd made off with a big heist. Taking a bite of the pastry, she gave a little moan of delight and began scrolling through her email.

A half hour later she'd answered a few emails and helped one frantic PhD student who'd been up all night finishing her dissertation and was panicking when she lost one of her graphs. She was on her second cup of coffee when the phone rang.

"ScholarTech help desk."

"Ah, yeah. Is this Dawn?" a baritone male asked.

She didn't recognize the voice, but she hadn't been here long enough to have met everyone yet. "Yes. May I help you?"

"This is Luca Fierro. The cop you talked to the other day."

Wow! She'd never thought she'd hear from him. From the way he'd looked at her after she'd warned him, she could have sworn he thought she was a nutcase. And she couldn't blame him. What normal person walks up to a complete stranger and warns him about a terrible thing that might happen? "I remember. Is everything okay?"

"Yeah. Can I meet you somewhere?"

"Um, I'm at work, but you knew that. Is it something I can do from here?"

"No. I can't talk about it over the phone, in case we're being recorded."

And she thought *she* was paranoid. "Well, I can't just leave. I only got here an hour ago."

"I wouldn't bother you if this weren't important."

"Is it more important than me losing my job?"

After a brief pause, he said, "It might be. Is your job a matter of life and death?"

That was not only cryptic but rude. "My job is what stands between me and starving to death. Is that enough?"

He made a sound of frustration.

"Look, I don't know much about you, Luca, but you're acting kind of entitled. Do you mind telling me what this is about?"

"Sorry. I don't mean to sound demanding, but time is of the essence, and I think you might be able to help. I guess I should have said please."

"Saying please is nice and everything, but it doesn't change the fact that I have to work. Why can't you just tell me what it's about over the phone? No one is recording us."

"As far as you know. I might get in trouble for working on a case that isn't mine, but I have to do something. There are no leads, and someone's life is hanging in the balance. I thought of your psychic senses, and you said you like to help people."

"Shit. I guess I could get a stomachache." She glanced at the half-eaten Danish and formulated an excuse. "Hopefully, my boss will let me go home."

"Yeah. That would be great."

"I'm not exactly sure about this, but if it's really that important…"

"It is. Trust me."

She sighed. Oddly enough, she did trust him—at least based on the vibes he was giving off right now. He was genuinely concerned for someone else and was willing to disobey the rules and put his own job in jeopardy. "Where can I meet you?"

"I can pick you up out front. I'll be there in twenty minutes."

"Okay, I'll see you downstairs." Dawn believed in fate, to a point. She still believed people had free will, but some opportunities weren't coincidences. Maybe this was one of those opportunities to fix her own karmic past.

The weirdest thing had happened a week ago. Dawn had been walking home from the subway at her usual brisk pace, head up, alert, clutching her baton stick with the keys jangling. Ready to swing it at anyone who would dare get into her personal space. That's when she had seen her: an old woman, crumpled on the front stoop of her house. Thinking it was her grandmother, Dawn had rushed up the steps to the woman and helped her sit up.

"Are you okay?" Dawn asked anxiously, relieved it wasn't Annette but concerned nonetheless.

The old woman opened her eyes and smiled. "I'm okay now, dearie. I was waiting for you."

"Who are you?" Dawn sat on the top step, her back against the railing.

"I'm Lynda from Karma Cleaners, and I'm here because you called us."

"I think you're mistaken."

"Oh no. There's no mistake."

Dawn's eyes widened. "First of all, what's Karma Cleaners, and secondly, when and how did I call you?"

The old woman's twinkling blue eyes stared into hers. "At Karma Cleaners, we help you change your bad karma to good karma. All anyone has to do is express a desire to change. The message goes out into the universe and ends up on our switchboard." She whipped out a tablet from the pocket of her threadbare coat and started tapping and swiping on the surface of the electronic device. "Ah, here we are. Six months ago, you were walking home from your shift at Keene Street Convenience, and you said, 'Fuck my life. I wish I could change everything.' So here I am."

"Why should I believe you?"

"Did you say that?"

"Yes, but that was six months ago. And now you show up?"

"We had to be sure you meant it and that you had the stuff to succeed."

"I got myself a way better job."

The old woman grinned as she tucked the tablet back into her pocket. "Yes, I know, and we're so proud of what you've accomplished, going to night school and working the day shift at that hellhole that fronts for the Keene Street Gang. And then extricating yourself from their influence. Very impressive."

"Yeah, hellhole is the nicest term you can use to describe that place," Dawn said. It was a well-known secret that Keene Street Convenience didn't just sell cigarettes and lottery tickets. Downstairs in the basement were the bathrooms and storeroom. It was also where the gang did most of their deals. Dawn had been stuck for years acting as their psychic lookout when it came to the undercover narcs. So many times, she regretted letting them know of her psychic ability. She'd been trying to be cool and show off a bit. Naturally, they exploited her talent.

"We're short-staffed and backlogged right now. You wouldn't believe the number of people who've reached out since the election."

Dawn crossed her arms. "Okay, so how do I know you're actually from this place, Karma Cleaners, and not just some drunk old lady who wants money?"

The old woman gave Dawn a cheeky grin. "I was hoping you'd ask me that."

She stood up, spread her arms out, twirled in a little circle, and in the blink of an eye, shifted into a tall, lithe young woman with straight black hair tied up in a high ponytail. She had the same bright-blue eyes but this time peeking behind a pair of retro-style black-framed glasses. She wore a crisp white blouse tucked into high-waisted tailored black pants and a pair of sky-high heels.

"What the…"

"Try to relax. You of all people know there's more to this world than meets the eye."

"Yeah, but…some kind of shape-shifting thing?" Dawn could barely speak because of her throat going dry. "You must be some kind of magician."

"Oh, it's magic all right, but not an illusion. What you saw really happened."

After another shocked hesitation, she had to ask. "You...er...actually have to twirl in order to change... um...forms?"

"Well, it's a choice. I love Lynda Carter, so I always go for the twirl."

"Lynda Carter from the *Wonder Woman* TV show?"

"Yes!" Her eyes glittered with excitement. "She's my favorite."

Dawn couldn't help but smile. "Okaaaay... So what's your name?"

"Lynda Carter. I had it legally changed."

"Nice touch."

"Thank you."

"So are all the Karma Cleaner caseworkers women?"

"Yup."

"No men?"

"Nope. And that's how we like it." She leaned in again. "Don't get me wrong. There are different outfits out there that *do* have men, but we have the highest rate of karmic shifts. And just between you and me, if you wanna get a job done right, you send in a woman." She lifted her hand for a high five. "Am I right?"

Dawn humored her and slapped her hand. "Don't take this the wrong way, but this is the weirdest thing I've ever heard of. So what is the protocol?"

"You need to erase your past bad karma and start to rebuild good karma."

"Aren't there other people whose karma is worse than mine?" Dawn thought of her own mother. She would never rat on her, despite her mother's drug-dealing activities. But she had to admit, jail was the best place for her mom right now. At least she was getting the help she needed…or so she'd said.

"Sometimes the choices are not easy, are they?" Lynda said softly.

"I guess you know about my mom too?"

"Yes," she replied. "We make a point of knowing everything about those we help. And just so you know, she's doing great. Trust me on this one."

"Thanks." Dawn blew out a breath. "So what do I need to do?"

"You need to keep doing what you're doing. Stay away from that gang, and be of service to those who need your help."

"I guess I'm on the right track?"

"You most certainly are." Lynda nodded. "We're just here to offer you a little guidance."

"Okay, so do I need to keep written reports on my good deeds or something?"

Lynda laughed. "Well, you can if you want, but we automatically know when you do something good. It gets logged in our system, and we keep excellent records."

"I guess that's a good thing? So how do I get in touch with you if I need you? Or do you automatically know that too?"

Lynda took a card from her pocket and handed it to Dawn. "Our address and phone number are there."

Dawn glanced at the card. It read: *We fight the stains on your clothes and the tarnish on your karma.*

"You mean you're actually a dry cleaner as well?"

"We can get grease out of silk like you wouldn't believe."

"Well, that's good to know, I guess. I've never owned any silk."

Lynda smiled. "You will."

Dawn couldn't really respond to that. Apparently, this woman was way more psychic than she was. "So what's the next step?"

"You have to check in once a week in person for a session. I'm sort of like your probation officer but with cookies! Plus, it's a great excuse for a good gabfest. Deal?"

Dawn would love to have someone to talk to when she didn't want to worry her grandmother. "Deal."

Amazing how your life can change in a week. First, she had met Lynda from Karma Cleaners, and now she had met a cute young cop who needed her help.

Dawn hoped lying to her boss and pretending to be sick wouldn't count against her karma if it was for a good cause. She took a few moments to look up symptoms on WebMD. Something that could be serious but not *too* serious.

At the appointed time, she grabbed her backpack, strode to Nancy's office, and remembered to place her hand over her abdomen before she knocked on her door.

No answer.

Shoot. She'd have to go to Nancy's boss, Mr. Addison. *Oh, wait. That might be even better!* Men tended to shy away from "lady problems."

With a look of discomfort on her face, she made her excuse of a worsening pain in her abdomen.

Addison took one look at her and said, "You should see a doctor."

"Yeah. I was thinking the same thing." *Huh? I know I'm pale, but do I look sick even when I'm not?*

She was slightly insulted, but at the moment, it served her purpose.

"Do you have someone who can drive you? Or would you like me to call an ambulance to take you to the emergency room?"

"An ambulance? No! I can see the nurse practitioner who works with my doctor right away. Their office isn't far."

"Okay. Let me know how it goes."

"I will. If it's nothing, I'll even come back today."

"Good. I hope it's nothing serious."

Dawn walked to the elevator, trying to decide if she should shuffle slowly, holding her stomach, and possibly look like she needed an ambulance, or just walk normally and risk being seen as a faker.

She decided on a fast shuffle and got on the elevator before the big boss changed his mind. When the doors closed and she began descending, she muttered, "This better be important, Officer Fierro."

She stepped outside and spotted Luca waving from his car. She strode to it briskly and got in.

"Thanks for meeting me. I need your help."

"With what?"

"A missing child. You can't tell anyone else, or it could mess up the investigation."

Her eyes widened. "Oh no. A missing kid? That's awful. Boy or girl? How old?"

"A four-year-old girl, and there are no leads. We're trying to find her quickly, before anything worse happens. You can't tell anyone."

"I wouldn't know who to tell, except maybe the cops. But—oh wait, here you are."

He smiled at her joke.

"Do you have anything that belongs to her?" Dawn asked.

"No. The detectives would have that stuff. But I'm afraid they won't consult a psychic."

"Yeah, I doubt that too, but I need something to go on. Just some way to latch onto her energy." *And, hopefully, see out of her eyes.*

"Would it help if you saw her home from the outside?"

"Maybe. Do you know where she lives?"

"She's actually sort of a neighbor. Her place is around the corner from where I live, but I don't know the family well."

"Take me there."

"This may be tricky. I can't be seen at or near the house. It might look like I'm interfering with someone else's investigation."

"Isn't that exactly what you're doing?"

"When you consider the first priority is preserving life, I don't really have a choice. I just have to be careful not to compromise the case. If someone took her and procedure isn't followed, no matter how guilty he is, the perp could walk away unpunished. That's the last thing anyone wants. For someone like that to be free to do it again would be a crime in itself."

"I get it." Dawn understood what he was saying, and she even knew some people who had gotten off on a technicality—Ice Spider, for one—but it seemed cumbersome to follow procedure when a child's life was at stake.

Luca drove her to his house and gave her the Richardsons' address around the corner. Dawn couldn't help but stare at the outside of Luca's home. The neighborhood was definitely upscale and a far cry from her run-down area. The four-story brick building had beautiful wrought iron railings and sconces on either side of the large front door. Clearly, his parents had done well. Or they'd inherited a fortune.

"Remember, don't look conspicuous," Luca said as Dawn got out of the car. "The forensics team could still be there gathering evidence."

Dawn nodded and tucked some loose wisps of her punk pixie hair behind her ears. Not that that would make a difference. They had decided while she was doing her psychic thing outside the missing girl's house, Luca would change and meet up with her at the Starbucks two blocks away in about half an hour. Dawn had no idea how long it would take, but half an hour would be plenty of time for her to *try* to get some vibes about the little girl.

Luca was tired, but he imagined the detectives on this case weren't getting much sleep either. Dawn had said she needed something that belonged to the girl. Maybe he could transform again early tomorrow morning after his shift, search for an open window, and fly in to grab something from the girl's room. The Richardson family had been renting the upstairs apartment of the old Bixby home. The owners had passed away a few years back, and their kids had turned the massive house into three separate apartments. Smart move.

Even though Luca's dad had inherited their brownstone from his grandfather, who'd inherited it from his great-grandfather, Antonio complained that the taxes were like paying a mortgage that never ended. Phoenixes could live to be five hundred years old but not in the same place. People got suspicious eventually, so after a good number of years, the house was passed on to the next generation.

Luca hoped Dawn could glean something from the facade of the residence itself—also without attracting attention. Chances were the detectives had gathered many of the little girl's things, but if he could fly in and grab a T-shirt or a toy that could be helpful to Dawn, he'd have to be careful not to be seen. A bird flying around with a stuffed animal in its beak would look pretty weird. Besides, the detectives probably took her favorite toys and recently worn clothing for the K-9 unit to sniff.

Luca wished he could share his shape-shifting ability with Dawn. She'd probably understand, right? One weirdo to another. But the stakes were too high. He'd never even told Lisa about it. Now, he was glad he hadn't. Her father would probably have him committed to the state hospital.

He jogged up the steps to his home and let himself in.

"Luca! I was getting worried," his mother greeted him. "How was your night, honey?"

"Good, Ma, but I'm on my way out again. I just have to change clothes."

Gabriella leaned back and studied his face. "So soon? Aren't you exhausted?"

"Not really. I got a second wind."

She tipped her head. "Well, I hope you get some rest before you get the wind knocked out of you."

"I will." Despite wanting to protest her fretfulness, he kissed her cheek. Then he jogged downstairs to his bedroom in the finished basement.

As soon as he had tossed his uniform in the hamper and put on a pair of jeans and a well-worn Patriots T-shirt, he went to the kitchen. Even though he was going to meet up with Dawn, he was starving, so he grabbed a package of Pop-Tarts and a banana from the bowl on the counter.

Antonio didn't look up from the morning newspaper. "Your brother and his family are moving back in. Did you know about that?"

"Who, Gabe?"

"Yup. He's the only one with a family."

"So far," Gabriella said. She refilled Antonio's coffee cup and then raised the pot in Luca's direction. "Want some?"

"No. I don't have a lot of time. I just need to chow down and go. I'm meeting someone."

Gabriella's eyes lit up. "Meeting someone? Like a young lady, perhaps?"

Antonio glanced at his wife. "Of course it's a woman. He wouldn't be so anxious if he was just hanging out with a guy."

"Well, that's wonderful, honey! We were wondering when you were ever going to start dating." She glanced at her husband. "Unless you *are* meeting a guy. In which case, we're okay with that too."

Luca almost choked on the banana. "Mom, stop."

Gabriella shrugged. "It used to be a worry to the older generation who wanted grandchildren, but now that gay couples can adopt…"

"I'm not gay!" he groused.

"'Bout time somebody asked him," Gabe said as he entered the room. "You might want to keep your voice down though. Misty was up with Tony half the night. She just got to sleep."

"Sorry. Is Tony okay?"

"Yeah. He just has the sniffles. Who came up with the idea of toddlers needing playdates, by the way? The minute they share their toys, they share germs too." He'd aimed the question at their mother.

"It's about socialization. None of you needed to worry about socializing. You had each other," she said.

"And how." Gabe chuckled. "I had three older brothers and three younger bothers."

"You mean brothers," Gabriella corrected.

"Nope. I mean bothers." Gabe messed up Luca's hair as he walked by.

Luca rolled his eyes. "Why are you back here anyway?" he asked as he bit off a piece of pastry and then chewed the large chunk in his mouth.

"My studio apartment isn't big enough for a family of three—or four."

"Four?" both parents said at once.

Gabe smiled. "Yeah. Misty's pregnant again."

"Oh my goodness!" Gabriella hopped up from her seat and hugged her six-foot son around his neck despite her being only five foot three.

Luca knew his mother wanted nothing more than grandchildren. "You must be in seventh heaven, Ma."

She chuckled. "Yes. Who knew having seven sons would only produce a couple of grandchildren?"

"There's plenty of time for more," Antonio said and rose to shake Gabe's hand.

"True, but it looks like the three oldest aren't having kids," Gabe said. "That leaves Dante, Noah, and gay Luca here to help out."

"I am not gay!" Luca shouted.

"He has a date this morning," Gabriella said happily.

"It's not a date. I—I'm consulting with a woman on a case. That's all."

"What kind of case?" Gabe asked.

"An ongoing investigation. In other words, I can't tell you," Luca said smugly. He'd always wanted to say that. Before anyone questioned him further, he guzzled down a glass of juice and jumped up from the table and headed out. "See ya," he tossed over his shoulder.

"Have fun...consulting," Gabriella called after him.

Luca strode down the street, hoping Dawn was at the corner coffee shop to meet him. He didn't feel like waiting around, since he could possibly bump into one of his family members. There were enough of them floating around.

The idea of a date with Dawn had occurred to him but only fleetingly. Was he ready to give up on Lisa after two years of being together? It suddenly occurred to him that maybe Dawn could tell him if Lisa might have a change of heart. Maybe it was just "taking the next step" jitters that had prompted her to break it off.

Following Luca's directions, Dawn made her way to the Richardson place. Luca had told her the Richardson couple rented the apartment on the third floor in the sprawling, red-brick, four-story townhouse, so she focused on that as she strolled down the street. There were several cars out front, including a police cruiser. Luckily, the house was across the street from a park, so Dawn found a bench and sat down. Gazing up at the apartment, she noticed the curtains were drawn in every window. She could understand that, given the tragedy that had befallen the poor woman and her child. There was one thing Dawn understood, and that was how life sometimes dealt the cruelest blows, and somehow, people needed to find the strength to carry on. She supposed her strength came from her grandmother, who raised her to be strong and self-reliant, to stand up to troubles…something Dawn's mom seemed unable to do.

Dawn shook off her musings. The sun came out, so she put on her sunglasses and gazed at the house. Dawn took a few deep breaths, focusing on her breathing. Her body began to relax. All she heard was the sound of her own breathing and around her the wind whistling through the long grass, tickling the leaves…

A young man sat slumped on the floor in a little girl's bedroom, a pink unicorn held tight to his chest. The soft pink walls decorated with princess decals seemed incongruous to the utter grief emanating from him in waves. "Why? Why didn't I go with you? Why did I have to stay for a stupid guys' football weekend?"

A knock on the door, and a police officer entered. He spoke quietly to the man and helped him up. They left the room, the man forgetting the unicorn on the floor.

The unicorn looked so lonely.

A sweet, girlish giggle echoed in the room. A young girl, blonde hair, blue eyes, in a purple polka-dot tunic and purple tights, bent to retrieve the unicorn. "Mama, we gots to take Sparkles with us to Grammy's."

"Honey, we've already got your two besties, Binky the elephant and Rommy the turtle," a woman said from the other side of the room. She was packing a small child's suitcase. Wearing a nurse's uniform, she had the same golden hair and blue eyes as her daughter. "Besides," she went on, "Sparkles would miss her playmates here."

"I guess it's okay if she stays here. She gots lots of friends here too."

"She sure does, honey. Now, do you want to take your blue dress or your green dress? Grammy wants to take us out tomorrow night."

"I want my blue dress, Mommy. It's so much more fancy than the green one."

The woman giggled and agreed that the blue dress was certainly more fitting for a night out.

The laughter faded away...

The pink room turned black.

"Mommy?" the little one whispered brokenly. "W-where are you?"

Dawn arrived at the Starbucks before Luca and ordered for both of them. If he didn't like her choice, she'd take it home to her gran. After receiving her order, she scored two plush chairs in the corner and sat down, feeling the weight of the vision heavy on her shoulders. She took a sip of her coffee and didn't notice when Luca arrived.

"Hey." Luca plopped down across from her.

"Hey, yourself." She quirked a half smile. "I took the opportunity of ordering for us. I like their cinnamon dolce latte, so I got one for you too."

"Thanks," he said, picking up the coffee and taking a sip. "This is good. Are you okay?"

"I'll be okay after I have a bit more of this latte," she replied.

"I take it you sensed something?"

"Yes. I saw the father in his daughter's room, crying… He was holding a pink stuffed unicorn. He said he wished he had gone with them and not stayed home for a guys' football weekend."

Luca nodded, and pulling out a small notebook from his pocket, he began to take notes.

Dawn told him everything, every detail she could recall right down to hearing the little girl's tiny whisper in the dark calling out for her mom—and how her heart broke when she heard it.

"Did you get a sense of where the girl might be? Any flashes of light or noises?"

Dawn shook her head, her frustration mounting. "No, it was pitch-black. I'm pretty sure I was looking out of the little girl's eyes. Either she was blindfolded or stuck in a room with no windows. I had this feeling of helplessness. What that poor little girl must be going through."

"Not panic? Or fear?" Luca asked.

"Not really, but she might still be in shock or just exhausted. Maybe they drugged her?"

"Crap. On the other hand, if she's not fearful or panicking, maybe she feels she's not in any real danger. Maybe she knows her abductor."

"At least she's alive. I wish I could tell you more."

Luca's smile encouraged her. "You told me the most important thing: she's still alive. And you gave me a lot of details. If I can get hold of a personal item, would you be willing to try—?"

"Of course," Dawn jumped in. "I want to do everything I can to help rescue this girl. Her dad was so devastated." Dawn wrapped her arms around her middle, still having a hard time letting go of the feelings and images in her vision.

Luca fidgeted in his seat. "I, uh…I was wondering if you might be able to tell me something else. It's unrelated, but it's bugging me."

"I'll try. What is it?"

He hung his head. "It might sound stupid."

"If it's bothering you, it's not stupid."

He gave her a weak smile. "Okay, here goes. I've been secretly dating this girl since our junior year in college. Suddenly, she dumped me out of the blue. I can't think of anything I've done to upset her. In fact, everything I've done has been for her, including becoming a cop, hoping to please her father."

Dawn had sensed loneliness and wondered why this great-looking guy seemed unattached. Apparently, he was recently detached against his will. *Dammit*. She didn't want to be anyone's rebound. Not that they had any kind of relationship or future together. But she couldn't help being attracted to him. He was really cute. And a nice guy. Not the kind of guy she used to date. But certainly the kind of guy she'd love to date someday when her karma was cleaned up.

Mentally shaking herself out of her self-centeredness, she grasped his hand across the table. "I'm sorry." His hand was warm, and he didn't pull away, but she had to. It wouldn't do to fall for a guy who was pining away for another woman. "Is that what you were upset about the day I met you?"

"Yes. She'd just dumped me an hour before."

"You were hurt and angry. I knew that for sure."

"So…um… Do you think you could maybe see if Lisa and I might get back together?"

Dawn blew out a breath. "Do you have anything of hers or a photo?"

He pulled out his wallet and slipped out a photo booth picture of him and Lisa.

She was pretty. Just the kind of girl that Luca—or any guy, for that matter—would be drawn to. Long blonde hair, sparkling blue eyes, chic off-the-shoulder outfit. She looked like Barbie.

Dawn held the photo and closed her eyes. Red Corvette speeding along. Lisa was in the driver's seat, laughing. The car came to a stop, and she leaned over and kissed someone. Darker blond hair, green eyes, tanned. If Barbie's Ken were living and breathing, it would be this guy.

Damn. What am I supposed to tell Luca?

She opened her eyes and stared into Luca's baby blues. His dark lashes and brows made the unusual color stand out even more. And then it hit her. Like a scene from a sexy movie trailer, she saw herself in bed with Luca. *Holy moly!*

"Did you see anything about Lisa?"

"Um…I'm not sure right now." She could feel herself blushing and averted her eyes. "I think it's all the people here. Like static interference. I've had to develop this psychic thing on my own, and it's not an exact science."

He slumped in his chair a little and looked like a sad puppy dog. "That's okay. I get it."

Steady, Dawn. If she got too close to him, she'd be liable to lose her head and her heart. She had to focus. *Remember, your goal is to clean up your karma. Falling for a guy who's hung up on his ex-girlfriend is not a smart move.* She pasted a sunny smile on her face. "You seem a lot more open-minded than I would've expected."

"Just because I'm a cop?"

"Yeah. I don't mean to stereotype you, but cops aren't usually willing to entertain anything in the realm of the supernatural."

He sat up and seemed to consider her comment. "In training, we talked about a cop's gut feeling and how that could be a help or a hindrance. I've heard everyone is a little psychic. Some people are just more in touch with it."

She shrugged. "I can't speak to everyone, but I've been aware of something different about me since I was a kid. I think the first time I predicted something, I was about the same age as this girl who was taken."

"Taken? You're sure?"

"No, actually. I shouldn't have put it that way. All I know for sure is the little girl from that home is alive, and for whatever reason, she can't see." Dawn had finished her coffee and noticed that Luca's cup was empty too. "I should let you get home. You already worked a full shift, and you must be tired."

"Yeah, and I should let you get back to work. Thanks for meeting me. I didn't know if there was anything you could do or not, but I figured if there was a possible lead you could give us, it would be worth pursuing."

"I doubt the police will welcome my help, so it's a good thing I know you, in case I get a vision later."

"Do you think you might?"

"Anything is possible."

They threw their cups into the recycling bin. Luca held the door open for her, and she stepped out ahead of him.

"Remember, you can't let anyone know that I asked you to get involved, but I'm grateful you were able to answer a couple of questions for me."

"I'll remember. And there's something I'd like you to remember too."

"What's that?"

She turned back to tell him, but her words died in her throat.

Blood. All she could see was blood.

Then everything went dark.

Chapter 4

"GIVE HER SOME SPACE."

"You give her some space. You're crowding her."

"I'm a cop. I know what I'm doing."

"I've been a firefighter for ten years. You've been a cop for, what? A day?"

"He started Monday, dear."

"Ma, you're not helping."

"Okay, everyone move back. I'm older than all of you, and I was a firefighter before you were born."

The voices woke her up, but she couldn't decide if they were voices in her head or actual real voices. They were still arguing. She decided to chance it and opened her eyes.

"There she is. Can you tell me your name?"

A man who looked a lot like Luca but about thirty years older was hovering over her. Concern flickered in his eyes. She had an instant feeling of comfort and protection. It was a good feeling. Not something she was used to.

"Dawn Forest." Ugh, her voice sounded like a frog.

She heard a snicker but couldn't see who was laughing.

"Shut up, loser."

That sounded like Luca.

"Sorry, but it sounds like a stripper name."

"Didn't I raise you to be a gentleman?" A lady's voice, maybe the wife and mother?

"Yeah."

"Good. Now be quiet and let your father do his work."

"Take a sip of water." The older version of Luca handed her a glass.

Dawn took a sip. She was feeling better. She remembered what had happened.

She gazed around her, and standing behind the nice, older man, she saw a petite, older red-haired woman with the same concern etched on her sweet face. Kindness exuded from her. Dawn guessed they were Luca's parents. He must have taken her back to his house.

Standing behind the couple was another tall, broad-shouldered guy who could only be Luca's older brother. *Holy moly, is everyone in this family good-looking?* "Luca? Are you here?"

"I'm here, Dawn." Luca shoved the hunk to the side and crouched down in front of her. "How're you doing?"

"I fainted again?"

"Yep. Right in the middle of Mass. Ave. I figured I'd bring you home."

"Shit. I—I mean, shoot. Did you carry me?"

"Yeah." Then he shrugged. "My house was basically across the street."

"I'm sorry I fainted. I guess I was just…" What could she say among these people? Certainly not that she had seen Luca covered in blood.

"It's okay. It's not your fault. I'm just glad I was there to help."

Dawn nodded and took another sip of water. For some ridiculous reason, it felt good being surrounded by these people. "Thank you."

"You're welcome." Luca turned to the older couple. "She's okay now. Can you guys give us some privacy?"

"Luca, aren't you going to introduce us?"

"Ma, this is a *friend* of mine. Dawn."

The older woman took Dawn's hand between her own. "I'm Gabriella Fierro, and this is my husband, Antonio, and one of our sons, Gabe."

"Pleased to meet you all," Dawn replied, embarrassed. "Thank you for your concern and your help."

Gabriella's sweet smile lit her beautiful features. "You need to eat something. I have some nice, homemade Italian wedding soup."

"I don't think I've ever tried that," Dawn said.

"It's delicious," Antonio added.

"Mom makes the best wedding soup," Gabe chimed in. He gave Luca some kind of smirk, and Luca narrowed his eyes at his brother.

"Antonio, Luca, help Dawn to the dining room table, and I'll get some soup." Gabriella marched to the kitchen, clearly expecting her orders to be followed.

Antonio and Luca each took an arm and helped her up. They both had a firm grip on her, and soon she was settled in a comfortable, straight-backed dining room chair. Dawn glanced around her and noticed the beautiful details of the elegant and sprawling dining area. The table, which must have been custom made, was large enough to seat at least twenty people. A tall glass-fronted cabinet flanked one wall. It was filled with pretty china and crockery that may have been passed down for generations. She had a feeling of lasting endurance. A permanence she rarely felt anywhere.

"Are you feeling better?" Luca asked. He sat beside her. Antonio sat at the head of the table and Gabe across from them.

"Yes, much better," Dawn replied.

"You'll be good as new after you try Ma's soup," Gabe said with a grin.

Dawn couldn't help smiling back. How could she not? Surrounded by three kind men. Apparently, all first responders.

A delicious aroma wafted from the kitchen, and a few moments later, Gabriella walked in with a tray. Setting it on the table, she lifted a steaming soup bowl and placed it in front of Dawn, along with a side plate with a thick slice of Italian bread drizzled with olive oil. Dawn inhaled appreciatively, closing her eyes.

"This looks and smells like heaven," she breathed.

"Thank you. Pardon my asking, but have you eaten recently?"

"Ma!" Luca warned.

Gabriella shrugged. "She's just so skinny."

"I have a very fast metabolism. Some people can't lose weight. I can't gain it."

"I wish I had that problem," Gabriella said.

Personally, Dawn thought she had a lovely figure. Maybe she just struggled to keep it that way.

Antonio chuckled. "She's always complaining about a few extra pounds."

Gabriella whapped Antonio's arm with the back of her hand, and he laughed. "Now, dig in, Dawn," she said. "The soup will make you feel much better."

Dawn blushed, glancing around. "I'm the only one eating?"

"Don't worry about us," Antonio piped up. "We'll eat later, but you need to get your strength back."

"It's okay, Dawn." Luca placed his hand over hers, which only made her blush even more. "Mom's soup cures everything."

Dawn lifted the heavy, silver spoon and scooped up a spoonful of broth and meatballs mixed with spinach and some kind of small pasta. She tasted it and sighed in pleasure. She dipped her spoon again and made an appreciative *mmm* sound. "This is so good, Mrs. Fierro."

"I'm glad you like it, Dawn, and please call me Gabriella."

"Thank you, Gabriella."

The older woman beamed and sat on the arm of her husband's chair. His arm automatically snuck around her waist, holding her close. Dawn swallowed a sudden lump in her throat. It sure would be nice to have that kind of easy loving relationship. Her glance strayed to Luca, who was smiling encouragingly at her.

"Eat up," he said, gesturing to the bowl.

Dawn tasted another spoonful of the delicious soup. She was feeling almost herself again, thanks to these good people. She wondered if maybe her involvement with Karma Cleaners was already starting to pay off. She'd never had anyone do anything nice for her except her grandmother, and Annette was family.

"Is this the first time you've had a fainting spell, dear?" Gabriella asked.

"No, I've had them before." Dawn felt her face flush again. She didn't want to seem like a weakling. That was far from the truth. She hadn't had a fainting spell in a while, but since she'd met Luca, she'd had two—correction, three. She'd had a quick addendum to the vision with Luca. He lay on the ground in front of thick black bars...like a prison. She'd have to figure this out. She couldn't keep fainting every time she had a vision.

"So what do you do for a living, Dawn?" Gabe asked just as Dawn filled her mouth with a big bite of bread.

"She works for ScholarTech, at the Pru," Luca jumped in. "She's really smart."

He really thinks I'm smart? She suddenly felt like she was floating on a cloud. "I just run the help desk," Dawn replied.

"I've heard of them," Gabe said. "They do software for students, right?"

"Yes, to help with their studying and term papers. SAT prep. All kinds of career testing. It's really cool and very useful."

"Well, that is a wonderful thing you do...helping students," Gabriella said with a nod.

"So is Dawn the one helping you with a case?" asked Antonio.

"I was just asking her a few questions, Dad."

"Son, what's this all about? What are you keeping from us?" Gabriella asked.

Luca blew out a breath. "Patricia Richardson, who lives around the corner, was found dead yesterday. It looks like her car had been run off the road. Her little girl, Mandy, was in the back seat. When they found the car, the little girl was missing."

"Oh my God!" Gabriella exclaimed.

"Man, Jack must be going crazy right now," Gabe said, glancing at his parents. "If you'll excuse me, I'm going to check on my wife and son." Gabe's face had blanched with what could only be the fear of a young husband and father when they heard about such a tragedy. He stood up and, with a polite nod at Dawn, said, "Nice to meet you, Dawn. Take care of yourself."

"Thanks. You too."

Gabriella stood up and hugged her son. "It's okay, Gabe. They're safe here."

He glanced at his dad again, who nodded at him, and then he turned and left the dining room.

Gabriella sat in Gabe's empty chair and heaved a deep sigh. "Every time I hear about this kind of tragedy, I just can't help but wonder who these animals are who prey upon innocent people."

Antonio reached out and grasped his wife's hand. As he stroked it with his thumb, he asked, "What does Dawn have to do with it?"

Luca hesitated, glancing at Dawn. She for one didn't mind if his parents knew about her. They seemed like good, open-minded people.

"I'm a psychic," she blurted.

Gabriella and Antonio didn't look shocked at all. In fact, if not for Antonio's slightly raised eyebrow, you'd think she had just told him it was going to rain.

Antonio turned to Luca. "Are you investigating Patricia's death and Mandy's disappearance?"

"Technically, I'm not on the case, but the entire squad was briefed this morning. We're all on the lookout."

"And that's why you contacted Dawn?" Gabriella asked.

"Yes," Luca said. "I asked Dawn to walk by the Richardson place to see if she could get any vibes, then

I met up with her for coffee to discuss any leads she may have found."

"And then I fainted," Dawn finished. "Sorry about that."

Gabriella glanced at her husband, concern etched on her face.

"Did you have a vision of the missing girl?" Antonio asked.

"Yes," Dawn replied. At Luca's nod, she told them everything she'd seen—except their son covered in blood. "Then at the end, I just saw blackness and I felt her confusion, but I think she's okay, unharmed."

"Is that why you fainted?" Gabriella asked. "Does it take a lot out of you?"

"Uh…" Dawn glanced at Luca and then back at his parents. "Sometimes."

"You've been up all night, and it's already past eleven a.m.," Gabriella said to Luca. "Why don't we take Dawn home so you can get some sleep?"

"Thanks, but I want to drive her home."

"Don't worry about me," Dawn piped up. "I'll just hop on the subway."

"No, we can't let you do that," Gabriella said. "You just came out of a dead faint, and Luca said it happened in the middle of the street. I'll drive you home."

"Ma, I can drive Dawn home." Luca raised his eyebrows at his mother, giving her a look that meant he wanted to talk to Dawn.

"Okay, okay." She swiveled enough to smile at Antonio.

"Thank you for the soup and…everything," Dawn said to Antonio and Gabriella. "I really appreciate your kindness."

Gabriella hugged Dawn and whispered in her ear. Luca couldn't hear what she said, but he was sure it had something to do with him.

"I'll be back soon." Luca escorted Dawn out to his car parked on the street.

"I'm sorry I caused such a fuss," Dawn began as Luca held the door for her. "Your parents are such good people. I saw blood in a vision, and you know what happens then…"

"You faint." Luca blew out a breath. "It's okay. Thanks for not telling them anything about seeing blood."

"Uh-huh." When he hopped into the driver's seat, she said, "Luca?"

"Yeah?"

"Don't freak out, but I think the blood was yours."

"Whoa. I'm *really* glad you didn't say anything back there. It's not exactly news that my parents—heck, my entire family—disapproves of me going into law enforcement." He turned to her. "Are you sure you saw me covered in blood?"

"Yes, but I don't think there was a bullet wound, so there is that."

He rolled his eyes. "Yeah, there is that. Did you see anything else besides the blood?"

"Sometimes I'll just get a quick flash of something. I saw bars, like maybe you were at a prison. The second vision—the one that happened in the middle of Mass. Ave.—confirmed the bars and you lying on the ground beside them. I might get another vision. If I do, I'll call you."

"Yeah. After you wake up," he teased. "So what did my mom whisper in your ear?"

Dawn blushed and plucked at the backpack on her lap. "She just said she appreciates me helping you."

"Hmm…" he said, glancing at her pink face. *I bet there was more to it than that.*

"So if everyone in your family is a firefighter, why did you decide to become a cop?" Dawn was clearly trying to change the subject.

Luca put the car in drive and maneuvered out of the tight space. "Like I said, it has to do with my ex."

"Seriously? She was the whole reason?"

Luca glanced at Dawn. "Lisa's dad is on the force. He's a sergeant."

"That must make it tough at work. Is he harder on you than the other cops?"

"Remember, he's not supposed to know I was dating his daughter." Luca kept his eyes on the road. "So let's keep that little secret between us."

"Sure, I understand—I think. Why did you never tell your parents? From what I can tell, they seem understanding."

Luca glanced at her and then back at the road. "It's kind of complicated. We started dating when we were in college, pretty young. So we kept it quiet, because we were both living at home, and she said her dad was an overprotective hard-ass." He hesitated, thinking back on his relationship with Lisa. Maybe it was for the best that he hadn't told his parents. His mother might have had them halfway to the altar by now.

"Oh, I haven't given you my address. But you're headed in the right direction anyway." She told him her address on North Street.

He already knew where she lived. Damn. He hoped she couldn't read minds too.

"Why are relationships so complicated?" Luca asked, changing the topic.

"I don't know. But what I do know is if you can't tell your family about someone you're dating, then that's kind of a warning sign, isn't it?"

"Yeah. Hey, how come we're always talking about me?" He turned to her with a grin. "What about you? Are you dating anyone?"

Dawn shook her head. "Nope."

"That's all you're going to say on the subject?"

"Yep."

He laughed. "C'mon, there's no one you like? No up-and-coming financial whiz or tech guy you see on the elevator every day? Maybe an old boyfriend you'd like to have back?"

"Ugh. No." She crossed her arms and stared out the window.

He'd obviously hit a sore spot. Maybe she was just getting over a bad breakup too. "I'm sorry. I didn't mean to pry."

Dawn turned back to him. "I'm sorry to snap at you." She hesitated. "I used to hang out with this guy who was in a gang. It wasn't a healthy relationship, but I didn't really have a role model for what one of those might look like. He gave me a hard time when I started turning my life around. I bumped into him the other night. Or rather he was waiting for me. Told me he wanted to get back together—or something. Guys in gangs don't exactly date."

Luca was quiet for a moment. "Do you?"

"Do I what?"

"Do you want to get back together with him?"

"Hell no. I never did have deep feelings for him. I'm glad I'm not with him anymore. And the gang... Holy shit. I don't know what I was thinking. I guess I just liked feeling like I belonged—somewhere."

He smiled at her. "I'm glad you're not dating a guy in a gang."

A few minutes later, Luca pulled up front of the old colonial duplex she'd directed him to.

He got out of the car and escorted her up the steps. "Hey, would you be interested in going out sometime?"

He liked Dawn. She was interesting and easy to talk to. Maybe they could become friends. Hell, he could use a good friend. It was hard to share stuff with his family. They meant well, but sometimes he just wanted someone to listen and not lecture.

"You mean to discuss the case?"

"No, I mean to discuss the merits of pepperoni versus Italian sausage pizza."

She laughed. A small dimple appeared in her right cheek. And it didn't hurt that she was really cute.

"Okay, but I draw the line at anchovies."

"Don't tell my mother, but I consider anchovies on pizza an abomination. I always take them off. You're a woman after my own heart."

———～———

"Whew!"

Dawn leaned against the inside of her door. She placed her hand over her racing heart.

"Dawnie, is that you?" Her grandmother's voice floated down the stairs.

"Yes, Gram, it's me. I'll be right there."

Dawn hung up her jacket and purse, then jogged up the stairs to her grandmother's bedroom. "Hi, Gram." She gave her grandmother a kiss on the check. The older woman was in her rocking chair, knitting woolen mittens. She was always knitting for the homeless and usually made a few dozen scarves and mittens every fall and winter and donated them to the local shelter. If that alone could change your karma, Annette should have five gold stars by now or whatever system Karma Cleaners used. She'd have to ask Lynda.

"Honey, why are you home from work? Are you okay?"

Dawn sat on the edge of her grandmother's bed. "Yes, just feeling a bit dizzy, so I came home early."

Annette gave her one of her shrewd *I ain't buyin' what ye're sellin'* looks. "What's this really about?"

"I'm helping a guy look for a missing girl." Dawn tapped her phone, searching for a news article. She found it and handed her phone to her grandma.

"Oh no," Annette said with a shake of her head. "What a terrible tragedy. But who is this guy you're helping? The father?"

"No, he's a cop who knows the family."

Annette's eyebrows shot up at that.

"Yeah, I know. But I just met him by accident, and we had coffee this morning and he took me to the girl's house, which happens to be in his neighborhood."

"Did you see where she is?"

"Sort of, but it was kind of vague. I could sense the little girl, but all I could see was darkness. Maybe she's in a dark room?"

"Did you get dizzy after that? You came home in a car."

"Yes, Luca, the cop I met with, took me to his parents' house, and they were home and gave me some soup. They were very kind."

"But there's more to this…" Annette reached for Dawn's hand. Her eyes widened, as she seemed to sense what Dawn had been through. "You had another vision, didn't you? About the young man."

"Yes, I saw him covered in blood."

Annette nodded. She'd seen enough bad stuff in her lifetime; Dawn knew that for a fact. Nothing shocked her grandmother anymore.

"You get into bed and get some rest. I'll wake you when it's dinner time. I'm making a casserole for dinner."

"Grandma, what am I going to do? I can't miss work every time I have a psychic vision."

"You need to figure out how to keep the visions from affecting your heart, mind, and body. You can still help people without making yourself sick. You need to train your body to do that."

"How? How do I do that?"

"Practice, sweetie. When you get a vision, write it down and date it. Don't hang onto it emotionally like it's part of you. That vision doesn't belong to you. It's not about you. You're like a radio transmitter or a TV set.

And you have to learn to step back and allow it to come through and then record it and move on. That's what I was told to do."

"Did you faint?"

"Not really. I'd get dizzy sometimes. But right now, I want you to get some rest. We'll talk more about it later over dinner, and I'll tell you some tricks you can use to keep yourself grounded."

Dawn hugged her grandmother and went to her room. She wished she'd told Annette about her abilities years ago. Her grandmother had probably figured it out anyway but had waited for Dawn to come forward. Annette was like that. She'd learned not to interfere, just to offer wisdom when asked. Dawn hoped Gram could help her through this inner turmoil she felt every time she had a vision, especially one involving blood.

Chapter 5

THURSDAY NIGHT—OR WAS IT FRIDAY MORNING? LUCA was having a hard time keeping his days straight, because he left for work on one day and returned home the next, even though it was just an eight-hour shift.

He and Joe were getting breakfast before the commuters began clogging up the fast-food lines. He took a bite of his breakfast sandwich and dropped the rest of it onto its paper wrapper. All this grease wasn't doing his stomach any favors.

"You okay, kid?" Joe asked.

Luca thought about that. Was he okay? Police work wasn't what he'd thought it would be, but something else was bugging him. Something important was missing.

He shrugged. "I guess."

"You've been quiet all night. What's eating you?"

"Besides the ulcer all this fast food is going to give me?"

Joe laughed. "You don't get ulcers from burgers, Fierro. You get them from stress. Are you feeling stressed? Or more stressed than you should be from your first week on the job?"

"I...uh...it's hard to put into words. I guess I had hoped the job would be more fulfilling. I mean, yeah, we answer a robbery call, but when we get there, the perp is long gone. And he's always medium height, brown hair and eyes, wearing jeans and a black hoodie, no scars or—"

"Look, kid, it's easy to get discouraged. You can't win 'em all. Some days, you can't win any of 'em. But you gotta be ready. I know this job comes with long stretches of boredom punctuated by moments of sheer terror. There aren't a lot of people who'd put up with the shit we do. But if we weren't here, the rest of the population would be defenseless. And there are always people out there who'll take advantage of chaos. Sometimes, just by our presence, we're stemming the tide of chaos, and we don't even know it."

Luca nodded. He hadn't quite thought of it that way. Even if it wasn't very exciting, there was the very real possibility they were deterring crime just sitting here in a fast-food restaurant with their cruiser outside.

"Help!" A woman burst into the restaurant, glancing around wildly until she found them. "Police! A guy just snatched my purse."

Luca was up and running for the door. "Which way did he go?"

She pointed to his right. "That way."

Rushing out the door, he caught sight of long legs in a pair of jeans running around the next corner. Putting on the best burst of speed a human could manage, Luca took off after the suspect.

When he rounded the corner, he spotted a guy who was indeed carrying a woman's purse. The guy was fast, but Luca was faster.

The guy disappeared around the next corner, but Luca spotted him as he tried to enter a business from its back door. He tackled the guy on the linoleum floor of a bakery, and the two of them went sliding into a metal table covered in flour. It tipped just enough to coat both of their dark blue pants in white powder.

"You're under arrest," Luca said, whipping out his handcuffs and immobilizing the guy in record speed.

A portly older gentleman walked back to where they were with his hands on his hips. "I knew I should have locked that door this morning."

Luca yanked the guy up off the floor, looped the leather purse over his shoulder, and recited his Miranda rights as he marched him back to the cruiser. Joe and the woman were standing outside the restaurant. He was taking notes as she answered questions for the report he'd have Luca write up later.

"My purse! You got it!" And as he handed it to her, she babbled, "Thank you! I had my mother's ring in there. I was getting it sized to fit my future daughter-in-law."

Luca nodded. "Glad to be of service, ma'am. Did you want to check and make sure it's still there?"

"Yes," she said quickly. She opened the zipper and fished out a small box, revealing a sparkly diamond ring inside. She let out a deep sigh of relief. "Oh, thank goodness."

As Luca stuffed the guy into the back seat of the cruiser, the perp said, "Damn, you can run. I didn't even see you until you were on top of me."

Joe smiled and offered one nod of respect in Luca's direction.

Almost as if the universe had heard his apathy, Luca took the compliments with ease and felt like he understood what Joe had been trying to tell him a little better.

Their presence had stopped this guy from getting

away with grabbing the purse. Luca had been able to prevent a personal tragedy. Okay, maybe tragedy was a bit of an overstatement, but as they pulled away and he saw tears glisten in the woman's eyes, he felt damn good.

"Hey, Fierro?"

"Yeah?"

"Better clean your pants as soon as we get to the station. Otherwise, they'll think you made a cocaine bust."

———

TGIF. Dawn did a little twirl in her office chair when 1:00 p.m. rolled around.

She'd got to work that morning without any mishaps and no visions, thank goodness. She couldn't afford to miss another day.

Last night, Annette had made her some chamomile tea and told her a cup of tea after a vision would help. She did feel better after the tea, but that could also have been due to the fact that she was curled up on the sofa with Annette, watching an old movie at the time.

Work was pretty uneventful. Her manager asked her how she was doing, and Dawn came up with some twenty-four-hour bug excuse. Dawn's mind kept wandering to Luca. She didn't have any more bloody visions, so that was a good sign. But what was more telling was she kept glancing at her phone, to see if he might have texted her about going out. Would he call her? Why was she so nervous about it?

Dawn always finished work at 1:00 p.m. on Fridays, since she started every day at 8:30 a.m. and worked until 5:00 p.m. Monday to Thursday. Those extra three hours came in handy, especially given her new "extracurricular activities." Dawn hopped on the subway and headed to her first weekly check-in at Karma Cleaners. Today, she would talk to Lynda about Luca and the missing girl.

The dry cleaner was busy with a line that reached the door. She looked around and tried to discern if the people in line were there because they had spilled wine on a shirt or because they had a shitload of bad karma in their lives. When she got to the front of the line, she smiled and greeted a petite brunette wearing a pair of neon-pink 1950s secretary glasses.

"Hi. I'm supposed to ask for May."

"Hi, Dawn. Are you here for pickup or drop-off?"

Dawn leaned in and gave the code phrase. "I'm here to pick up my wedding dress."

"Just go down the hall to the back where we have our special orders."

"Right. Thanks." Dawn smiled and opened the door on May's left. The code phrase would change every week, but she understood it was the easiest way to avoid any odd looks by the dry-cleaning customers. Before she and Lynda had parted after their initial meeting, she had been given the code phrase and a three-digit code. She walked down the long hallway, barely noticing the gray floor tiles and off-white walls. The door at the end of the hallway had a sign that read SPECIAL ORDERS. She had to punch in her three-digit code to unlock it. Then she walked down a shorter hallway that led to two sliding glass doors. Dawn sighed in pleasure as she stepped through the doors.

The other side of Karma Cleaners was an oasis of calm. A huge atrium featured a fountain with a massive

porcelain statue of a woman holding a watering can
that poured crystalline water into a shimmering glass-
bottomed pool. Dawn was in awe, considering from the
outside, Karma Dry Cleaners was tucked between a foot
clinic and an H&R Block. *That's some big-ass magic*,
Dawn mused as she strolled past the busy food court
area where people were tucking into their lunches from a
dizzying variety of food kiosks that included fresh sushi,
vegan soups, exotic salads, and even a gourmet cupcake
cart. Lynda had told her the flavors changed every
month. This month's special was a chocolate cupcake
with mocha hazelnut buttercream icing and a dollop of
Nutella inside. Mmm. As far as Dawn was concerned,
you couldn't have enough Nutella in your life.

Dawn stepped onto the elevator and rode up to the
third floor where the Karma caseworkers' offices were
located. She greeted the bubbly brunette receptionist
with a smile.

"Lynda said to go right in," Amanda, according to her
name tag, said with a smile.

Dawn thanked her and walked down the short hallway to Lynda's office. Opening the door, she noticed
Lynda was on a video conference call, but Lynda waved
her to her seat.

"Oh, it's absolutely heaven. Wait till you taste it,
Karma."

Dawn's eyes widened. Lynda was actually talking to
Karma?

"Dawn Forest just walked in. Do you want to meet
her?"

"Absolutely," said a woman's voice from the monitor.

Lynda gestured for Dawn to come around the desk.

"Karma, this is my new superstar recruit," Lynda enthused. "She's doing such an amazing job in such a short time."

Dawn didn't realize she had done anything yet.

"Good to meet you, Dawn." Karma smiled. She was surprisingly normal-looking. She had auburn hair, pulled back as if she wore it in a bun or chignon.

"It's wonderful to meet you, er, Ms. Karma."

Karma laughed and it made Dawn think of tinkling bells.

"You can call me Karma. Although I do like the sound of Ms. Karma. Maybe I should use that at the annual convention. What do you think, Lynda?"

"Love love love it."

"There are conventions?" Dawn asked.

"Oh, of course," Karma replied. "We have them in different places every year. This year, we'll be at Machu Picchu. I let it slip to Oprah over breakfast this morning, accidentally on purpose."

"Oprah?"

"Karma and Oprah are very good friends," Lynda said. "You know whose idea it was to give out cars?" Lynda pointed to the screen.

"Stop," Karma said, waving her hand. "We were just chatting, and I said wouldn't it be cool if you gave everyone in your audience a car? I made sure the recipients deserved one, and Oprah made it happen."

"Will Oprah be attending the event?" Dawn asked.

"Oprah has attended in the past, but her schedule is pretty full. This year, our keynote speaker will be Melinda Gates."

Dawn's eyes widened. "As in Bill Gates's wife?"

"Well, we prefer to say Bill is Melinda Gates's husband," Lynda quipped.

"It sounds amazing. Do all the caseworkers attend?"

"We hope so," Karma replied. "We have caseworkers all over the world working with people who are just as determined as you are to change their karma."

"We're so proud of you, Dawn," Lynda gushed.

Humbled, Dawn thanked them for their faith in her.

"Oh, trust me, this is all you," Karma said. "You're doing excellent work with your psychic abilities. Once you learn to control them, there is no telling the kind of positive impact you can have on the world."

"Thank you again," Dawn said. "I'll keep working as hard as I can."

"And just so you know," Karma added, "don't worry about your visions. You're stronger than you think. We have someone you can work with."

Dawn nodded, wondering just how much Karma knew about her psychic abilities. They seemed to know everything about her. Did they know she was helping Luca find the missing girl?

"By the way, that cop, Luca Fierro, is a hottie," Karma said with a wink.

Well, that answered that.

"I have to run. A polar ice cap is melting, and I'm tired of all the 'climate change isn't real' crap. Now I have to go and bang a few heads."

They said their goodbyes, and Lynda shut off her monitor. "Isn't she a kick?"

"She certainly is," Dawn replied, sitting in the plush leather chair across from Lynda's desk.

"Now, let's talk about you." Lynda leaned forward

and pushed a bowl of brightly wrapped candies at Dawn. "I have a sweet tooth. Have one. They're from the Twists and Turns Candy Shoppe downstairs, and they have no calories!"

Dawn reached for a striped orange-and-white wrapper.

"Oh, that's a good one," Lynda said as she reached for a sweet wrapped in shiny blue foil. "Tell me how your week went."

Dawn popped the candy in her mouth and immediately tasted a blend of orange citrus with a creamy, swirly undertone. "I was thinking of reaching out to one of the community youth organizations that help street kids. I want to be able to help kids on the street and get them away from drugs, prostitution, and gangs."

"I love that idea, and given your background, you're the perfect person to do it." Slipping on her Wonder Woman glasses, Lynda turned back to her computer. Punching the keys like a madwoman, she printed up a sheet and handed it to Dawn. "We have a contact at the Youth Community Center: Tansy Miller. I'll let her know who you are, and she can plug you in. They're having an open house this weekend. So you can go and introduce yourself."

"Is Tansy a caseworker or someone like me?"

Lynda leaned back in her swivel chair. "Tansy is a transgendered former prostitute and former heroin addict. Aphrodite found her on a rainy night in a dark alley. She'd just been raped and was barely conscious."

"Aphrodite, as in the Greek goddess of love?"

"The one and only. Well, she goes by other names in different pantheons, but our goddesses go by whichever name they like. She likes Venus too. Anyway, Dee Dee brought Tansy into our karma clinic, and after she recovered, we put her in a drug rehab program. Now Tansy's kicking butt in the Keene Street area where a ton of street kids hang out. I'm sure you know the area."

Dawn nodded. "Yes, I do. I used to hang out there myself. But I didn't know goddesses existed—and that they took an interest in grassroots work too."

"Oh yes," Lynda replied. "Aphrodite goes out regularly to keep herself grounded, so to speak. She can get rather daydreamy otherwise." She grinned. "Now, tell me more about Luca Fierro."

Dawn told Lynda everything about her first meeting with Luca then about him calling her at work. She was embarrassed to mention she faked being sick, but Lynda just gave her a knowing smile and told her to continue.

"You have a remarkable gift," Lynda said after Dawn had finished her story. "And I know you're going to help Luca find little Mandy."

"I hope so," Dawn replied. "I wish I had the ability of those psychics on TV. They seem to know everything right away."

"Well, that's partly true and partly showbiz," Lynda said. "Besides, you're just as talented as they are, and you are determined to help. I think your grandmother's advice was excellent. We do have a psychic division here led by Minerva." Lynda picked up her iPad and began swiping and tapping. Dawn's phone beeped. "I just sent you Minerva's contact info. She's the best of the best and can help you nurture your ability."

"Isn't she in this building?" Dawn asked, checking her texts.

"No, she has her own space. It's just as wonderful as Karma Cleaners. It's called The Crafty Candle. It's a real craft store, and in back—"

"It's just as huge and amazing as Karma Cleaners?"

"You got it."

"Minerva? Isn't she also known as Athena, the goddess of wisdom and war?"

"Yes," Lynda said with a grin. "You know your mythology." Then she giggled. "Which isn't so mythical."

"Wow." Dawn's eyes widened. "So, they're all real?"

"Yes, but they're all independent. Karma and Minerva have a lot in common and help each other with clients and special projects."

"I have a feeling this is only scratching the surface."

"Oh, you better believe it, baby," Lynda quipped.

"Well, I will definitely reach out to Minerva if I need her help."

"You can just show up any time. She'll know when you're ready. Until then, you have a lot on your plate, so dig in." She chuckled at her own joke.

An hour later, Dawn stepped on her subway, feeling good about her session with Lynda and what she needed to do in order to clean up her karma. She had also learned next week's code phrase was "I'm here to pick up my son's ninja costume."

She glanced at her watch and noted it was just after 4:00 p.m. on a Friday and she would be part of the usual commuter traffic. Her baton firmly in hand, Dawn reached the steps to the subway terminal when an arm grabbed her shoulder from behind. Lifting her baton, she turned, ready to strike.

"Whoa, Dawn! It's just me."

Luca's wide blue eyes looked a little startled.

"Oh. Sorry. I thought…"

"Yeah. You can relax. Those are some impressive reflexes you have."

"I…uh…I was just thinking about my past. Where I came from, I had to be tough and ready for anything."

"Have you been attacked?"

She worried her lip. How much should she tell him? Probably enough to explain herself and maybe even let him get a glimpse of the real Dawn. Hopefully, he wouldn't run in the opposite direction. "I don't mind answering your question, but this isn't really a great place to talk."

"Yeah." He glanced around. "Do you have time for a coffee? Or a short walk?"

"Sure. I'll just text my grandmother so she doesn't worry."

They walked toward Copley Square. As soon as Dawn had sent the reassuring text, she stuffed her phone in her leather jacket's pocket. "So, how are you doing?"

"Not bad. My training officer, Joe, said he'd take me to JJ Kelly's for dinner. It's a cop bar."

"That's nice of him."

Luca chuckled. "Yeah. He said it's because I didn't quit or get killed during my first week on the job, which would have made him look bad."

Dawn grinned. "Is that typical cop humor?"

"Pretty much. So, not to get distracted…you were saying something about being attacked? Was it recent?"

"No. I didn't mean to alarm you. I've never really been attacked—at least not by a stranger."

His brows lifted. "By someone you know?"

She stopped. "It's not what you think."

"What do I think?" He just gazed at her.

"I may be able to sense things, but I can't read minds."

"Neither can I."

They just stared at each other for a few moments. At last, she heaved a sigh. "I think I told you about my involvement with a gang at one point. Right?"

"Yeah. Was it one of them?"

"Sort of. I mean, it wasn't really an attack. They used me."

His brows shot up.

"Not like that! Jeez."

"Well, the term 'gangbanger' comes from somewhere."

"Not from me. Sure, I lost my virginity to one of them when I was fifteen, but—"

"Fifteen? That's statutory rape."

She snorted. "Ask a gangbanger if he cares." She walked on in silence.

"I'm sorry. Go ahead. You were saying they used you?"

"My psychic ability. I should have never told them about it. The next thing I knew, I was their lookout. When I said I wanted to finish high school, they tried to entice me to quit school, saying they'd give me a cut of the profits."

"You weren't making any money?"

"I got a pittance compared to the others before that. They thought I'd quit school as soon as I learned how easy it was to support myself and my grandmother once I got my hands dirty. I have to admit I thought about it." She sighed. "It wasn't an easy time for me."

"So how did you get out? Most gangs claim you for life—not that it will be a long one."

"I had to make a deal with the leader."

"What kind of deal?"

She didn't want to tell him the rest. He didn't need to know that "Little Bobo," who was over six feet and 220 pounds of steroids, made her deal his drugs at school during her senior year.

"Let's just say I worked for him for a year, and then when he didn't want to let me go, I had a hissy fit."

"And what does a hissy fit look like?"

She smirked. "Picture all 110 pounds of me jumping on the back of a guy twice my size, trying to choke him with one arm and beat him black and blue with the other."

"Wow. And you're still alive?"

"Yeah. He was laughing the whole time until one of his guys cocked a gun. Then he yelled at him to put it away, and three other guys peeled me off of him."

"Weren't you afraid he'd retaliate?"

"At that moment, I was so angry, I didn't care if he did."

"Wow. And did the others do anything to you?"

"Mostly just verbal threats, flexing their muscles and that kind of shit."

Luca shook his head, looking amazed. "You really are a badass."

She grinned. "Oh yeah. Be afraid. Be very afraid."

Friday night. The last night shift of his first week. He'd have a three-day weekend and then switch to day shifts.

He didn't know if he'd like the day shift better than the night, but he did know one thing—his first week went pretty well. Except for the missing little girl and her murdered mom. Even though it wasn't his case, he knew he could help.

The detectives didn't have what he had, his paranormal powers and a friend who was psychic. If only he knew a detective on the force he could trust, someone he could confide in who'd let him help solve the case. Well, if he didn't know anyone now, maybe he could get to know them.

He and Joe were let out of their briefing, and before Joe reached the outside door, Luca grabbed his arm, stopping him.

"Hey, before we take off, do you mind if I talk to the detectives for a minute?"

"The detectives? Why?"

"It's about the missing girl."

"You have some information?"

"Maybe."

Joe hesitated but eventually nodded and said, "Sure. They're probably upstairs."

Luca had been given a tour of the whole station a few weeks before, but he didn't have any reason to go back to certain areas of it.

They walked all the way down to the end of a long hall, passing the lieutenant's office on the way. Beyond that were cubicles, and at the very end, two cops talking to each other seemed surprised to see anyone coming their way.

"Can I help you?" one of them said.

"Hi, I'm Luca Fierro, and this is my TO, Joe

Sorenson. I heard about the missing Richardson girl. Is that your case?"

They glanced at each other. "Yeah. I'm Detective Morrow."

"Detective Griffin," said the other one, and they both shook his hand.

"Do you have any information for us?" Morrow asked.

"Not sure. I just wanted you to know I live near the family. If there's anything I can do, I'd like to be of help."

The two detectives smirked at each other. "Yeah, well, if you see anything suspicious, like if the father suddenly shows up carrying a new teddy bear or something, let us know."

Surprised, Luca asked, "Are you suspecting the father?"

"No. We don't have any suspects at the moment."

"Oh. Hey, I've heard psychics can sometimes be of help. Is that something you'd be open to?"

The detectives cracked up, laughing.

"Don't mind him, guys. He's new." Joe seemed to think he needed defending and acted as if he were naive.

Luca glanced around the detectives' area. One of them had a file called "Unsolved Mysteries" on top of his inbox.

A picture of Morrow's face superimposed over the face of Glinda, the Good Witch of the North in *The Wizard of Oz*, hung on the outside wall. Luca pointed to it. "What's that about?"

Griffin chuckled. "Someone Photoshopped that when Morrow busted a satanic cult last spring."

Joe laughed, and Luca smiled. "Congrats. I guess you guys have to maintain a sense of humor to deal with some of the crap that goes down in this city."

"Yeah. It helps," Morrow said. "Listen, thanks for coming up and offering your support."

"Sure thing. I want to help any way I can."

"You say you live around the area where the family lives?"

"All my life. Right on Mass. Ave. near Tremont."

"Nice. Well, if you hear anything, let us know. We can use a lead right now."

"You didn't get anything from the accident scene?"

"Nothing. You'd think there would be a print from someone trying to get a child's car seat unbuckled from the back, but the only prints belonged to the victim."

"Damn. I'm sorry to hear that. She's a cute little kid, and the mom seemed nice."

"How about the father? How well do you know him?"

"Not well. He says hello when he sees one of us neighbors, but not much beyond that."

"Okay, thanks for keeping your eyes open," Morrow said.

"Nice to meet you both." Luca shook their hands again and left.

Joe gave him a strange look when they were out of earshot. "Did that accomplish what you'd hoped?"

Luca shrugged. "I wasn't hoping to accomplish anything, really. I just wanted to know if they've had some progress in the case."

"You don't know that they haven't."

"They just said they had no leads."

"They also don't want a rookie working their case.

You can get in a lot of trouble for interfering in someone else's shit, especially with something like this. If you don't follow procedure, you could fuck up a sting, ruin evidence, or blow the whole court case in a number of ways. Not only that, you could get fired."

Luca looked over at him, surprised. "I wasn't planning on interfering."

"Good. See that you don't."

So much for a good end to his first week. The detectives seemed cool enough, but was Joe right? Could his desire to catch who did this interfere with the case? He wished Dawn had given him more to go on. Maybe he'd text her on his break and ask if she'd had any more visions. Hell, even a flash of something or someone might help.

He wouldn't know what to do with the information though. He didn't want to lose his job.

Chapter 6

"ARE THERE ANY NICE YOUNG MEN AT YOUR WORKPLACE?"

"Graaaaan."

"Dawwwwwn."

Dawn and Annette were curled up on the sofa and had just finished watching *Sleepless in Seattle*. It was one of her grandmother's favorite movies. "I wish you could find someone like Tom Hanks," Annette said. "I think he should have married Meg Ryan for real. I always thought they made such a cute couple."

"Grandma, it's called acting. Besides, he's been happily married forever."

"Well, I'm not surprised. The good ones usually are." Annette gave her a playful swat on her leg. "But seriously, aren't there any nice boys at your job or even in the building where you work?"

"I don't really pay attention to the men in my building. I've only been there a little over a month." Dawn cuddled the pillow closer to her, Luca's cute grin and bright-blue eyes flashing through her mind.

"Oh…" Annette said with a sly grin.

"What?"

"There *is* someone. Is he nice?"

Dawn blew out a breath. "Actually, I did meet a nice guy this week, but not at work."

"Well, he can't be from around here, because most

of the young men in this neighborhood aren't the 'nice guy' type."

"He's not from around here."

"Well, good. Tell me about him." Annette looked like an excited teenager. Dawn hadn't seen her grandmother so energized in a long time. She sure as heck didn't want her to get her hopes up.

Dawn fidgeted. "I already did. The cop I mentioned to you. The one I'm helping with the missing child case."

"A police officer. Hmm."

"His girlfriend just broke up with him. I doubt he's even interested in dating anyone right now. Not seriously anyway."

"His girlfriend broke up with him? What's wrong with him?"

"Nothing is wrong with him. He said they started dating in college, and she wants to meet other people before settling down." Dawn remembered the vision she'd had of Lisa with another guy, driving around in a red Corvette.

"If you ask me, I think there are far too many young people wanting to let loose. It gets you nowhere. Look where it got me, and look where it got your mother—"

"And look where it got me."

"What do you mean?" Annette wrapped her arms around Dawn. "You are doing so well. You finished college, and now you have a good job. You are going places, young lady, and don't you forget it."

"Thank you for being my biggest cheerleader, Gran."

"Always." Annette gave her a kiss on the forehead, then stood up. "I'm going to make us some herbal tea."

Dawn stretched her legs and closed her eyes. She

was looking forward to heading over to the Youth Community Center tomorrow, but she hoped she wouldn't mess up. She wanted to make a difference, not screw up lives. They had enough screwed-up people in this area, let alone around the world.

Pop! Pop! Pop!

"Grandma, are you making popcorn?"

"No, why?" Annette called back from the kitchen.

Dawn heard the popping sounds again, followed by screams and cursing.

"Grandma, it's gunshots!" Alarmed, Dawn jumped up, ran to the kitchen, and pulled Annette down on the kitchen floor. They had thought about setting up a panic room in a closet but never did it. You could get shot just by sitting in your living room.

"Are you okay?"

"I'm fine, dear," Annette said, out of breath. "I wish they would stop with these guns. Too many senseless deaths over the years."

Pop! Pop! Pop!

Dawn called 911, and then she texted Luca. She knew he was working tonight, and she trusted him.

Shots fired on my street. Very close.

Within seconds, her phone pinged back with a text from Luca: On my way.

———⁓———

Luca and Joe were parked at a McDonald's. It wasn't Luca's favorite restaurant, but the sandwiches hit the spot, and they could get their food in a hurry. Joe was a good guy, and Luca liked him. But unlike his father, Antonio, who could probably still keep up with any of his sons, Joe's twenty-five extra pounds thanks to the night shift and twenty-four-hour fast-food places slowed him down some.

He was about to chomp into his burger when the dispatcher alerted them to a 10-71, shots fired in the area of Dorset Ave. and North Street.

"That's where Dawn lives!"

"Who's Dawn?" Joe asked, shoving the last bite of his sandwich in his mouth as he put the car in gear and pulled out of the parking lot.

"A friend of mine."

Joe flicked on the siren at the same time as a text came in on Luca's phone.

It was Dawn, asking for help. He texted her back, hoping they would get there before anyone was hurt.

"I know a shortcut," Joe said.

He made a left and drove down an alley behind an old warehouse, then out the other side onto Dorset Ave.

Luca's heart was beating fast. He hoped Dawn was okay. If there was one thing he knew from his training and experience, it was that sometimes a situation could escalate in a matter of seconds.

They arrived only a couple of minutes later, just as another police cruiser was arriving.

Joe radioed the officers in the other car. "You guys cruise the main drag, and we'll go on foot and check out the houses on North. Over."

"Copy that," Amanda Tillson replied from the other vehicle. Luca had met her the other day. She was a ten-year veteran on the force and before that was in the Air

Force, with two tours in Afghanistan under her belt. She was one badass chick. Her partner was Delvin Jordan, who, like Luca, was a trainee. Luca liked Delvin and thought he was a good guy. They came out of the police academy together. He was married with twin boys.

Amanda and Delvin drove away, and Joe and Luca stayed in their car and started cruising along the street, keeping a lookout.

A chair smashed through a window just down the street from where they were.

"Change of plans," Joe radioed Amanda. "We may have found the location. Double back." Joe gave them the address as they got out of the car and ran toward the disturbance.

"Copy that."

As they approached the run-down three-decker, they could hear shouting and cursing. The house was just two doors down from where Dawn lived. Luca wanted to go check on her, but he had to do his job first. Luca and Joe ran toward the steps at the front of the house. A man was standing by the broken window.

Joe called out, "This is the police. Lay down any weapons and put your hands in the air."

The man on the porch followed Joe's orders immediately. Luca was behind him in a split second and cuffed the man.

A woman screamed for help from inside, followed by a man yelling at her to shut up. "I'm not going back there again," the same man's voice shouted.

"If you come out, we can talk this through. Just put your weapon down and come outside with your hands up."

"Fuck you!" Gunshots riddled the front door, followed by more screaming.

Luca and Joe stood on either side of the door, looking at each other.

"Go around back and see if there might be a way in," Joe said.

Luca nodded and took off around the back of the house.

When he returned, he said, "Joe, I can get in from upstairs. There's a second-floor window next to the flat porch roof. The window is open a few inches."

"And then what?" Joe countered. "Get shot on your way down the stairs? This is your first week on the job, kid. I can't risk it."

"Joe, please, I know I can do it."

He sighed. "All right, go ahead. Then we'll proceed from there. Don't get shot. That's an order."

"Yes, sir." Luca stayed low as he ran around to the back of the house. The postage-stamp-sized yard was full of junk: Luca could make out old tires, a rusted-out wheelbarrow, and a mattress. He glanced up and spotted the open window on the second floor of the house. In a split-second decision, he did what he had to do. He opened the top button of his shirt, transformed into his phoenix form, grabbed his uniform, including his duty belt, in his beak and talons, then flew onto the porch roof. As soon as he shifted back, he opened the window wider and slid right in. He dropped his clothes on the bedroom floor, changed back into his phoenix form, then glided down the stairs, where he spied a man with his arm wrapped around a woman's neck.

"You bitch." The man pressed the gun to the woman's

temple. "You made me do this. You fucked my best friend when I was in jail. In my own bed. MY BED!"

The young woman whimpered, tears streaming down her face. "Please don't hurt me."

Joe called, "Why don't you come out and we can talk about it," from the other side of the front door.

The man pointed his weapon at the door and cocked the gun again. "I'm not coming out, and I'm not going back to prison! You figure it out!"

Luca took the opening and swooped in. He landed on top of the man's head and dug his claws in.

"What the fuck?" The shooter screamed and began flailing at him. Luca let go, circled the man, who by now had covered his head, and plucked the gun out of the shooter's hand before he even knew what hit him. The suspect ran out of the room, cursing all the while. Luca flew back up the stairs with the gun in his beak, then dropped it out the window.

He transformed back into his human form, dressed in seconds, pulled his own gun out, and rushed back downstairs.

He whispered to the woman, "Where is he?"

She whispered, "Probably the kitchen, getting a knife."

Luca peeked around the corner, saw the man, and yelled. "Hands up! Now!"

The man had a drawer open but apparently hadn't had time to locate a suitable knife.

Luca strode forward with his gun pointed at the shooter.

The suspect's eyes were wide, and thankfully, he put his hands in the air.

"Don't shoot!" the man said.

Luca cuffed him, then pulled out his radio and pressed the button. "All clear."

Moments later, Joe came in through the front door, followed by Amanda and Delvin. Joe raised an eyebrow that said *I don't know how you managed to pull this off, but we'll talk about it later*.

Luca knew he had to come up with a cover story, and he wasn't looking forward to writing up *that* report. His mind was already churning, trying to come up with something plausible. Saying he climbed the pile of junk to the window should work. He saw an opportunity to save lives and acted. He had to.

They took the shooter back to the squad car while Amanda and Delvin escorted the woman out. They were both babbling about a large bird with bright red and yellow tail feathers that had flown into the house and grabbed the gun.

Two more squad cars arrived. While Joe was speaking to the other officers, Luca texted Dawn that it was all clear. He asked her to come outside.

A few moments later, Dawn appeared on her front stoop. Luca was standing at the base of the stairs and tried to keep from smiling at her appearance. She looked adorable in flannel pajamas decorated with penguins. She'd thrown a coat over her shoulders and was gazing at the activity around her.

"You okay?" Luca asked.

She nodded, coming down the three steps and standing in front of him. "Are you okay?"

Her eyes reflected worry, and he wanted to allay her fears. "I'm great." He grinned. "Nice outfit."

"Hey, I was ready for bed when the commotion

started. I never thought about staying dressed for a neighborhood shoot-out."

Luca nodded. "Yeah, unfortunately, this happened too close to you. We got him though. Did you hear anything else before we arrived?"

Dawn shook her head. "No, just the shots and lots of shouting and swearing. It sounded like he was in some kind of Wild West movie, making threats and shooting up into the air. I'm sure he must have hit a few poor birds with all the shots he fired."

Luca tried to clear his expression at her comment about birds. He wondered if she sensed or had had an actual vision that exposed him as a shape-shifter—or was she simply making a joke? "Well, I have to get these people to jail. I'm glad you're safe. Call me if anything else happens, okay?"

She smiled. "Thank you. Trying to keep this neighborhood protected seems like an impossible task. I feel better knowing you're around."

"I wish you didn't live here. It's not safe, Dawn."

"Well, I'm not exactly flush with cash, am I? Besides, I've lived here all my life. I can take care of myself and my grandmother."

"I know you're tough, but promise me you'll always call or text me if you're ever in trouble."

She gazed at him, and he wondered what she was thinking. Her pretty gray-green eyes glowed in the moonlight, and he had the sudden urge to kiss her. *Damn! Not here, dummy.*

"Fierro, we need to get going," Joe called out.

"I've gotta go," Luca said.

"It's okay. I know you're on the job. Thanks for

getting here so fast." Dawn gave him a sweet smile and then a little wave as she trotted back up the steps and inside. He heard locks snap into place and felt a sense of relief that she was safe. In that moment, he decided he would help Dawn and her grandmother get away from this area…somehow.

Dawn heaved a deep sigh, leaning against the inside of her front door. Relief washed over her. And fear as well. She had to get her stubborn grandmother out of this neighborhood. It was becoming far too dangerous. Thank goodness she knew Luca. She felt safer knowing he was just a phone call away, but at the end of the day, she could only rely on herself and Annette. Besides, it wasn't like they were dating or anything. He was still hung up on his ex-girlfriend, Lisa. She shook her head and went back into the living room. Annette was probably exhausted by now.

"Gran, are you okay?" Dawn flicked on the lamp, and her grandmother poked her head up from the couch where she was lying down.

"I'll be fine, sweetie. I've been through worse before and likely will again."

Dawn helped Annette stand and then held her arm as they started upstairs. "That's just it, Gran," Dawn began. "I don't want you to go through anything like this ever again. You already got shot in the leg before I was born. You still limp sometimes."

Annette patted Dawn's hand. "Don't you worry about me, dear. I'll be just fine. I want you to focus on your career and your own life. Maybe even a nice young man."

Dawn rolled her eyes at Annette's twinkly expression.

"Was that police officer the same young man you were telling me about?"

"Yes. How did you see him from inside? Did you peek out a window?"

"I just heard his voice. Seems like you're sweet on him and vice versa."

"Oh, Gran." Dawn laid her hand on Annette's shoulder. "I do like him, a lot, and that's what scares me. I'm not exactly a great catch."

Annette suddenly stopped and grabbed Dawn's shoulders. "Don't ever say that, young lady."

When Dawn hesitated, Annette gave her a little shake. "You are an amazing and strong young woman. Any man would be proud to have you in his life. Don't ever doubt that. Okay?"

Dawn smiled at Annette. "Okay, okay. You're one tough cookie."

"Well, it takes one to know one." Annette tapped Dawn on the nose. "And speaking of cookies. Since we never got our tea, how about one of my home-made peanut butter cookies and a cup of hot chocolate before bed?"

"That sounds fantastic right now."

As her grandmother limped back downstairs, Dawn followed and pulled out her cell phone to check her messages. Her heart skipped a beat when she saw a new text from Luca: I like the penguins BTW ;)

She texted back her own smiley face and thanked him again. Then as she waited for her snack, she stretched out on the couch and thought about those blue eyes.

She sighed again. She was in big trouble as far as Luca Fierro was concerned.

A cop and an ex-gang girl? Talk about opposites!

~~~

"You could get in big trouble for doing what you did tonight."

After Luca and Joe hauled the shooter in and processed him, they went back out on the road, stopping for a quick coffee at a Dunkin' Donuts drive-through.

"I'm sorry, Joe. I don't want to disappoint you." Luca glanced at the older man as he bit into a cinnamon cruller.

"Don't give me that look, Fierro."

"What look?"

"That 'you shouldn't be eating a doughnut' look," Joe said around a mouthful. "This is stress eating."

"What about the other eleven doughnuts in that box?" Luca asked with a grin.

"I've got a lot of stress," Joe replied, licking his fingers and reaching for a Boston cream. "Besides, we're talking about you, not me. What happened in there?"

Luca sighed. "It's like I said, I climbed up a pile of junk, got into the upstairs bedroom through an open window, and as I was making my way downstairs, the perp swung his gun away from the woman and pointed it at the front door. That's when I made my move. He had his back to me, so he didn't see me coming. I had no choice. He could have shot her or whoever came through that door."

Joe wiped the side of his mouth with a napkin and then reached for his coffee. Taking a sip of the strong brew, he said, "I believe you, but next time, wait. We have protocol for a reason. I won't say anything in the report about it."

"Thanks, man. I appreciate it."

"You've got good instincts. Just be careful. There are a lot of wolves out there who don't like heroes. They get jealous when someone like you comes along."

Luca contemplated Joe's warning later on when he was driving home after his shift. Wolves? Interesting word choice. He had heard there were werewolves on the force.

As he turned onto Mass. Ave., he passed the corner pub and spied a man lying in the gutter.

Luca pulled over and got out of the car. Making his way to the prone figure, he squatted down and bent to check for a pulse. The man groaned. At least he was alive.

"Hey, man, you okay?" Luca shook the man's shoulder, trying to wake him up.

The man groaned again and started to move. Luca helped him turn over and then recognized him. The man's eyes opened and widened, clearly recognizing Luca as well.

"Hey, I know you. You live aroun' here," he slurred.

"Hi, Jack. Are you hurt?"

Jack burst into tears. "Hurt? You're asking me if I'm hurt? My wife was killed, and my little girl is missing. Hurt doesn't even begin to explain what I'm feeling."

"Sorry, man." Luca hooked his arm around Jack's elbow. "I meant, have you sustained any injuries?"

"Nah, just had too mush to drink and then I guess I mush have passed out."

"My car is right here. I'll drive you home."

"Thanks."

Luca helped Jack to the car and eased him into the front passenger seat. As Luca drove him a couple of streets over and down the block, Jack rubbed his forehead and glanced over at the uniform. "You're a cop?"

"Yeah, just started my first week."

"I don't think those detectives are doing a damn thing."

Luca hesitated. There was a protocol. He didn't want to overstep, but at the same time, he was feeling frustrated himself. "It takes time, Jack."

"I don't have time. I went online to see if it's true, what they say about the forty-eight-hour thing, and it's not good. After forty-eight hours, it becomes even harder to find a missing person. She's just a little kid, and there's no ransom call. Maybe you can help me? I keep calling those detectives, and they say they're working on it, but I need to find my daughter. Sh-she's all I—"

Jack broke down, his shoulders shaking as he sobbed.

Luca reached out and awkwardly patted the man on his shoulder. "I promise I'll do my best to find your daughter. But you have to do something for me."

Jack looked up at Luca, his eyes red from crying. "Anything."

"You have to give me something of Mandy's, a stuffed toy or a doll."

"Are you gonna use sniffer dogs?"

"No, I've got something else in mind, but you can't tell anyone. I mean it. I could get fired."

Chapter 7

"'BYE, GRAN. SEE YOU LATER."

Dawn grabbed her keys and slipped on her leather jacket. She figured it was a thirty-minute walk to the Youth Community Center, plenty of time to get there and avoid the subway. She loved to walk as much as possible. It was the only exercise she ever got, and it helped her sort out her feelings. That and her visits to the Christian Science Center kept her sane. Now that she had Karma Cleaners to help her, she hoped her path would be easier, and she could finally live the life she'd always dreamed of, helping others—and free from the Keene Street Gang.

It was early yet, so most of the people in her neighborhood were either sleeping one off or already at work. Keene Street had always been that way. Most were decent, working-class people usually with two, sometimes three jobs to make ends meet, while the others wanted a quick fix, in more ways than one. Distracted by her thoughts, she didn't notice the footsteps behind her and felt a sudden tug on her arm.

She growled and swung around with her baton key chain, ready to do battle.

"Hey, take it easy. It's just me."

Ice Spider. Great. Just when I think I'm headed in the right direction… "What do you want?"

"Out for a morning stroll and just happened to run into you."

"You're never out for a morning stroll. More like you were behind that building waiting for me." She gestured with her chin at the tenement a few feet away.

"I figured it's the only way I can talk to you."

"Well, you figured wrong, Ice." Dawn turned away from him and started walking again, faster than her usual pace.

"Where you headed?" He sped up and matched her stride. *Damn him.* Even with all the booze and drugs he consumed, he still had the stamina to keep up with her.

"None of your business." She wished he would go away. She didn't want him knowing about her volunteer work at the community center. The center probably had to deal with gangs trying to infiltrate it on a regular basis, and Dawn didn't want to be one of those conduits.

"C'mon, Dawnie," he cajoled. "You're hiding something from me. You wouldn't be working with the cops, would you?"

"Are you crazy? Why the hell would I be working with the cops? I've got a mom doing time for dealing." *Shit! He knows something. The question is what.*

"Little Bobo said he saw you talking to a boy in blue the other day. He was running an errand in the South End. Said you looked pretty cozy."

"I'm not cozy with anyone. Now leave me alone." She kept walking, facing forward, not even looking at him. Hoping he would slink away.

Instead, he grabbed her arm and pulled her close, hindering her ability to swing her keys at him. "You better not be fuckin' anyone, especially a cop," Ice said with a leer. "You and me were real hot together once, babe. We can be that way again. We can do great things together, both in and out of the sack."

"The only reason you slept with me was because you wanted to win a bet. Oh yeah. You didn't know I found out about that, did you?"

He shrugged. "Doesn't matter how it started, babe."

She rolled her eyes, pretending a bravado she didn't feel. His face sported a smirk, but his grip was steel. She suddenly wished she'd taken the subway instead of walking.

"Ice, we're done. I'm not interested in you or anyone else for that matter." Well, that wasn't entirely true. An image of Luca's handsome face flashed through her mind. "I don't know who Little Bobo saw, but he must have been mistaken. As you know by my address, I don't associate with people in the ritzy part of town."

"Well, just in case, I wouldn't want you or your grandma getting into any trouble down the road."

She managed to yank her arm out of his grip. "Don't threaten me," she began. "And do *not* threaten my grandmother. I'm still good with Carla, and she wouldn't like hearing about this little conversation. Do you think she doesn't know about your deals in the back of her store?"

"Carla's in Florida," he shot back. "She might not return until spring."

"Doesn't matter," she countered. "Ever hear of cell phones?"

Ice's lips thinned as he stepped back. He held his hands up in a gesture of innocence. Yeah, like anything Ice Spider ever did was innocent. "I'm just trying to look out for you, babe."

"Don't bother, okay? And don't threaten me or my

grandma again. Carla would be royally pissed if she knew." That was true. Carla owed Annette her life. Annette had hidden her when Carla's husband had beaten the shit out of her. She'd managed to get away from him, and Annette had taken her in and called the cops.

Dawn's mother had been only thirteen when it happened. Carla's husband had been stinking, reeling drunk at the time and got into a fight with the officers who showed up at their house a few doors down. He had pulled a knife and lunged at one of the cops, and the other officer had shot him in the chest. Carla had lived with Annette and Elise for the next few months until she got back on her feet.

Carla's job at Keene Street Convenience resulted in her marrying the owner a year later. He was twice her age, but he was good to her. She had inherited the store and the building after he died, but she had never forgotten what Annette had done. Even though the years had toughened Carla, she was still good to Annette and sent her a gift basket every Christmas with a one-hundred-dollar bill slipped into a candy tin. Annette had saved it up over the years, not telling Dawn's mother about the money. It had helped Dawn pay for her clothes and shoes. Dawn's mother would have squandered it on drugs.

"Easy, Dawn. We're cool." Ice smiled and added, "Let's pretend we didn't bump into each other."

"I have a better idea," Dawn shot back. "Let's pretend we don't know each other."

She turned and walked briskly toward the subway entrance a block down the street. She didn't want him to keep following her and find out where she was headed, so she decided to take the subway a stop past the community center and then walk back.

So much for a peaceful morning walk.

Venti white chocolate mocha. Two Sweet'N Low packets.
Venti white chocolate mocha. Two Sweet'N Low packets.
Venti white chocolate mocha. Two Sweet'N Low packets.

Luca kept repeating it like a mantra in his head. According to the unofficial rookie rules, it was his job to get their captain her favorite coffee drink from Starbucks on Saturday morning at 8:00 sharp along with the Saturday edition of the *Boston Globe*. Glancing at his watch, he noted it was 7:42 and there were four people ahead of him. *Shit! What's with all the crazy people up early on a Saturday?* Finally, it was his turn.

"Hi, what can I get you?" The perky blonde barista with a high ponytail smiled brightly at him.

"Venti…" He hesitated. "Venti…" *Oh no! What's the name of the drink?*

"We have a wide array of coffee and tea beverages as well as a great selection of breakfast sandwiches."

"*Mocha latte for Amanda!*" a male barista shouted from the end of the coffee bar.

"White chocolate mocha," Luca said in a rush. The blonde barista asked his name and processed his drink order. Two minutes later, he was out the door and on his way to Captain Moore's brownstone on Marlborough Street. He wished he could turn on his siren, but this early on a Saturday morning? The upscale neighborhood wouldn't appreciate it.

Score! Spying an empty parking spot right in front of

the captain's house, he jumped out of the car, gripping the newspaper in one hand and the coffee in the other. He rang the doorbell and waited a few moments. When no one appeared, he rang it again. A man answered the door dressed in scrubs.

"Can I help you?" he asked, brow furrowed.

"Yes, I'm here to see Captain Moore. I'm Officer Luca Fierro. I have her Saturday morning coffee and newspaper."

The man's face creased into a grin. "Oooookay. I think I know what this is about." He turned back and shouted, "Hon, a rookie is here."

Captain Moore appeared a moment later with a sympathetic smile on her face.

Luca handed over the coffee and newspaper. "Here's your coffee and newspaper, Captain. Venti white chocolate mocha with a couple packets of Sweet'N Low on the side." Luca smiled, hoping for a compliment.

"Thank you, Fierro. You do realize you've been had."

"Huh?"

"The guys at work are just busting your chops because you're a newbie."

Luca could feel the heat rise to his cheeks. "Shit."

"Besides, I only drink tea."

Her husband plucked the cup out of her hand and took a sip. "Mmm…they picked a good flavor this time. Thanks!"

This time?

"Fierro, this is my husband, Lloyd. He's just on his way to the hospital, aren't you, dear?"

"Yep. This will certainly perk me up on my rounds." With a peck on his wife's cheek and a nod at Luca,

Lloyd made his way down the steps to a car that had double-parked a moment before. Apparently, he was carpooling to work.

Luca rubbed the back of his neck, feeling like a fool. "Sorry, Captain Moore. I guess the guys are enjoying a good laugh this morning."

"I would say they are," she replied with a grin. "Don't worry about it, Fierro. You're doing a great job."

"Thanks, ma'am. That means a lot."

She reached out her hand with an expectant look on her face.

Realizing what she wanted, Luca handed her the newspaper with a sheepish smile.

"Might as well make good use of it." She wished him a good weekend.

Making his way back to his car, Luca wondered how long he'd be getting the rookie treatment. He hoped they weren't planning any more shenanigans. But he'd put up with it if it meant being accepted as one of them…soon.

He got into his car and drove in the direction of his station, feeling silly but pleased at Captain Moore's comment about his first week on the job. Normally, he would have called Lisa to talk about it. But after his last phone call with her, he wondered if she would even answer her phone—and if he even wanted to talk to her about his job.

Would it be worth calling Lisa and asking her if she'd had a change of heart? They'd dated for two years, and it was hard to let go of someone you'd spent so much time with.

Would Dawn have told him he'd played right into their hands? He doubted it.

A vision of Dawn in her penguin pajamas popped into his head, and he couldn't help smiling.

He glanced at the bag on the front passenger seat of his car. Jack had let him into Mandy's room, where Luca had found the pink unicorn on the bed exactly where Dawn had seen it in her vision. He had asked Jack if he could borrow the toy, that he had a friend who might be able to help. Jack had agreed, telling him he'd do anything to find his daughter.

—∞—

"Mind if I sit beside you, young lady?"

Dawn glanced up at the old woman standing before her and grinned. "Good to see you, Lynda."

"Good to see you too." Lynda eased herself down beside Dawn as the subway car filled up.

"Are you going to the Youth Community Center too?"

"No, I just wanted to wish you luck. I heard about the shooting in your neighborhood."

"Does Karma Cleaners know everything?"

"Only as it involves our clients."

"How?"

"We have our ways." She gave her a Mona Lisa smile. "So how are you doing?"

Dawn blew out a breath. "I just ran into an ex-boyfriend. He was sniffing around, asking if I was getting cozy with a cop."

"What did you tell him?"

"I told him to buzz off." Dawn shrugged.

"Good girl." Lynda nodded and opened her large quilted bag. She rooted around in it for a few moments and then pulled out what looked like a pager with a red button.

"Here. This is for you."

"What it is?"

"If you're ever in trouble or you need to talk, you can press that button, and I'll find you."

Dawn frowned at her. "Are you serious?"

"As serious as these galoshes I'm wearing."

Dawn glanced down at Lynda's hideous boots. "Those are seriously ugly."

"Like I said."

"Do you know something that I don't?"

"Well, you're the psychic. You tell me."

Dawn made a face. "Okay, I am a little worried. I've become friends with a cop, and I texted him when I heard gunshots. I also called 911, but I just felt safer texting Luca."

"Luca is the young man you're helping locate the missing girl."

"You remembered. Can you help?"

Lynda gave her an indulgent look.

"We can't interfere. We just keep tabs… But if you need our help desperately, we'll step in. Nobody wants you getting killed while you're trying to do the right thing."

"I appreciate that."

"And by the way, he's a real hunk." Lynda winked at her.

"I think so too. Trouble is he seems to be hung up on his ex-girlfriend."

"Well, the operative part is 'ex'. Besides, sometimes it takes guys a little longer to recognize a real wonder woman when they meet her."

"Thanks, LC."

"You're welcome." She smiled and patted her hand. "Oh, this is my stop. Have fun today." Lynda gave her a little wave and then hobbled out the door.

Dawn hoped Lynda was right, about everything.

"Hey, it's me."

"What do you want?"

"Good morning to you too, Lisa."

"It's Saturday morning. Most normal people are still asleep."

Luca rolled his eyes. Lisa was definitely not a morning person. Her Saturdays consisted of getting up late, spending the afternoon at the spa, then going out and partying half the night.

That may have been fun while they were in college, but now that he was a cop, he had to focus on keeping a healthy routine.

"I just thought I'd check in and see how you're doing." After dropping the captain's newspaper off, he'd gone home, grabbed a quick shower and a PowerBar, and decided to call Lisa, because he just had to know once and for all.

"I'm doing fine, Luca. Why are you really calling?"

"Look, this breakup is just weird and unexpected. Is there any chance you've changed your mind?"

A sigh at the other end of the phone was his answer. "It's over. I'm already sleeping with someone else."

He said nothing.

"I think what we had was fun when we were in school," she continued. "It was exciting to sneak around behind our parents' backs, but look, we're not kids anymore. At some point, we either have to get serious or end things. And I'm not ready to get serious with anyone right now. I need freedom. Some space to figure out what I really want."

Translation: You want to sleep around and party all night.

"I'm only twenty-two years old. I just graduated from college. I want to take some time off before I have to start looking for a job. This is the time to live my life before I have to settle down."

Luca was becoming irritated. How could he have not seen it before? She was lucky she could afford to just laze around at home and hang out with her friends at night. The rest of the world had to get up and go to work.

"Besides, do you really think my father would have approved of you? You're just a rookie cop. My dad expects me to marry an investment banker or a lawyer. Not a police officer who works a beat."

"Your dad's a cop."

"He's a sergeant, and of course he wants me to marry a sophisticated, wealthy man."

"Whatever. I hope you and your sophisticated investment banker have a very nice life together."

Luca hung up and grunted his frustration. What did he ever see in her? Yeah, she was hot, and the sex—when he could get it—was great, but you can't base a life on that. She was shallow, spoiled, and selfish.

How did his brothers manage to find such wonderful women?

He snorted. If his brothers could read his mind, they'd say, "You're still young."

Reading minds... Hadn't Dawn said she couldn't do that when they had coffee the other day? And last night when he had watched her come out of her house in her penguin PJs, he'd just wanted to wrap his arms around her...

"I'm such an idiot."

"Are you Tansy?"

"Honey, do you see any other six-foot-tall, half–African American, half–Irish wolfhounds around?"

Dawn chuckled. "I suppose not."

Tansy was the very picture of casual glamour. Her impossibly long legs looked like they went on forever in her blue denim skinny jeans and black pumps.

An olive-and-gold top set off her creamy mocha complexion and startling hazel eyes. With her sleek, long dark hair in a high bun, she looked like she should be strutting down a catwalk instead of running a community center in a poor neighborhood. Tansy was quite possibly one of the most stunning women Dawn had ever met.

"You must be Dawn Forest." Tansy smiled back. "WW told me all about you."

"WW?"

"Wonder Woman," Tansy said with a wink.

Dawn nodded. "Ah, Lynda. Yeah. Well, I'm here to help in any way I can."

"Let me show you around." Tansy escorted Dawn to the back office, passing the kitchen and games room. There were three main areas where the kids could hang out: a quiet computer room for doing homework and getting extra help, a gymnasium where they could play various sports, and they even passed by a room that said POOL.

"Is there really a pool here?"

"Well, it's not an Olympic-size pool. It's about half that. Just a place where they can learn to swim."

There was also a restaurant-size kitchen and dining room.

"We teach them some basic cooking skills, and that provides a hot meal. We all eat together."

They finally reached the back offices for the staff, including a room with a sign that said CLINIC.

Dawn pointed to it. "Clinic?"

"A retired nurse practitioner volunteers every Tuesday and Thursday and on Saturday afternoons. She's here for wellness checks, plus confidential advice regarding health and sex education. I've seen her slip some condoms to the teenage boys."

Dawn was impressed at the setup. If a place like this had existed when her mom was a kid, she might not have lost her way. Then again, Dawn might not be here had her mother received sex education.

"This is such an amazing place," Dawn said. They settled at a table in the dining room with two cups of coffee and a plate of two oversize churros dipped in white and dark chocolate on either end.

"We're pretty lucky here," Tansy said. She pointed to the pastry. "Have one. They're damn good."

"Thanks." After one big bite, Dawn nodded in agreement. "Mmm."

"You're a tiny thing, but I like the way you eat."

Dawn felt her face heat up.

Tansy laughed. "Don't worry. There are plenty more in the fridge. We have a very generous benefactor who prefers to remain anonymous, but he makes sure we have everything we need."

"One person was so generous, they donated all this?" Dawn's eyes widened as she glanced around at the expansive kitchen and dining room.

"Not all of it. We received a grant to build the center, but most of the programs are kept going by one family." Tansy leaned in, giving her a sly smile. "You would certainly have heard of a few of them. A couple musicians and actors. A famous chef…"

Dawn knew exactly the family Tansy was talking about. They might be in Hollywood now, but they grew up right here in Dorchester.

Tansy had a dynamic presence and seemed like she could run a ship like this easily. It couldn't be an easy job though.

"In my experience, people are just looking out for themselves and usually breaking the law to do it or struggling not to," Dawn said.

"And yet you're here. Ready and willing to make a change. Maybe the benefactor was also like you, ready and willing to make changes. You don't have to remain poor even if growing up in lousy circumstances."

"True." Dawn sighed. "Do you really feel like you're making a difference in the lives of these kids?"

"Let me ask you something instead," Tansy countered. "If you'd had a place like this when you were a kid, do you think it would have made a difference?"

Dawn thought about what she'd seen in the lounge area. It was early on a Saturday morning, and yet there were kids of different ages hanging out, chatting, doing their homework. They looked happy and relaxed. She was a latchkey kid. Came home from school to an empty house, locking the door behind her. That was how her mother and grandmother kept her safe when she was young and they both had to work.

When she'd peeked into the lounge, her eyes had landed on a lone girl sitting by herself with her feet tucked up under her on an overstuffed chair. The girl was immersed in a book, but she looked...sad. Dawn understood all too well what that felt like. "I think it would have," she said softly.

"Some of these kids come here for food, and others are here for a different kind of nourishment."

Dawn cleared her throat, nodding her understanding.

Tansy laid her hand over Dawn's. "I know how special you are."

Dawn's brows lifted in question.

"You can sense things in other people."

"How did you know? Did Lynda mention it?"

Tansy nodded. "She told me because she knows you can help us."

"How can I help? I didn't study social work. I'm not a counselor."

Tansy waved away her question. "Honey, we already have plenty of those here. We need more people like you. People who can relate to the kids—and spot trouble before it happens."

"I'm just worried I'll make mistakes and maybe make things worse. What if I say the wrong thing when I'm talking to them?"

"You won't. If your heart is in the right place,

they'll know it. Trust me on that one. Are you ready to get started?"

Dawn blew out a breath and nodded. "As ready as I'll ever be."

"Good. Are you done with your churro?"

Dawn popped the last bit of churro into her mouth. "Mmm. I'll bet a professional bakery couldn't make better."

"Another one of our benefactors owns a successful bakery. Sometimes he helps out, just for fun."

"Wow! So you know all the benefactors well?"

"Honey, that one I do. I married him."

Chapter 8

"Hey kid!" Luca slowed his car alongside the boy walking his bike along the sidewalk. DeVaughn Washington, the kid he'd saved from the speeding car. "I'm glad I ran into you." Luca had finished his shift and on impulse bought a box of doughnuts and swung by DeVaughn's street to drop them off and introduce himself to his parents. Maybe if he couldn't help Mandy, he could help a kid who needed someone to look out for him.

"I didn't do nothin' wrong, I swear." The boy looked alarmed as he stopped.

"It's okay, DeVaughn. I just wanted to ask you something."

The boy nodded, and Luca got out of the car, grabbing the box of doughnuts.

"Where were you heading with your bike?"

"To the gas station to pump air into my tires. I think one of my wheels got something sharp stuck in it."

"Let me take a look." Luca hunkered down and spun the front wheel. Sure enough, he found a small nail embedded in the wheel. Pulling it out, he held it up to DeVaughn. "Here's your culprit."

"Aww man. I have to try to patch it up now." DeVaughn heaved a sigh.

"I'll help you fix it."

DeVaughn's face lit up. "Really? Thanks. You're pretty cool for a cop."

Luca laughed. "Why don't we go back to your place so I can meet your family, then I'll take you to get your bike fixed. I know a great mechanic."

"I don't have any money for a mechanic." DeVaughn looked deflated.

"It's okay. It's on me. You can do me a favor."

"Like what?"

Luca almost laughed at the suspicious look that flashed in DeVaughn's eyes.

"Take me to meet your family. I just want them to know where we're going."

"That's the favor?"

"Yup."

"Okay. But does it include those doughnuts?"

"Yup."

"Deal."

DeVaughn and Luca walked back up the street to a small row house. DeVaughn took a key out of his pocket and unlocked the door, bringing his bike inside. He leaned it against the wall in the tiny entryway. "Mama, someone wants to meet you and Grandpa."

A woman stepped out of the kitchen, just off the entry, wiping her hands on a tea towel. "What happened?" The tiny, stout woman wore the same alarmed expression the boy had when he saw Luca.

"Nothing happened, Mama. This is Luca. He's okay."

"DeVaughn is right, ma'am. I'm Officer Luca Fierro, and your neighborhood is part of my beat. I'm just getting to know some of the residents in the area. Just finished my first week on the job." He flashed her his trademark grin, which of course had the desired effect on the woman, who automatically smiled back.

"I'm such a mess. Just cleaning up in the kitchen."

The sound of a toilet flushing followed by a hacking cough greeted them. A man, who looked considerably older than DeVaughn's mother, shuffled down the stairs, holding onto the wall for support. Luca noted the lack of a bannister. Homes here weren't always up to code.

"Why are the police here?" He held up his hands.

"Abe, it's okay."

Luca reached out his hand and introduced himself to the old man, who reluctantly shook it.

"What is that box?" The elderly man gestured to the box of doughnuts with his chin.

"I thought you might enjoy these," he said with a little shrug.

"If you offer, I'll enjoy." The old man cracked a smile.

An hour later, Luca had learned that DeVaughn's father, Vaughn Washington, had died in a truck driving accident when DeVaughn was five years old, and his mother's father, Abe, a widower, had moved in to share the expenses and make sure the boy got to school. DeVaughn's mother, Ida, worked housekeeping in a "fancy hotel" on weekdays. Ida frowned at DeVaughn when he accidentally let it slip that she also worked for cash on Sundays cleaning a rich lady's apartment.

"I told you not to tell no one that," she admonished him.

"It's okay, Mrs. Washington. I didn't hear anything." Luca grinned at the lady, who smiled her relief.

"So what do you want with our DeVaughn?" the old man asked bluntly.

"I was hoping you'd let me take him to the Youth

Community Center later today," Luca suggested. "It's a
great place for kids to hang out."

"We heard about that place," Ida said, refilling Luca's
coffee. "But we like that DeVaughn stays close to home
when he's not in school."

"I can understand that. But they offer supervision,
help with homework, and organized activities. It's a
positive environment, and he can meet kids his own age.
I'll keep an eye on him."

Ida glanced at her son's eager expression. "You want
to go to this place with Luca?"

"Yes, Mama. I promise I won't get into no trouble."

Ida set the coffeepot down and wrapped her arms
around her son. "You promise to be good?"

The boy nodded, and she kissed him on the head.
"Okay, you can go, just to see what it's like for now."

"Thanks, Mama." DeVaughn beamed at his mother
and turned to Luca. "Can you still help me fix my bike?"

"What happened to your bike?" Abe asked.

"A nail got stuck in the tire, and Luca said he would
fix it for me."

Abe nodded. "I used to be good with things like that,
but now I'm too old."

"It's okay, Grandpa. You can watch TV and rest."

Abe smiled. "Yes, watching TV shows is about all I
can do now. That and dream about winning the lottery."

Ida rolled her eyes, and Luca laughed at the twinkling expression in the old man's eyes. As far as Luca
was concerned, an important part of his job was helping
the community. Some cops did it while other cops just
drove their beat, hauled drunks into jail, and then went
home. But Luca wanted to make a difference. Even if

he could only help a few families, he would do what
he could.

———~~~———

It was now or never.

Dawn walked up to the girl sitting alone.

"Hi there."

The girl didn't look up. "Hullo."

"I see you're reading." *Oh, great first opener*.

"Yeah."

"*A Separate Peace*. That's a tough book for a kid
your age."

The girl shrugged. "It's okay. I have to read it for
school. I already saw the movie."

"I used to hate reading, and then a couple of years
back, I kinda got into it."

The girl finally looked up at her. "You don't have to
try so hard."

Dawn scrunched up her face. "That obvious?"

The girl nodded.

"Okay, how about I start again. Hi, I'm Dawn Forest.
Can I join you for a bit?"

The girl giggled. "You've got a funny name."

Dawn laughed too. "So I've been told."

"I'm Rita Devalos."

"Nice to meet you, Rita." Dawn pulled up a big bean-
bag chair and plopped herself down on it. "This is my
first day."

"Yeah, I noticed." Rita smiled.

"Have you been coming here long?"

"Three months. Tansy came to talk at our school a few
times. On her third visit, I said, 'Okay, okay, I'll go!'"

Dawn grinned. "Do you like it here?"

"I don't really like sports, and I can't swim or anything. So I just come here to hang out and do my homework."

"Well, I don't think I would ever make the Olympic team or anything, but I saw the schedule, and they offer beginner swimming classes on Sunday mornings. Would you be interested tomorrow?"

"My sister drops me off here on her way to work on Saturdays. She doesn't want me walking anywhere by myself. And Sunday is the only day she gets to sleep in."

"Well, what if I came by your place, and we could take the subway here together?"

"You would do that?"

"I sure would."

Rita's eyes lit up. "Okay."

Dawn knew she was smiling ear to ear. She was doing it. She was making a difference. And it felt good.

"Hey, I know those kids over there from school."

"Do you want to say hi?"

DeVaughn's excitement was contagious. Luca ruffled his hair and told him to go and play with his friends, and he would be waiting for him in the lounge. He decided to stroll through the place first.

Spotting a canteen at the far end of the large lounge, Luca made his way over to grab a coffee. He heard a noise but didn't see anyone around, so he leaned over the counter.

"Hi. Is anyone back there?"

A familiar spiky brunette head popped up from below. Wide gray-green eyes stared into his.

"Dawn." Luca felt just as surprised as she looked.

"Luca! Are you here on police business?"

He wondered why she seemed so flustered. She'd been rummaging around in the cupboards and was holding two bags of Hershey's Kisses.

He gestured to the chocolate. "Got a sweet tooth?"

"Always." She grinned. "I was going to put them out in bowls for the kids. Tansy said I could jump right in, and that's what I'm doing."

"You know Tansy too?" he asked.

"I just met her this morning. This is my first day volunteering here. How do you know Tansy?"

"We met when she came to talk to the cadets about getting involved in the communities they serve. She told me to come by sometime, so I brought DeVaughn here."

Her brow furrowed in confusion.

Luca grinned. "DeVaughn is the kid you saved."

"What?"

"You told me to watch out for a kid on a bike. I told you he was okay when we met for coffee, and I decided to bring him here today."

Her smile lit up her face. "Can I meet him?"

"Sure. Come with me."

They approached a group of kids huddled around a gaming console.

"Hey, DeVaughn." Luca laid his hand on the boy's shoulder. "I want to introduce you to a friend of mine."

He brought DeVaughn over to Dawn. "DeVaughn, this is my friend Dawn. Dawn, this is my buddy DeVaughn."

"Pleased to meet you." Dawn smiled.

"You got really cool hair and tattoos," the boy said to her.

"Thanks. I'll tell you about my tats sometime if you're interested."

The boy nodded.

"I guess I'll be seeing you around here then?" Dawn asked.

The boy turned to Luca, his eyes hopeful.

"You bet, kiddo. I'll bring you every Saturday, if I'm not working and your mom says it's okay."

"Hey, DeVaughn, it's your turn," one of the boys said from the console.

"I gotta go. I'm up next. I'll see you, Dawn."

"Later, DeVaughn."

They watched the boy join his friends.

She turned back to Luca, and his heart contracted at the tears glittering in her eyes. "Hey, it's okay. You saved him. *You* did that." He reached for her hand and squeezed. He wanted to reassure her. Wanted her to know how amazing she was.

She nodded, wiping at her eyes. "But what about Mandy? We've got to help her too."

"We will. We'll find her together." He was operating on impulse today, and so far, it was working. "Do you want to have dinner with me?"

She gaped at him. "You mean tonight?"

"Yeah, tonight, tomorrow—whenever you're ready."

"Sure. I'm ready when you are."

"In that case, could you be my date to an engagement party tomorrow? Unless you have other plans…"

"Yes and no."

"Huh?"

"Yes, I'd love to go, and no, I don't have other plans."

He thought those were the best words he'd heard all week.

———————

"Oh, sweetie, you look so pretty!"

Dawn did a little curtsy. "Thanks, Gran. You don't think it's too much?"

"It's perfect, darling. Where did you find that dress? It looks like it cost a fortune."

Dawn winked at Annette. It had certainly cost *some-one* a fortune at some point, but Dawn had paid only eighteen dollars for it at Goddess Fashions, a thrift store she happened to walk by a few weeks ago on her way to the grocery store.

The store had just opened, and they were offering twenty-five percent off everything in a grand open-ing promotion. The sales woman, who called herself Venus, was an absolute expert stylist and had helped Dawn create the perfect look. At the time, Dawn was just shopping for work clothes, but Venus had assured her the dress would come in handy one day.

"You look like Audrey Hepburn," Annette exclaimed.

"Do you think so?" Dawn asked, feeling a bit unsure. Her look was usually more modern, and this look was definitely out of her comfort zone.

"*Petite enfant, t'es bonne.*"

Dawn grinned at Annette's use of the Cajun slang. "I think you're referring to a grandbaby."

Annette giggled and shrugged. "It's still the truth." Annette had grown up in Boston, but she still on occa-sion used the slang she'd learned from her mother, who was from New Orleans.

Dawn smoothed her hands down the front of the deep burgundy dress. She did feel like a star in it. With a form-fitting bodice underneath a delicate lace overlay of the same color, the dress was belted at the waist and flared out in a slight pouf. It looked like the kind of dress Audrey Hepburn would have worn, and Dawn loved it. She'd managed to wrestle her spiky hair down and part it on the side, bringing out the Hepburn style even more. Her makeup was perfect. Liquid eyeliner, mascara, and cherry-red lipstick. A black satin clutch purse and black pumps rounded out her ensemble. Her entire outfit had cost less than thirty dollars, and if that wasn't a statement to her frugality, she didn't know what was.

"All I can say is your young man is going to do a backflip when he sees you."

"Thank you, Gran." Speaking of backflips, the butterflies in her stomach were doing just that. She'd already met Luca's parents and brother, but going to a family event was a big deal. She began to feel panicked about seeing everyone in his large family.

"Honey, I'm so happy for you. I hope his family is just as nice as the ones you already met. Just remember when out in public, keep it to yourself that Luca is a police officer. This isn't the right kind of neighborhood to be dating a cop."

Dawn laughed. "He's not going to be wearing his uniform on dates." After a quick look at Annette's *you know what I mean* face, she put on a more serious expression. "I know. I'm being careful."

She didn't tell Annette about Ice Spider confronting her on the street yesterday, asking her about her "cop friend." She was not about to go down that road. If she did, her grandmother would insist she move to a safer neighborhood, maybe even out of town. She would not leave Annette behind. It just wasn't up for discussion.

"I just want you to be safe, honey."

"I know and I am. Honest." Dawn crossed her fingers behind her back and hoped the Karma Cleaners weren't watching. She certainly didn't want any dings against her karma by lying to Annette.

This karma cleaning was tough business. Sometimes you had to do little bad things for the greater good. At least that's what Dawn kept telling herself. She needed to ask Lynda more questions. Like, is a little white lie okay? Is bopping someone over the head okay, if it's in self-defense?

In the meantime, she would keep her baton of keys with her at all times. She managed to shove it into the clutch purse along with her bank card, some cash, and her cell phone, snapping it shut at the same time as the front door bell rang.

"Let me get it," Annette said. "You go upstairs and come down when I tell you to."

"Gran, what are you up to?"

"Nothing. Just do as I say, young lady."

Dawn sighed and shook her head. "Okay." She scooted up the short flight of stairs to the tiny landing and stood there waiting for her grandmother to call her.

"Welcome, young man." Annette's voice floated up to her. "Come in, come in. Dawn is just finishing getting ready."

Dawn grinned at her grandmother's lie. She was making it look as if she hadn't been ready an hour ago and was just casually slapping on a coat of lipstick.

"Thank you, ma'am," Luca's voice replied.

"Well, aren't you handsome. I'm Annette, Dawn's grandmother. And you must be Luca Fierro. I've heard so much about you."

Dawn heard a catch in Annette's voice and wondered why she sounded so odd.

"These are for you, ma'am."

"Oh, I love pink roses. How lovely. Please, call me Annette. What a nice young man you are."

Dawn couldn't wait any longer. She knew she was wading into unknown territory, so she took a deep breath and dived in. As she made her way down the steps, she caught Luca's expression and almost tripped.

Chapter 9

HE HAD NO WORDS. THE VISION WHO FLOATED DOWN THE stairs was gorgeous. Like, movie-star gorgeous. He swallowed a nervous lump in his throat and said the first thing that popped into his head. "Wow!"

Luca caught her around the waist as she stumbled on the last step. Lifting her down, he gazed into her wide gray-green eyes. "Are you okay?"

She nodded, blushing the same shade as her dress. It only made her look prettier…if that were possible.

"You look incredible," he told her.

"Th-thank you."

She seemed out of breath. He guessed it was because she'd almost tripped.

"Look at these beautiful flowers Luca brought me." Annette waved the bouquet under Dawn's nose.

She sniffed them. Taking the time to smell the roses…that was a good thing, right?

"Oh, Gran, they are lovely. Let me get a vase for them."

"Don't you dare," Annette said. "I'll put them in water myself."

"I have something for you too," Luca told Dawn.

"Oh, you didn't have to do that," she replied, shaking her head.

"No, I wanted to." He pulled out a slim box from his pocket and handed it to her.

She opened it up and gasped. "Oh, I love it. Thank you, but you didn't have to do that."

He wanted to pat himself on the back at the wide-eyed look of happiness on her face. He'd just had a feeling she didn't receive many nice gifts from men.

"It's partially a thank-you for helping me with Mandy."

"Partially?"

"Yeah. And it's partially because it made me think of you."

He'd discovered the silver charm bracelet in the window at a little shop while he was on duty.

He'd gone back after work, and the saleswoman, Venus, who looked an awful lot like someone he knew but couldn't place, had gushed over the bracelet and told him it would make a great gift for a special woman. Maybe not now, but in the future.

Showcasing delicate silver charms of the sun, moon, and the stars studded with garnets, the bracelet seemed to be made for Dawn. What was it about Dawn that attracted him? She certainly wasn't the typical girl he usually liked, but she was stunning. Lisa had been sweet as honey on the outside and then tough as leather on the inside. Dawn was the exact opposite, tough on the outside and sweet and sensitive on the inside. He suddenly realized that's what made her special.

"My family is going to love you," he whispered in her ear as he helped her into her trench coat.

"Dawn is the most lovable girl in the world," Annette echoed, clearly having heard his comment.

It didn't matter. He agreed with her and flashed her a grin.

"Okay, you two, get on out of here before you make me cry."

"Gran, why on earth would you cry?"

"You two just look like I'd always imagined you would if Dawnie had attended her prom."

"Aww…" Dawn wrapped her arms around Annette. "I'll text you later if I'm going to be home late."

"Don't you worry about me. I'm going to make some popcorn, watch an old movie on TV, and enjoy my roses." Annette beamed at them.

Luca thought she was a sweet woman. He changed his vow. He would do everything he could to get them *both* out of this neighborhood.

As he helped Dawn into his car, he noticed she looked at him with a special glow in her eyes. He'd never had a woman look at him that way.

He got into the driver's side, started the engine, and reached for her hand. "They're going to adore you. Don't worry."

"Now who's psychic?"

"I'm just imagining someone brand-new walking into not one but two families who all know each other now—and one of those families with seven sons and various daughters-in-law. Please don't worry. Many of them have been in your shoes, and they'll welcome you with open arms."

She gave him a tremulous smile. "I hope so."

"Try to relax. We're going to meet up with some of them at my home first, and you've already been there. Besides, you've met my parents, and they really like you."

"What about Gabe?"

"Gabe doesn't count, but he thinks you're great too."

"Everyone counts. I don't want to make a bad impression on anyone."

"Well, you're the psychic. How do you think they're gonna react to you?"

"I'm too nervous to feel anything. Besides, it's harder to sense things when it relates to myself."

"Speaking of sensing things, I have something for you that I was hoping you could have a look at."

She raised a fine brow. "Is this about Mandy?"

"Yes. I ran into Mandy's father, Jack, and he asked for my help. He gave me Mandy's pink unicorn, the one you saw in your vision."

"Do you have it with you?" Her eyes were alight with excitement. "Maybe if I held the unicorn, I could figure out where she is."

"It's in my trunk. When we get to a place and time where you can concentrate, I'll get it for you."

"Do you think Jack would allow me into his home?"

"I don't know. He's pretty raw." Luca appreciated her desire to help, but he remembered the warning Joe had given him. It was the firm, no-nonsense, forbidding type. "And I need to tell you something. You need to leave me out of it. I could get fired for interfering."

"Seriously? Even if you save the child's life?"

"Yes. I'd probably get a commendation one day and a pink slip the next."

"Shit."

All he could do was advise and look out for her. What if she wasn't able to get anything from the unicorn? He didn't want her to be inside Jack's house if that happened. Jack might react badly, and he didn't want Dawn to get hurt. He cared about her too much.

The revelation surprised him and made him nervous at the same time. He'd only known Dawn a short time, and given his recent breakup with Lisa, he wasn't ready to jump into another relationship. Was he?

"Okay. Maybe you're right. Now is probably not the right time anyway. I'm feeling too nervous about meeting your family."

She gave him a wobbly smile that made his heart melt. *Shit. So much for jumping in too soon.*

"Maybe we could go somewhere quiet after dinner, and I can hold the unicorn then. I should be able to concentrate as long as nothing terrible happens during the party."

"I have an idea." He told her his fellow new recruit cop friend, Delvin, and his wife were out of town for the weekend and asked him to house-sit. Taking a few minutes there before he brought her home might give them a clue. He hated to wait any longer than she did.

"You don't think they would mind?"

"I'm doing him a favor, watering their plants and taking care of their cat, Bubbles. So, nah, they won't mind."

She grinned. "Bubbles? What a cute name."

"He's a white Persian, with big round blue eyes. I guess they must have looked like bubbles to someone. Or they just liked the name. He's really...strange around me, but pretty. Maybe you can feed him, and he'll like you better."

She chuckled. "Okay, that sounds like a plan."

"Good, we'll do that later after dinner. And it will be a good excuse to leave early if my brothers start razzing me."

"Do you get along with all your brothers?"

"When they aren't being stupid, I do."

She giggled at that, and he had the sudden urge to kiss her. *Man, I've got it bad.* He had to keep a handle on his attraction to Dawn. He didn't want to mess anything up if he moved too soon.

He knew his entire family would love her. His gut instinct told him he could trust Dawn with who he really was, a shape-shifting phoenix. But what he didn't know was how she'd react when she first found out. Would she accept him for who and what he truly was? Or would it be too much for her?

In the Fierro living room, Sandra asked, "So how did you and Luca meet?"

Dawn had found herself whisked into a warm, welcoming group of young women who introduced themselves to her as the Fierro wives and girlfriends. And they'd wasted no time peppering her with questions.

"We met by the fountain outside the Christian Science Center."

"So he saw you sitting there, came up to you, and laid on the Fierro charm?" Kristine asked.

The other women giggled. Dawn smiled. It sounded like each one had a story she'd enjoy hearing at some point.

"No, it wasn't exactly like that..." She hesitated, unsure how to proceed. She didn't know if Luca's parents had told anyone else in the family about her psychic abilities. Not everyone responded well to that sort of information. She was rescued by Luca's mom, Gabriella, who smoothly stepped into the conversation and wrapped a comforting arm around Dawn's shoulders.

"Luca of course noticed how pretty Dawn was, and when they started talking, he knew he couldn't let this girl get away. Give her a chance to breathe, girls."

Dawn gave Gabriella a grateful smile, although she felt as red as her dress. The daughters-in-law all gave her knowing smiles, their eyes twinkling.

"There'll be a quiz on our names later," the one they called Chloe said in a lilting Irish accent.

Dawn was trying to remember them all, but she couldn't guarantee she wouldn't make a mistake or two.

Gabriella gave her shoulders a little squeeze and whispered that she wanted to show her something. Dawn's eyes met Luca's across the room. Luca seemed to be on the receiving end of some good-natured ribbing from his father and older brothers.

Dawn's mouth practically fell when he'd introduced her to everyone. Luca had told her the Fierro family gatherings were a challenge to pull off, since everyone was so busy and some were scattered in other countries, but since Mallory and Dante hadn't had a formal engagement party and now Noah and Kizzy had announced their engagement, Antonio and Gabriella had insisted on celebrating the special occasions with a huge family dinner, which would require a restaurant's function room. They'd all be going there shortly.

Dawn followed Gabriella upstairs to the sprawling master bedroom. A seating area consisting of a red love seat and two matching plush chairs sat facing a cozy fireplace.

"Have a seat," Gabriella told her. "I'll be right back."

Dawn sat on the comfortable love seat and gazed into the fire. Relaxing back into the sofa, she closed her eyes and allowed the warmth of the fireplace to envelop her.

Feeling the familiar pull of a vision, she allowed her mind to follow and saw herself walking down a hallway into a bright, sunny kitchen with a patio door leading onto a back deck and beyond that, a big backyard with a swing set. Luca was pushing a little girl on a swing. The only trees in the yard were palm trees. "*Push me higher, Papa,*" the little girl squealed with delight. He grinned and complied. Then he looked up, and his eyes met hers. He winked at her, and she melted with a feeling of love so strong, it almost took her breath away.

"Here we go." Gabriella sat down beside Dawn, and the vision floated away. "Are you all right?"

Dawn read the look of concern on Gabriella's face and sought to reassure her. "I'm fine. I just had a vision."

"Was it about the missing child?" Gabriella reached for Dawn's hand. "Luca told me not to tell anyone you were helping, and I haven't, but naturally, I can tell you...you already know."

Dawn shook her head. "No, it was about Luca."

Gabriella's eyes widened in alarm. "What did you see? Is it his job? Can we stop something awful from happening?"

"No, he was happy. He was pushing a little girl on a swing. His daughter."

Tears sprang to Gabriella's eyes. And she gasped. "No female child has been born into this family in generations. You can't imagine how much I've craved a little girl to spoil."

Dawn didn't want to tell her that she was in the vision

as well. She didn't want Gabriella to think she was trying to angle her way into this amazing family.

Gabriella placed a hand on her chest and breathed deeply. "Thank you for sharing your vision with me. We'll keep it to ourselves for now. But it makes me so happy to know you saw Luca with a little girl."

"You're welcome," Dawn replied, smiling.

"I hope you were in that vision too," Gabriella added.

Dawn's gaze dropped to her lap. She had little experience dealing with so many members of a big, extended family, and all the emotions pinging around were a little overwhelming. Now, to have Gabriella say something so wonderful to her almost made her break down in tears.

Gabriella must have realized what Dawn was going through, because she wrapped her arms around her in a fierce hug.

"I know you have been through some difficult times in your life, but now, you're part of us. No matter what, we *all* have each other's backs. And I want you to know I'm very happy Luca brought you with him tonight."

"Th-thank you," Dawn stuttered in a whisper. She didn't know what else to say. She was touched.

Dawn's own mother had tried, she really had, but the pull of heroin had been too much for her, and Annette had had to fill the role of both mother and father for Dawn. Being welcomed into this loud, loving, boisterous family was more than Dawn could have ever imagined. She'd never even realized how badly she needed this.

"I noticed your lovely bracelet, and I think I have something that goes perfectly with it." Gabriella opened a small velvet sack and pulled out a beautiful silver necklace with the same matching charms on it. A few links were studded with garnets as well. It matched the bracelet Luca had given her perfectly.

"I bought this necklace on a whim," Gabriella said. "I was shopping and stopped by this new little shop called Goddess Fashions, and the saleswoman was so kind. I ended up buying something for each of my daughters-in-law, and then I saw this necklace and just knew I had to have it, even though I didn't know why at the time. Isn't that a remarkable coincidence?"

Dawn nodded in agreement. "I have something to tell you, Mrs. Fierro."

"Uh-uh, I'm Gabriella." The older woman wagged her finger at Dawn.

"Okay, Gabriella. Luca gave me this bracelet earlier tonight. He bought it at the same store. Did you know about that?"

"No, I didn't. I swear." She crossed her heart.

And it's the same store where I bought my dress. Dawn wondered if Lynda and company had something to do with this coincidence. It certainly seemed a little too odd to be a complete accident. She would ask her at their next meeting before jumping to conclusions.

"Imagine that!" Gabriella's eyes widened. "I knew my son had good taste. Let me put this on you." She draped the necklace around Dawn's neck and fastened the clasp, then she sat back. "It suits you perfectly. Maybe it's a sign." Gabriella's eyes glittered, and Dawn wondered if the older woman was going to start crying.

"I'm just so happy you're here." Gabriella sighed. "You are a very special young woman, and Luca is a very special young man. I can tell you care about my son, and I can see that he cares about you. That is a very good place to build from." Gabriella squeezed Dawn's hand. "I'm very worried about Luca's job. I know it's dangerous. I'm counting on you to keep him from trying to be a hero. He can be very stubborn and doesn't tell us even a fraction of what he goes through. And while I'm not psychic like you are, a mother has certain intuitions about her children."

"Mrs.—Gabriella. I'll...do what I can. I promise." Dawn put her other hand over Gabriella's. "Luca means a lot to me."

"I know he does. I can see it in your eyes when you look at him."

"But you should know, I don't have the perfect background," Dawn said sadly.

"Hush." Gabriella shook her head. "I don't want you to disparage yourself. We don't have any power over where we come from. But we do have power over where we're going. And you, my dear girl, seem to have a great future."

Dawn was so moved by Gabriella's faith in her. She would do everything she could to make sure Luca was safe. The image of Luca covered in blood was a memory she wished she could shake. She wouldn't tell Gabriella about that. Instead, she vowed she would do whatever she could to keep Luca from getting hurt.

"Hey! It's time to get going." Antonio was leaning around the doorjamb, smiling.

"Coming, darling," Gabriella said as she rose.

Dawn wondered if he'd overheard any part of their conversation. They rejoined the others, and Luca met her at the bottom of the stairs with her trench coat over his arm.

The restaurant efficiently brought out each course and whisked away the remains of the last one. Not an easy feat considering the number of people involved. The head table consisted of Dante and Mallory—the soon-to-be married couple—Noah Fierro and Dr. Kizzy Samuels, plus her sister, Ruth. One would assume that the couple who'd been engaged were probably part of the wedding party to come. Luca had told her that Dante and Noah had been roommates, best friends, and firefighters in adjacent houses, not to mention brothers.

When all the dishes had been cleared from the dinner but before dessert, Dante stood and tapped his champagne flute to get everyone's attention.

"Excuse the interruption, but I have an important announcement to make. As most of you probably know, Mallory and I are planning our wedding on Thanksgiving Day, which is coming right up. And in a surprise turn of events, I'm happy to announce that our *other* engaged couple have caved to the pressure my lovely fiancée and I applied repeatedly and will share our wedding day as theirs too. In other words, it's a double wedding!"

There was much cheering and clapping. Luca leaned over to Dawn and asked, "Will you be my *plus one* to the wedding?"

Dawn wanted to, more than anything, but what if their relationship imploded before then? It was still new. Then she decided she was being silly. Luca was perfect.

"Of course I'll come. Thank you for inviting me."

Luca couldn't help touching her. "You're beautiful

and surprisingly sweet." He cupped her face and leaned in to kiss her. He hesitated just a second before his lips touched hers. She closed her eyes, and her lips puckered. *Yep. That's the go-ahead signal.*

He kissed her, gently but intentionally. This wasn't the place to make a passionate overture, but at least they'd had their first kiss, and it seemed like the right time.

As soon as he leaned back, they smiled at each other.

Luca jumped when he got an elbow in his ribs. Glancing over his shoulder, he caught Gabe's expression.

"Don't even say it," Luca growled.

Gabe laughed. Fortunately, he didn't say a word. He just turned back to Misty, picked up her hand, and kissed her knuckles like an old-fashioned knight.

All Luca's brothers had found true love. He was the last one, and with any luck, Dawn was it.

"They all love you, but then again, I knew they would."

Dawn and Luca were sitting in Delvin's kitchen, sharing a cup of coffee.

"Thanks." She blushed again. She was doing that a lot lately. He thought it was adorable.

With her spiky hair and tough girl attitude, he'd never realized how beautiful she was, but sitting across from him was a girl who made him think of one of those old-time movie stars. He wanted to lean in and kiss her so bad and then do other things…

"Do you want to do this here or in the living room?"

Luca blinked.

"The unicorn."

"Oh!" Now it was his turn to feel the heat rush to his

face. "Maybe in the living room. I left the bag there on the couch."

A few moments later, they were sitting on the sofa side by side. He took the unicorn out of the bag and handed it to her.

Dawn blew out a breath and closed her eyes. She sat quietly for so long, he was wondering if she was even having a vision. But he didn't want to interrupt her in case she was getting something.

It was the strangest thing, like she was there with him, but she wasn't. Kind of like she was asleep but awake at the same time.

He gazed at the fluttering of her eyelids, and she suddenly gasped. Her eyes opened wide as she turned to him. All he could see was fear.

Chapter 10

"I SAW HER. I SAW MANDY. I-I MEAN, I LOOKED DOWN AND saw little legs in purple tights, and a piece of clothing with a purple polka-dot hem. Then she must have lifted a blindfold, because I could see a little more."

Dawn clutched the unicorn close to her chest. She could feel the little girl's fear and confusion.

"Tell me exactly what you saw," Luca urged.

Dawn closed her eyes once more and revisited her vision. "She's on a cot. The walls are kind of dingy. There's a lamp on the floor plugged into an open wall socket. A side table with a juice box on it and what looks like the remains of a kid's burger meal. She's sitting up on the cot, rocking back and forth. I feel like she's been crying, but she's all cried out now."

Dawn's eyes filled with tears, and she opened them again.

Luca enfolded her in his arms. "It's okay. We're going to find her. You did great."

Bubbles the cat jumped into the space between them, purring his way to Dawn's lap.

"See, even Bubbles thinks so."

Dawn smiled through her tears and stroked the beautiful white cat sitting contentedly on her lap.

Luca kept his right arm around her as Dawn tucked her head into the crook of his arm and shoulder. She relaxed into his warmth. Just having his arm around her made her feel better. But it wasn't just any man's arm around her. It was Luca's warmth and protection making the difference. She felt safe, special, cared for. Something she had never felt before, except with her Gran—and sometimes when she was little, her mother. She closed her eyes again and let his warmth surround her.

"Are you feeling better?"

"Yes. Thank you. These visions. Sometimes they take a lot out of me, especially this one."

Luca swept a lock of unruly hair behind her ear. "Did you see anything else in the room that could tell us her location?"

Dawn concentrated but couldn't remember anything. She shook her head, letting out a groan of frustration. "I'm sorry. I'll keep trying. I have to connect with the person, and sometimes I can only see what they see. But now that I have the unicorn, I can keep concentrating on it."

She leaned back and looked into Luca's eyes. "Do you think Jack would let me into his home, into Mandy's bedroom? Maybe that would help."

Luca blew out a breath. "I don't know. I mean, you're just getting bits and pieces. If we go to Jack and tell him this now, without any concrete info, he might overreact, demand the cops use a psychic or something that will point to interference."

"But if I could go into her bedroom, maybe I could get a better sense of things."

Luca scratched the back of his neck. "I have another idea. Why don't we drive to the location of the accident? Do you think maybe that could help?"

"Yes. I imagine her energy is strong there. Can we go now?"

Luca glanced at his watch. "It's going on midnight. Are you sure?"

Dawn nodded as she picked up Bubbles and set him on the floor. "Yes, I want to find Mandy, and the sooner the better. Who knows what these kidnappers are capable of?"

"Okay, let's do it."

Luca drove them to the scene of the original accident, and they parked at the side of the road. A few flowers had been placed at the base of the pole where the car had hit. Luca grabbed his flashlight and went around to the passenger side, letting Dawn out.

Still holding the unicorn close, Dawn walked slowly around the area.

"Honey, don't cry."

"Mama, you're driving fast. Daddy doesn't like fast driving."

"I know, honey, but I have to get to Grandma's fast."

"Mama, I'm scared."

"It's okay, honey. I love you, Mandy." She felt a hand squeeze her knee.

Screams filled Dawn's ears, followed by a car screeching and the loud crash of steel hitting steel.

Then darkness.

"Dawn…Dawn, wake up, hon."

Dawn opened her eyes and for a moment didn't know where she was. "I saw the accident. I s-saw Mandy's mom fly into the windshield. Blood everywhere." Dawn felt the dizziness overtake her again, and she fought to stay conscious.

Luca lifted her up and carried her back to the car. "You need to get some rest. This was too much."

"We need to find her."

"We will find her. But this is the third time you've fainted doing this, and I'm worried about you."

"I didn't faint."

Luca buckled her back into the front passenger seat, then got into his side and drove her home.

"I don't think my fainting is because of having visions. I only faint at the sight of blood. It's always been that way. I just haven't seen blood this often in a short amount of time—until hanging out with you." She smiled, hoping he'd take that as a joke.

He was quiet the entire time, and she was too tired to carry on a conversation, still trying to process everything she'd seen.

As he was helping her out of the car, she began to get teary.

"I ruined our night, didn't I?"

Luca wrapped her in his arms again. "Are you kidding? You're the most amazing woman I have ever met. I'm the one who should be apologizing for pushing you too hard."

"We did what we felt was right at the time. No apologies needed."

Luca helped Dawn into the house and told her to lock the door after him. She didn't even roll her eyes. She understood why he'd remind her. He gave her a quick, fierce kiss and told her he'd call her tomorrow.

Dawn dropped her purse and the unicorn in the closet by the front door. "I have to stop this fainting thing," she mumbled to herself. Dawn remembered the name Lynda Carter had given her—Minerva. Maybe Minerva could help her stay focused long enough to see what she needed to see instead of fainting all the frickin' time.

She would go tomorrow after work and hope Minerva could help her.

"Dawnie, is that you?" Annette's voice floated down the stairs.

"Yes, Gran. I'll be right up." Dawn picked up the unicorn and placed it in a cloth grocery bag and hung it over a coat hanger. Then she draped her coat over it and scooted up to her room. Once she'd hidden the unicorn in the closet, she felt it was safe from Annette seeing the toy and asking questions. She popped into Annette's bedroom and plopped down at the foot of her bed.

Annette was sitting propped up against a bunch of pillows with a book facedown on her lap.

"How did your date go?"

"Luca is amazing, and so is his family." Dawn showed Annette the necklace that Gabriella had given her and recapped some funny highlights from the engagement dinner.

"Sounds like you had a wonderful time."

"I did, Gran. I really did."

Annette seemed to hesitate for a moment, then said, "Sweetie, there is something I need to tell you." She patted the bed next to her, and Dawn cuddled up beside her.

"Okay."

"Now, I'm kind of rusty with the extrasensory thing. I don't get out as much as I used to, and I certainly don't have the same abilities you do, but when I shook hands with Luca earlier this evening, I got a strange feeling from him."

"What do you mean?" Dawn's heart kicked up a beat. Did her grandmother sense something bad about Luca? No, it couldn't be. He was wonderful.

"There's something supernatural about him. Unique."

"Supernatural?" Dawn's eyes widened.

"I don't mean anything like ghosts haunting him or anything… I sense some type of superhuman ability."

"Like a superhero?" She laughed. "Gran, you're not making any sense."

"I know. I just can't put it into words. That doesn't mean I'm wrong."

She'd been completely open about her past with him. Was he keeping something from her?

Annette must have seen the alarm in Dawn's eyes, because she wrapped her arm around her and hugged her close. "I don't sense anything bad or mean about him. He has a good heart. Who knows? Maybe he doesn't even know this about himself. But I think he does. I felt like he could fly like a bird."

"Holy moly."

"Or maybe his spirit was soaring because he's in love. Or…maybe I've been watching too many of those romances you keep recommending. But I think whatever quality that boy has, it sure is special. I don't know what else to say. Just keep your eyes and mind open."

―⁂―

"Which one of you brave rookies is going to volunteer?" Sergeant Butts's eyes skewered Luca as he walked in with his new day shift training officer, Mary Beth Gulliver. "Hey, I think Fierro just volunteered. Didn't you, Fierro?"

"What now?"

Mary Beth had gone over their route in the hallway, so they were a few moments late for the morning briefing.

Luca had no idea what Butts had volunteered him to do, but he could tell by the cold gleam in his eyes that it wouldn't be fun. He decided to grin and bear it. "What would you like me to do, Sarge?"

Luca heard a chorus of chuckles around the squad room. *Uh-oh. This can't be good.*

"Well, Officer Fierro," Butts said in an almost gleeful voice, "today we're hosting the new class from the police academy. And we're going to demonstrate the protocol for tasing. And *you're* going to play the perp."

Luca swallowed hard. Certainly not his idea of a good start to a Tuesday morning, but he had no choice. It was one thing to get fooled into delivering a coffee and newspaper to the captain; it was quite another to have to get tased. "Okay, no problem."

"I'll make sure the Taser is on its lowest setting," Mary Beth whispered to him. "Don't worry. A lot of us have been through it."

Luca shrugged. "I guess it's all part of the rookie treatment."

"All right, Wonder Boy," Butts said, rubbing his hands together. "The students are waiting for us in the workout room."

Luca wondered at the sergeant's attitude. He could always sense that Butts didn't care for him, and since his breakup with Lisa, it almost seemed to have skyrocketed. Did Lisa tell her dad about their relationship? She was pretty nasty to him on the phone the other day. Was that for show? *Maybe she told her dad and blamed the breakup on me. I wouldn't put it past her.*

His mind drifted back to the night before last. Dawn. She was unlike any girl he'd ever known. She wanted so badly to help find Mandy. He was worried about Dawn though. Every time she had an upsetting vision, it caused her to faint. Luckily, he'd been with her each time, but what if he wasn't?

What if, one day when she was waiting for the subway, she had one of her visions and then fell onto the tracks? His heart kicked up a beat as he thought about her getting hurt. He would text her not to hold the unicorn unless he was with her or unless she was safely lying down at home. He hoped that would keep her out of trouble for the time being.

So why did he keep feeling like something terrible was going to happen? He wasn't the psychic one, except he'd heard that everyone was a little bit psychic. Some had honed their skills and others called it intuition.

Everyone was gathered in a circle for the demonstration.

"I'll do the tasing," Mary Beth offered.

"Oh, now why should you get all the fun?" Butts said, taking the Taser from her hands.

Mary Beth clearly didn't want him to do it. An odd look passed between her and Butts. Luca couldn't help but feel the tension between them. Mary Beth was glaring daggers at Butts, who just smirked at her expression. Luca wondered… If he'd noticed it, did anyone else? Should he bring it up with her later? He didn't want to overstep. He'd play it by ear. In the meantime, he braced himself for the tasing.

They'd set up a scenario where Luca played the role of someone resisting arrest. Luca was apprehensive, wondering if his phoenix abilities would keep him upright. Mary Beth and Butts played the roles of the arresting officers. Luca stood with his back to them. Mary Beth approached on one side and pulled Luca's arm behind his back to cuff him. Luca pulled out of her grip and turned around. Mary Beth took a step back, and Butts fired the Taser into his side. Luca felt the jolt shock his entire body, and the next thing he knew, his knees were locked, and he toppled over like a tree.

"Move back. Give him some air."

Luca heard Mary Beth's panicked voice from a distance. He groaned and wondered if his phoenix abilities had saved him at all. It sure felt like he'd experienced the full effect.

Mary Beth was hovering over him on one side, her eyes filled with concern, and on the other side, Sergeant Butts was staring at him with what could only be raw hatred. Luca blinked to clear his vision, and Butts's expression was now one of humor. *He has the right name. He's a pain in everyone's butts.*

"He's just fine, Gulliver." Butts gave her a smirk. "Don't worry. I didn't hurt your pet trainee—permanently."

Mary Beth motioned for two of the students to help her lift Luca up onto his feet, then walk him slowly to a chair.

"You okay?" Mary Beth asked, her hand resting on his shoulder.

"Yeah, I'll be fine." He turned to the group of wide-eyed students and flashed them a grin and a thumbs-up sign. They broke into spontaneous applause.

Sharing a joke with the class, he said, "All in a 'tase' work, folks."

Good-natured laughter followed as Luca rose and left the room with Mary Beth. He glanced over his shoulder on his way out, and his eyes met Butts', who stood there with his arms crossed, looking like he'd just swallowed a glass of vinegar.

"Welcome. I've been expecting you."

Dawn looked around to see where the voice was coming from, but she didn't see anyone.

Then she felt a tug on her jacket and turned around. She saw a stunning woman who looked like she'd been in a movie at one time, but she couldn't place her—and she was sitting in a wheelchair.

"Most people don't know where to look," the regal lady said.

"Are you Minerva?"

"I am indeed."

"How did you know I was coming?" Dawn realized what a silly question that was.

Minerva smiled at her. She wore a robin's-egg-blue-colored shift dress that would have made Jackie O proud.

"Let's get down to business, shall we?" the older woman said with an accent Dawn was unsure of. Everything about this woman—or goddess—was unexpected.

Minerva turned and briskly rolled her way to the back of the store, with Dawn following.

As soon as they arrived at a door, which Minerva

locked behind them, she rose from the wheelchair and walked. Her shiny black pumps made a tapping noise on the hardwood floor. Glancing over her shoulder, she said, "Are you coming?"

Dawn hurried after her. "You don't need the wheelchair?"

"No. It's just to see what my wounded veterans have to go through."

"Oh." She had no idea what she meant by *her* veterans, but she figured if she needed to know, it would be explained later.

When Minerva threw back a curtain, Dawn gasped at what she saw. She shouldn't have been surprised though. Minerva was connected to Karma Cleaners, so it was no wonder that the back of her store resembled a serene woodland forest. Tall leafy green trees, lush grasses, myriad multicolored flowers. Dawn even heard birds chirping. Minerva led her down a cobblestoned path to a quaint cottage. Opening the door, she gestured for Dawn to follow.

Dawn gaped at how pretty the cottage was, from the floral-patterned wallpaper to the cobalt-blue glass vases filled with an abundance of colorful blooms.

Minerva sat down on a muted-green sofa. A white porcelain tea service adorned with a green floral pattern had already been set on the carved wooden table, which was painted the palest of pinks and covered with a pretty white embroidered cloth. A matching three-tiered tea plate, laden with pastries and finger sandwiches, sat temptingly next to it.

Minerva poured the fragrant orange and spice brew into two cups, adding a drop of cream to each one.

She placed two tiny sandwiches and a pink-frosted cookie on each of two side plates and handed one to Dawn. "Now we can enjoy our tea and have a civilized conversation."

"So you live here?" Dawn asked, taking a bite from the delectable cream cheese and cucumber sandwich.

"Yes, I do. I've been here in this home for many years. But I travel often. Wherever I am needed, my lovely cottage goes with me."

Dawn almost choked on her sip of tea. "How?"

Minerva gave her a look as though to say *You even have to ask?*

"Sorry. I'm still having some trouble taking it all in. I've just gotten used to Karma Cleaners, and now meeting you has been kind of out of the ordinary for me."

"Well, given that you are an *extra*ordinary young woman, it's high time you start to believe in the *extra*ordinary." Minerva's bright-blue eyes twinkled at Dawn over the rim of her teacup.

Her cheeks heated.

"You want to know how to keep from fainting when you have visions, correct?"

Dawn nodded as she set her teacup down on the table. "It only happens at the sight of blood."

"Hmm…"

"What are you thinking?"

Minerva sighed. "Just that I've seen more than my share of blood. I'm the goddess of wisdom and war."

"Oh. I thought that was Athena."

Minerva chuckled. "At your service."

Dawn slapped herself upside the head. "Oh, right. You guys pick whichever name you like best. So I guess you prefer being called Minerva instead of Athena?" Dawn would have chosen the other way, but who was she to tell a goddess what to do?

"Yes. I like having a nickname with my sisters. Some of them call me Mini—and we all get a kick out of it."

"Ah. I see." She really didn't, but she might be able to figure it out. *Let's see. Powerful goddess of war and wisdom. Mini. Has to be ironic.*

"Quite so."

"I can't get used to having my mind read."

"I'll keep it to a minimum then." She smiled. "It comes in handy when a soldier can't speak but desperately wants to communicate his last wish."

"Oh."

"But you didn't come here to discuss war. You came for wisdom. There are several key points I will tell you, and they are all here in this book." She snapped her fingers, and a slim leather-bound book appeared in her hand.

Handing the book to Dawn, she continued, "I want you to close your eyes, sit back, and breathe deeply in through your nose and out through your mouth. Breathe deeply from your very core, your diaphragm. Not your chest." The goddess took Dawn's hand and laid it where her chest met her abdomen.

"Feel it expand as you draw in nature's life-giving force. Feel it contract as you expel all that nasty negative energy that humans absorb throughout the day."

Minerva's soft voice floated through Dawn's mind. Was she speaking aloud or in Dawn's head? It didn't matter, as Dawn felt herself becoming more and more relaxed.

"I want you to picture yourself in a garden surrounded

by nature's beauty and concentrate on one flower in that garden. Picture each petal, see the dewdrops trickling down, the long, elegant stem…"

Minerva continued to guide Dawn through the meditation, lasting about a half hour. When she was done, she instructed Dawn to open her eyes.

"How do you feel?"

"I feel calm. Peaceful."

"That's a different feeling for you, isn't it?"

Dawn blinked a few times, tears coming to her eyes. "Yes."

"You have had a difficult life, my little dove. But you have a special gift that lifts you up and that must be used wisely. I want you to practice this exercise every night before you go to sleep and every morning, sitting in a comfortable chair just as you are now. The moment you open that book, you will hear my voice in your head, guiding you through the exercise. Some people might call this meditation, while others might call it simply being in the moment. You must learn to clear your mind of the buzzing nonsense of everyday life. All the stresses and problems of your day. Let it all go. So that when you have a vision, you will remain calm, and it won't cause your body such physical distress. When you see blood, fear makes you hold your breath. You may not even realize you're doing it."

"I can't thank you enough for your help."

"No, it is I who must thank you. Ours is not an easy path. But it's an important one. And you have much good work still to be done. You will do it all, but from this point on, you will do it with clarity of mind and strength of spirit."

"What about your other suggestions?"

"*Sleep well. Eat well. Move well. Play well. Meditate well.* These are my five pillars of living that make up the five points of a star." Minerva lifted the book from Dawn's lap and opened it. It wasn't a book at all but a cleverly created box. Inside was a gold star with five points. Each point had a symbol that Minerva pointed out to her. "Practice these five things, and your inner force will grow strong."

Dawn must have looked skeptical, because Minerva wagged her finger at her. "Tut-tut. You would be surprised how many people like you had that exact same expression on their faces. Eventually, they all follow my creed. You cannot do one without the others. I have looked into your past, and I have seen that you have turned away from darkness and are capitalizing on the good foundation your grandmother already set in place. Oh, and make certain you follow up on those weekly sessions with that girl at the community center. She needs you."

"Is she going to be okay?"

"I don't know. But you'll be helped by helping her."

―∿―

"Are you okay, Fierro?" Mary Beth asked. "You're too quiet."

"Nothing gets past you, does it?"

"Nope. I've got three sons and a daughter at home. Nothing much gets by me."

Luca and his new TO were driving back to the station after a grueling shift. Two muggings, one stolen car, and a street fight between two prostitutes, and that was just in the morning. He'd managed to send a quick text to Dawn, asking her to be careful with the unicorn, not to try another vision unless she was at home and in bed.

She replied that she wouldn't and was getting some advice from someone who could help with her fainting problem. Also that she would call him later in the evening.

It felt good. Natural. Texting or talking with Dawn. She was fast becoming an important person in his life. He asked her out for that pizza they hadn't had yet, and she'd said yes, instantly. None of those *Let me check my calendar* games.

Once he'd come to realize the kind of person Lisa really was, it made him see what he'd been missing. His brothers' girlfriends and wives were all wonderful women. Their concern for each other outweighed all other priorities. He sensed Dawn was like that too.

Man, what a moron he'd been. An immature fool who could only see with his dick and not his mind and heart.

Mary Beth startled him out of his reflective mood.

"Look, I know Butts was hard on you this morning," she began.

"Yeah, but I guess it's all part of the rookie hazing process."

"No, it's not. He isn't usually that enthusiastic with the Taser. I barely got out of the way in time."

"Yeah, he seemed more than ready to take me down."

"Just be careful. I've been doing this job for ten years, and I know what Butts is capable of. This seemed above and beyond mere 'rookie hazing.' Avoid him if you can."

Luca nodded and flashed her a grin.

"Ah, my kids give me that smile when they listen but

don't plan on obeying. I'm serious. Butts is not someone you want to mess with."

"Have you had a run-in with him?" Luca knew he could be overstepping, but she seemed to know a lot about Butts.

"He's a slimeball who doesn't respect boundaries. I've spoken to the captain about it, and she's reprimanded him at least once already. Being a cop is tough. Even more so if you're a woman or minority."

Luca was about to state that he wasn't a minority until he realized he was—a paranormal shifter is a rarity. Of course, she couldn't know about that, right?

"Hiring practices may have changed, but there are still cops out there who have the 'old boys club' mentality," Mary Beth was saying.

"Yeah, but Captain Moore's a woman."

"True, and she's also in a tough spot. She has to answer to the higher-ups, who are powerful men, and the union reps, who can be intimidating."

"So you have to just put up with his bullying and inappropriate behavior?"

"We have our ways of dealing with guys like Butts that sometimes piss him off. I'm not usually passive-aggressive like he is, but sometimes it seems to be the only language he understands. And believe me when I say this stays between you and me."

"You got it. Thank you for the warning. I'll steer clear."

"Good. Now let's fill out our reports, and then we're done for the day."

Luca wondered if Butts's harsh hazing had to do with him finding out about Lisa or something else.

Antonio had warned him when he'd made his decision to become a cop that there were shape-shifting wolves on the force. Could Butts be one of them? Could Butts have sensed the shifter in Luca? Did that make him defensive?

How could Luca figure out for sure if Butts was a wolf or not? He'd have to do some investigating and fast. If Butts had it in for him, he'd have to figure out how to deal with him or risk something even more extreme than a tasing. Wolves could eat a phoenix if one didn't stay out of reach.

"Please don't say you love white sauce on pizza."

"I don't. Please don't say you love pineapple on pizza."

"I don't."

Dawn and Luca had just settled into a cozy booth at Ronaldo's Pizzeria, an old traditional pizza place in Boston's North End. Luca had told her it was one of his favorite restaurants. She had never been there, but it was well-known. The place was packed.

Perusing the menu, she couldn't decide what she wanted. "Spicy Italian sausage and roasted red pepper with caramelized onions looks good."

"That one's actually my favorite." He grinned.

"Really?"

"I love it."

"Wanna get it?"

"Let's do it."

She giggled at the double meaning. "You want to do it? Right here?"

He rolled his eyes, but his subsequent grin meant he

didn't mind her deliberate misinterpretation in the name of humor. They ordered a large pizza, and in the meantime, they sipped the local craft beer Luca had recommended and tucked into the warm, crusty Italian bread, dipping it into the plate of seasoned olive oil.

"This bread is delicious," Dawn said as she broke another piece off and dipped it into the oil.

"Focaccia," he said around a mouthful of it. Luca stared at her as she licked her fingers.

Feeling self-conscious, she took a sip of her beer. "Um, you're staring."

"I'm sorry." He seemed to shake himself out of his reverie. "It's just that you eat with such gusto. Like you really love food."

"Uh, yeah, I do." She frowned. "Why, is that weird?"

"No, it's not weird at all." He leaned in and whispered, "It's super hot."

"Oh." Her face heated, and she took another sip of her beer. "I never thought my appetite was sexy."

"Oh, it is. Believe me."

"Well, in that case…" Feeling a little daring, she broke off another piece of bread, swirled it into the oil, and lifting the dripping oil-soaked bread, opened her mouth and popped it in.

Luca groaned in reply and took another swig of his beer.

———~~~———

Their first official just-the-two-of-them date. Luca was relieved that it was going well.

Dawn was wearing a tight black top with crisscross straps at the back, black skinny jeans, and black leather boots. She looked hot. Her hair was spiked a bit, but not as severely as when he'd first met her. He hadn't realized how sexy short hair could be on a woman, but she rocked it.

Dawn had a tight bod, but she was definitely not a "dressing on the side" kinda girl. Being Italian with a mother whose cooking could rival a religious experience, he loved that about her. *Man, I really dodged a bullet with 'salad only' Lisa. Why the hell didn't I see it sooner?*

And Dawn was fun to be with. He didn't have to try so hard. He was having a great time with her, and he didn't want it to end.

They were halfway through their dinner when a commotion broke out in the booth next to them, a clatter of cutlery followed by a yell.

"Help!"

Luca leaped up and rushed to the next booth. Assessing the situation in moments, he saw an older man, about his dad's age, choking and struggling for air. The woman he was with, no doubt his wife, was frantically slapping him on the back. Luca went into rescue mode, pulling the man out of the booth and standing behind him. He wrapped his arms around the man's middle and pushed in and up just beneath his diaphragm with one strong movement. A piece of meat flew out of the man's mouth, landing on the floor. The man breathed in great gulps of air, teetered, and slumped to the floor, unconscious.

"He has a heart condition," the woman cried, falling to her knees.

"Someone call 911."

"I called." It was Dawn's voice, from behind.

Luca felt for a pulse and watched the man's chest to see if it was rising and falling. When it was clear the victim had gone into cardiac arrest, Luca tore open the man's shirt, knelt by his side, located the correct spot on his sternum, then began CPR, alternately compressing the man's chest and opening his mouth to breathe life-saving oxygen into his air passage.

The man didn't respond, but Luca kept it up. He could keep the blood circulating until the paramedics arrived. Not giving up was key.

Finally, he heard the welcome words "Stay back. Get back, everyone."

Within moments, two paramedics rushed up. Luca knew them both. Jeff Dresden and Bob O'Rourke, both friends of his brothers and long-time paramedics.

"Hey, Fierro, good thing you were here."

They quickly went into action using their portable defibrillator and Ambu bag.

When the man came to, everyone in the restaurant cheered.

Luca helped the paramedics lift the man onto the stretcher. Jeff slapped him on the back. "Good work, Fierro."

Bob grinned. "You Fierro guys. You're always making first responders look good with your heroics."

The man's wife turned to Jeff. "Is my husband going to be all right?"

"He's stable, ma'am, thanks to this hero cop here."

She turned to Luca and hugged him. "Thank you for saving my husband. I don't know how I can ever repay you."

"I'm just glad he's stable. They're going to take good care of him."

She nodded and left with the paramedics.

By then, a crowd had gathered around him. Strangers were slapping him on the back, congratulating him. The manager came up to him. "You... Fantastico! Grazie. Pizza on the house for a month!" He pulled him aside and lowered his voice. "We'd love to have you come back and give our staff some training. You are amazing."

"Sure. I'll mention it to my captain. I'm sure she'll approve someone giving a class to your staff. If not me, someone who does it regularly."

"Dinner's on us tonight too, of course."

"Thanks, sir."

"No, thank you." The manager slapped him on the back and then with enthusiastic hand gestures, he shepherded the spectators back to their seats.

Luca glanced around, searching for Dawn. He found her standing behind a cluster of people chatting about the events of the night.

He reached for her hand and pulled her up beside him. "Thanks for calling 911."

"You saved that man's life."

"I just did what I'm trained to do."

She stared at him wide-eyed, as though she'd just seen a miracle.

"I'm not a hero. This is what cops are trained to do. We don't just give people speeding tickets." He chuckled, feeling a little embarrassed at all the attention.

"You are a hero," she whispered, giving him a peck on the lips.

"Do you want to get a coffee somewhere quiet?"

She nodded.

"Let's go."

Dawn glanced up at Luca. She was feeling kind of shy. Watching him in action had left her speechless. She'd never seen anything like it. In her neighborhood, she'd only seen people try to hurt or evade each other, and she'd never seen a cop act with kindness, let alone heroically.

They were sitting at a Starbucks in the corner, sipping lattes.

"I think what you did was wonderful."

"Shoot, you're making me blush." He grinned.

"No, it's true. You're a natural. Yes, you're a cop, but you have an instinct to save people. Most people freeze for a few seconds. Or wonder if they should get involved, *even* if they know what to do. You didn't lose a second. You just went into action and did what needed to be done." She smiled. "You're amazing."

"If I'd known I'd get this kind of reaction from you, I would have saved someone a lot sooner."

She shook her head at his joke. "Don't underestimate what you did."

"Hey, the manager gave me free pizza. And he asked me to come in and teach his staff."

"That's great!"

"Of course, I'll need some help eating all that pizza."

"Oh, really?"

"Yeah, a month's worth."

"Well, if you insist."

"I do."

"Any time you want a pizza date, I'm your girl."

"Deal."

"So, can I ask you something?" Dawn felt awkward, unsure of her words.

"Sure, anything."

"You didn't hesitate back there. Was that just all about your training or was it something inside of you that switched on? Something supernatural. I was just wondering, since your whole family are first responders."

He blew out a breath. "I never really thought about it that way before. Sure, the training prepares you and makes you ready for action. But in the moment when it happens, we just kind of know it's up to us. I don't think it's anything supernatural. I think some people are just made that way, and some aren't. Does that make sense?"

Dawn nodded. "Yeah, I think it does. But some people are afraid they might be sued if something goes wrong, or that their involvement might be unwelcome."

"Maybe that's where the training comes in. When you're faced with a situation where someone's life hangs in the balance, you don't stop to think about consequences. You just do what you have to do, because you can."

"That makes sense, I guess." She'd never known people who approached life that way. To her, doing what had to be done meant looking out for number one. Even she was guilty of that. Well, except for Annette.

Now, that meaning had shifted for her. She was no longer just thinking about herself. She had Rita and the community at large to think about. Maybe her karma had been altered too. And finding Mandy was part of it.

Chapter 11

"C'MON, PINK UNICORN, HELP ME OUT HERE."

It was early on Saturday morning, and Dawn was sitting up in bed, holding Mandy's unicorn in her lap. She'd done everything Minerva had told her to do, the breathing exercises and meditation, over several days. So today, she would try again. She didn't have to rush to the community center, because they were closed for a couple of weeks for renovations. So she had time to concentrate and focus.

It had been almost a week since she'd had her last vision. She wanted—needed—something to happen. Was this how detectives felt when they were on a case and trying to locate a missing person or solve a murder? It must be maddening.

She wanted it to happen now. But her empath abilities didn't work on demand. She knew that, but it was still frustrating.

Luca was being super supportive, in addition to his usual cute and sexy self. They'd gone out for pizza last week—their first official date—and then texted the rest of the week. She knew she should be patient, but she couldn't wait to see him again.

"Okay, time to concentrate." Dawn closed her eyes and began taking deep breaths. She held the unicorn close as she relaxed, clearing her mind of all the stuff that pinged around every day...

I feel you, Mandy. I know you're out there. Show me where you are.

Deep breath in.

Deep breath out.

Mandy…tell me…show me…

Everything was dark. Pitch-black. Dawn kept taking deep breaths, kept holding onto the unicorn until she saw a flash of light. It was like a window blind pulling up. Dawn saw a wall in a small room. A mop leaned against the wall, and beside it was an old, faded poster of Bettie Page.

Dawn gasped and her eyes flew open. "I know where she is!"

———

"The kid's asleep."

"I don't care if she's asleep. We need to fix this problem."

Ice Spider scratched the back of his neck as he leaned against his truck in the parking lot behind a burned-out warehouse.

Sergeant Butts was pacing back and forth. "Drive up to Canada and dump the kid in front of some church. She'll get adopted by a nice Canadian family, and we'll be rid of the problem."

Yeah, like Ice was going to spend hours driving up to the border with a kid in his trunk and get nabbed by Customs. No way. The kid was his insurance policy. No way in hell he would let her out of his sight. He wasn't going to take the fall for the woman's death. He was the one taking care of the girl. Keeping her alive. Butts wouldn't. Ice and his gang were heroes. The kid stayed with him or his boys.

Butts was one mean SOB, but Ice wasn't afraid of him. He'd never been afraid of anyone except his father when he was a kid. The man who sired him and raised him for the first ten years of his life was a brutal sociopath who murdered two prostitutes he was pimping before the cops caught him and put him behind bars. The cops had no idea when they burst into Drey Douglas's dump of a home on Keene Street East that he had a son hiding in a secret hole in the back of a closet. A crawl space the boy had created to hide from his father's rampant rages.

After the arrest, Ice crawled out of the space and ran to Keene Street Convenience and never looked back. Carla had taken him in and let him sleep in the basement. Eventually, it became his hangout, and when other street kids started showing up, like Mick and Bobo, kids with nowhere else to go, they formed a gang and vowed to be the rulers of Keene Street.

"Look, Carla's cool. She doesn't know everything, okay?" Ice ran his hands agitatedly through his curly hair. "She doesn't ask no questions, and she gets a cut of the deal. She stays quiet. I told her the kid is the daughter of one of the prostitutes who OD'd and is now getting clean at a city-run clinic."

"Are you a fucking idiot?" Butts spat. "The missing girl has been all over the news. Do you really think Carla bought your lame-ass story?"

Ice lit a cigarette and took a drag. "We've been doing business with her for years. We do our thing, and she looks the other way. Carla's never gotten her hands dirty, but she likes the proceeds from our business and the protection we provide. It's made her enough to buy a condo in Florida."

Butts shook his head. "You better be right about her. Or she's gonna end up as a midnight snack for an alligator in Florida."

"Hey, Carla, how was your trip to Florida?"

"Dawnie! Good to see you." The older woman stubbed out her cigarette and stepped out from behind the counter, wrapping her arms around Dawn.

Dawn smiled when they let go. "Now, if only we can get you to wear sunscreen and stop smoking."

Carla barked out a laugh. "What doesn't kill me only makes me drink more gin."

"Why not retire for good?" Dawn smiled, leaning against the counter. "You could sell this place and just bask in the sunshine."

"Well, where's the fun in that? There's too much excitement up here." Carla strolled back to the other side of the counter when an old man hobbled in.

"Hey, Carla, gimme two of those scratch tickets I like and a pack of Marlboro."

"Sure thing, Bart." Carla pulled up the lottery tickets from underneath the glass for the old man, then rang up his order.

"When are you gonna marry me and make me a happy man?" Bart winked at Carla.

"When you win the Powerball, I'll be yours forever." She leaned over the counter and grinned.

The old man's chuckle turned into a raspy cough. He turned and tipped an invisible hat at Dawn and went on his way.

"See, if I retire to Florida, I wouldn't be around to

make Bart's day." Carla opened an old fridge behind her and pulled out a bottle of vodka and a container of orange juice. She poured two glasses of juice, handed one to Dawn, and added a healthy dose of vodka to the other. Taking a sip, she sighed. "Now that's the way to start the day."

Dawn grinned as she drank her juice, but inside, she was feeling panicked desperation. She had to get down to the basement storage room. Mandy had to be there. Dawn had recognized the tattered old poster of Bettie Page on the wall and supply shelves that had been in the same place forever. So she had thrown on some clothes and told her grandmother she was going for a walk. She remembered her conversation with Luca after he'd saved that man's life at Ronaldo's. Luca was a cop, but it was more than just his job. Despite what he said, he just seemed to know what he had to do and he did it without hesitation. That was what Dawn wanted to do for Mandy. She simply had to be careful not to involve Luca and get him fired.

"How's Annette doin'?"

"She's on her fifteenth pair of woolen socks to go with the hats, scarves, and mittens she knits for the homeless."

"Saint Annette. That's what we used to call her behind her back." Carla chuckled and lifted her glass in a toast. "There's nobody like her." She downed the rest of the screwdriver and poured herself another.

"I'll drink to that." Dawn took another sip of her juice. "So what's the excitement downstairs these days? Are the guys up to their usual shenanigans?"

Carla's eyes narrowed. "You know my motto. I don't ask questions I don't wanna know the answers to."

Was she onto Dawn? She knew Dawn had the "second sight." *Easy, Dawn. Keep playing it cool.* "Mind if I top up my juice?"

"Sure thing." Carla lit another cigarette and leaned her hip against the counter. "What are you really doin' here, Dawn?" Carla crossed her arms over her ample but sagging chest.

Dawn felt a chill go down her spine. She had to keep Carla chatting, keep it easygoing. "Man, it's tough getting anything by you, isn't it?"

"That's why I'm still alive and kickin'."

"Why come back here, when Florida has all the sunshine?" Dawn tried changing the topic.

"Oh, you know me." Carla took another sip of her drink and waved her arm, gesturing at the store around her. "I can't stay away from the place I love."

"Didn't Mick's girlfriend run the place while you were away?"

"Suzie?" Carla snorted. "That one. She spends more time shooting up or shooting the breeze than she does stocking shelves. Nothing like you. When you were working for me, I could leave here for days and know nothing would be missing and the place would be spotless when I got back." She raised her glass in a toast. "But now? I found discarded needles in the bathroom downstairs, courtesy of Suzie. That's what happens to the kids on Keene Street. Some grow up to sell drugs, and others grow up to use them. A lot turn tricks to afford an expensive addiction. But that never happened to you, did it?"

"Ha! Annette would have killed me."

"Hey, plenty of these kids have tough parents, but the

kids lose their way despite whatever threats or guidance they're given."

"I guess the problem with growing up on Keene Street is no one tells you there's always another choice. And even if they do, you have to follow through on it yourself. The deck is stacked against these kids."

"I was worried about you for a while."

"Really?"

"Yeah. I was hoping you'd pull Ice up and that he wouldn't pull you down."

Dawn nodded.

"Ah well, sometimes that's the hardest choice of all, isn't it?" Carla topped up her glass with more vodka and skipped the orange juice. "So you never answered my question. Why are you really here?"

Dawn gulped more of her juice and set the glass down on the counter. *Shit. Think fast.* "I just wanted to say hi and buy Annette some lottery tickets."

"I don't remember Annette ever playing the lottery."

"Well, I got a hunch, so here I am."

"A hunch, huh? Maybe I should play too. Okay, take your pick." Carla pulled up the tray of scratch tickets for Dawn to peruse.

Dawn picked a bingo ticket, a crossword puzzle ticket, and two tickets with a joker on them. She paid for the tickets and then reached for her glass to finish her juice. *Please, someone come in. Please, someone come in.*

"Well, good luck. I hope Annette wins—or better yet, me!"

Dawn laughed. "I hope so too."

The bell over the door rang, and Dawn almost sighed

with relief. A young teenage couple with a crying baby came in to buy junk food, diapers, and cigarettes. Carla had to serve them, so Dawn said, "I just have to use the bathroom. Be right back." Dawn didn't think Carla even heard her, the baby was crying so loud and the couple was bickering.

Dawn scooted down the stairs at the back of the store to the basement. The storage room was the second to last door down the narrow hallway.

Almost there. Dawn's heart was pounding in her chest. She would grab Mandy and then hightail it up the back stairs that led to the alley. She'd deliver her to her father before Carla even knew she was gone. Just as Dawn reached out to grasp the doorknob, she felt a hand on her shoulder. Gasping, she swung around, and standing before her was the last person she wanted to see.

"Hello, beautiful. What brings you back to this hellhole?"

"Hello, Ice." Dawn slipped her hand into her pocket and gripped her keys. "I was just stopping by to say hi to Carla and came down here to use the bathroom."

"You passed it. How long did you work here?" Ice slipped his hands in his pockets. His leather jacket fell open as he did so, and Dawn glimpsed the handle of a gun poking up from his waistband.

"Well, I was preoccupied and walked right by. Look, I really have to pee." She turned around and hoped he couldn't hear her heart pounding. It felt like it was going to burst out of her chest.

"If you have something on your mind, tell it to someone who cares." He gestured with his head back in the direction of the stairs.

"Uh, yeah, I get it." She shrugged, giving him a little smile. Hopefully, he wouldn't misinterpret it.

There was no way she would be able to rescue Mandy at the moment. She had to get out of there.

"Your hair looks good like that." Ice reached out and ran his hand along her bangs and down the side of her face. *Ugh*. He could always be counted on to think with his dick.

Maybe she could distract him and get him to wait for her upstairs if she played along. "Do you think it makes me look hot?" *I think I'm going to gag*.

"Short hair or long, you are always one hot piece of ass."

Ice stepped in so close, she could feel the heat of his body. Her mouth had gone dry, knowing he was going to kiss her.

Ice wrapped his arms around her and pulled her close, pressing his cock against her thighs.

Shit. Shit. Shit. I've got to get away from him.

Just as he was leaning down to press his lips to hers, Carla appeared at the bottom of the stairs.

"I think it's time for Dawn to go. Isn't it, Dawnie?" Carla said in her raspy voice. "It was nice going down memory lane with you. But that's the thing with memories—they're better left *buried*."

Dawn nodded like a bobblehead doll. She couldn't speak. A little girl was on the other side of that door, and she'd blown it. Saying anything now could get them both killed.

Ice gave a frustrated groan as she began to pull away from him. Leaning down, he whispered, "We should finish what we started."

Suppressing her gag reflex, she gave him a weak smile and yanked herself out of his arms.

She brushed passed Carla, standing at the bottom of the stairs with her hands on her hips and glaring at her. Rushing up the stairs, she made a beeline for the door and ran as fast as she could, not looking back.

She ran until she got home. Tears rolled down her cheeks. *What the hell am I going to do now?*

—∿—

Craig Butts was no fool. So when he walked into the precinct and saw Fierro chatting it up with Morrow and Griffin, the two detectives assigned to the Richardson case, he knew he had to put a stop to it. He'd assigned his two worst detectives to the case, and he didn't want anyone else nosing around. Morrow and Griffin were good guys, but they tended to be lazy and didn't investigate as deeply as they should, exactly the way he liked it.

Butts had counted on that in the past when he himself was connected to a crime, and it had worked every time. But that was before Fierro showed up. And now he was asking too many questions.

"I really admire what you guys do," Fierro said. "I want to see you in action. Would you mind if I just hang out with you today?"

"On your day off?" Morrow glanced at Griffin. "Hey, this kid wants to work on his off day. What do you think about that?"

"I think he's a rookie, and by this time next year, he'll be in bed sound asleep at 9:00 a.m. on his day off," Griffin said and chuckled.

"Look, kid, this is, what…your second week on the job?" Morrow crossed his arms. "Why not just do what everyone else does? Keep your head down, and learn how to be a cop before thinking you're a detective."

"Morrow is right." Butts stepped up to the trio. The pipsqueak glanced at him and straightened. "One thing at a time, Fierro."

"Sorry, Sarge." The pretty boy visibly swallowed. "I was just killing some time before I had to pick up my suit for my brother's wedding."

"Well, instead of bothering these two good men and keeping them from doing their jobs, why don't you go home and get dolled up for that wedding?" Butts slapped Fierro on the shoulder and gestured with his head to step into the hall. "Fierro won't be bothering you two again."

In the hallway, Butts took his most imposing stance, feet planted wide apart, leaning forward with his hand resting on his gun, and glared at the rookie. Fierro was maybe three inches shorter than him. At six three, Butts was big and imposing, and he never failed to use it to intimidate. "I hear you already approached Morrow and Griffin once before."

"Yes, sir, I was just trying to help."

The kid looked nervous, and that was how he liked these anxious-to-please newbies. "Well, I let the first time go, but I'm gonna write you up this time. It's going in your file. Fair warning. Don't do it again."

"Sir, with all due respect, I didn't think it was against protocol to ask questions, and I want to learn. I thought that was what we were supposed to do."

Shit, this kid is a piece of work. Butts glared at Fierro, wondering how he was going to get through to the Goody

Two-shoes without making him suspicious. He decided on righteous anger. "You know, for every upstart kid like you who goes to college and thinks he knows everything because he's taken Criminology 101 and written a term paper about Ted Bundy, I have a dozen cops like Morrow and Griffin who worked their way up the old-fashioned way and know a hell of a lot more than you could read in a textbook." He shoved his finger in Fierro's face for good measure. "So don't 'with all due respect' me. I know a brownnoser when I see one. And if you think Captain Moore is gonna be impressed by your Boy Scout charm, you've got another think comin'. I'll be writing you up, and you better understand something—I don't condone smart-asses. So shape up or ship out."

"My apologies, sir." Fierro stood up straight and stiff as a pole. "I promise not to overstep again."

"Good." Butts sneered. "Now get the hell out. I don't want to see you ever nosing around here on your day off again."

"Yes, sir."

Butts nodded in satisfaction. And watched Fierro turn and walk out the door. He should have amped up that Taser to full throttle. But if he'd really hurt the bastard, there would have been an investigation. He just couldn't help thinking that this kid was fucking his daughter, and she thought he was so stupid he couldn't figure it out. He was a cop, for God's sake. He'd followed her to see who she was meeting at the so-called library.

No, he'd have to be careful. He'd have to make it look like an accident, an on-the-job thing. Maybe set up a robbery and a fire at Keene Street Convenience. He could off Carla, Fierro, and those two buffoons guarding the kid, then get rid of her himself, niece or no niece. He'd worked too hard for the money he'd never make on the job to get caught now.

He'd have to think this through carefully. Plan everything out.

I feel like time is running out for Mandy.

"You *will* find her and free her. I know you will."

Dawn was sitting on a bench at the Christian Science Center, talking to herself. After the incident at the convenience store, she needed to think, and what better place to wrestle with her thoughts. After a half hour of kicking herself, she remembered the pager that Lynda had given her. Dawn rooted around in her purse for it and finally pulled it out. She pushed the button and waited. "Hmm. I wonder if this thing really works?"

"Of course it works. I'm here, aren't I?"

Dawn glanced behind her and saw a grinning Lynda approach. She wasn't in her old-lady garb this morning. This time, she looked young and vibrant, wearing a body-hugging teal jogging suit with silver trim. Her sleek black hair was tied up in a high ponytail. Dawn looked down at her own garb—a black turtleneck, faded jeans with rips, and her usual leather jacket.

"Everything's going to be okay. I'm here to help." Lynda plopped down on the bench beside Dawn, crossing her sleek legs. Her wedge sneakers even matched her outfit.

"How do you know? Are you psychic too?" Dawn asked.

Lynda laughed softly and reached into her matching

purse. She pulled out some toffee candy and handed one to Dawn. "I know because I know you. I know you don't give up. You care deeply about this little girl. Finding her means saving her life and saving yours."

"What do you mean—saving mine?"

"You know what I mean. Deep down inside, you believe if you don't find this little girl, your karma will be crap forever."

Dawn frowned. "That would make me a pretty selfish person to be thinking about my karma when a little girl's life is at stake." It was true, though. She had thought about it and hoped she wasn't a terrible person.

"Oh, please, you're a tough girl from the streets of Boston. You're not Snow White." Lynda took a deep breath. "You know deep in your heart what the right thing to do is. Maybe it's not the easy thing. But it's the right thing." Lynda leaned back on the bench with a sigh, nodding as though she'd just shared the secrets of the universe.

"I get it," Dawn said. "Okay, lesson learned. Getting Mandy back is the right thing to do, and good karma or not, I'm going to rescue that little girl, because I am dedicating myself to doing so. I have a gift and I'm using it for good. But what good did it do?" Dawn filled Lynda in on her vision with the unicorn and then rushing off to the convenience store. "I was so close. I could have just opened that storage door and yanked her out of there."

"And gotten yourself killed in the process?" Lynda shook her head. "You have to work smart. You can't just rush into danger like the Lone Ranger. You have to think before you act. That's what we need to teach you."

Dawn's eyes filled with tears, and she wiped them away in frustration.

Seeing her reaction, Lynda gave her a side hug. "Look, you know where the girl is. I think they're keeping her around as a safety net. Whoever Ice is in cahoots with must be a VIP. I can only guess that Ice is keeping a close eye on the girl for a good reason. You know what I mean?"

Dawn nodded. "Yeah. But I also know Ice. If he starts to feel panicked, he's going to do something rash. Stupid. And that's why I have to get back to that storeroom."

"They have the place guarded. Why don't you stop and think of a plan first?"

"Like what?"

"Like maybe confiding in that hunka-lovin' boyfriend of yours."

Dawn's face flushed. "He's not my boyfriend."

"Really? Then why are you going to yet another family event with him tonight?"

"How did you know?"

Lynda gave her one of those looks again. "Puh-leeze. I know stuff. A lot of stuff."

"I should tell him, shouldn't I? I just didn't want to put him in danger. He's already been told he shouldn't interfere with someone else's case. I wanted to get her out of there myself."

"You wanted to be the heroine."

Dawn nodded, tears blurring her eyes. Why was she always crying lately? It was really pissing her off.

Lynda took Dawn's hand in hers. "You got this, girlfriend. Sometimes you have to settle for the silver medal before you can get the gold."

Dawn leaned her head onto Lynda's shoulder. "Thanks, LC. You always have my back."

"Speaking of which, do you have a dress for the wedding?"

"Uh, no. I've been a little busy trying to work, date, and be a heroine and all."

Lynda giggled. "I forget how sarcastic you are. Well, I think you need a kick-ass dress to wear so you knock Luca's socks off."

"But Mandy—"

"There's not a thing you can do right now."

"Are you sure?"

"Positive. Let's get your mind off of it for now."

"I guess it couldn't hurt."

"A little retail therapy never hurt anyone except in the pocketbook." Lynda's eyes gleamed. "You just got paid, so you must have some money burning a hole in your pocket by now."

Dawn chuckled. "Speaking of Luca…"

"Yes?"

"Um, regarding karma stuff, do I have to…uh… abstain from sex in order to keep my karma clean?"

"What?" Lynda stood up, hands on her hips and fire in her eyes. "Sex is not *dirty*. It's as natural as breathing when a couple is young and in love."

"Okay, okay, just checking. I thought maybe there was some code book for sex."

Lynda sighed and shook her head. "The only thing you have to worry about is making the right decisions for yourselves. Now let's get shopping. There's an amazing little shop around here called Goddess Fashions."

"You don't happen to know the owner, do you?"

"Venus?" Lynda winked. "I may have heard of her."

Chapter 12

OVER THE MUSIC AND CHATTER OF THE RECEPTION, LUCA teased his brothers.

"Do you, Dante?"

"I do."

"Do you, Mallory?"

"I do."

"Do you, Noah?"

"I do too."

"Do you, Kizzy?"

"I do too."

Dawn didn't feel enough a part of the family yet to chime in. Fortunately, his sister-in-law did.

"It was cute!" Sandra insisted.

"I thought so too," Kristine said.

At least Dawn was beginning to put the correct names with all the faces. Sandra was a willowy blonde nurse married to Miguel. Jayce's wife, Kristine, was tall and had golden-red hair. Not exactly strawberry blonde... more like bronze. She was a Boston fire captain. Misty was Gabe's wife and a stay-at-home mom. She was on the shorter side and had long brunette hair and big blue eyes. Now adding Mallory, a stunning blonde artist of medium height, and Kizzy, a shorter brunette—and a doctor! What an amazing, eclectic group of women!

Is that all of them? I must have missed a couple. She remembered Chloe and Ryan were in Ireland

and couldn't attend. So yes, she must have met almost everyone.

"How did you manage to join the wedding with only a couple of weeks to plan?" Kristine asked Kizzy. "Jayce and I needed every minute of those four months to get our wedding together."

"I already had my mother's wedding gown," Kizzy said and stepped back to show off the full-length satin and lace white dress.

"It's gorgeous," Sandra said. "So that must have been all you needed?"

"Since Noah and Dante were best friends as well as brothers, Mallory's guest list was pretty much the same as ours, so that was already taken care of. We added my bouquet and contributed another bride and groom to the top of the cake."

"Pretty much everything was all set," Noah added. "Dante had to get a new best man though. I suddenly had other plans." Everyone laughed.

Dawn remembered Dante and Noah had been roommates and firefighters in adjacent houses when they began dating their brides, and the two women seemed close too. The newly married couples gazed at each other, smiling. Anyone could tell they were in love and happy.

"I had to add a few people to the guest list," Kizzy said. "Especially my sister, Ruth, who was my maid of honor."

"And your father," Noah added.

"Yes. And my overprotective father, who learned to love you when you saved my life."

Gabriella Fierro wandered over and slipped her arm around Dawn's waist.

"Are you all being inclusive to Luca's date, Dawn?"

"Yes, Mom. Why wouldn't they be?" Luca asked.

"Good. I just noticed she seemed kind of quiet. I didn't know if you were all talking about people she didn't know. Of course, even if that wasn't the case, it can be hard to get a word in edgewise with such a large group. Right, Gabe?"

Gabe coughed. "Right, Ma. Somebody has to be the quiet one."

"Well, I hope you're all making Dawn feel welcome. I'd like to keep her around." She smiled, gave Dawn a side squeeze, and returned to her husband, Antonio.

"Ha! You're next, Luca. And it looks like Ma's already picturing Dawn in a white dress," Dante said.

Dawn groaned before she realized how it could be taken. She was actually thinking that white was the last color she should be wearing. Her appropriate color would be more like gray.

Luca rubbed her back. "We've only been officially dating for a couple of days."

"Oh, so not long enough for her to realize you're a dweeb and run for the hills," Gabe said.

Luca narrowed his eyes. "Maybe there's another reason you're the quiet one…"

Everyone laughed.

"I was only joking. He's a good kid, Dawn. Don't run off yet."

She smiled at Luca, but she was nervous and hoped her voice remained steady. "I wasn't planning on it."

"I think I'll go where I'm welcome," Gabe said. He wandered off toward Misty, at which point his son began wiggling out of her arms. When she set him down, he ran right to his daddy. Gabe swept him up and held him above his head. The toddler's laugh was adorable.

"He seems like a good dad," Dawn observed.

Luca snickered. "Yeah. You'd never know he didn't want kids at all."

"A lot can change in a short time around here," Noah said.

Kizzy chuckled. "You can say that again."

"Um, I need to excuse myself for a moment," Dawn said.

"Me too." Luca walked with her toward the restrooms. "I hope my family didn't scare you."

"Oh, not at all. They're wonderful! I just…"

There was a line for the ladies' room, and he drew her aside.

"What is it, Dawn? I know you well enough to see that something's bothering you."

She sighed. "Yes. But this isn't the time or place to talk about it."

His brows shot up. "Are you dumping me?"

"No! Oh my God, no. I—it's about the case. But I don't want to ruin your brothers' wedding reception by pulling you away from it."

"Is it something that can wait?"

She worried her lip.

"Okay. I can see it's important. As soon as you're out of the ladies' room, I want you to tell me."

She hesitated.

"Please. I have something to tell you too. I'll wait for you right here."

She sighed. "Okay, we'll talk. But go back to your family and socialize. I'll find you."

He nodded and returned to the festivities.

When she returned from the restroom, Luca was dancing with his mother. She hung back and watched. It was obvious from their smiles that mother and son were comfortable together.

As soon as the dance was over, he glanced around, probably looking for her, so she went right to him.

He gave her a quick kiss and swept her into the next dance.

"So, what did you need to tell me?" he asked.

"I'd rather you go first."

He tipped his head and gazed at her with curiosity. "Okaaaay. I'm glad we're here with my family, because you may not believe me at first. They can confirm my story. No one else can know, though. Can you promise to keep a secret? I'm about to share something you *must* keep to yourself, no matter what. You may be in for a shock."

She leaned back and studied his face. She saw *and* sensed his expectant anxiety. "Not much shocks me anymore. Go ahead."

"Promise you won't tell anyone first."

"I promise."

He took a deep breath and glanced around. She followed his eyes, and when he was apparently assured nobody was listening, he leaned next to her ear and whispered, "I'm a shape-shifting phoenix."

He leaned back for a moment to check her reaction. She was careful not to react at all.

"Did you hear what I said?"

"Yes. I'm not sure what it means, though."

"It means…I have a special ability. I can shift into

my other form, which is a bird about the size of a hawk but with long, colorful tail feathers."

Again, she was trying not to react, even though she was silently wondering if he was completely crazy. But if so, why would he say she could check with his family? Did they humor him? Then Annette's words returned to her mind. A few questions were in order.

"Can you fly?"

"Yes. My dad discourages it, because we age faster in bird than human form. There are advantages, though. Even if we get old or if anything happens to us, we can reincarnate in fire."

Her brows shot up. "Have you ever witnessed this?"

"Yes. It happened to Gabe…right in front of my face."

She paused, mulling that over. "I see. So this ability includes everyone in the family?"

"Just my dad and brothers. My mom is human."

Her eyebrows shot up. She couldn't help it. "So, you're telling me you're not human. Are you from some alien world?"

He laughed. "No. Of course not. You've heard the legend of the phoenix, haven't you?"

"Yeah. I think it's a Southwestern Indian thing, right?"

"Not just there. Ancient Romans and Greeks had stories about firebirds. That's another name for us."

"Firebirds."

"Yes."

Dawn glanced around the dance floor, picking out Luca's brothers and their dad. They were all somewhat similar in looks. Dark hair, olive skin, and except for Luca, they all had brown eyes. She'd learned that the name Fierro meant "fire" in Italian. She'd wondered about so many of them working for the fire department. If the legend was true, that would be a pretty obvious job. If it weren't true, a job with the fire department could be something that supported a delusion.

Then she remembered. *Shoot. I've been accused of being delusional too.* That's why she didn't share her psychic abilities and photographic memory with many people. Luca just happened to catch her in the middle of a vision—literally.

With an expectant look on his face, he said, "Are you okay?"

"Um, I think so. You certainly surprised me, but I'm okay...not in shock or anything. I'm just processing."

He let out a deep breath. "Good. You'll need a little while to process, I'm sure. But like I said, if you want to talk to any of my family members, please do. They've all been through this. They don't usually tell anyone they're dating until they're sure they can trust them, and I don't know why I feel that way with you so quickly, but I do."

"You're a cop with good instincts about people. And don't worry. I promised I wouldn't tell anyone, and I won't."

He smiled and leaned in for a kiss. She imagined he was greatly relieved she didn't run screaming from the reception hall. A part of her wanted to hold back her kisses until she'd had a chance to check out his information, but a bigger part of her knew he wasn't lying.

She leaned in and met his kiss with her own. Suddenly, it was as if everyone melted away. It was just the two of them, sharing a warm, tender kiss—right on the dance floor.

A few whoops and hollers brought her back to the moment. She leaned away to see the two grooms surrounding them, smiling and applauding. Their wives were smiling too.

She gazed farther and saw Gabriella with her hand over her heart and tears in her eyes. But she was smiling too. Antonio put his arm around her and kissed her on top of her short, dyed red hair.

When Dawn turned back to Luca, he was grinning. "Maybe we should take a short walk, so you can tell me whatever you wanted to get off your chest."

"Yeah." She giggled. "Yeah, that would probably be a good idea."

Out on the sidewalk, she began her story. "So there's something I haven't told you."

"You're a shape-shifting bunny rabbit?"

Dawn smirked. Now that she knew he was a shape-shifting phoenix, as were his father and all his brothers, she felt strangely elated. Her boyfriend was like some kind of superhero.

Boyfriend. That made her feel all warm inside. Was that what it felt like to have good karma? She'd have to talk to Lynda about it at her next session. Could you tell when your karma was shifting? Did you feel differently inside? Did good things start to happen? So many questions whirled through her mind. She wished she could ask Lynda about shape-shifting, but she had promised not to.

First things first. "I had a vision about Mandy. I know where she is, and I went there but wasn't able to rescue her."

"You what?"

"I had a vision about Mandy."

"I heard that part. That's not the part I'm worried about. You tried to rescue her by yourself? Hang on. I need to sit so we can talk." Luca pulled her over to a nearby bench, and they sat. Then he turned to her, his eyebrows raised. "Why didn't you tell me?"

"I'm telling you now."

"Yeah, after the fact."

"Look, I knew you'd get in trouble if you were involved."

"Fuck that. A little girl's life could be hanging in the balance. And holy shit, Dawn, *your* life may have been endangered too! You should have told me."

"Well, excuse me, but I was a little busy earlier, trying to process that big news that you dumped in my lap about being a shape-shifting bird."

"Phoenix."

"Yeah, and I find this out at your brothers' double wedding, and now, I'm sure everyone thinks we're next, because I kissed you at the reception." She huffed and crossed her arms over her chest.

"You didn't change anything. My mom already loves you, and if you hang in there, everyone else will too." He grinned.

"So you don't think your parents will be pissed off at me if we break up?"

"They'll be pissed off at me, not you. Are we breaking up?"

"No. Of course not. I still need time to talk about your abilities with your parents, but not today."

"I should have told you at some later time, but we were coming clean…"

"I'm glad you did tell me."

"Good. Now it's your turn. Tell me everything that happened from your vision to going to her rescue. And don't leave anything out."

Dawn filled him in on her vision and her trip to Keene Street Convenience and how she'd almost been able to rescue Mandy but was stopped by Ice and Carla.

"Shit." Luca shook his head, his eyes laced with concern. "You could have been hurt or worse. They could have just thrown you in that storage room with Mandy and then hauled you out to a dump in the middle of nowhere and offed you."

Dawn swallowed the lump of emotion in her throat. She'd never had someone care so much about her, other than Annette. Even her mother had cared more about getting a fix than her own daughter. On the other hand, she wasn't used to having to answer to anyone. That kind of rankled her.

"Look, thank you for caring, but as you can see, I'm fine." She didn't tell him about the part when Ice leaned in for a kiss nor about the gun he had tucked into his pants.

"Thank you for caring?" Luca shook his head. "You could have been killed."

"But I wasn't. I got away. So it's fine. At least I'm fine. Mandy is still stuck there. And we need to rescue her before it's too late."

"We will rescue her, but we'll do it the right way. Not like some half-cocked crazy action movie or waltzing in there like Robin Hood."

"I couldn't let Mandy just stay there when I knew where she was."

"You going over there only made them suspicious," Luca countered. "For all we know, they could have moved her to another location by now."

Dawn blew out a breath. She hadn't thought of that. She may have jeopardized Mandy's life. Tears sprang to her eyes. "I fucked up, didn't I?"

"No, I understand," Luca said, placing his hands on either side of her face. "You're a brave woman. But I could have lost you. You mean too much to me. I don't want you putting yourself in danger like that again."

Luca leaned in and kissed her, underscoring what he'd just told her. When his tongue slipped along her lips, she soon forgot about their argument. His breath mingling with hers, the heat of their bodies, made her wish one of them had an apartment. She'd never felt so attracted to a guy like she did Luca. He did things to her insides that no other guy ever had. Luca pulled away from her, his blue eyes hooded, like he wanted the exact same thing she did.

"Please don't keep things like that to yourself, babe," he whispered. "I don't want you getting hurt."

Dawn wanted to kiss him again just for that, but instead, she reached up to the side of his face and whispered back, "Yeah. So you've said. You mean a lot to me too."

Dawn stretched and yawned. She glanced at her iPhone and saw it was just past 9:00 a.m. She rarely ever slept in this late, even on weekends, but by the time Luca had dropped her off, it was almost 1:00 a.m. Her phone beeping alerted her to a text message. No doubt that's what had woken her.

Hey babe, just wanted to check in to see how
you're doing. I'm glad we talked last night.

She sighed at Luca's endearment. It felt good.
Texting back, she said she was just waking up and then
paused before she hit send. *Should I use the emoji heart?
Or XO? Or…love? Or what?* Hmm…would that make
her seem too pushy or needy? On the other hand, he'd
called her *babe*.

She groaned in frustration. XO meant a hug and a
kiss. Yup. They'd already been there. She hit send and
waited. Her breath caught when he texted back with
a heart and asked her out for brunch. They could also
plan what they would do about Mandy. She texted back:
Sure, I'll reach out when I've had a shower.

Heading downstairs, the aroma of cinnamon wafted
up to her. She breathed in deeply of the sweet and spicy
scent. Walking into the kitchen, she spied the muffins
cooling on a rack. Annette was dressed and packing a
thermos and some sandwiches along with a container of
six of the muffins. "Morning, Grandma. Those muffins
smell and look delish." She kissed Annette on the cheek.

"Morning, sweetie." Annette gave her a sideways
hug. "Freshly baked cinnamon-apple coffee cake muffins. Help yourself."

"Oh, I will." Dawn picked up one of the warm muffins and laid it on a plate, inhaling the incredible scent.
She picked off a chunk from the still steaming top and
popped it into her mouth. "Mmm. So good! No one can
bake like you do."

"Thanks, dear. Now grab a glass of milk, sit yourself
down, and tell me about last night."

"Okay, but where are you heading today?"

"I'm heading over to Sheree's place. She's been feeling low since her husband died six months ago, so I'm bringing her a little care package. Thought I'd spend the day with her, playing cards."

"You're such a good friend." Dawn took a sip of her milk to wash down another bite of muffin.

"Well, Sheree was there for me when Lissie was sent to prison, and I'll never forget that." Annette finished packing the food, then pulled out a chair and joined Dawn at the small kitchen table. "Now, spill it. Tell me everything."

Dawn told her grandmother about the wedding, leaving out the part about Luca and his family being shape-shifters. She didn't want to worry Annette, but at some point, if it turned out to be true, she'd have to tell her. She also left out the part about her vision of Mandy and her failed rescue attempt at the convenience store. She hated lying to Annette, even by omission, but she didn't want to put her in danger. The less she knew, the better.

"Well, it sounds like you had a great time. The Fierros seem like a wonderful family." Annette patted Dawn's hand.

"They are," Dawn agreed.

"I just want you to be careful. The women in this family seem to have bad luck when it comes to men."

"Hopefully, our luck is about to change."

"If anyone is going to change it, it's you, sweetie."

"Aw, thanks, Gran." Dawn stood up and wrapped her arms around Annette. "Speaking of luck." She remembered the scratch tickets she had bought at Keene Street

Convenience. Grabbing her purse off the hook by the front door, she went back to the kitchen and pulled out the scratch tickets and handed two to Annette.

Annette shook her head. "Oh, now you've gone and done it. You have labelled me a typical old lady who sits in her kitchen and scratches lottery tickets."

Dawn chuckled. "Well, at least you don't play bingo on Saturday nights."

"No indeed. Okay, hand me a quarter and let's get to work."

The two women scratched off all four cards. Dawn didn't expect to win, but then Annette let out a squeal of delight.

"Did you win?"

"Well, wonder of wonders, I actually won."

"What did you win?"

"Here, look."

Dawn saw the amount: $20.

"Cash it in, honey. We can move to Hawaii." Annette chuckled.

"I will cash it in, and I know just what to get with it."

"What?"

Dawn smiled to herself. She'd seen a beautiful old cane at Goddess Fashions on sale for $19.99. It was black with an ivory handle and an ornate bird design down the length.

"I'm going to surprise you."

Annette smiled. "Okay, you do that, but promise me one thing."

"Yes, anything."

"That's the first and last time you buy me lottery tickets."

"Deal. Now, you promise me one thing."

"What's that?"

"Let me walk you to Sheree's place, okay? We're supposed to get rain later today, and they say after dark, it could freeze."

"Oh, I'll be fine. You enjoy your day off." Annette patted Dawn's hand, still around her shoulder.

"I intend to, after I walk you to Sheree's. And when you're done visiting, text me and I'll come get you."

"Never mind about that. I'll be fine."

"Oh, all right. I have no idea where you get your stubbornness from."

"Really? And where does your stubbornness come from?"

Dawn grinned as she was about to take her last bite. "I'm looking right at her."

Annette chuckled.

~~~

"Are you going to finish that bacon?"

"You bet I am." Dawn picked up her last piece of bacon and waved it in front of Luca's face.

"Damn, I thought women didn't eat bacon. My sisters-in-law say it's too fatty and high in calories."

"Really." She grinned. "Well, this woman loves it." Luca made a puppy-dog face, and Dawn burst out laughing. "Okay, okay! But you have to come get it."

"Ah…challenge accepted."

She put one end of the slice in her mouth, and Luca leaned in and, with a little growl, opened his mouth and took a big bite. Dawn giggled, loving his playful face. He lifted one eyebrow like a villain in a silent movie.

"Why don't we order more bacon to satisfy your appetite?" she said.

He waggled both his brows. "I have many appetites that need satisfying. Bacon is only one of them."

Dawn was about to reply when her phone rang. Lifting it off the table, she recognized Sheree's number. She swiped to answer. "Hi, Sheree. Is everything okay?"

"Honey, it's your gran. She slipped and fell just outside my door. I called 911, and some nice paramedics just took her to Boston General Hospital. I'm sorry, honey. I feel terrible."

"Oh my God! I didn't think it was going to ice up until tonight."

"It wasn't ice. Wet leaves were covering one of my grandkid's marbles that he left on the steps."

"Shoot. Thanks for calling."

"I'm so, so sorry."

"It's okay. It's not your fault. I'll head over now."

Dawn hung up and looked at Luca. "My gran fell, and they took her to Boston General. Can you drive me there?"

"Absolutely. Let's go."

As they made their way to the car, Dawn felt terrible that she wasn't there when it happened. "I told her not to leave Sheree's on her own. I told her to text me. I was going to stop off at Goddess Fashions and pick up a really cool old-fashioned cane for her that I saw there. It would help her get around and keep her from slipping. And here she went and slipped."

"Everything will be okay, I promise."

Luca drove like a speed demon to the hospital and dropped Dawn out front, telling her he'd meet her inside.

Dawn ran in to the ER and spoke with someone at the nurse's station. "Can you tell me about my grandmother, Annette Forest?"

The nurse glanced at her computer monitor and a few moments later said, "She's been taken to the OR."

"They're operating? On what?"

"I need to see if you're on the list before I release personal information."

"I'm definitely on her list. Dawn Forest."

The secretary flipped to the next page and nodded. "Yup. You appear to be the only one we can talk to. Do you want the nurse or doctor to talk with you?"

"Maybe later. Can you just tell me what they're operating on?"

"A broken hip."

"Damn," she breathed. "Oh, sorry. Where can I wait for her?"

The nurse told Dawn where to check in, and Dawn texted Luca to meet her on the fifth floor in the waiting area.

Three hours later, Dawn and Luca were standing by Annette's bedside in a hospital room. Another lady was in the room. Dawn had pulled the privacy curtain around them, not liking the fact that her grandmother was not in a private room, but they couldn't afford it.

Annette was groggy but waking up. Dawn held her hand and glanced at Luca. He smiled reassuringly at her.

"Gran, how are you feeling?"

"Like a silly old woman." She asked Dawn to give her some water. Dawn held the cup with the straw to her grandmother's lips so she could take a sip.

"You're not a silly old woman. But please, next time when you want to try a cartwheel, text me first?"

Annette chuckled. A good sign. "Oh, I'm so sorry to put you kids through this. I ruined your date."

Luca crouched by the side of the bed. "Mrs. Forest, you have nothing to apologize for. We're just glad that you're okay."

"You're such a nice boy, Luca." Annette reached out for Luca's hand, then her eyes widened.

"Gran, what is it?"

Annette glanced at both Dawn and Luca. "Is there something you need to tell my granddaughter?"

"Are you psychic too?" Luca asked.

"Li'l bit."

Luca must have realized what Annette sensed. "She knows, Mrs. Forest. I told her last night at my brothers' wedding."

Annette visibly relaxed. "I could feel something about you when you reached for my hand. But I can't explain what it is."

Dawn looked at Luca, a worried expression on her face.

"It's okay, Dawn." Luca glanced behind the curtain to make sure the other woman was sleeping. With a lowered voice, he explained his abilities to Annette, who listened patiently.

"Why didn't you tell me?" Annette eyed her granddaughter.

"I promised not to, and even if I could, I didn't know how. I figured I'd know when the time was right, and then you fell. Please forgive me."

Annette sighed and nodded. "I understand." Annette reached for Dawn's hand and Luca's. "Luca, you need to watch over my Dawn. She's got a big heart and has a notion she can change the world we live in."

"I promise to look out for her, Mrs. Forest."

"And promise me you'll call me Gran from now on."

"I promise, Gran." Luca grinned.

"I can see why my granddaughter is so taken with you."

The nurse interrupted them and told them visiting hours would soon be over.

"Honey, tomorrow morning, bring me my nightgown and robe. I can't abide these hospital gowns. And my knitting. I need it to pass the time here or I'll go batty."

Dawn nodded, saying she'd be in first thing in the morning before work. She placed a gentle kiss on Annette's forehead, but she was already falling asleep.

"Good night. Sleep well."

Dawn sighed and leaned her head on Luca's shoulder as they made their way out of the hospital.

So much for the Forest women's luck turning. The nurse said her grandmother would have to stay in the hospital for at least a week and then go into a rehab facility for two weeks after that. She would be safer in the hospital than at home. Dawn would be able to focus on finding Mandy, knowing her grandmother wasn't in harm's way.

"Are you okay?" Luca asked in a soft voice as he pulled up to her house.

"I'm okay." She turned to him. "I don't want to be alone. Will you come inside?"

Luca nodded.

Dawn felt overwhelmed by what had happened to Annette. She blamed herself. She wasn't able to rescue

Mandy, and she wasn't able to stop her grandmother from breaking her hip. Somehow, she had to make it right. But for now, all she wanted was Luca's arms around her. She wanted his heat. His kisses, his body close to hers. She turned to him. And leaning in, she whispered in his ear, "Stay with me tonight. Please."

Luca followed Dawn inside her house. He had been here before, but it seemed strangely quiet without Annette bustling around. Without saying a word, Dawn opened the hall closet, then reached toward him for his jacket.

After handing it over, he ambled around the living room, taking in features he had missed before. A bookshelf against the far wall was crammed with books of different sizes and no knickknacks. It looked as if Annette and Dawn were serious readers. The sofa appeared to be one that could be opened and made into a bed, not that that meant much. Somehow, he doubted Dawn would make him sleep on the couch tonight.

After hanging up her own leather jacket, Dawn walked over to him and slipped her arms around his neck.

"Thank you for staying with me tonight. I'm really upset about what happened to my grandma, but I put on a brave face for her."

His arms automatically pulled her closer. "I know. It's okay. She's going to be fine. In the meantime, you have me." He stroked her back and placed a gentle kiss against her neck.

She leaned back slightly and looked up into his eyes. "You have the most beautiful blue eyes. But you're the only one with blue and the rest of the family has brown eyes. Right?"

Luca smiled. "I know. I must've had an ancestor on both my parents' sides who had blue eyes, and I got the recessive gene."

"Yeah. I know how it works." She brushed his hair away from his eyes and just stared into them for a moment.

He felt like an idiot. Of course she knew how it worked. She was a smart woman, and that was basic high school biology stuff. About the only way he could think of to recover was to use his own knowledge of chemistry. Either way, she met his lips halfway, and they shared a deep, warm, comforting kiss.

Her mouth opened, and he gained access to her tongue easily. They stood close, tasting and touching each other for several moments. At last, they broke the kiss and just hugged. He found himself wanting to comfort her, but how? She seemed so tough, it was unusual to see her so vulnerable.

"Would you like anything to eat?" she asked.

"Not unless you want something. I'm not really hungry for food." He realized how that sounded as soon as it left his lips. But hey, when the truth comes out…

She smiled shyly, then simply stepped away, took his hand, and led him upstairs. Her room was utilitarian. A full-size bed, handmade quilt, two pillows, a nightstand with a decorative lamp on top and books piled on the shelf beneath. There was a desk under the window, and that was about it. The only artwork on the walls was a couple of posters of the Arizona desert. At least, one of them said "Arizona," as if it were a travel poster. The others were just desert landscapes.

"Do you like the desert?"

"I like warm weather."

"But Arizona gets hot. Like, a hundred and twenty degrees hot. Is that what you like?"

She smiled. "Not really. I'm just not a fan of Boston winters. If I could spend summers here and winters in Arizona or New Mexico, I'd be a happy camper." Then she laughed. "Camping is the only way I could afford to do it."

They stood beside the bed, and she began unbuttoning his shirt. He wasn't quite sure what to do. Should he help? Should he start pulling layers off her?

It didn't much matter as it turned out. He undid his belt and let it drop to the floor, and as soon as he did, she pulled her own sweater over her head and dropped it behind her.

She had a toned body, perfectly proportional and a little on the petite side. How she managed to eat so many calories and not show it was beyond him. Most of his female friends and family members were concerned about the calorie count of everything they put in their mouths. Apparently, Dawn didn't need to worry. Her metabolism must just take care of it all.

She slipped off her bra, and his breath caught. She was lovely. Her skin was a natural creamy tan. The freckles on her face didn't extend to her chest, just her arms. Places the sun hit, so he'd guess she didn't do a lot of nude sunbathing.

As he peeled off his own pants and she her jeans, all their clothes turned into a messy pile on the floor. He stepped into her space and pulled her against him, letting his hands mold to her body over her buttocks and back up to her shoulders.

Their mouths found each other automatically. He didn't know how long they stood there kissing and fondling each other before she moved a couple of feet, leading him toward the bed. Eventually, she sat down on it and he followed her. Soon, he resumed kissing and nipping his way along her neck and shoulder.

Dawn pulled back the covers, and they scooted underneath. He loved the feel of her. She was soft and satiny. His hands couldn't stop traveling over her every curve, every dip. He wanted to memorize all of her, as if he were blind. They kissed and nipped and licked until he couldn't wait any longer, and then he had to find her center and taste her there.

Luca kissed his way down her torso and then pushed her legs apart, positioning himself between her knees, and when he licked her folds, she arched and gasped.

"Are you okay with this?" he asked.

"More than okay," she said breathlessly.

He parted her folds and laved the small bundle of nerves, which sent her arching and moaning in reaction.

She was so responsive…so easy to make love to. She didn't demand or try to call all the shots, as Lisa used to. In fact, no directions needed to be given at all. She writhed beneath him, occasionally gasping or cooing. It seemed as if he was doing just fine without any help.

When he knew she was sensitive to the slightest touch, he concentrated on the center of her pleasure and flicked his tongue back and forth as fast as a hummingbird's wings could go. In seconds, she came apart. She screamed and gurgled and screamed and gasped and screamed and writhed. Her head thrashed from side to side as she climaxed over and over. He was not sure if she would ever stop, until at last, she pushed on his forehead and gasped out, "Enough…enough!"

Her chest was heaving with deep huffs and puffs. He wiped his mouth on the back of his forearm and scooted up beside her.

She gazed into his eyes, looking awestruck. "That was amazing… I've never…like that…before."

"Stick with me, kid," he said. "There's lots more where that came from."

She grinned. "Lie back. It's your turn now."

She scooted down until she was eye level with his sex and took his engorged cock in her hand. He almost jumped with his own sensitivity.

She spent a few seconds admiring him before she took him into her mouth. The warmth and suction drove him crazy. He knew it wouldn't take much, he was already so turned on.

He let her torture him a little longer though. Knowing the kind of joy he got from watching her reaction, he wanted to let her have some of that enjoyment as well… to feel her feminine power.

Letting out his own moans of pleasure and trying not to spill his seed prematurely was a bit of a balancing act. He wanted to come so badly, but he would give her every ounce of pleasure he could before taking his own.

When at last he couldn't take any more, he scooped under her arms, lifting her right off of him and yanking her up to his face, then he rolled her onto her back and stared into her bright-green eyes.

Without having to say a word, she opened her legs for him. He positioned himself between her bent knees and entered her slowly, inch after luscious inch. Her warm, wet channel engulfed him completely. The glorious friction of withdrawing and plunging again and again was incredible. As if this ancient dance had been choreographed specifically for them, they followed each other's lead, meeting each other thrust for thrust.

The pressure built at the base of his spine like a hot ball of fire. He knew he wouldn't last much longer. He hadn't brought a condom to bed with him. They hadn't had the talk. And it seemed like a terrible time to stop. *Damn.* But he had to.

"I'm sorry. I forgot all about having a condom available. There's one in my wallet in my pants pocket."

She nodded. "Sure, go get it. I'll just wait right here," she said with a smile.

He chuckled but withdrew quickly and grabbed what he needed. When he returned to her, she parted her thighs and welcomed him back with her arms opened wide.

"You know, maybe it's a good thing we had to pause. I almost forgot something else," he said.

"What's that?"

He looked deeply into her eyes and, seeing no guile at all, decided to risk it. "I love you."

She smiled up at him. "I love you back."

He kissed her soundly, and without another word, he reentered her and resumed his rhythm. She picked right up where they'd left off. Their movements soon intensified, becoming harder and faster, more urgent and passionate.

He kissed her ear, her cheek, whatever he could reach of her, as he thrust into her warm, willing center. The sensation grew so quickly and so desperately that he found himself pounding deep into her without even realizing it. However, she was not complaining.

She appeared to be in the throes of her own passion. With eyes closed and unsteady breaths, she began to shiver. Her voice became a crescendo of moans, climaxing into a scream. Her sex clenched his as she orgasmed around him.

He couldn't have held back any longer if he'd wanted to. But coming together seemed so perfect, he just let go and rode the wave of his own deeply satisfying climax. He let her milk every drop from him before he stilled and then continued with aftershocks from a few more surprise spasms.

At last, he collapsed beside her and rolled to the side. They were both breathing heavily, staring into each other's eyes, and grinning.

"That was…" He had no words to describe the best orgasm of his life.

"Yeah. It was."

She smiled, and he knew she understood. He tucked her head under his chin and held her close. This wonderful woman, someone he never would have seen himself with, was now someone he couldn't see himself without.

Chapter 13

"I LOVE YOU."

"I love you back."

Dawn had just shut down her computer at work and was on her way to the hospital to visit her grandmother when Luca called. She was practically walking on air as she made her way to the elevator.

"I'll meet you at your place, okay?"

"Okay."

"Promise me you'll go straight home after you visit your grandmother."

"I promise." Luca's concern over her made her feel loved and cared for. But it did take some getting used to.

It had been exactly six days since they had first made love…and about ten hours since the last time. She'd lost count of how many times occurred between. Sometimes it was just once at night and once in the morning. Sometimes, well, more. A lot more.

Annette had been recovering at Boston General all week, affording them the kind of privacy they usually didn't have, considering their living situations. Although she missed Annette and worried about her day and night, Dawn had never slept better than she had wrapped in Luca's arms after a hot night of sex with her stud.

The only sadness between them was that Mandy was still missing. Luca had followed up with the detectives on the case. He gave them a bogus story about a tip he got from someone who wanted to stay anonymous. The supposed tipster said he'd heard from a gang member about a little girl hidden in the basement of Keene Street Convenience. The detectives brought along Luca, Officer Gulliver, and a few members of the gang squad to back them up when they went to investigate, but they came up empty-handed. If the girl had been there, she wasn't any longer.

When Luca told Dawn about it, she was spitting mad, knowing full well Carla and Ice had moved the girl. Dawn had held the unicorn several times after that, hoping for some kind of vision or flash of insight, but nothing had come to her.

Frustrated, she wondered if her so-called gift was a curse at times. Or if it was only good for stupid shit like keeping tabs on the cops when she was hanging out with Ice. She told Luca as much, and he tried to reassure her.

He said they were getting close, and the reason the gang had moved Mandy was because they were nervous. Luca also hoped they would not harm the little girl and were most likely keeping her hidden as they tried to decide what to do.

He figured a ransom demand would be forthcoming, but why hadn't they received one already? Dawn prayed she was okay. Otherwise, she would never forgive herself for not having the guts to rescue Mandy when she had the chance. Gun or no gun.

Dawn had stopped off at Goddess Fashions and bought the walking cane to give to her grandmother when she visited her. Stepping off the elevator, Dawn made her way to Annette's room and was shocked to discover another woman in her bed. Rushing to the nurse's station, she frantically got the attention of the nurse on duty. "Where is my grandmother? Annette Forest?"

"She was taken to the sixth floor, rehab. She'll be staying there for the next week while we get her back on her feet. They'll be teaching her some exercises she can do at home. You can go up there to see her. Check in at the nurse's station first."

"Thank you!" Relieved, Dawn made her way up to the sixth floor. She found Annette sitting up in a chair, knitting. "Grandma, you gave me quite the scare. Why didn't you text me that they moved you?"

"Oh, sweetie, I'm sorry." Annette laid her knitting aside on the small side table next to her. "Everything happened so fast. They came in this morning and told me it was time to get to work and then they wheeled me up here. They had me walk up and down the hallway and then they gave me a nice massage. I feel almost as good as new! Of course, the painkiller they gave me afterward didn't hurt any." She winked.

Dawn laughed. "Grandma, that's wonderful. Do you know how long you'll be here?"

"Well, at least a few more days. They're going to be showing me some exercises I can do at home. Now tell me, how was your day?"

Dawn filled Annette in on the usual mishaps at work with frantic students calling up and asking for help for their software woes. "Honestly, I think I could design a better system. I know all the glitches and how to fix them. But the engineers don't want to even listen to my suggestions. They think just because I didn't go to MIT that I have no business telling them how to do their job."

"Honey, it just goes to show you how smart and

talented you are. In time, you can look for another job, one better suited to your abilities."

Dawn pondered that for a few moments. The pay was pretty good, but it was a starting salary, and given all the extra work her manager threw at her, she wished she were in a position to either ask for more money or start looking somewhere else. But she had only been there a couple of months.

"I'll think about it, Gran. Oh, by the way, I have something to give you."

"Oh, more gifts? I don't have any more room," Annette said with a chuckle. "The orderlies had to make two trips to get all the presents and flowers in my room and bring them here."

"Well, you'll have to make room for one more." Dawn reached under her jacket and pulled out the cane in three pieces. Fitting them together, she handed the practical work of art to her grandmother.

"Oh my. Now if that isn't a pretty cane, I don't know what is."

"Do you like it?"

"I love it. I'll be able to scoot up and down the hallways in no time with this." Annette waved the cane around like a wand. "And look at how beautifully it's carved. All these birds. What craftsmanship. It looks like it cost a fortune."

"I got it with our lottery winnings." Dawn grinned. "And I have a penny left over."

Annette's eyes widened in delight. "Now, whoever said the women in our family were unlucky must have been mistaken."

Dawn stayed with Annette through dinner and helped

her back into bed after a brief walk so she could get some rest. Annette used her new cane, greeting all the nurses and orderlies and showing off her gift, eliciting oohs and aahs from all of them.

After giving her sleepy-eyed grandmother a kiss on the cheek, Dawn left, hopped on the subway, and made it home before Luca arrived.

She had some time before she expected him, so she decided to try to channel Mandy once more. Sitting cross-legged on her bed, she held the unicorn and began to breathe deeply as Minerva had instructed her to do.

Breathe in...

Breathe out...

Dawn found herself sitting in a cage. A large, sprawling cage. Looking around, she spotted a worn sign on the brown patchy grass just outside the cage. GREEN PARK ZOO. She kept breathing in and out, staying focused in the cage even though she felt scared and cold from being outside. She saw a blanket wrapped around her shoulders and heard a siren in the distance, and then Luca's voice floated in the wind.

"She's in the lion's cage." She heard yelling, and then she saw Luca topple to the ground near the abandoned sign. Blood poured from his head. Fighting nausea and dizziness, Dawn kept breathing deeply in and out as she opened her eyes. "Oh my God."

I can't wait to see her.

Luca should have been listening to Mary Beth's advice about dealing with sociopaths, but his mind kept wandering to Dawn. They'd had one amazing week of hot sex followed by nights of sated sleep, cuddled in each other's arms. He had to get his own place and fast. Was it too soon to think of moving in together?

What about Annette? He knew Dawn would refuse to leave her grandmother in such a bad neighborhood, and he agreed. An elderly woman living alone practically invited a home invasion. They'd have to find a place for her too, but could he afford that yet? He wanted to start looking around but was a little hesitant to bring it up with Dawn.

"So you need to watch out for him, Luca. He can be vicious." Mary Beth glanced at him, a frown on her face. "Did you hear what I just said?"

"Uh, sorry. I've just got some stuff on my mind."

She smiled. "Uh-huh. I'll bet it has to do with Dawn Forest."

Luca couldn't help smiling at the mere sound of her name. "Yeah, it's going really well. She's terrific." Her weird name. She could get rid of the teasing if she wanted to become Dawn Fierro. *Whoa! Too soon.*

"I'm glad. But just stay aware of Butts, okay? He's a real SOB, and he's already written you up once. Don't think he won't do it again. He could get you suspended."

"Got it, thanks." Luca glanced at his TO. "You said before that you had a few run-ins with him. Any you can share?"

She blew out a breath. "Let's just say he's not exactly pro-woman. He was pissed when Wanda Moore got the captain's job. He made it plain he thought she was given preferential treatment because she's a woman. And he's an asshole. A bully at best."

"No argument there."

"You may hear rumors among some of the female support staff and junior cops about him being handsy. Nothing has ever been reported though. If he tried anything with me, I'd break his arm." Mary Beth glanced at Luca with a grin. "I think on some level he knows that. He's been wary of me."

Luca smiled. "I guess he knows you take a direct approach."

"The thing about bullies is you need to stand up to them. But you have to do it right. Don't let him get under your skin, no matter how hard he tries. Got it? It's almost easier for a woman, because of our smaller size. If a woman loses her temper and punches him, no one will worry. People would doubt she could really harm him as long as a weapon isn't involved. They'd be wrong, but they wouldn't be as concerned."

Luca was about to reply when the dispatcher announced suspicious activity coming from the abandoned Green Park Zoo.

"Let's go." Mary Beth sped up, and even though it was out of their usual area, she got them there in under ten minutes. They were the second car to arrive, so she consulted with the Hyde Park unit.

The first officer on the scene motioned for Luca to go around behind the main building to the right, Mary Beth to the left, and he would enter through the front.

Luca nodded in agreement and, crouching down, ran to the back of the building that had housed an interactive zoo until the owners moved locations.

He radioed that everything was clear from the outside. Mary Beth responded all clear from her end. He told her he was going in and would meet her inside.

Opening the back door, Luca cringed when it made a squeak and groaning sound from the rusted-out hinges.

Slipping inside, he didn't have to wait for his eyes to adjust to the light. His phoenix abilities gave him great eyesight in the darkness. Being able to avoid using a flashlight and possibly alerting a perp to his presence came in handy. He made his way down a dark hallway toward a door at the end.

Remembering trips to this zoo when he was a kid, he knew there was an open area in the main hall where some of the animals had been kept, including a huge lion's cage. Opening the door, he stopped for a moment and thought he heard a child crying.

Shit! Could this be where they had taken Mandy? He felt his phone buzzing in his pocket. He'd put it on silent back in the car. He would answer it later. Right now, he needed to stay focused. The area was a bit like a maze with barrels and bales of hay stacked in places. It was hard to discern which direction the crying was coming from.

He made one turn and found himself at a dead end, looking into a glass enclosure. A huge painting of a wolf snarled back at him. The image was so detailed, Luca almost thought it would come to life. Turning back the way he'd come, he took a left and walked down another hall in the maze. In the almost pitch-black, Luca's instincts kicked into high gear. Hearing scuffling sounds behind him, he turned around and felt a hard object smash into his skull.

That was the last thing he felt, saw, or heard…

———◦∾◦———

I knew this would happen. I just knew it.

Dawn paced back and forth in the ER waiting room at Boston General. Luca's mother, Gabriella, was sitting beside his father, Antonio.

Gabriella patted the seat beside her. "Come, Dawn. Sit down. You're going to wear a path in the rug."

She gave her a weak smile, then lowered herself into the chair beside the kindly woman. "Thank you for calling me, Mrs. Fierro."

"Gabriella, please. I know how much you care about Luca."

"I wish they would let us in to see him," Antonio muttered, running his hands through his salt-and-pepper hair. "They're taking too long. If they aren't out in five minutes, I'm going in."

"Antonio, be patient. They had to stop the bleeding and stitch up a nasty gash. The nurse told us they were just doing a CT scan to make sure everything is okay. I'm sure the doctor will be out soon."

Antonio snorted. "I could tell if everything is okay. Just give me a flashlight and a chance to ask him a few questions. If he says the president is George Bush, we know he has more than a slight concussion."

Dawn didn't dare tell the Fierros about her vision earlier. They might not forgive her for not letting them know in advance.

She'd frantically tried texting Luca, even calling him. She'd felt an overwhelming sense of impending danger, and she had seen him covered in blood again. Luckily, she hadn't fainted, but she hadn't been able to stop Luca from getting hurt.

He'd been dispatched to the abandoned Green Park

Zoo with his training officer. She was there in the ER, talking to Luca's parents when Dawn arrived. Police were now in the process of combing the zoo, looking for clues as to who had been there and why they'd attacked Luca.

Dawn already knew the answer to that. Ice. He'd taken Mandy there, and he had probably moved her again after Luca and the other officers showed up.

She hoped Mandy was unharmed. Hoped the blood she saw on Luca was just because of his head wound and not something worse that was looming. She'd have to try holding the unicorn again tomorrow when she was feeling calmer.

She doubted Luca's parents would let him go home with her tonight. They would insist on taking him back to their house where they could keep watch on him overnight. Concussion victims needed to be woken up periodically just in case they'd lapsed into a coma.

Dawn was feeling frustrated to no end. This was the second scare she'd had at Boston General today. First when she went to her Gran's room and saw another woman in her bed, and now this.

She glanced at her watch. It was 10:30 p.m. Annette would be sound asleep by now. She would stop by in the morning to visit her before she went to the Youth Community Center. Life marched on, no matter what curveballs got thrown at you. She was committed to her volunteer work at the center, and besides, she was positive Luca wouldn't want her to shirk her responsibilities just to pace and wring her hands over him.

"How is your grandmother doing, dear?" Gabriella was such a caring woman. She'd sent a container of biscotti over with Luca for the nurses and a gift for Annette, a warm flannel nightgown and robe. Dawn had taken it in to Annette a few days ago, and her grandmother had insisted on writing a thank-you card to Gabriella. Fortunately, the gift shop had plenty of them.

"She's doing much better, thank you for asking. They moved her to the rehab floor today, and she's progressing really well."

"That is such good news. All this must be stressful for you…first your grandmother, and now Luca."

"I'm okay. I'm just worried. I wish I could snap my fingers and make it all better."

Gabriella laid her hand on Dawn's. "They're both going to be fine. I know it."

"Hey, there's the man of the hour now," Antonio said. He rushed up to greet his son's doctor. Both Dawn and Gabriella shot out of their chairs as well.

"Your son was lucky. He has a concussion and a broken nose, but the CT scan showed no serious brain injury."

"Can we see him?"

"Yes. Follow me. I'll go over his discharge orders with all of you."

As Dawn trailed behind, she was glad she didn't have to defend her need to go in with them. She wanted to see her love as badly as his parents did.

Luca's head was wrapped in a thick bandage, and his eyes sported purple circles. The discolorations made his eyes look even bluer. Dawn wanted to run up and hug him, but she stayed back a little, knowing his parents were anxious to talk to him.

After a few moments, Gabriella moved aside, and Luca

called out to Dawn. She ran up to him and leaned down, placing a gentle kiss on his lips, then gingerly laid her hand on the side of his face. "I'm so sorry you were hurt."

"It's okay, babe. I'm fine. Just a little banged up."

Then she did what she'd promised herself she wouldn't do. She started blubbering. Everyone tried to make her feel better. Gabriella insisted Dawn come home with them and spend the night.

"We don't want you alone and worrying," Gabriella said, hugging her.

"Thank you so much. I would love to stay over." Dawn wiped her tears, wondering what she'd done to deserve such good people in her life.

Maybe good karma wasn't about only good stuff happening. Maybe it was about having people around you for support when the bad stuff happened. She'd have to ask Lynda about that next time she saw her. For tonight, she would curl up beside Luca and watch him sleep. There was nowhere else she wanted to be.

―――

The next morning, Gabriella made them all a big breakfast, and other than his bandaged head and black eyes, Luca was back to his usual self. He ate well and cracked jokes with his dad. But when the topic came around to his injury, Antonio had a few things to say.

"I'm sorry, Son. This job's just too dangerous."

"Dad, being a firefighter is just as dangerous as being a cop."

"When you go into a burning building, you are with your brothers. Even the ones who aren't biologically related are like family. They have your back."

"Mary Beth *did* have my back. She called the paramedics, and I'm fine."

"Why do they keep putting a rookie into these dangerous situations?" Gabriella asked, wiping her hands on a tea towel and throwing it over her shoulder as she leaned against the kitchen sink. "You just started. Why do you have to be the one always going to these places?"

"I'm on duty. When you're on duty, you have to go where the dispatcher sends you. I'm a cop now. Not a cadet. I respond to calls like any other cop."

"I don't think so. I heard about this sergeant of yours. Butts. I heard stories about him," Antonio said. "He tased you on purpose at the precinct. I think he's the one putting you into these situations. Maybe I'll go down there and have a little chat with this SOB." He pounded his fist on the table.

"Dad, you can't do that."

"If this guy has it in for my son, I have to do something. Would you rather I talk to the commissioner?"

"Shit no. Who told you he had it in for me?"

"I hear things. I have friends in a lot of places, okay?"

Luca glanced at Gabriella. "Mom, tell Dad not to go beat up Sergeant Butts, please."

Gabriella shrugged. "I'm not sure I want to stop him."

Luca turned to Dawn, his eyes begging her for help. "Can you talk some sense into these two?"

"I just want you to be happy and safe in your job," she said, laying her hand over his.

"And why does this Butts man have to single you out?" Gabriella waved her hand in the air.

"It's hazing. They do it to all the newbies."

"I doubt that," Antonio said. "I hear he doesn't like

firefighters. Fierros are legendary in Boston, and *all* of us are firefighters, except you."

"Look, I'm going to be home for a few extra days, but when I go back, I'll have a talk with Mary Beth and Joe and ask if Butts is acting out of character. I really think he's an ass to everyone, not just me. But if I'm being singled out, I trust them to tell me. They're good people."

"Well, I don't want the next place I see you to be a morgue. So if this guy doesn't change, he's toast." Antonio pounded his fist again. "*Capisce*?"

"*Capisce*, Dad." Luca turned back to Dawn. "Can you help me back downstairs? I want to lie down for a bit."

"Okay." Dawn wrapped her arm around his waist and was surprised at how heavily he leaned on her as they made their way back down to his room in the finished basement.

"Help me break out of here," he whispered with a tired smile.

"No way. Your parents are just worried about you. And so am I. I texted you so many times yesterday and even tried calling but you didn't answer."

"I couldn't. I was in that maze, trying to find whoever was crying in there."

"I had a vision of Mandy being held there." She helped Luca back into bed and cuddled beside him.

"I had a weird feeling she was there too. I heard weeping as soon as we got there. My paranormal hearing helped, but I couldn't look like I knew exactly where she was by making a beeline for her."

"I know it was Ice who hit you with the shovel. I just know it. I hate that prick."

"It was a shovel?"

"Yeah, that's what Officer Gulliver said. Ice probably didn't want to shoot you, because the noise would attract your partner—but he's always armed. I'm worried about you."

"You're worried about me? I'm the one worried about you. I don't want you going back home alone. It's too dangerous. They probably know we're onto them."

"They only suspect I'm onto them."

"Yeah, but they probably figured out that you're working with the cops."

"I'm not working with the cops. I'm working for Jack Richardson."

"Even so, Ice might come looking for you. He knows you have visions."

"Or maybe that's why he's staying away. He would have already come looking for me after I paid Carla that little visit. Maybe he's just trying to lie low."

"Promise me you'll be careful."

"I will. I have to go to the hospital to check on Gran and then over to the community center."

"Okay, but keep in touch with me. Are you going to come back here tonight?"

"Do you think your parents will let me stay?"

"Are you kidding? You're already part of the family. The only thing is that you'll have to sleep in one of my brothers' rooms."

"They let me stay in here with you last night."

Luca laughed. "That's because I was zonked out on painkillers. Tonight is another story, though." He waggled his eyebrows at her and leaned in for a long, hot kiss.

"*Dawn, do you want a ride to the hospital?*" Gabriella's voice floated down the stairs.

Luca groaned in frustration. "See, my mom has this supersensory radar thing. I swear she knew we were getting close."

Dawn giggled. "I'll be right up, Gabriella," she called out.

"Promise me you'll be careful." He gave her one more fierce kiss.

"I promise. Promise me you'll get well soon. I'll miss you in my arms at night."

"I promise."

Dawn kissed him back just as fiercely and then, grabbing her jacket and purse, went upstairs.

Gabriella insisted on meeting Annette, and the two women got along as though they were long-lost friends. Dawn announced she had to get to the community center, but Gabriella stayed to chat a bit longer with Annette. It felt good. All of it. Luca's family was actually accepting her. It was wonderful being part of a big, noisy, loving family. Weird, but wonderful.

When Dawn arrived at the Youth Community Center, Tansy gave her a big hug and asked her how Annette was doing.

More good karma. Dawn helped out with a group meeting with some of the kids who'd started getting together to talk about their issues at home. A parent in jail was something Dawn could relate to. She was setting up the chairs for the meeting when she spied a girl talking to Rita. The girl looked kind of tough. Dawn knew the type… Hell, she *was* the type. The girl nodded at Rita and then went off to talk to a group of older kids.

Dawn made her way over to Rita, who'd gone back to reading her book. "Hey, Rita, how are you doing?"

"Hi, Dawn." The teenager smiled, but she looked a little nervous.

"So who was that girl you were talking to? I've never seen her around here."

Rita's eyes skittered away. "Um...she goes to my school. Her name's Joanie. She's okay. She was just saying hi."

"Hi, huh?" Dawn sat down across from Rita. "Look, I know it's great to make new friends, especially with kids who seem a lot cooler than you."

"Hey! I'm cool," she said with a sardonic smile.

"Yes, you are. Much cooler than some kids who have ulterior motives." Dawn made a mental note of talking to Tansy about Joanie.

Rita stiffened and looked a little hurt. "I don't have many friends, and she was being nice."

"I'm sorry, Rita. I may have been wrong. I hope so. I could be projecting, because I was kind of tough at that age. I turned my life around, but not all the tough kids in the world do that. Just know you're really special. You've got straight A's, and you're a good kid. You help out here on weekends. You've got a good future ahead of you. Just be aware is all I'm saying."

"I understand." Rita tipped her head. "Were you really like Joanie?"

"Oh, much worse. You don't want to know how I was. But just remember where you want to be in ten years and *who* you want to be. Don't forget that. Keep that dream in your head, and you'll keep shining like the star you are."

Rita grinned. "Thanks, Dawn. You're pretty cool, even when you're being corny."

Dawn clutched her chest. "You wound me!" Then she chuckled. "Just remember to send us a postcard from all the amazing places you'll be travelling to when you're all grown up." Suddenly, she had a flash of Rita at a podium, grinning and waving. Red, white, and blue balloons were released and fell all around her. She was celebrating some kind of political win!

Dawn gave Rita a tight hug. She felt the good karma glowing around her.

Chapter 14

IT WAS TIME.

She'd been putting it off for too long. Taking a vacation day, Dawn decided to visit her mom. So much had happened since she had last seen her five weeks ago. She was overdue for a visit. And if she was going to get a handle on her karma, she needed to talk to her mom and make sure she was doing okay.

Her mom had left a phone message last night while Dawn was at the Fierros'. Dawn didn't answer it. Didn't want to be reminded of who she was and where she'd come from. Didn't want to think about the fact that Lissie was her mother. She'd told Luca about her, but his parents had no idea that Dawn's mom was a drug addict and was doing five years at Framingham for trafficking and possession. But at least she was getting treatment, albeit minimal and forced. But she seemed to be trying. Finally.

Dawn asked Luca if she could borrow his car. He wanted to go with her, and it was all she could do, short of tying him up, to get him to stay in bed. He was nearly healed, thanks to his paranormal abilities, but his parents insisted he stay home for the rest of the week, since recovering so quickly would raise red flags. The police department's doctor had prescribed bed rest and told him he wanted to see him in a week's time.

Over breakfast, when Luca worried about getting

fired after only a few weeks on the job, Gabriella wisely changed the subject before Antonio could launch into another diatribe against Butts and the police department. His parents had been vocally against Luca's getting involved in law enforcement, but now that he was there—and saying he loved the job—they were trying to be supportive. Some times with more success than other times.

Before Dawn drove to the prison, she thought about what she'd say to her mom. Would she tell her about Luca being a cop or just say she was dating someone? Better to keep things in as general terms as possible.

She stopped off to see Annette at the rehab before hitting the highway. Framingham wasn't far, only about forty minutes depending on traffic, but she wanted to make sure her grandmother was okay, and she wanted to tell her where she was heading.

Annette said, "Give my love to Lissie, and tell her I'm fine. She's been calling here whenever she can to check on me, poor thing. She blames herself for our circumstances." Annette stopped talking to wipe her tears and blow her nose. "Told me when she gets out, she'll get a good job and work to make our lives better."

Dawn reserved judgment on that one. Her mother had said stuff like that in the past. Many times. But her jobs never lasted more than a few weeks before she started using again or she fell into some big scam or drug deal. This was her second stint at Framingham, and this time, she was actually getting somewhere with counselling. It was one thing to detox, another to actually own your shit and right your wrongs.

Dawn hugged her grandmother and told her she'd

text her when she got there. When she got to Luca's car, a familiar figure was leaning against the driver's side door.

"Hiya!"

"Lynda. What are you doing here? My appointment with you isn't until Friday."

"Well, I thought I'd just pop by to see how you're doing."

Lynda was in full regalia—skinny jeans with bling up and down the seams, a red sweater, and a sleek black jacket. Not to mention the sky-high stacked black boots she had on.

"Wow! You look…" Dawn grinned.

"Thanks! I thought I'd go along with you for the drive at least." Lynda grinned back.

"Hop in."

Dawn filled Lynda in on her vision of Mandy at the zoo and then Luca getting hit on the head.

"Do you think it was that Ice Spider and his gang?" Lynda asked, offering her a crinkly chip bag. Dawn grabbed one and popped it into her mouth.

After munching and swallowing the chip, she said, "I'm positive it was them. They obviously moved her, and I don't know where they've taken her—yet, that is. It seems like they're always one step ahead."

Lynda seemed to ponder that one for a moment. "Do you think Ice will come after you?"

"He hasn't so far. Just a couple of warnings. I think he's lying low. Trying to figure out how to deal with this one. He could have killed Mandy right off the bat, but he didn't." Dawn shuddered at the thought of the child being murdered. "Maybe she's his insurance policy if the cops catch him? Who knows. But the sooner I figure out where she is, the better I'll feel."

"You've got a lot on your plate, Dawn."

"Yeah, what else is new? I've got Gran in the hospital, my mom in prison, Luca stuck at his home with a concussion, and I still need to find Mandy." Dawn blew out a breath.

"Didn't Minerva give you advice on destressing?"

"Yeah, but that doesn't change anything."

"Of course it changes everything." Lynda shook her finger. "No matter what happens, you need to take care of you. Your center, your core is the light. Don't let it go out. That's why you need to meditate every day, morning and night. Have you been doing that?"

Dawn cringed. "Not really. At least not since Luca got hurt. I've been staying at the Fierros' place all week."

"You can still meditate. You can get up a few minutes early. Excuse yourself for a few minutes before you go to bed. You have to commit to it."

"I am committed to it," Dawn said indignantly. "I volunteer at the Youth Community Center, I am trying to help find Mandy, and I'm trying my best to be a good person."

"You *are* a good person, Dawn," Lynda said gently, patting her knee. "But it's not just about doing good deeds. Lots of people do good deeds, and they lead miserable lives. You have to find a way to balance your deeds with who you are and how you feel. No matter what happens in your life, you need to know that inside, your soul will not change. You are constant."

"Okay, I get it. Being centered and all that. The difference between intention and actually doing and being. That's always been my mom's problem."

"The road to hell is paved with good intentions."

Dawn glanced at Lynda. "My gran always says that. Do you believe in heaven and hell? Or good and evil?"

"You mean the big guy upstairs and the hottie in the basement?" Lynda grinned. "I can't tell you about the afterlife. We're all sworn to secrecy, but I can tell you the battle between good and evil isn't like the ongoing battle between Coca-Cola and Pepsi."

Dawn chuckled at that. Lynda's humor was a welcome relief.

"By the way, you're doing great at the community center. Tansy gave me a glowing report about you."

"She did?"

"Yes, she did."

"So why were you yelling at me about meditating a few minutes ago?"

"I don't yell. I never yell. I just gently reminded you to stay on track."

"Am I really making a difference?"

"You are. You can't imagine the impact you've had on Rita."

"I really like her. She's a good kid."

"More important, she's going to pay it forward and be there for Joanie when Joanie needs a good friend."

Dawn's eyes widened. "You mean the tough girl with the tats and the skull earrings?"

Lynda nodded. "Yes. Joanie was the one who needed help. And your support of Rita gave her the confidence to reach out."

"Well, I'll be damned. I told her to be careful around Joanie."

Lynda chuckled. "You also reassured her about her

own strengths. Joanie confided in her about something very traumatic, and Rita spoke with Tansy. They're getting Joanie the help she needs."

"But that wasn't my doing." Dawn swallowed the lump in her throat. "I thought Joanie was bad news."

"You set everything in motion. You were an agent of karmic change, and that is truly a feat. Sometimes you'll never know what little things you did or said that made a difference."

A tear streamed down Dawn's cheek. "If I'm so psychically centered, how come I couldn't see that about Joanie?"

"Maybe because you were a lot like Joanie? You couldn't sense what she was going through, but you projected your fears about what your life could have been. You just saw a tough girl, like the tough girl you used to be?"

Dawn blew out a breath. "Okay, I get it. I get it."

"So that's why I need you to stay focused and keep doing your meditation. If you're in a good place, the impact you have on others is unique and positive."

Dawn didn't say anything to that. But it sure felt good.

A few minutes later, she pulled into the visitor parking lot at the prison.

"Well, this is my cue to leave."

"You don't want to come into the prison? You might get some fashion ideas…orange is the new black and all that."

"I have too many former and future clients in there," Lynda said with a sigh.

"Shoot. I never thought of that. You probably get a lot of business from places like this."

"I wish even more of them asked for help and meant it with all their hearts."

"Can you tell me if my mom—"

Lynda held up one hand to stop her. "That's up to her, and don't forget your own sworn secrecy. The best thing you can do is to continue the power of your example."

"Understood."

They got out of the car, and Lynda wrapped her arms around Dawn for a tight hug. "You've got this."

Dawn hugged her back and walked to the entrance. As she approached the sliding doors, she turned to wave at Lynda, but her karma caseworker had already disappeared.

———◆———

"You're just in time for birthday cake," Dawn's mother said.

"Seriously? They give you birthday cakes?"

She smirked. "No, sweetie. I'm sorry. I'm just being a smart-ass. See Thomasina? She's the young woman over there."

Dawn glanced in the direction her mom was pointing. A petite African-American girl was chatting animatedly with her visitor.

"She looks like a teenager."

"She just turned nineteen today."

"Oh no. What's she in for?" Dawn turned back to face her mom. They were seated at a corner table by the window. The sun was streaming in through the glass pane, giving her mother's brown hair a soft halo effect. Dawn sometimes forgot just how young her mom truly was. Only sixteen when she had Dawn, Lissie was now thirty-eight. Dawn didn't think prison would have such a positive impact on her mom, or was it that her mother was actually clean and coherent for the first time in, like, ever?

"She stabbed and killed her pimp. She's kind of a hero around here, but she's not a violent person. He raped and beat her one too many times. Everyone has a breaking point. And get this…she wants to become a pastor."

"Wow, that's amazing."

"Yeah, it is pretty amazing. She's been counselling me as part of her experiment…to see if she's any good at it."

"Is it going well?"

Lissie nodded. "That girl is only nineteen, but she's an old soul. She's getting me to admit things I knew were wrong and remember things I blocked out."

"Like what?" Dawn really wanted to know. A part of her had held onto her anger toward her mother for a long time. But maybe it was time to let go of that anger, if her mom was ready to meet her halfway.

"I blamed my circumstances on you and Annette. I felt sorry for myself. I couldn't stay at any job longer than a few days, because I didn't want to…and not because I lacked an education. I always ended up back on the street, dealing. I'm ashamed of what I did, but most of all, I'm ashamed of how I treated you, my own daughter and my mother. I let you both down so many times. For that, I am so very sorry."

Dawn wanted to wrap her arm around her mom's slender shoulders, but on opposite sides of the table, it would have to wait until they said goodbye. She could see her mother trembling, the emotion overtaking her.

"Has the drug counseling helped you?"

Lissie's eyes filled with tears. "Yes. It's helped me now that I'm taking it seriously. I doubt I'd have lived much longer going the way I was... I'm so glad you're here, punkin."

Punkin was what Lissie had called Dawn for as long as Dawn could remember. Lissie said she'd started calling her that after they went to a pumpkin patch when Dawn was five years old and Dawn kept saying she wanted the biggest punkin they could find—even though they couldn't put it on their doorstep. It would have been smashed in minutes.

"What about the other stuff? Are you doing okay with that?"

Lissie nodded. "Better than I thought I would. It's hard, don't get me wrong. The psychologist has me doing the journaling thing, but I have to keep the notebook in her office. Nobody wants those thoughts shared with the whole cell block if the journal got stolen. It's helping, I think. Plus they have an AA and NA group here. They call me on my bullshit. It takes one to know one, as they say. I guess I needed that."

"I'm so glad, Mom."

"Punkin, I know I've said this before, but I really mean it now. When I get out of here, I'm going to make some major changes."

"I know. Gran believes in you, and I believe in you too." Dawn surprised herself. She actually did believe her mom this time. Some kind of shift in her mother's eyes. They used to look like nobody was home. Now, she was *present*. Also the way she sat, relaxed instead of half listening and fidgeting in place like she was itching for a fix.

"I'm worried about my mother. Is she really okay?"

"Gran told me you've been calling her. She's doing great. She's the most popular old lady on the rehab floor and is knitting baby booties for one of the pregnant nurses."

Lissie giggled and shook her head. "That's my mother for you. Knitting her way into everyone's heart."

"She's—well, just a good person." Dawn was about to say something about her gran's good karma but didn't want to accidentally give away something she shouldn't.

"And this young man you're dating? Is he a good guy?"

"Yes. He has Gran's stamp of approval."

"Good. I can't wait to meet him."

"You will." Dawn didn't say any more than that. Despite her mom's progress, some ghosts continued to linger. Lynda was right. She did need to meditate and concentrate more on her inner self. Changing karma wasn't just about doing good deeds. She did feel like she'd turned a corner with Lissie, and that was a relief. One that she hadn't felt in a long time.

⁓

"Hey you!"

Dawn turned toward the voice shouting at her. She'd just parked Luca's car on a side street and was making her way back to the Fierros' home.

"I know you. You're Luca's girl, right?"

Dawn recognized Jack Richardson, Mandy's father, walking toward her. "Yeah. Can I help you with something?"

"Uh, yeah. You still have my daughter's unicorn."

Dawn worried her lip.

Dressed in wrinkled jeans and jacket, he looked like he'd slept in his clothes, at least what little sleep he did get. The poor man had bags under his eyes the size of craters.

"Yes, I still have it. Would you like it back?"

"You were supposed to find her. That's why I gave Fierro the unicorn. He said you could help. That was two weeks ago. What happened?" He looked anxious and hurt, his eyes holding the pain of a man who'd lost far too much and couldn't afford to lose anything more.

Dawn blew out a breath. "Can we go somewhere to talk?"

Mandy's father ran his hands through his unkempt hair. "Yeah, I live just around the corner."

Dawn nodded. *This is it. I finally get a chance to go inside Mandy's home.*

A few minutes later, Dawn was sitting in the Richardsons' kitchen. For all of Jack's rumpled state, his house was immaculate, as though he was channeling all his grief into cleaning—or maybe he had a housekeeper.

Dawn could feel the energy swirling around her. Could she convince Mr. Richardson to let her into Mandy's room? Sometimes a chance presented itself, and she had to go with her gut. This was one of those times.

"Can I get you a coffee?"

Mr. Richardson was already popping a K-Cup into a Keurig machine.

"Thanks, Mr. Richardson."

"I only have milk."

"That's great, thanks."

"Sugar?"

"Yes, please."

"One or two?"

"Two."

He finished making her cup and set it down on the table, then sat across from her. "Jack."

Dawn took a sip of the brew and glanced at him, a question in her eyes.

"My name is Jack. You can call me Jack."

"Thanks, Jack. My name is Dawn."

"Dawn, I know Mandy is out there somewhere. Can you help me find her?"

She took another sip of coffee to steel her nerves. "I can only try. This is not an exact science, but being in her home," she said, glancing around, "is helpful. I can feel Mandy's energy."

Jack leaned forward, his eyes alight, like a starving man being offered a steak dinner. "Can you see her?"

"I can sense her but—would you let me into her bedroom?"

He didn't hesitate. "Come with me."

Leading her down a hall, he opened the second to last door on the right. "This is Mandy's room."

"May I?"

He nodded, and Dawn stepped into the room. She felt light-headed as soon as she crossed the threshold. Turning to him, she whispered, "Can you leave me in here for a few minutes with the door closed?"

Jack hesitated.

"I know you don't know me, but I swear I won't take anything."

"Of course. Forgive me for my city cynicism." He closed the door, and she heard his footsteps retreat down the hall.

Dawn turned in a slow circle, her eyes taking in everything in the room, from the princess quilt on the bed, to the pink walls, to the large number of stuffed toys lovingly sitting on a shelf, waiting patiently for the little girl whose imagination could bring them to life.

Everything she'd previously seen in her mind was right in front of her.

Dawn sat down on Mandy's bed and closed her eyes. She began to breathe deeply, in and out... "C'mon, Mandy, show me something."

A series of images flashed in her mind. A bedroom. A dump, really...drug paraphernalia scattered on the nightstand. A woman was sitting hunched over on a chair. She looked familiar, dirty blonde hair, skinny. She had a badge pinned to her shirt that said HOUSECLEANING STAFF, and below it the name SUZIE BAXTER. *Mick's girl-friend...but where are you, Mandy? Show me.*

She approached a dingy window. A neon sign flashed: DORC T MOTEL.

"Dorcet! Good girl, Mandy. Good girl."

––––––

Mandy looked around at her new place. At least it was warm and there was a bed for her to sleep on.

"Here, kid, drink your juice."

Finally, the woman was awake. "Are you gonna take me home, lady?"

She didn't look like any lady that Mandy had ever known, like Mommy or Grandma or any of the ladies at Sunshine Day Care. This lady had a mean look on her face and dots up and down her arms.

"Why do you have purple dots?"

The mean lady smiled, but it didn't make her look nicer.

"Cuz I like how they make me feel. Don't you have anything that makes you feel good?"

Mandy took a sip from her juice. "My mommy and daddy. And my friend Elizabeth and my toys."

"Yeah, well, I don't have a mommy and daddy or an Elizabeth."

The lady poked a needle into her arm, but she didn't start crying like Mandy did when she got a needle. The mean lady closed her eyes and went to sleep.

Mandy took another sip of her juice and looked around, wondering if the door was unlocked. Maybe she could try. Maybe she could find her own way home. It felt like so long ago since she was home. Was Mommy back home? Or was Mommy in heaven like the lady told her at the store? The lady who brought her ice cream on a stick.

She wondered what would happen if she tried to turn the doorknob. It was probably locked. Every time she tried to get away, she was always stuck.

After being in the room with lots of boxes and food on shelves, the nasty man took her to a zoo. It wasn't a good zoo. There were no animals or ice cream anywhere, just a big empty cage. She didn't stay there long. He ran off with her, just telling her to shut up. Then he put her in his car and drove her to this place. He had a fight with the mean woman until she finally threw her hands in the air and said, "Fine. But I don't babysit for free." The man handed her a plastic bag and left.

Mandy finished her juice and stood up. She walked to the door and reached for the handle, glancing over her shoulder to make sure the mean lady was still sleeping. This time, when she turned the knob, the door opened! And then she walked right into someone with big boots.

Glancing up, she saw a big gun, then a face that she knew. She gulped.

Chapter 15

"I NEVER THOUGHT I'D BE SPENDING MY FRIDAY NIGHT ON a stakeout." Dawn was sitting beside Luca in his car. Empty burger wrappers littered the dashboard. They were parked across the street from the Dorcet, a seedy motel generally used by prostitutes and drug addicts. "Why can't we just go in there and get her ourselves?"

"Babe, we can't just waltz in there. It's dangerous, and we have no warrant. We could be prosecuted for breaking and entering. We need to plan this out with people we trust."

Luca was back to his old self, much to Dawn and Gabriella's relief. He'd gotten the okay from his doctor to go back to work on Monday. He had never been so miserable as when he had to spend a whole week hiding out at home to look like he was healing as a human.

"What about Mary Beth and Joe?"

"I can't put them in that kind of situation. They're veteran cops, and what we're doing could get me repri-manded or worse."

"Can't we tell the detectives on the case?"

"The last time I did that, they showed up and Mandy was gone. It's really odd. It feels like this gang is one step ahead of us."

"Maybe they have a psychic working for them," Dawn joked.

Luca smiled, and then his eyes widened. "Or

maybe they have someone on the inside working against us."

"Are you serious? There's a dirty cop on your force?"

"Look at what happened at the convenience store."

"Yeah, but that may have been because I showed up a few hours before."

"True, and you were lucky. I think they were willing to give you the benefit of the doubt because of your history with Ice and Carla. And then it was as if they were tipped off about the abandoned zoo, but I wasn't so lucky. If they think you're working with the police, pretty soon the gang will stop cutting you breaks."

"You know your dad said something the other day that made me wonder."

"What did he say?"

"Remember we were in your kitchen and your dad mentioned Sergeant Butts. He said he found out you got tased—"

"I think Mary Beth must have told Mom or Dad when I was in the ER."

"Yeah, but what if there's something to that? Butts wrote you up when he saw you talking to the detectives about Mandy."

Luca shook his head as though not willing to believe it.

"Luca, I didn't tell you at the time, because I didn't want to hurt you, but I had a vision of Lisa driving a Corvette—with a blond guy in the passenger seat. I didn't think of it then, but have you ever known a cop to be able to afford a car like that?"

Luca turned to Dawn. "I don't know that he bought it for her."

"Is there any other way she could have afforded it?"

"Not that I know of. She doesn't have a job yet, and it doesn't sound like she even wants one." He took a deep breath. "Do you think Butts is working with the Keene Street Gang? That he's involved in Patricia Richardson's death and Mandy's kidnapping?"

"What else could explain why they keep moving her?"

"He's Mandy's uncle, Dawn."

"What? I had no idea!"

"His wife is—was—Patricia Richardson's sister. Well, half sister."

"How do you know this?"

"Mary Beth told me. So if Butts is behind all this, that would be so effing twisted. His own family."

"Do you think Ice knows that too?"

"I don't know." Luca blew out a breath. "But if he does, that could explain a lot."

"What do you mean?"

"Keeping Mandy alive is an insurance policy for Ice. He could use her against Butts if it came down to an arrest."

"So Ice is the one keeping Mandy alive, and Butts is the one who wants her killed?"

"Maybe."

"That's psychopathic."

"That's a scary thought, but you could be right."

"Do you think he also found out about you and Lisa?"

"If he had, I probably wouldn't be alive right now. She was adamant he shouldn't know about us, back when she cared what happened to me."

"We have to stop him, Luca, and we need to save Mandy."

"I have an idea. But I need to do it now, or it might be too late. You've never seen me transform before. Do you think you can handle it?"

———⁓———

"This deal is going down tonight."

"No go. We've dealt with the Bronx guys before. We want some assurance that their guns can't be traced."

"You have my assurance. Where's the coke?"

"Carla has it secure. It's pure. She brought it back from Florida. Smuggled in by boat."

Butts paced back and forth in the alley behind Keene Street Convenience. He looked agitated, nervous. "I want the kid here."

"She's with a friend." Ice leaned against the brick wall, his arms crossed over his chest.

"Call your friend and tell him or her to bring Mandy back here," Butts growled.

"Why the fuck would I do that? Rocco and his crew are gonna be here soon. The kid would only distract us."

"I want her here."

"You don't run the show, *Sergeant* Butts." Ice smirked and gave him a police salute.

"Oh, yeah? One phone call and I could have this place swimming in blue uniforms."

"Really? Then what would happen to the kid? You forget I know she's your niece. I know you ordered Mick to run down her mom."

"I told him to pick them up—not run her off the road and get her killed."

"Doesn't matter. She's dead and Mandy is now in *my*

custody. Safe and sound. One wrong move from you, and you're the one who's going down."

From his perch on the roof, Luca could see everything. He had all the proof he needed—for himself. Nothing to prove a case against Butts though. He was working with the Keene Street Gang—probably had been for a long time, and he was responsible for Patricia's death. His own sister-in-law. And what did he want his niece for?

"You get that kid here." Butts pushed Ice against the brick wall in the alley.

Ice shoved him back. "Drop dead."

"You text whatever whore you have taking care of her to bring the kid here. Now!"

"I'm not handing over that kid. She's fine where she is."

"You better make sure she gets lost permanently, or the Tyler Street Dogs might find out you cut the cocaine with baking soda."

"Man, you are one cold son of a bitch." Ice crossed his arms over his chest. "You're not even human. You're some kind of freak of nature."

Luca was keeping a close watch on the two men from his perch on the rooftop. He'd missed the meeting with the Tyler Street Dogs…another gang. *Shit, all we need is a gang war in the streets.*

Butts stopped pacing. "You have no idea what I'm capable of. You think you have the upper hand? Think again. You had your meeting with the Tyler Street Dogs. You got your shipment of guns. Now, it's time to pay up. I want the money and the kid."

"You can get your money today. The kid will have to wait until tomorrow."

"You better get that kid to me today, or your entire operation here, including Carla, is going down."

Ice glared at him. "You can't threaten me, Butts. I know all your dirty little secrets."

"Your bravado won't be worth shit in court. Who are they gonna believe? A veteran cop without a single blemish on his record, or a lowlife gangbanger? And when your bunkmate is a 350-pound guy named Bubba, you'll wish you had done things differently."

Butts turned and rushed Ice, pushing him against the wall. They grappled for a few minutes, and then something strange happened. Luca saw a flash of gold emanating from Butts's eyes. A fierce growl came from his throat, his hands grew claws, and then his whole body transformed. The wolf cornered Ice, who screamed in fear. He snapped his jaws at the frozen man and then shifted back into his human form. His uniform was a little uneven, but it hadn't fallen off.

Fuck. The bastard is a werewolf!

"Did the big bad gangbanger just poop his pants?" Butts laughed. "Don't try me, or I'll turn you into a midnight snack."

"Fine. I'll go get her, but it may take a while. If you follow me, it's off."

"Just remember, I know where to find you."

Screw protocol. Luca had to get back to Dawn. They had to rescue Mandy while Butts was waiting for Ice.

The motel room where Mandy was being held wasn't far, just a few streets over. He would fly back, switch to his human form, get dressed quickly, and get Mandy and Dawn out of danger. *Fast.*

—◌◠◡◠—

"I'm coming to get you, Mandy."

Dawn couldn't wait any longer. An hour had passed since Luca had flown away in his phoenix form. When she had watched him transform into a phoenix, her eyes had nearly popped out of her skull. But seeing him fly was unbelievable. He was majestic and powerful at the same time. She was in awe of him and his whole kind. He was beautiful.

She and Luca had watched Ice leave the motel more than an hour ago, which was why Luca had transformed, to follow him. He'd told her to wait for him to get back, but she was worried about Mandy.

Then her chance came. A woman shuffled out of the same room Ice had left. Dawn recognized her from her vision. Suzie, Mick's drug-addict girlfriend, must be who'd been watching Mandy. She seemed fidgety, nervous as she peered around and then started walking down the street.

Is Mandy alone? Dawn wondered. She held the unicorn and closed her eyes once more. Looking out of the little girl's eyes, she scanned the room and saw no one else.

Dawn remembered what Minerva had told her the last time she stopped by for a visit. "You're a light warrior, and that can be a burden. But it is also a gift. You have within you the power to save lives. Trust your instincts. You know what you have to do."

"I do," Dawn whispered to herself.

She got out of Luca's car. The street was eerily silent. It was almost midnight. She ran across the street to the row of rooms facing out.

A few moments later, Dawn was standing just outside the door to Room 5. There was a row of about ten rooms on the street side where she was and another twenty on the other side. Windows facing the street all had curtains drawn. Of course, Dawn thought, in order to keep prying eyes away from drug deals and prostitution.

Even from outside, it reeked of urine and other stale odors Dawn didn't even want to think about. From the looks of it, Suzie did a terrible job cleaning.

She tried the door. *Shit!* It was locked. She knocked softly on the door, hoping Mandy wasn't afraid to open it.

Dawn glanced toward the street, worried that Suzie was on her way back. Even if she were, Dawn was prepared to fight her. Do whatever it took. "Mandy, are you there, honey? Your dad sent me," she whispered through the door. "My name is Dawn. He misses you. He wants you home. I'm gonna take you home."

A few moments later, the door creaked open, and standing there was the sweetest sight Dawn had ever seen.

"Where's my daddy?"

Big blue eyes stared at her, bright and hopeful. Wearing a dingy purple polka-dot dress and stained purple tights that no doubt she'd been wearing for weeks. Her hair was in knots, and a few braids were coming undone.

"I'm going to take you to your daddy right now."

"What about my mommy?"

"Your daddy will tell you everything."

Mandy nodded. "I know who you are."

"You do?" Dawn leaned down and picked up the little girl.

"I saw you in my dream. You were an angel princess, and you told me you were going to save me."

"Well, I kept my promise, didn't I?" Dawn grinned.

"Yeah, but where's your pretty sparkly dress?"

"I left it at home. It needed washing."

"Okay." Mandy yawned and laid her head on Dawn's shoulder. "I've been wishing and wishing, and now my wish has come true."

"Yes, it has, honey." Dawn hugged her close, tears in her eyes. *I hope.*

"Hey, what are you doing?"

Dawn turned around with Mandy in her arms.

Suzie was walking toward them, a paper bag in her hand.

"That's the mean lady," Mandy whispered, holding tighter to Dawn's neck.

"I'm taking this little girl back home to her dad," Dawn said firmly. She wasn't scared. She didn't know if Suzie had a gun or a knife, but she was ready to fight.

"Fuck you." Suzie pulled out a gun and pointed it at them. "Get back in there, both of you."

Mandy started trembling and crying into her shoulder. "Please don't make me go back in there."

"You don't want to do this, Suzie."

"Do what? Shoot your Goody Two-shoes ass? I know who you *really* are. You used to work at Carla's store. Now you think you're too good for us. Ice told me about you. Said you had some psychic powers. That you might come by and try to steal the kid."

"I'm not stealing the kid. I'm taking her back home where she belongs."

Dawn could sense Suzie's fear. She was holding

the gun, but she was shaking. Or maybe she just needed a fix.

"I can help you, Suzie. Let me help. You can turn your life around."

Suzie snorted. "Yeah, Ice told me you'd try that bullshit on me too. What he saw in you, I'll never know. I guess you're a good lay or something."

Dawn was about to reply when out of the corner of her eye, she saw a bird swoop down from the sky.

Luca! He was moving so fast, Suzie didn't even have time to react. His talons grabbed her by the shoulders and hauled her away. She screamed and dropped the gun. He deposited her in the dumpster across the street.

"That big bird just grabbed the mean lady," Mandy said, her eyes wide. "It's like he knew she was mean."

"Let's go." Dawn tightened her hold on Mandy and rushed to pick up the gun. She ran across the street to the car. Luca had transformed back to his human form and pulled on his T-shirt and jeans. Sounds of yelling and cursing were coming from inside the dumpster.

Dawn could tell Luca was pissed.

"What the heck were you doing?"

Yup. He was definitely pissed. "I was rescuing Mandy," she replied calmly.

"I told you to wait."

"Yes, but then Suzie left, and I couldn't let another chance slip by."

"Yes, but then she came back with a weapon."

"Yes, but then you showed up and saved us." Dawn grinned.

Luca sighed. "It's hard to stay mad at you." He

opened the back door for Dawn to strap Mandy into the back seat.

"*Get me the hell out of here!*" Suzie yelled from inside the dumpster. "*Help!*"

"The mean lady is yelling," Mandy said.

"She'll be fine." Dawn gave Mandy a kiss on her cheek.

"Is he your boyfriend?"

"Yes, he's my boyfriend," Dawn replied. "His name is Luca."

"Is he nice?" Mandy said.

"Yeah, he is." Dawn nodded.

Luca pulled out his cell phone and made a call. "Dad, I have a situation here. Can you bring Gabe? I'm on Waverly Street in front of the dumpster across from the Dorcet Motel."

"What happened to the pretty bird?" Mandy asked Dawn while Luca was talking to his dad.

"He had to fly home to be with his family. I need to buckle you in, honey. We'll be heading home soon."

Luca finished up his call.

"Okay, everything's set. I called Dad, and he's going to call Captain Moore with an anonymous tip. SWAT is going to swarm Keene Street Convenience."

"Why? What's going on there?"

"I'll tell you in private."

He opened the passenger-side door, and she got in. As soon as he was in the driver's seat, she asked, "What about Suzie?"

"Joe will come with backup to haul her out of the dumpster and take her in."

Dawn reached out and placed her hands on his cheeks. "Does that mean this is over?"

"I think so."

"Thank you." She kissed him fast and fierce. "Oh, here's the gun by the way. It wasn't loaded." She handed it to him.

He shook his head and shoved the gun under his seat. "Let's get Mandy and her dad reunited."

Luca pulled out onto the street and drove like a maniac to the safest place he knew…

The Fierro family home. From there, he'd call Jack.

"What happened?" Dawn whispered as soon as they were inside.

Gabriella came bustling out of the kitchen, bent over Mandy, and gave the girl a big warm hug. "Sweetheart. Your daddy is on his way over. He's so glad you're safe. We all are. Would you like a glass of milk and a cookie?"

"Yes, please!"

Gabriella chuckled and gave Luca a smile that conveyed relief, gratitude, and something else… Awe?

Luca filled Dawn in on what he'd overheard in the alley behind Keene Street Convenience.

"I can't believe it," Dawn said. "I mean, I *can* believe it, but it's so crazy. That horrible sergeant actually had his own sister-in-law offed and wanted to do the same to his niece?"

"I had no idea how ruthless he is. But I guess part of it is trying to save his own neck. I heard him talking to Joe the other day about his upcoming vacation to Cancun. I bet he's looking to make a getaway and disappear for good."

"You mean leave his family?"

"In order to escape jail time? I'm sure of it. Psychopaths really don't think of anyone but themselves. He's probably doing this one last deal to get a big cash haul."

"I hope they can stop him before he gets out of the country," Dawn said.

"Don't worry. Someone in that gang will roll on him for a lesser sentence."

There's only one problem with that…on the full moon, he'll tear his cellmate apart.

"What are you planning? Whatever it is, I'm going with you."

Luca shook his head. "No way. You are going to stay with my parents. I don't want you in harm's way."

"You can't order me around. If I say I'm going with you, then I'm going with you."

Luca gritted his teeth. "I love you, Dawn, but you have it in your head that you have to save the world, and you could get yourself killed in the process. I can't risk it."

"I don't have that mindset. You do!"

Mandy overheard the couple and poked her head around the kitchen doorway. "Don't fight. That's what the mean man and lady did all the time."

They gazed at each other, chagrinned. "We're not fighting, honey," Luca said. "Not really. Sometimes grown-ups both want the same thing, but they just want it to happen different ways."

Dawn took his hand and said, "It's okay. I know you're right about wanting to keep me safe. But you aren't right about me wanting to save the world." Then she winked. "Just my little corner of it."

"Tomorrow, you can get your grandma out of the hospital and bring her here."

"Why? Do you think they'd go after her?"

"Babe, if it's known that you had something to do with it, the gang might try to retaliate."

"Maybe we shouldn't wait...and shouldn't you ask your parents?"

Antonio breezed into the living room, wearing his bathrobe. "Ask your parents what?"

"Can Dawn's grandmother stay here until this all blows over—or until we find her another place to live?"

Antonio nodded gravely. "She can stay here as long as she likes. You too, of course, Dawn."

Dawn threw her arms around Antonio's neck and spoke through a throat thick with tears. "Thank you." Then she turned to Luca. "We have to catch them."

"We will. I promise."

The doorbell rang.

Luca answered it, and Dawn was happy to see Jack Richardson on their doorstep.

"Is she here?"

"Yes," she and Luca said at the same time. They didn't have a chance to say another word before Mandy came running, yelling, "Daddy! Daddy!"

The man dropped to his knees in front of his daughter and burst into tears. He pulled her into a tight embrace and held her as if he'd never let her go. She was holding onto him just as tightly.

Gabriella waited until they had pulled apart, sniffling,

and handed them both some tissues. "Let me make you some coffee, Jack."

"No, thank you. I just want to get my little girl home—where she belongs."

"That's completely understandable."

Jack rose, lifting Mandy and resting her on his left hip as he stuck out his right hand to Luca. "I can't thank you enough." After shaking his hand, he turned to Dawn and shook hers. "And you... You're amazing. I don't know how you found her, but I'll be forever grateful."

Dawn shrugged. "I'm just glad I could help."

They all said their goodbyes and ushered the happy reunited family out the front door.

As soon as the door was closed and locked, Antonio shouted, "You both could have been killed!"

"Dad, I told you over the phone, we're fine."

"Well, I was saving my yelling until now."

"Shh..." Gabriella tucked her hand in the crook of her husband's elbow. "I think he knows you were worried. We both were. But please take a moment to tell our son how proud you are of what he did."

Antonio hung his head. "I'm sorry. Yes, what you did, Luca, rescuing that child, was...miraculous. I've rescued plenty of kids, but they weren't in the same kind of danger, and neither was I."

"Yes," Gabriella breathed. "Who knows what would have happened to that precious little girl if you hadn't acted."

"I just hope I don't get in trouble for not following protocol."

"Son," Antonio said, "even if you get fired, you did the right thing."

"That's what I believe too. But it wasn't all me."

Then he gave Dawn a look. She was beginning to interpret his subtle body language.

"I'm afraid if anyone messed up the investigation, it was me. I saw an opening and rushed in, grabbing Mandy without even thinking about any protocol that should be followed."

"And I'll bet you'd do it again if you had to." Gabriella smiled.

"Yup. I'm afraid I would. And now I have to rescue my own grandmother. I don't want to wait until tomorrow."

Antonio's cell phone beeped, and he pulled it out of his pocket. After a few short responses, Antonio thanked the caller and hung up. "Joe wanted you to know he picked up that woman in the dumpster and hauled her to jail."

"Great. Now hopefully Captain Moore and half the BPD are on their way to arrest Butts and Ice," Luca said. "In the meantime, we need to get Annette. Carla is still out there, and she could do something dangerous to save her skin."

Hearing that broke Dawn's heart, but Luca had a point. She had been colluding by looking the other way. Who knows what Carla had participated in knowingly?

Dawn was on pins and needles all the way to the hospital. They might have to sign Annette out AMA— against medical advice—but if that was what it took to keep her gran safe, so be it. Luckily, there was a young nurse on duty, and Luca worked his charm while Dawn went into Annette's room to wake her up.

She was scheduled to be released the next day

anyway, so she was just leaving a few hours early. Dawn found a wheelchair in the hall and took it into her grandmother's room while Luca distracted the night nurse with his tales of working the streets at night. It sounded as if he'd been on the force for years, not weeks.

"Gran, wake up."

Annette opened her eyes and stared at Dawn in surprise. She glanced at the clock on the wall. "What are you doing here? What's wrong?"

"We have to leave. I need to take you to Luca's parents' house. Antonio is in the car, and Luca's just outside at the nurses' station. It's not safe for you here."

Annette nodded. If there was one thing about her grandmother, it was how smart and alert she was. Given her background and her experiences in her lifetime, she was no fool when it came to danger. Dawn helped her grandmother up and quickly packed up her bag, then helped her into the wheelchair and wheeled her out while Luca still talked with the night nurse.

"Thank you," Annette said to Antonio when she'd been helped into the family's SUV. "For looking after my granddaughter and now me! I don't want to be a burden!"

"Don't look at it like that. We don't," Antonio assured her. "Besides, my wife loves having people to cook big Italian meals for—and I benefit too!" His big grin reassured her.

By the time they got back to the Fierro house, Luca's brother Gabe and his wife, Misty, were up with their toddler, Tony. Apparently, he had decided to wake up early—or perhaps the chaos woke him.

They were in the dining room, chowing down on the huge breakfast Gabriella had set on the table.

"Welcome, Annette." Gabriella wrapped her arms around Annette and gave her a warm hug. She helped her sit on a chair with a cushion added and offered her some tea or coffee.

"Oh, I'd love some coffee. Thank you."

"I thought I'd make up the sofa bed in the living room for you, just until you can go up the stairs to our guest room. You'll be very comfortable."

"Thank you, dear Gabriella. I hope I'm not causing too much of an inconvenience."

"Not at all. We're used to family staying here whenever they need or want to. Your Dawn is part of our family now, so that means you are too."

"I'm so grateful." Annette's eyes watered, then she cleared her throat and said, "My, those muffins look delicious."

Gabriella quickly put one on a plate and placed it in front of Annette. "I adapted the recipe, based on the Italian spumoni cake Antonio's mother used to make."

Annette took a bite and groaned in delight as she chewed.

Dawn and Luca told her what was going on. Annette shook her head and wiped her eyes when Dawn told her about Carla.

"What's the next step?" Gabe asked.

"There's something I have to tell you, Dad," Luca began. "But we need to talk about it privately."

"I'd like to come too," Gabe said.

Antonio grabbed a muffin, rose, and said, "To the man cave!"

Before he'd even had a chance to get comfortable, Luca told his father, "Dad, when I was watching Sergeant Butts and one of the gang argue, Butts shape-shifted into a wolf."

"Holy shit!" Gabe said. "Will a regular jail cell hold him? And what about the full moon? Do you know anyone who might know what to do, Dad?"

"I have an idea. Something that Butts will never expect," Luca said. "We'll need a little help from an unusual source, and I think we'll get a unique brand of justice."

Luca glanced at his dad, whose eyes were gleaming. "I think I know what you're getting at, Son," Antonio said. "Besides, I promised her I'd report any violations of her rule number one. Never reveal your paranormal identity to a human—outside of the human wives, that is."

"Oh no," Gabe said. "You're not talking about who I think you're talking about, are you?"

A whirlwind sprang up in front of them. Gaia appeared, wearing a white toga belted with a green vine. "I hear you need a kick in the Butts."

Antonio shot to his feet. "Mother Nature. Welcome!"

Chapter 16

"FIVE CRUISERS PULLED UP TO THE KEENE STREET Convenience store."

Joe was on the phone, describing the scene Luca had missed soon after he left. "The officers rushed in and dragged out Ice Spider and Butts along with several other Keene Street Gang members. Gulliver and Captain Moore were the first ones in. You would have loved it, kid.

"Ha, Butts thought he was smart," Joe continued. "Picking the time during shift change, when most officers were back at the precinct. Only instead, it seems as if both shifts were busting up his operation. Captain Moore personally read Butts his rights and handcuffed him. Butts yelled, 'You bitches. You think you can get me? I'll be out on bail in an hour.' Then Captain Moore said, 'Butts, for once in your life, shut the fuck up,' as she put her hand on his head and shoved him into the back of the cruiser."

We got them. Luca breathed a sigh of relief. "Did your guys get the Tyler Street Dogs too?"

"Yup," Joe replied. "The stash of coke was in a false bottom in the trunk. They might help implicate Butts."

"What about Carla?"

"We got her just as she was trying to get through security at the airport."

"Joe, I owe you a beer or two."

"You got it, buddy. And look, I know you're a rookie, but you are one damn fine cop."

"Thanks, man." As he hung up, he felt like he'd achieved what he was meant to do.

A short while later, Luca peeked into the living room and saw Annette sleeping on the pullout sofa. Dawn was watching from the dining room table.

"How's Annette doing?" he whispered.

"She's sound asleep." Dawn suppressed a yawn, and Luca wrapped his arms around her.

"You should be sound asleep too. Why don't you get some rest?"

"I'm not going to bed until all this is done."

"This one is just like your mom." Antonio grinned, lifting his chin at Dawn. He carried a full coffeepot out of the kitchen and set it on the dining room table's trivet.

"Who's just like me?" Gabriella strolled out of the kitchen with a tray of mugs and spoons, plus cream and sugar.

"Dawn is as stubborn as you are." He softened his statement with a kiss to her cheek.

"Good," Gabriella replied, winking at Dawn. "We need to be that way to handle the Fierro men."

Dawn chuckled at their banter. Luca hugged her even tighter. It was good to hear her laugh.

"What about Butts?" Dawn asked Luca.

"He's been arrested along with Ice and Carla. He was calling himself Blue Wolf as a code name."

"He'll be out on bail and on a plane to Mexico by tomorrow morning," Antonio added.

"We can't let him get away with it! He's going to escape." Dawn's eyes were wide with alarm.

"It's okay," Luca said in a reassuring voice. "We have a little surprise for him when he gets to his destination."

"A surprise?" Dawn tilted her head, a gleam beginning to flicker in her eyes. "What sort of surprise?"

"I'll tell you later," he whispered.

"You know what I just realized?" Antonio said.

"What?" Dawn and Luca asked together.

"The blue sheep just took down the blue wolf."

Luca rolled his eyes, then couldn't help laughing anyway.

———

Two days later…

"Room service. How may we help you make your dreams come true?"

"I'd like a deep tissue massage, and make sure you send in the same girl as last time. Then in one hour, I'd like another bottle of champagne, a steak rare, and a slice of your chocolate mousse cake."

"I'm sorry. The masseuse you had last time is off. I have someone else you'll like just as much."

"Are you sure?"

"Positive."

"All right then. Send her up."

"Right away, Mr. Mooney."

Butts grinned at the use of his pseudonym. He hung up and stretched out on the king-size four-poster bed. He picked up the remote control and flicked through the channel selection, landing on an adult film site.

He'd been coming here on vacation for the past five

years. He was here for one more quickie before heading to a country where there was no extradition treaty with the United States. He had a stash of money, a luxury condo picked out, and would soon find a hot mistress who would satisfy his needs for the rest of his life.

He unbuckled his pants and chuckled in pleasure as he watched three buxom women cavorting in a hot tub with a pizza delivery guy.

Ice and Carla would no doubt rot in jail, while he would bask in the sunshine, sitting on his terrace with an ocean view. Luckily, he knew the judge personally, and his bribe had worked to get him bail. He'd had to turn over his passport of course. No problem, since he had two other passports under different names. His suitcase had been packed and ready.

If he never saw his wife again, it would be too soon. Damn woman was like a nun. As for his daughter, well, she was already engaged to a congressman's son with a tidy prenup. He'd made sure that if the prick broke the engagement, and he no doubt would after hearing of Butts's arrest, Lisa would get a cool million. That would keep her satisfied until she found another idiot to marry. And he was sure she would. She'd inherited her father's instincts.

He raised his glass of champagne in salute to his daughter. "The apple doesn't fall far from the tree." Would he miss his daughter? Nope. She was a pain in the ass who went through his money like it was growing on trees. The million wouldn't last long. Well, she was his wife's problem now. He couldn't very well have stayed in Boston. He would have ended up doing time, and he couldn't risk that. No way he was going to spend the rest of his life in jail with the same lowlifes he'd put there.

A knock sounded at the door. A muffled female voice announced, "Massage for Mr. Mooney?"

He grinned and got up, opening the door. Standing there was the most gorgeous redhead he'd ever seen. Wearing a tight white sheer blouse with a black bra underneath and a short black skirt showing off a pair of legs in sky-high red heels, her hair was in a bun near the top of her head. He couldn't wait to run his hands through it. He loved redheads. "Now this is what I call room service." He opened the door wider as she waltzed in with a portable massage table.

She gave him a perky smile and said, "You'll have to strip for me, Mr. Mooney, so I can give you the best massage you've ever had."

"Sure thing." He quickly removed his clothes, dropping them on the floor as she efficiently and expertly set up the massage table. He was already rock-hard as he watched her bend over and adjust the legs of the table. Her ass was round, and her tits were huge, just the way he liked.

She stood up and saw his erection, a slow smile spreading across her face. "You're a very naughty boy, Mr. Mooney." She wagged her finger at him.

"Well, I hope you can teach me to behave." He grinned wolfishly.

"You'll just have to get onto the table and find out."

He quickly hopped onto the table and lay there on his back, knowing full well what she'd be massaging first. He was fairly agile for his age. Wolves usually remained in good shape well into their later years. He had a slight paunch, but that wouldn't keep him from indulging in a good fuck.

"Now, let's get started," she crooned. "I'm going to give you something you'll never forget."

"Ooh, I can't wait," he breathed.

She reached under the table and pulled up two heavy straps, buckling them over his chest and legs.

"Wow, this is new." He chuckled as she tightened the straps.

"Oh, yes," she replied, bending over, her lips hovering over his. He groaned as her breasts rubbed against his chest. "I'm the best there is."

"I bet you are."

The redhead stepped back and proceeded to unbutton her blouse. He was so hard, he'd probably come the minute her lips touched his cock.

She popped open one button and then reached up to unfasten her bun.

All of a sudden, her skimpy outfit changed to a long white tunic.

"What the fuck?"

"Tsk. Tsk. Tsk." She crossed her arms over her chest and walked around the table. "Did you really think you could get away?" She strolled to the door and opened it. In walked four burly blond men wearing dark sunglasses and black suits.

"Who are you?"

She walked closer to him and bent close to his face. "I'm Karma. I was sent by my sister, Gaia. It's not nice to fool Mother Nature...or try to."

His eyes widened. "Your sister is Mother Nature?"

"Yes indeed. Now that you know who I am, I'll tell you what I'm going to do with you."

"Y-you don't have jurisdiction over me. You can't do this. There's a council. I'll notify them."

She narrowed her eyes and said in a cold voice, "*My sister is the council*. It's called GAIA, which stands for Gods and Immortals Association. And when she turned you over to me, she said, 'Karma, do what you will.' In other words, whatever I say goes. The council has heard about how you purposely exposed your wolf to a human, plus your other illicit activities. It stops now. You, Sergeant Butts, are finally getting what you deserve."

He began to struggle against the straps but stopped when the burly men surrounded him.

"Wh-what are you going to do?"

She snapped her fingers, and the room began to spin. Feeling dizzy and nauseous, he closed his eyes. When he opened them again, he was no longer in the hotel. He was in a cage with bars. But it wasn't a jail cell. No, it was much worse. There was very little light, but on the other side of the bars were the blond men and the sound of a loud engine whirring. It seemed as if he was in the cargo hold of an airplane. He was still completely naked and strapped to the table. Panic set in as he realized he was fucked.

"We'll be in the Arctic circle before you know it. Enjoy the rest of your life, Mr. Mooney," Karma said with a smirk. "Oh, by the way, we created a little accident back home in Boston. A terrible tragedy. Your car went up in flames. Not enough human remains left to identify you. I'm afraid you're now deceased." She chuckled. "Oh, well, at least your long-suffering wife will have all your money to console her. I made sure all that cash you wired into that secret offshore bank account got wired back to her. After all, she won't be getting your pension anymore, given what a rat you are. Speaking of rats..." She stepped out of the cage and stood beside her burly bodyguards. "Enjoy your new roommates."

A scratching sound echoed from the corners of the cage.

"You can't leave me here!"

"Oh yes, I can, Sergeant. This is what you get for causing a child to become motherless. My sister Mother Nature and I take exception to any harm done to the nurturers of this world. You were fucked the minute you ran that woman off the road."

"It wasn't me."

"You ordered it."

The scratching grew louder and louder.

"Not to mention all the lying and cheating you put your wife through. Your daughter grew up into a brat, thanks to you. I'll have to see what I can do about her."

"Who called you? How did you find out about this?"

"A little birdie told me."

The scratching echoed all around him. He pissed himself when he felt the first nibble on his leg.

"Get me out of this cage!"

"Soon. Sven has the key."

One of the blond bodyguards held up a thick metal key to the heavy padlock.

She snapped her fingers, and the straps holding him to the massage table disappeared.

"You're an idiot. I can just shift into wolf form, and these rats become my lunch."

"That's the idea. When you parachute out into the Arctic, you and your new pack—who don't like you very much, I'm afraid—will have a snack before you have to spend the rest of your long-ass life hunting down caribou."

"So where's my parachute?"

She shrugged and gave him a wave. "Toodles. Enjoy your new home."

He cursed. He would be cursing for the rest of his "long-ass life."

Dawn's eyes widened. "You're kidding."

"Nope," Luca said.

"Karma herself?"

"Yup."

"How did you manage that?"

"Her sister, Gaia, asked my dad to keep her informed of significant paranormal crimes, since she gets pretty busy and can't be everywhere at once."

"I had no idea how well-connected your family is."

Luca chuckled. "The important thing is that bastard won't be scheming and taking advantage of humans ever again."

Dawn and Luca were lying side by side in bed at her place, cuddling.

Annette would be staying with the Fierros for a few more days, which thrilled Gabriella, since she had someone new to fuss over. They had notified the hospital administrator to let her know about the circumstances of the midnight release, telling her the night nurse should not be blamed for a missing patient. They couldn't have been talked out of taking her.

Earlier that day, they had all had lunch in the Fierros' dining room, including Jack and Mandy. Mandy didn't seem too badly off, considering what she'd been through. She was grieving the loss of her mother, certainly, but she was obviously happy to be with her daddy. Jack had taken an emergency leave of absence to help them both bond and heal.

Gabriella had promised to check on them later and told Mandy she could come over and play whenever she liked. Mandy had nodded, shoving a huge forkful of pancake, dripping with syrup, into her mouth, making everyone burst into laughter.

Luca and Dawn had dropped off Jack and Mandy, letting them know they would stop by soon. "I can't thank you enough," Jack had told them as he held Mandy tightly in his arms. "You're a hero," he had said to Dawn.

"Yes, she is," Luca had said, wrapping his arm around her shoulders.

Later that night in bed, Dawn swallowed a lump in her throat. She was no hero. She'd almost failed to rescue the girl. It took three tries to find her. She never wanted to go through that again.

"Hey, what's wrong?" Luca tipped her chin up and drew her gaze to his. "Why so gloomy?"

Her eyes filled with tears. "Jack called me a hero."

"You *are* a hero."

"No, I'm not. I should have rescued Mandy that first time."

"You tried, remember? If you'd gone into that room, Ice might have killed you both." He tucked a wisp of her hair behind her ear. She hadn't realized how much longer it had gotten. With so much happening over the past weeks, her hair was the last thing on her mind. Luca had told her he loved the soft waves, so she decided to let it grow.

"What if I failed on the last attempt? Mandy could have been killed. I can't make that kind of mistake again."

"You sound like a cop," he said, kissing her on the forehead. "If anything like this happens again, we'll work together as a team and get it right the first time. We were both rookies at this—me a rookie cop and you a rookie psychic detective. But we learned a lot, didn't we?"

Dawn sighed. "Yeah, we did."

"And Mandy is with her dad, where she belongs. And Butts is in…well, Karma put him where he can't hurt anyone."

"What about Ice and Carla?"

"They're in jail. Most likely, it won't go to trial. Lawyers love plea deals. Even if it does, I think Mick will flip on them to save himself. They'll be put away for a long time."

"Carla could have turned it around," Dawn said quietly. "She could have done the right thing, but she didn't."

"I guess she'd gotten so used to doing the wrong thing that she didn't know any other way. Or she let the gang talk her into colluding with them."

"I almost went down that same road."

"No. You're nothing like Carla." Luca pulled her into a tight embrace and kissed her fiercely. "You're an amazing, caring, courageous woman, and I love you."

"I love you back," she whispered thickly. "I love you so much."

Luca kissed her tears away, then moved back to her mouth. He kissed her tenderly, like he was handling a precious gift.

She almost couldn't take it. "Let me show you how much I love you," Dawn said.

Luca grinned. "What did you have in mind?"

"Roll onto your back," she whispered.

Luca gladly did as she asked and folded his hands behind his head. "And now?"

"And now, just lie there and enjoy."

She took his already erect cock in her mouth as far as she could, then applying suction, she drew back almost all the way to the tip.

He groaned and arched slightly. She took that as a good sign and kept going. She circled the shaft with her tongue, and when it was good and wet, she pushed down until she was almost all the way to the hilt. She didn't want to choke. There was nothing sexy about a good gag reflex.

Apparently, she was doing it just right. He moved his hands from behind his head to her hair and gently ran his fingers through her silky strands.

"Oh, babe. I love that."

She didn't respond, but no reply was needed. His moans of pleasure guided her.

When at last he said, "I can't take any more," and pushed her shoulders away, her mouth let go with a pop.

"Ahh… That was incredible. Now it's your turn." He flipped her over onto her back and crept down the bed until he was eye level with her sex.

He returned the favor with gusto, bringing her to an earth-shattering orgasm. And another…and another! She was limp when he finished.

He let her recover—sort of. While her chest heaved, he took a nipple into his mouth and sucked the sensitive bud until she was arching and moaning again. After giving the other one equal treatment, he cupped her face and said, "Are you ready for me?"

She giggled. "I don't think I could be any more ready. But do we need a condom? I'm not ovulating."

"I don't know, do we? Shifters don't get diseases."

"In that case, I'm ready when you are."

With a broad smile, he moved to kneel between her spread legs. Entering her slowly, they maintained eye contact. He rocked into and out of her until she had to close her eyes and moan. She could feel the incredible sensual tension building again.

At last, she shattered. She had to hold a pillow over her mouth to scream out her powerful climax without alerting the police in three counties.

While she was coming, Luca's body jerked, and she knew he was finishing with her. He had incredible stamina, but she doubted many men could hold out much longer, since her vaginal muscles were squeezing and pulsing like crazy.

At last, they were both spent. As they lay side by side, sweating but holding hands, he said, "You must love me a lot."

She laughed. "More than even that."

Chapter 17

"YOU DID IT," LYNDA SAID.

"Did I?"

Dawn was sitting on a bench, gazing at the fountain at the Christian Science Center. It was early in the morning, quiet and peaceful. She'd left Luca sleeping at her place, putting a note and a bagel for him beside the bed.

Lynda sat beside her. "Of course you did. You did everything you were supposed to do."

She was wearing a light-blue tracksuit as if just going for a run, yet not a hair was out of place.

"What if Suzie hadn't left? I wouldn't have been able to rescue Mandy. Or what if her gun was loaded? What if Ice had come back?"

"And what if a spaceship landed on your head as you were crossing the street?"

"Huh?"

Lynda smiled.

Dawn shook her head. "What's the use of having good karma if so much is out of your control?"

"You can't control the world. You can only control your own actions."

"It sounds so easy, but it's harder than I thought it would be." Dawn blew out a breath.

"What is this really about?" Lynda asked her, reaching into her purse and handing Dawn a Hershey's Kiss.

Dawn popped the chocolate in her mouth and welcomed its soothing, chocolatey sweetness. "What if I don't deserve any of this?"

"Of course you do. You worked very hard to get where you are. You're amazing. Do you know that? You inspire everyone around you, even people you don't know. You may get a 'thank you' at your job when you help someone wrangle their software program—or not. That doesn't mean you're not doing your job. Right?"

Dawn snorted. "That's just computer stuff."

"Really? Just computer stuff? Most of those students who call you are desperate for help, with a lot riding on that assignment or term paper. Many are adult learners who didn't grow up with computers and haven't the faintest idea what to do when there's a glitch. You help them get through it.

"Not to mention the loving care you show Annette, the kids you help at the Youth Community Center, and," she said softly, "the love you feel for Luca. He's a gem, but you make him even better. He does the same for you.

"And look at your determination to rescue Mandy! Even though cops have to face things like that every day, do you think they could have solved that crime as quickly? Especially with someone on the inside making sure they didn't? No, it might have lasted months or years, eventually becoming a cold case."

"Saving someone's life is awesome, but failing to must be hell."

"Welcome to life. Nobody bats one thousand. Not cops, not doctors, not social workers. Neither can we."

Dawn stared at Lynda, and now it was she who gazed at the fountain. "Remember when I told you that not everyone can make that change?"

"Yes."

"Well, Carla was one of my people."

"What?"

"Years ago, I found her. A few weeks after Annette saved her from that asshole husband. I approached her and tried to bring her into the organization. She tried at first. But after a month, she stopped coming in for her weekly meetings. I reached out to her many times, and she just blew me off. She said she liked her life the way it was. She didn't want to complicate things. I told her she had an opportunity to help all those runaways and street kids who ended up in her store. She refused to listen. So after a while, I just had to wipe her memory of Karma Cleaners and let it go."

"I—I'm sorry."

"So you see, all we can do is try. And if we fail, we move on to the next person and try again."

"I think I understand." Dawn wrapped her arm around Lynda's shoulders. "You know what, LC?"

"What?"

"You're pretty amazing yourself."

"Thanks, kiddo. Now, how about we do a little retail therapy? My treat. Goddess Fashions is having a flash sale today." She glanced at her watch. "It'll be starting in about fifteen minutes."

"I love that store! I might actually do all my shopping there in the future."

"You won't, but I can't tell you why not. Just know the sacrifice will be for the greater good."

—✺—

"Sweetie, it's time for me to go home."

"Gran, you're still not a hundred percent, and what if you fall at home when I'm at work?"

"The Fierros are lovely people, but I can't keep imposing on them. You know that's not my way. It's best for me to go home."

"What's this I hear about you leaving?" Gabriella walked into the guest room that Annette had, at last, been able to reach by the stairs, as long as she used her cane. Their hostess was holding a tray with tea and some delicious-looking cake that made Dawn's mouth water. *Yum. I don't care how fast my metabolism is, I could gain ten pounds here, easy.*

"You have been so good to me, Gabriella," Annette began. "I just can't put you out like this."

"You are doing no such thing." Gabriella set the tray down on the coffee table and rested her hip on the daybed beside Annette. Reaching for Annette's hand, she held it between her own. "Annette, I don't want you to go. I know I'm being selfish, but I want you right here."

"Me?" Annette's eyes widened.

"Now that almost all my kids are on their own, I have very little to do. It gets lonely, especially when Antonio is off visiting his old firefighting buddies. And that's only part of it. Since you've been here, I can't help but notice he's a lot more thoughtful. Why, just this morning, he brought me my morning coffee in bed with a red rose on the tray. When I asked him what the special occasion was, he said *just because*. Now I *know* that was *your* doing."

Annette blushed.

"And when Gabe had that silly disagreement with little Tony, you had a nice chat with them and smoothed things over." Gabriella patted Annette's hand. "You are so very special. I can see why Dawn is such an amazing young woman, because she was raised by her very wise grandmother."

Annette's eyes teared up. "I don't know what to say."

"Say you'll stay."

"I would love to. Thank you."

Gabriella wrapped her arms around Annette's shoulders.

Dawn sniffed and wiped her eyes, moved by the love the Fierros had shown both her and her grandmother.

"Really? He brought you coffee in bed with a rose?" Annette asked. "All I said was how lucky he was to have you and I hoped he let you know it."

"Yup. First. Time. Ever." Gabriella opened her arms to bring Dawn into the embrace, and the three women began to laugh. When they broke apart, she said, "Now, let's have some tea and cake."

"In a minute." Annette held up one hand. "I need to know more about this shape-shifter stuff."

"You've heard of paranormal abilities? How there are a few individuals who are stronger, faster, and live longer than regular humans?"

"Well, no. To be honest, I hadn't until now."

"Ah. That's the way it's supposed to be. Humans as a general rule aren't allowed to know about it. But let me tell you what I know from my completely human point of view."

Annette nodded for her to go on.

Gabriella explained about how she was able to handle

her husband and so many of her sons being in a dangerous profession like firefighting because if the worst happened, they could reincarnate in fire.

She explained their extreme longevity and how they might reincarnate as many as a dozen times over their five hundred or so years on earth.

She even confessed her concern for Luca, since he could die by a bullet, and if no one was around to bathe him in fire, he might not come back.

That made a ball lodge in Dawn's throat. "I—I kinda wish he'd become a firefighter now."

"You and me both!" Gabriella said. "But Luca is Luca. He has always done things his own way."

"Is that a good thing or a bad thing?" Annette asked.

"Neither, really. I know the older boys and even my husband have accused me of babying him, but that has never been the case. If I wanted him to take the safe route, he'd make up his own mind and take the right route. Whatever that was for him. I'm so proud of my youngest. He's no sheep, despite the nickname—blue sheep."

"It never meant that," Antonio said as he poked his head in the door. "It was just a joke about the family's black sheep, because he chose a blue uniform."

"I know that," Gabriella said. "And by the way, that doesn't help."

Antonio laughed. "Well, I guess I'll butt out as quickly as I butted in."

As soon as he left, Gabriella said, "Now, where were we? Oh yes. Your concerns about my shape-shifting family."

Dawn reached over for Annette's hand, and they exchanged a smile.

"I don't have any more concerns. Do you, Gran?"

"Nope. It sounds like you landed in a well-feathered nest."

~~~

"Are you okay?"

"Yes. I think so."

In Dawn's living room, Luca was lying with his head on her lap. "You're amazing, you know that?" He reached up and caressed her face.

She fluttered her eyelashes at him. "Why, Mr. Fierro, are you flirting with me?"

He grinned. "I mean it. You've had such a tough life, and you—you have such a beautiful heart. You're the most caring woman I have ever met. I love you, babe."

"I love you back," she whispered.

Luca reached up and pulled Dawn's head down to his lips.

"You know what?" he asked between kisses.

"What?" she whispered.

"I think I fell in love with you the first moment I met you."

"You did *not*."

He sat up and faced her. "No, seriously. I think I did."

"You thought I was a freak. And you were pining after *Lisa*." She said the name in a mincing voice, making him chuckle.

"Well, maybe I thought I was still hung up on her. But I figured out she wasn't the girl for me once I got to know you." He rubbed the back of his neck. "I really dodged a bullet there."

"In more ways than one," she replied. "Imagine having Sergeant Butts for a father-in-law."

"No thanks." He shook all over as if a shiver had just passed through him. "So…" He grinned.

"So?" She grinned back.

"I think we should stay together. I'd say something like 'We make a good team,' but that's lame."

"I know what you mean. And yes, I agree."

He smiled. "When did you realize you loved me?"

"Hmm…" She leaned in close and touched his lips with her fingertips. "I think it was the first time you kissed me."

He kissed her fingertips. "I think we should celebrate our first kiss."

"Really?"

"Yep."

"How should we celebrate? With a kiss?"

"We can start with a kiss. Then maybe a surprise?"

"Oh, I love surprises," Dawn said.

"Good, because I have one for you right now." He rolled her onto her back and loomed over her. "Let's smash."

She giggled. "Such a romantic."

"Yeah. I'm a chip off the old Fierro block."

⁓

It was four in the morning, and Luca couldn't sleep.

He glanced down at the gorgeous woman tucked in under his arm and couldn't believe his luck. He was crazy about her. He kissed the tip of her cute nose and slipped out of bed.

An hour later, he had a pot of coffee brewing and a stack of pancakes warming, along with thick toast, bacon, and eggs.

"Hey, what are you doing up so early?"

"I thought I'd make us a big breakfast before I drop you off at work."

"You don't have to do that. Aren't you on the evening shift this week? You should be sleeping." She wrapped her arms around his middle as he filled two plates full of food. He leaned back and kissed her.

He was nervous. Really nervous. "Let's eat."

"Yum." She scooped up some scrambled eggs. "Mmm… You are *so* good to me. I think I'll keep you around." She winked at him as she popped a piece of bacon in her mouth.

He hesitated. Would she still want to be with him after he told her?

"Okay, what's wrong?"

He read the concern in her beautiful gray-green eyes. "I have something to tell you."

"This looks serious. Is it your parents? Annette? The gang? Butts? What's going on?" Her face was in full panic mode.

"No, it's nothing like that." To reassure her, he reached for her hand. "I just—"

"What?"

"I quit my job."

She gasped. "You quit?"

"Yes. I told them on Friday."

"That was two days ago."

"Yes, yes it was."

"Why didn't you tell me on Friday or even before you decided to quit?"

"I didn't know I was going to quit until Friday. I just… I realized I don't want to be a cop."

She sat there in silence, and that worried him. He began to speak and then couldn't stop. "I'm sorry. I should have told you. I was worried you would think less of me. That you'd think I was a quitter. After everything you've been through, I want to be the kind of man you can be proud of."

"Are you kidding me?" She stood up and planted her hands on her hips. "How can you even say that? You are the most wonderful guy in the whole world. Never, ever think that I'm not proud to be with you." She placed her hands on either side of his face. "I don't care that you don't want to be a cop. I care that you're happy. You're smart and brave, and you can do whatever you want with your life."

"Whew. So you're not mad I didn't tell you?"

"I'm only mad you didn't trust me enough to tell me. But I forgive you. Besides, I didn't tell you everything right away, so let's just call it even, and from now on, we'll tell each other everything as soon as possible. Agreed?"

"Agreed."

She kissed him and he kissed her back, and he knew without a doubt that she meant everything to him.

Dawn sat on his lap and took a bite of his toast. "So why did you quit?"

He blew out a breath. "I hated being so constrained. All the petty politics. I guess working under Butts really tainted my experience."

She giggled. "You said working under Butts."

He laughed. "Come on. I'm being serious here."

She cleared her throat. "Sorry. Go on."

"When you and I both used our special abilities to make a difference, I think I realized my actual calling."

"Really?"

"Yeah."

"So what are you going to do now? Become a fire-fighter like your dad and brothers?"

"I thought about it, but I don't think that's for me either. I want to try being a private investigator. What do you think?"

"I think that's a great idea."

"What do you think about working with me?"

"I think that's even better. But how are we going to make money? I hate to worry about it, but we should be practical." She made a face.

"It might be tight for a while, but I know we can make it work."

"I can keep working at ScholarTech while you get us set up so we have some money coming in."

"What did I ever do to deserve you?"

"I don't know." She grinned. "You're just one lucky dude, and I'm nuts about you."

"Can you believe it was only a few weeks ago that we met?"

Dawn took another bite of the eggs he'd made and thought for a moment. "It feels like a lifetime ago. So much has changed. Did you think we'd end up together when you first met me?"

"No, not that first time. I thought you were a freak, remember?"

"Hey!" She shoved his shoulder, and he burst out laughing.

"I figured it out pretty fast, though." He leaned in and kissed her. "Mmm…egg breath is so sexy."

"Aren't you glad I have mouthwash?" It was good

that they could laugh and tease. She was in a cheeky mood.

"You can't believe how glad I am about that." He grabbed another piece of his own egg and bit into it.

She glanced at him and asked the big question. "Are you worried about quitting your job and starting the PI biz? Is that why you couldn't sleep?"

Luca shrugged. "Kinda. But sometimes you have to take a risk, right? Jack would probably give us a great reference."

Dawn leaned her head on his shoulder. "I'll be with you every step of the way."

"I was hoping you'd say that...but you don't have to. I want you to follow your own dreams."

"I am." She sighed.

When she was younger, she had used her psychic abilities to help Ice and his gang get their drug deals made without interference from the cops. She hated where she came from, and she had hated her gift for a long time. But everything had changed.

"I have this ability inside me. A way for me to help make a difference. I want to keep doing that." She looked up at those cobalt-blue eyes that made her breath catch in her throat. "I want to be with you. If it works out and we have a successful supernatural PI service, then great. If not, we can do something else."

He kissed her, softly and sweetly. "We can always open up a pizza place, since we love it so much."

"Deal."

No matter where they ended up, they would be together, and that made her heart soar.

—⁓—

"Do you want to see the picture I drew of Mommy in heaven?"

"I would love to."

Dawn sat on the princess coverlet as Mandy opened a pink notebook and flipped the pages past several drawings.

Luca was chatting with Jack in the kitchen. Jack had told them he and Mandy would be visiting Patricia's mother for a few days and then moving to Rhode Island where Jack's parents were. He had two sisters who both had daughters close to Mandy's age. It would be good for Mandy to be around family. Jack's dad already had a job lined up for him.

They would live with his parents for a few months while they settled in. Mandy was glad when he told her they would be moving. She didn't want to leave Mommy alone. They'd buried Patricia in her mother's home town of Rockland. Jack had explained that Grandma and Grandpa would be there and they would keep Mommy's grave pretty. Also that Mommy wasn't really in there. She was in heaven, watching over her. That seemed to help her—a lot.

"I like your pictures. The colors are so pretty," Dawn said.

"Daddy said that too." Mandy carefully put the notebook away. She looked up at Dawn, her big blue eyes filled with sadness. "Do you think Mommy can see them?"

Dawn nodded without hesitation. "I know she can. I know she loves your pictures and she loves you. Forever and ever."

"I think I saw Mommy last night when I was sleeping."

"Did she say anything?"

"She just sat on the bed and smiled at me."

"How did that make you feel?"

"Happy and sad at the same time." Mandy glanced at Dawn. "Is that okay?"

"Yes, that's perfectly okay."

"Do you see dead people?"

"I sense things. I feel other people's emotions. So who knows? Maybe one day, I will."

"Maybe if you see Mommy, you can tell her I love her?"

"You can tell her yourself."

"Do you think she can hear me?"

"I know she can." Dawn tucked a curl behind Mandy's ear. "Do you want to tell her now?"

Mandy nodded.

"Close your eyes and tell her how you feel."

"Mommy? I hope you can hear me. I just wanted to say I love you so much. And I never want you to forget me, because I will never, ever forget you. I promise to take care of Daddy too. I love you, Mommy." Mandy opened her eyes. "Did I do good?"

"You did great."

～～～

Meanwhile, in the living room, Jack told Luca, "I can't thank you enough. If it weren't for you and Dawn, I don't know what would have happened."

"I'm just glad it's all over and Mandy is back where she belongs."

"I can't believe that bastard Butts." Jack shook his

head. "To do that to his own niece. You know that Patricia and Craig Butts's wife were half sisters, right?"

"Yeah, Captain Moore and my TO told me. Crazy."

"Yeah, Patty's dad had already been married once and divorced before he met Patty's mom. We spent holidays together."

"That is cold." Luca realized Butts was a sociopath who wielded his power like an old-school mobster. "But it all caught up to him in the end."

"I went to Butts," Jack went on. "I asked him what was going on with the investigation and if he could tell me anything. He told me they were doing everything they could do. Can you fucking believe that? That same night, I got drunk, and then you found me passed out."

"I'm so sorry. That guy was a bastard through and through."

"Then he ends up crashing his car in the same place where he had my wife run off the road. I just feel bad for his wife. She's a good woman. His daughter is another story. Butts spoiled her to no end. It all makes sense now. He was a dirty cop, and that was where he got all the money for his big house and fancy cars."

"Well, he got what he deserved." Luca left the part out about Karma and her own brand of justice, of course. Any mention of her existence to a human would have been met with instant and severe punishment. "The important thing is that Mandy is safe with you, and you guys can get on with your lives."

"What about you? Butts was your sergeant, and from what I know of him, he must have been brutal to have as a boss and a police sergeant."

"Yeah, it was no picnic." Luca told him about quitting the force. "It feels good. Now I have to get my own PI business up and running."

"I think you guys are gonna be great," Jack replied. "If you ever need a reference, you know how to reach me."

"Thanks, man. I appreciate it."

Chapter 18

"FAMILY MEETING AT THE FIERROS' CAN MEAN ANYTHING," Luca said. "But the one thing you can count on is Ma's great cooking and a dining room table groaning under the weight of it all."

Dawn smiled. "Are you sure we should be there? I mean, they've been wonderful to Gran and me, but we're not really part of your family."

"My dad told me what the meeting was about, in case I wanted to have you attend, and I do."

"Okay. Can you tell me what it's about too?"

The front door opened, and his brothers began filing in with their respective wives.

"Sorry. Not anymore I can't."

He greeted each couple and made sure Dawn was reintroduced, in case she had forgotten their names. Her grandmother was already sitting at the dining room table folding napkins, and Antonio was introducing her to each of his sons and daughters-in-law.

"What can I do to help with dinner?" one of the women called out.

"Damn. I should have offered to help your mother too," Dawn said to Luca.

"Don't worry about it. She's not shy about asking for help if she needs it. I think Misty's in there with her. She's been taking cooking lessons from Mom."

Dawn groaned. "I should probably do that at some

point. I can toast a mean bagel, but that's about it. Gran has always done the cooking."

"I can cook. Ma made sure I learned how as soon as she realized I wasn't going to be a firefighter. All firefighters learn to cook, since they're stuck at their firehouses for days sometimes."

"Yeah. I guess they'd starve if they didn't."

"Right. So no need to start your lessons yet. We can do that any time."

"Sandra?" Gabriella called out. "Can you set the table, please?"

"See? I told you she's not shy about asking for help."

"Okay. Well, I'll see if I can help Sandra then."

Luca nodded and went to take a seat at the table with most of the others. When Dawn asked Sandra if she could help, she glanced up from the silverware drawer and said, "Sure. You can place those glasses in front of everyone. Antonio will probably pass a bottle of red wine around. If someone asks for something different, maybe you can get that too."

"Great!" Dawn liked feeling useful, and she was happy not to be treated as a guest. Of course, she and her grandmother were practically living there now, so maybe they'd been absorbed into the family at some point without realizing it.

When everyone was seated, Gabriella brought out a large spiral-cut ham, surrounded by baked sweet potatoes. Misty came along behind her with a basket of rolls and a large salad. Sandra set another side dish on the table. It looked like broiled vegetables.

The wine was passed, and the only two who had

juice were Misty, who was pregnant, and little Tony. Gabe had a sippy cup for him at the ready.

Antonio said grace, and everyone dove in. A general happy chatter sprang up amid the family-style dining.

It was as if Antonio was waiting for everyone to finish the meal before any kind of subject was addressed. When everyone but Tony had cleaned their plates, he said, "The boys and I will clear the table, but don't anybody go anywhere. Gabriella made a wonderful dessert, and then we have an announcement."

Miguel, Jayce, and Gabe joined Luca in gathering the plates. Dante and Noah were already filling the sink and speculating over what the meeting might be about.

"Maybe it's someone's birthday," Noah said.

"Dude, it's always someone's birthday."

"Yeah, they wouldn't call a family meeting for that," Gabe said.

"Where are Ryan and Chloe?" Jayce asked.

"We're right here," Chloe said as they entered through the back door.

Dawn hadn't met Ryan yet. Luca had explained that because his eldest brother had "died" in a back draft and a very public funeral had been held for him, he and Chloe had moved to her home in Ireland soon after he had reincarnated. Now they had to wait until everyone in Boston who might recognize him passed away before they could be seen in public here.

It caused her to raise an eyebrow but only one. She had thought she was shock-proof before, but now that she'd been let in on the paranormal population, nothing much surprised her anymore. Apparently, other brothers had met with different types of disasters and found their way back to life without the whole city noticing.

Eventually, they were all sitting down again, and a scoop of gelato plus a piece of cake with whipped cream sat in front of everyone.

"Eat up," Gabriella said. "Before it melts."

She didn't have to ask twice. Everyone gobbled up dessert with enthusiasm, as if they hadn't just filled their stomachs with a big dinner.

When everyone was full and groaning, Antonio said, "Everyone satisfied?"

"And then some," Dante said, followed by a burp.

When the laughter died down, Antonio rose. "Good. Because your mother and I have an announcement. We're moving."

A beat of silence was followed by numerous voices all asking questions at once. Antonio held up his hands. "Quiet down. I'll explain." He took a deep breath. "Most of you know I've been trying to get your mother to move to the Caribbean with me after I retired from the fire department. Well, she didn't want to go until she knew all her sons were going to be all right. And by all right, she meant happily married or in a committed relationship."

"And I'm not ashamed of that," Gabriella said. "I'd have been miserable if I had to worry about any one of you."

"And apparently, we need a good woman looking after us in order for her not to worry," Jayce said, smirking.

Dawn wondered at that. Did Gabriella assume she and Luca were committed enough for her worries to be over? He was the youngest and the only son still unmarried.

As if reading her mind, Gabe said, "What about Luca? I thought you and Mom were twice as worried about him, because he decided to become a cop instead of a firefighter—and Dawn's great, but they aren't married yet."

"Well," Luca said, smiling at Dawn, "I know it's too soon in our relationship to ask her to marry me, but things are going well. I would like to ask her to come with us to Puerto Rico. I could live with Mom and Dad, but I'd rather get a place nearby—with Dawn."

Dawn's jaw dropped. He was asking her to live with him? In Puerto Rico?

Her grandmother clapped her hands over her heart. "Oh, that's wonderful! I always hoped she'd find a special young man like your Luca."

Luca gazed at Dawn expectantly. "She hasn't said yes yet...but I'll bet I know why." He rubbed her back. "Of course we want your grandma to come too."

Dawn laughed. "Oh yeah. The answer is yes. I'd love to go with all of you—as long as my grandmother comes too."

"Of course," Luca said.

"We expected nothing less," Gabriella added.

Annette's brows shot up in surprise. "Really? You talked about it?"

Please don't be stubborn, Gran. Please, please, please...

"I—I'd love to go. No more snowy winters!"

"Amen to that!" Antonio said.

"Um, can anyone else come?" Dante asked. He exchanged a quick smile with Mallory.

"Well, we won't have room in our place, because we want to downsize," Antonio said, "but I'm sure you and Mallory would want your own place anyway."

"If they haven't all been destroyed by Hurricane Maria," Jayce interjected.

"That's just it. Mallory's dad is a builder, and he was talking about possibly going down there and helping to rebuild the island. I was telling them I kind of wished I could go too. I enjoyed my shop classes and don't get much chance to build anything since we live in a brand-new condo."

"And I can work from anywhere," Mallory said. "All my design work is done online. Maybe I can get inspiration for some tropical prints and donate part of the profits for building materials."

Noah and Kizzy exchanged some kind of silent communication with their eyes. "If you go, maybe we can too," Kizzy said. She reached for Mallory's hand and gave it a squeeze. "We'd miss our best friends if we stayed here. I'm sure the island can use doctors and firefighters down there."

"And nurses," Sandra added. She looked hopeful as she gazed at Miguel.

"We should discuss it in private, but I'm not opposed to it."

She grinned and kissed his cheek. "In Miguel-speak, that means yes."

Everyone laughed, knowing the cautious nature of the third eldest brother.

"Oh my goodness!" Gabriella squealed. "If I could bring all my kids with me, the Caribbean would be my heaven on earth." Then her face fell, and she said in a somber voice, "Oh, but my grandchildren will grow up so fast, and I'll miss so many milestones."

Gabe shook his head, looking at Misty.

"I guess that headshake means you're not coming," Gabriella said with a tear in her eye.

Misty chuckled. "That's not Gabe's 'no way' headshake. That's his 'I know when I'm beat' resignation headshake."

"Gabe?" Gabriella waited, seemingly holding her breath.

"Misty's right. If the whole family is heading to the Caribbean, we may as well go too. I'll bet there's a job for a marine firefighter with experience working in Boston Harbor. If not, I have a strong builder's back. Besides, Tony would miss his Gammy and Gampy too much."

As if on cue, Tony wriggled off Gabe's lap and ran over to Gabriella. "Gammy!"

Gabriella swept him up into a hug. "Oh, my darling. You've just made me *so* happy."

"Oh, but…" Annette looked over at Dawn. "But my daughter…"

"Is in prison," Dawn said. "She can come down later and get a fresh start."

Annette smiled. "Yes. I guess she can."

"It might be the best thing for her too," Luca said. "New place and new people, with a whole new attitude."

"At this point, is anyone *not* coming with us?" Antonio asked.

Everyone laughed, but then Jayce, who'd been uncharacteristically quiet, looked at Kristine and put an arm around her. "We're both captains here, and it's what we love. If we move down there, we'd have to literally start over. Go through training all over again, then probation for however long, then work our way back up the ladder."

"You two could live here, Jayce," Antonio said. "I wanted to keep the brownstone in the family, and your little one-bedroom condo in Charlestown must be feeling pretty small with two of you in it now."

"I was supposed to take over as head of the family when you left. If there's no one in Boston but us..."

"I can do that now," Ryan said. "If I don't have to show my face in Boston, and with a wife who can transport me anywhere in the world at a moment's notice..."

Antonio leaned back in his chair and folded his hands over his expanding middle. "That's what I had intended long ago. That Ryan—our firstborn—would take over for me whenever I'm gone."

"*If* you're ever gone," Jayce said, and everyone laughed. "You're the only one who hasn't used up one of your many lives."

"I haven't," Luca said.

"Yeah, and you were the one Mom worried about. Go figure."

"Hey, you could start over, Dad," Gabe said. "Just let us have a barbeque on your head and come back as a young man."

Most of the room was laughing, but Gabriella gasped. "That's not funny, Gabe."

Antonio chuckled. "I won't waste a life just to come back looking like another one of Gabriella's sons. As it is, I have to fly around from time to time to speed up the aging process.

"No, I'm going to play the part of retired firefighter. I was thinking of starting a little wine-making business. I'm not the type to just sit around and do nothing."

"That's a great idea," Jayce said. "You'll need it to put up with a big family you can't seem to get rid of."

Kristine held up one finger. "I just thought of something. Puerto Rico has the largest tropical rain forest in the United States. You guys wouldn't even have to disguise your tail feathers down there. You'd just look like another tropical bird."

Antonio winked. "That's exactly what I was thinking and why I picked the Caribbean for retirement."

"So it looks like every one of your sons except Jayce and I are going to Puerto Rico," Ryan said. "And both of us can visit any time."

"You should still call first," Gabriella said. "We might be in the middle of…um…"

"Smashing grapes?" Luca asked.

Everyone burst out laughing, including Antonio.

If this was what Fierro family meetings were always like, Dawn figured she just might enjoy them.

"Hello there, gorgeous."

"Hi, LC."

Dawn arrived at Karma Cleaners for her usual appointment. But as soon as she walked in, it looked like a party was underway. People were milling about chatting and talking. Some were still wearing their work clothes, while others were all dolled up in fancy party clothes.

"What's going on?" Dawn glanced around the main

reception area. Tables had been set up and pastries from the bakery downstairs were laid out around a big punch bowl filled with a yummy-looking pink punch.

"Oh, we're just having a little celebration," Lynda said. She was wearing a gold-sequined minidress and sparkly gold heels. Her hair was down, looking straight and sleek and parted in the middle. "I'm glad you're here. C'mon. Let's grab a cupcake and go into my office to chat."

They strolled over to the refreshment table and perused the goodies. Dawn chose a double chocolate cupcake with chocolate ganache on top, and Lynda chose a white cupcake with buttercream icing and gold sprinkles.

"Matches my outfit." She smiled. "Okay, let's go somewhere quiet where we can chat."

They walked back to Lynda's office and sat across from each other in the overstuffed comfy chairs.

Dawn bit into her cupcake and closed her eyes in delight. "Oh. That is good."

"This one's heaven," Lynda said as she licked her finger.

"Can I take a few home with me for Luca and his family?"

"Of course, sweetie. We'll pack up a box for you."

"Thanks, LC."

Lynda nodded and placed the rest of her cupcake back on her plate. Wiping her fingers on a napkin, she took a deep breath. "I have something to tell you."

"Uh-oh. What's wrong?"

"Well, you see, it's about your karma."

"Shit."

Lynda stood up, walked over to her desk, and lifted a

file folder, then returned to her chair. She flipped open the folder, sorted through some papers, and cleared her throat. "I'm afraid we won't be needing you to come in anymore."

"What? What does that mean? Did I do something wrong? Rescuing Mandy was the right thing, wasn't it? Should I have waited for the police?"

"No. You saved her. That was the most important thing and what needed to happen."

"So having sex with Luca ruined my karma? You said sex was okay."

"I said it was your decision to make."

"So having sex with Luca ruined my karma?"

Lynda blew out a breath. "No, silly."

"No?" Dawn groaned in frustration. "But I can't think of anything else… What does that mean?"

"That means that you can have as much sex with Luca as you want. It makes no difference to your karma."

"So I'm okay?"

"I didn't say that."

"So I'm not okay?" Dawn was so agitated, she stood up and started pacing. "You know, I've been working really hard these past few weeks. Like, really hard. And yet here you are, telling me that my karma is still fucked."

"I didn't say that."

"Then what are you trying to tell me?"

"If you would just stop pacing and sit down, I will tell you everything."

Dawn flung up her hands. "Okay, okay." She plopped back down on her chair and slouched with her arms crossed over her chest. "What do you want to tell me?"

Lynda laced her fingers together, placed them on her

knees, and cleared her throat. "Dawn Forest, I hereby declare that your karma is officially clean!"

Dawn's jaw dropped. She didn't know what to say. She couldn't believe it. "Are you saying what I think you're saying?"

"I am indeed."

"You're serious."

"Yes."

Dawn stood and jumped up and down, whooping. "I can't believe it."

"Believe it, girl. You did it." Lynda stood up and danced along with her.

"My karma is clean. My karma is clean." Dawn sang and danced. Then she suddenly stopped. "Why did you lead me to think you had bad news?" She frowned, her hands going to her hips.

"I didn't. You just assumed it. I said we wouldn't be needing you to come here anymore. Maybe I should have said you won't be needing us anymore—as long as you stay on the right path."

"You are one of a kind, you know that, LC?" Dawn burst out in giggles.

"Yes, I've been told that many times." Lynda grinned.

"So what's the next step?" Dawn asked.

"The next step is you go on with your life and live happily ever after."

"But I still want to keep helping people. Using my psychic gifts."

Lynda reached for her hands. "I was hoping you would say that. In fact, I was pretty sure you would. And there's something else…"

"What?"

"Not that you have to do this or anything, but the girls and I have been talking, and we'd like to offer you a position at Karma Cleaners."

"Really? Oh, but I have something to tell you too, Lynda."

"You're moving to Puerto Rico?"

"How did you...never mind." She shook her head in disbelief. "So how am I supposed to work for Karma if I'm going to be living in PR?"

"Um, we do have offices everywhere, you know."

"Wow! But I'm supposed to be working with Luca on his PI biz."

"You can do both. I'm sure you'll find many candidates for karma cleaning with such a symbiotic situation. Oh, and one more thing."

"What's that?"

"The job comes with a salary, expense account, and three-bedroom home on the outskirts of San Juan. Plenty of room for you—and your kids." She winked.

Dawn's eyes filled with tears. "I can't thank you enough, LC. You saved my life."

"Honey, I didn't save your life. You did that all on your own. And I have to thank you. Your courage and tenacity have inspired me and everyone here. That party out there is for you, by the way." Lynda tipped her head, gesturing to the door.

"You're kidding."

"Would I kid you?"

They rose, and Lynda wrapped her in a big bear hug. "Come on. Let's go back out there. Everyone wants to congratulate you."

Lynda handed Dawn a tissue, and she wiped her

eyes. They walked arm in arm out the door and joined the fun.

Much later, Dawn lay in bed next to Luca after a particularly long session of hot sex. "I can't believe I'm a bona fide Karma Cleaner."

"I can." Luca grinned. "You're a natural. You're gonna kick butt in Puerto Rico."

She lay her head on his chest. "Are you going to miss Boston and being a cop?"

"Nope. Not for a second. Besides, most of my family is going to be living there, so it'll be just like home, except with sunshine and palm trees."

"And don't forget the noisy gatherings and your father joking and your mom cooking all the time."

"It'll be awesome."

"I know it will."

"But we can always slip away if they get on our nerves."

"Hmm…and what would we slip away to do?"

He flipped her over onto her back and proceeded to show her.

Three months later, in Puerto Rico…

Dawn dropped her keys on the console beside the front door and kicked off her sandals. Padding into the kitchen, she opened the fridge and pulled out a pitcher of iced tea. She poured herself a tall glass and took a few much-needed sips to cool down. With a sigh, she pressed the cold glass to her forehead, then opened the fridge again in search of the leftover tapas from the night before.

Two strong arms circled her waist from behind. "You're out of luck," a beloved male voice said softly.

She sighed and leaned back against the muscular chest. "Ah, the fridge bandit has struck again. I guess I'll have to get tougher on him next time."

"What do you plan on doing?"

She turned in his arms and looked into those gorgeous blue eyes that never ceased to make her heart do backflips. His eyes looked even more blue against his tan. "I'll have to think of a new punishment."

His eyebrows shot up, and a slow grin spread across his face. "Yeah?"

"Oh yeah."

"What kind of punishment?"

"Hmm…" She tapped her lips with the tip of her index finger. "This is going to take a bit of time."

"Well, we have about an hour before we have to leave."

"That should be more than enough time for what I have planned."

He leaned in and kissed her, and for a few moments, she was lost. Until her cell phone beeped. "Darn."

"Don't get that." He moved down her neck, nibbling as he went.

"I have to. It could be Gran."

"She's fine. She's at Mom and Dad's."

"I know, but she told me she was bringing her new friend, and she wanted my help picking out an outfit."

Luca sighed and stepped back. "You know, this whole living happily ever after on an island with our families isn't as carefree as I thought it would be."

Dawn grinned as she reached for her phone and answered. "Hi, Gran."

"Honey, it's down to two outfits, and I can't decide between the yellow-flowered print dress or my turquoise skirt and the white peasant blouse."

"I love that dress. I think it's a winner."

"Thanks so much, sweetie. I hope Diego likes it too."

"I'm sure he will. And I can't wait to meet him."

"Oh, he can't wait to meet everyone too. Gabriella said Antonio has a whole list of questions that he's going to grill him with."

Dawn chuckled. "If there is anything I know about the Fierro family, it's that they look after their own."

"They do indeed. But I'm sure Diego is up to the task, being a retired San Juan firefighter and all."

"I'm sure it's going to be a lively night."

Annette chuckled as they said their goodbyes.

"I don't know what Mom and Dad will do if Annette marries Diego," Luca said, picking up Dawn's glass and taking a sip. "They love having her living with them."

"Well, I've never seen Gran so happy in my life. She never had a chance really. This is completely new for her, and she's loving being courted by a gentleman. She wants to take it slow and appreciate it."

"Annette deserves all the happiness in the world." Luca wrapped his arms back around Dawn and kissed the tip of her nose. "And so do you."

"Well, I've got my knight in shining armor already. What more could I ask for?"

Annette was living with Gabriella and Antonio outside the city and had met Diego at a seniors' center in downtown San Juan. Antonio used to drive her there, but now her sweetie picked her up.

They'd been dating for the past month, and Annette was over the moon. Dawn was so happy for her grandmother. She was equally happy for her mom, Lissie, who was set for early parole. Her mom had become a model inmate and had a job lined up in Boston after she got out. She would be living in a halfway house and helping to counsel former drug addicts. Dawn was proud of her mom. She hoped that one day, Lissie could move to Puerto Rico too, but baby steps. Her mom had her own path to follow.

"I've got some news about our PI biz," Luca said.

"Oh? What's up?"

"Well, while you were working your karmic magic with your new client at Karma Cleaners, I got a phone call from the Foundation Against Human Trafficking. They want us to look into another case. A ring that's kidnapping girls from Haiti and bringing them here then to Miami."

Dawn shook her head. "That's horrible."

"I want to get these bastards."

"We will. We caught everyone who hid Mandy, didn't we?"

"We did at that."

Dawn was so proud of Luca. Since he'd decided to quit the police force and set up his own private investigation business, they'd been working with nonprofit groups who partnered with law enforcement to find missing children and women who were victims of violent crime. He was still using techniques he'd learned in college while majoring in criminal justice.

So far, between Dawn's visions and Luca's phoenix abilities, they had located five girls. It wasn't huge

money, but they didn't have to worry. Her salary from
Karma Cleaners was more than enough, and Dawn's life
couldn't be more fulfilling.

She spent half her day at the new location of Karma
Cleaners in downtown San Juan and then the evenings
working with Luca. Sometimes weekends too. But
she didn't mind. As long as they were together, she
was happy.

And if she couldn't get around to shopping or cooking, Gabriella and Annette made sure their fridge was
always stocked and they knew they were always welcome to a meal and a visit. Between those two mother
hens and Antonio's new wine-making business, the
elders were happy too.

After so many years of being alone with only her
grandmother, Dawn was lapping up all the attention
from the big family around her. She adored Luca's
family, the noisiness, the laughter, the camaraderie.
Luca shook his head at her when she told him that. But
his eyes sparkled with joy just the same.

"Tell me about your new client," Luca said, pulling
her onto their balcony and sitting down on their comfy
chaise.

She sighed and relaxed against him. She would
never get tired of the view of the Atlantic Ocean. It
truly was paradise.

Luca's brothers had been hard at work helping to
rebuild the devastated areas of the island after the hur-
ricanes. Luca and Dawn often took part in volunteer fun-
draisers and events to help the hardest-hit communities.
Luca donated his labor anytime he was free to do so.

Meanwhile, Antonio's wine-making business was

taking off, and part of the profits were donated to hurricane relief charities.

"She's struggling, but I know I can help her. Former prostitute and a single mom to the cutest boy. She's determined to change her karma. She wants to go back to school and study nursing. I'm so lucky to have Lynda helping me. She spends more time here than back in Boston."

"Lynda adores you and wants you to do well."

"I got an email from Jack and Mandy this afternoon. They're doing great in Rhode Island, and Mandy has a wonderful therapist who's helping her get over her mom's death."

"That's good…" Luca paused.

"What's wrong?" She leaned back and looked up at his pensive face.

"I'm so lucky. So lucky I met you, Dawn."

Dawn's eyes filled with tears, but she didn't care. She'd spent too many years keeping her emotions inside, and now she cried easily but laughed just as easily—and far more often.

Luca tightened his arms around her and kissed the top of her head. "You made me realize what I could do. If I hadn't met you that day in front of the Christian Science Center, who knows what would have happened?"

"You'd still be pining over Lisa and getting tased by Sergeant Asshole?"

Luca let out a mock groan. "Oh god, that would have been torture."

"Do you think your dad knows what Karma did with Butts?"

"If he knows, he didn't mention it to me. Whatever

she had planned for Butts was well deserved. I hear she can be very creative with her punishments."

From the open glass doors, they could hear a cell phone buzzing.

"Is that mine or yours?"

"Who knows? Who cares?" He grinned.

"I think we might have about half an hour before we have to get to your mom's."

"Hmm… What do you have percolating in that smart, sexy brain of yours?"

"Oh, just that I still have to punish you for eating the last of the sausage and pepper tapas."

"Oh yeah? What have you decided to do to me?"

"I'll race you to the shower and you'll find out."

"Deal."

They got up at the same time and ran, laughing, flinging off their clothes as they went. They ended up being late for dinner and had to listen to a lecture from Antonio, but they didn't mind. It was worth it.

Now for an excerpt of

I DREAM OF
DRAGONS

from Ashlyn Chase's Boston Dragons series!

THUNK.

"What the hell?" Rory picked himself up off the floor beside his bed, rubbing his sore hip. Three little men dressed in green stood by his bedroom door. One of them looked angry, and one of them was trying not to snigger. The other seemed like a neutral party with his hands in his pockets.

"Rory Arish, you're being charged with theft," the angry one said.

Rory blinked and stared at the little men. "Theft, is it? What is it I'm accused of stealin'?"

"Me gold. All of it."

Rory scratched his head. "Lucky, is it?" he asked, trying to put names to their faces.

"If you're talkin' about me name, it's Clancy. Lucky is me brother." The man with his hands in his pockets withdrew one and waved at Rory. "If you're talkin' about your day, I'd say this is the unluckiest of your whole long life."

The red-haired man who'd been trying not to laugh

moved his hand, uncovering his short, red beard. "Nobody steals from leprechauns and gets away with it—no matter how big you are."

Rory sighed. "There's been some kind of misunderstandin'. I haven't stolen anyone's gold—or anythin' else for that matter. Do you see anythin' worth stealin' here?" He spread his arms wide and swiveled, indicating the whole sparsely furnished room.

He and his sisters had moved from the crumbling castle on the cliffs to the caretakers' cottage a few years ago. The Arishes hadn't changed much, leaving the cottage about the same as when the caretakers had lived and died there.

"Move your arse, dragon," the angry one said. "March me to my gold!"

"I will not march anywhere," Rory said. "Especially when I don't know where your feckin' gold is."

Clancy balled his fists.

The gleeful one muttered, "Oh, *that* did it."

"Be quiet, Shamus," Clancy snapped. Then he focused his attention on Rory again. "Mr. Arish, I'm trying to be reasonable, but I'm not a patient man. Now, admit what you did and rectify the situation, or we'll be forced to end the treaty between our people."

Clad only in their nightgowns, Rory's sisters appeared in the doorway behind the little people. Well…behind and over them. Even at five foot five or six, the girls were easily twice the size of a leprechaun.

"What's goin' on here?" his sister Chloe mumbled as she rubbed the sleep out of her green eyes.

"Apparently I'm bein' accused of a crime I did not commit," Rory said.

His youngest sister, Shannon, piped up. "Crime? What crime?"

Clancy whirled on the girls. "Mayhaps one of you took me gold. We don't know if it was your brother or not, but it had to be the work of a dragon. Who else would have the strength to move it?"

Rory rubbed his forehead. "Now wait a minute. Me sisters didn't steal anythin' either."

Clancy pointed a finger at Rory. "Then you admit it! It was you!"

"I admit nothin'." Rory's annoyance was growing now. *Fine, wake me up. Accuse me of something I didn't do. But don't go pointin' fingers at me sisters!*

"It could have been any one of you…or all of you colludin' together. The punishment will be meted out to each and every one until somebody confesses."

"Punishment?" Chloe laughed. "I'd like to see you try."

Oh shite. That was probably the worst thing she could have said, but leave it to Chloe to poke the beast. Even though they came in pint-sized packages, leprechauns possessed powerful magic. Either Chloe didn't remember the treaty because it was signed when she was so young, or she didn't believe the leprechauns held the power to protect or expose her and her family. But how else could their castle in the cliffs have remained hidden from humans for all these centuries?

It's true that the bulk of it was built underground with entrances in the cliff's caves, but there was one turret, like a large rook on a chess board, in plain view. It was for the few humans brave enough to live near dragons, plus the royals had posted a sentry there to see anyone coming by land.

Clancy narrowed his eyes at the three of them. Finally he said, "You leave me no choice! You will march to the cliffs—now. If one of you doesn't confess to the crime before you get there, I will cast you into the ocean and ban you from ever setting foot in Ireland again! In fact, you'll be banned from all of the United Kingdom!"

"Ha!" Chloe said. "Nobody's goin' anywhere."

Moments later, dragons Rory, Shannon, and Chloe Arish bobbed on a raft just off the western shore of County Kerry, Ireland. They had been marched, against their will, to the edge of the cliff, and then magically transported to the raft. Rory, head of his clan, shook his fist at the little bastards dancing and laughing on the cliff above them, right next to his clan's, now fully exposed, ancient castle.

"You can't do this! Our people have coexisted for centuries. You're violatin' the treaty signed by our ancestors," he roared.

Shamus, the most gleeful of the three redheaded leprechauns, yelled back, "We don't know who signed it. We weren't there. Maybe the dragons forged our ancestors' signatures."

"Why would they do that?" Chloe yelled. "We were protectin' each other. Your people with your magic and our clan with our might."

"Ha! Look who's high and mighty now," Shamus called back.

"This is the same as murder!" Chloe yelled. "You know damn well this raft won't make it across the ocean. And look what you're doin' to poor sister." She pointed to Shannon, who was lying prostrate on the lashed logs, sobbing. The bastards hadn't even let her say good-bye to Finn, her intended.

Lucky elbowed Shamus. "She has a point."

"About a cryin' sister? Who cares?"

"Not that. About the murder part."

Clancy stroked his red and gray beard. "We should give them a worthy craft and enough food so they don't starve."

Shamus's delight faded fast. "You're not goin' soft on these thieves, are you? They took your gold!"

Clancy leaned in close, but Rory's superior hearing picked up what he thought was an admission of doubt.

"We didn't take your damn gold!" he shouted at the leprechauns.

"You did," Shamus insisted. "Who else but a dragon would covet our treasure?"

Rory set his hands on his hips. "Oh, I don't know... Everyone?"

Clancy finally addressed his brothers. "They should be kept alive. If we don't find the gold in their keep, we may have to question them some more."

Lucky nodded. "I agree."

Suddenly the dragons found themselves on a fishing trawler, probably large enough to make it across the sea *if* the weather was perfect the whole way.

"There. Now they have safe transport and all the fish they can catch," Clancy said.

Shamus let out a defeated sigh. "All right. I guess that covers our arses."

"Speaking of arses," Rory yelled. "What do you little shites expect us to do for money *if* we land somewhere? Are we to sleep on the docks and starve while we look for work?"

Lucky said, "Certainly not." He turned to Shamus. "There are women aboard."

Shamus rolled his eyes. "Fine."

A dozen plastic cards rained down on the dragons, bouncing off their heads.

"Ow," Chloe said. "You bastards did that on purpose." Then she picked up one of the credit cards and yelled, "Who the hell is Molly McGuire?"

Shamus shrugged. "Does it matter? She probably won't miss it for a bit."

"Surely we can have the treasure that you know belongs to us," Shannon pleaded. "All you're missin' is gold. We have jewels, antiques, silver…"

Clancy nodded and a jewelry box, a harp, and a silver tea set appeared on the deck. Suddenly the ship dropped a little lower in the water.

"There's more below," Lucky yelled.

"And what about our clothes?" Chloe called out. "Our instruments!"

Clancy tossed his hands in the air and said, "Do I have to do everythin'?"

"I'll get them," Lucky said. A moment later three small suitcases and their only means of income, the family's musical instruments, landed on the deck.

Suddenly Shannon shimmered off her nightgown, shifted into her dragon form, and flew at the cliff. Before either Rory or Chloe could scold her for changing in broad daylight, she bounced off an invisible barrier and landed in the sea, stunned.

Chloe gasped. "Shannon! Are you all right?"

A curl of steam escaped Shannon's nostril. She righted herself and flew at the cliff a second time—faster, as if speed could break through whatever magic barrier the leprechauns had created. Again she bounced off and landed in the ocean. This time her eyes were closed and her wings were limp as she floated on her back.

"You killed our sister," Rory yelled. He shimmered off his sweat pants, shifted into dragon form, and swooped down to grab his precious baby sister's limp body. After he'd returned her to the deck of the boat, he shifted back to human form and put his ear to the soft part of Shannon's scaly chest, listening for one of her two heartbeats. Rory always suspected her softer nature was a result of those two hearts. He sometimes wondered if she'd also gotten Chloe's, because his middle sister could seem a bit heartless at times.

He heard a few faint beats. *Ah, she's alive. Damn good thing too, or I'd have found some way around that barrier to toast every one of the little bastards and serve them as s'mores.*

Lucky and Clancy leaned over the cliff and appeared somewhat concerned. Shamus folded his arms and said, "If she's dead, she killed herself."

Clancy whirled on Shamus. "Shut your trap."

Shamus's back stiffened, but he didn't argue with his brother.

Shannon groaned and her eyes fluttered open. She shifted back to human form and touched her head. "Ow."

"What were you thinkin', Sister?" Chloe demanded as she rushed over with a tarp. "I get the first time, but the second? Did the first bump on the head knock the sense right out of you?"

"Finn... I need to see Finn. How will he know what happened? He'll think I've just run off and left him."

"No, he won't," Chloe said. "You two have been joined at the hip since you were sixteen. He'll know somethin' is drastically wrong."

"And that's supposed to comfort me?" Shannon moaned.

Chloe just held up the tarp while her sister shimmered back into her nightgown. Soon Shannon was bawling again.

Rory began fiddling with the controls in hopes of getting the boat started. He couldn't stand it when his sister cried. "Try to buck up, Shannon. I'll do whatever I can to get this vessel to a safe haven. From there you can call or text or whatever you want to do to him."

Chloe smirked. "I'm sure she wants to do more than that to him."

Shannon let out another wail, and Rory narrowed his eyes at his middle sibling. "You're not helpin', Chloe."

At last the engine caught and he pushed the throttle forward. They sped west. Eventually he'd figure out all the controls and possibly even hit Iceland.

———

Amber, along with the other flight attendants, boarded the plane from Iceland back to Boston.

She noticed a young red-haired woman with her adorable daughter—the resemblance couldn't be missed—seated in her first class section. She thought she heard the woman explaining to the little girl that she could have snapped her fingers and they would have been home instantly, but she didn't want the girl to think that was the normal way to get around. The little girl nodded and her big, blue eyes didn't blink, as if the explanation made perfect sense to her. It made no sense to Amber. She must have misheard.

All was going well until a bit of turbulence ruffled the plane's smooth path. Amber happened to be standing next to the mother's and daughter's seats.

The captain announced over the intercom, "Sorry, folks. We seem to be experiencing a bit of rough air."

At that moment the plane bounced dramatically, and Amber braced herself against the passenger's seat and the overhead bin. "No shit," she muttered under her breath.

The woman giggled as if she had superior senses and had heard the inappropriate comment over the engine noise.

"Please be sure your seat belts are fastened," the captain continued. "Flight attendants, return to your seats and buckle up. It's going to be a bit bumpy."

The woman seemed to be glancing at Amber a little more frequently than she'd expect—almost sizing her up.

Oh well… If she's going to lodge a complaint against me, it will take the decision to quit or not to quit out of my hands.

Amber had been flying the skies ambivalently for several years. After high school, she didn't have the money for college and didn't know what her major would be, so rather than waste her mother's hard-earned money, she'd decided to go to work. She figured as soon as she discovered her passion, she could go to college and by then she'd have a bunch of money saved up for school. Maybe it was time…

A few hours later they made a safe landing in Boston, and Amber waited to deplane after everyone else.

The redheaded woman and the adorable mini-version waited until they were the very last passengers.

Amber couldn't help being a little nervous. Did the woman want to confront her on her language? Chastise her privately? She wouldn't blame her. The little girl didn't act as if she'd heard Amber swear, but using such language was inappropriate nonetheless. Yup, it was definitely time to think about finding another job. This had to be a sign of burnout.

Ah, good. The woman walked past her and disappeared into the crowd. Amber headed for the airport bathroom.

When she entered the restroom, the redhead was washing her hands.

Damn it. She hadn't seen the woman enter, but here she was. It must be a sign. Amber would have to stop trying to avoid her and just face the consequences of her stupid remark. Or maybe the woman wasn't upset at all. Better to keep it casual and see.

"What a beautiful little girl," Amber said.

"Thank you," the woman responded, beaming. "She really is a great kid."

The little one giggled and nodded.

"Awww... What's her name?"

"Nikki," the mom said. "And I'm Brandee." She extended her clean and now dry hand to shake Amber's, so she grasped Brandee's hand for a firm handshake. Brandee held it a little longer than necessary and a smile spread slowly across her face.

What was that about?

A woman in a crisp business suit joined them and stood next to Brandee. She seemed happy to see her. It wasn't unusual for travelers to bump into people they knew at the airport, so Amber didn't think anything of it until…

"I might have a candidate for you," Brandee whispered to the businesswoman, who gave Brandee a smile.

"Do you now?"

Brandee tipped her head in Amber's direction, but she was already on her way to a stall. When she turned to close the door, she saw the woman pat Brandee on the head and say, "Good girl. I'll take it from here."

Brandee didn't seem to mind the businesswoman's condescending behavior. She simply smiled and then addressed her child. "Is it time for a diaper change, honey?" The toddler nodded.

When Amber exited the stall, Brandee and Nikki were gone and the businesswoman was washing her hands…again. *Must be a germophobe*.

She observed the flight attendant until Amber glanced at her and smiled. She was about to tell the woman to have a good day when suddenly she wasn't there. The whole restroom wasn't there! *She* wasn't there. She was surrounded by fog and couldn't see a thing. *Where the hell am I?* Suddenly the fog cleared and she was alone. What. Just. Happened?

By some miracle, Rory and his sisters made it to Iceland. They stood on the shore, shivering.

"I need a coat and a place to get out of this wind," Shannon said.

"We're *all* freezin' our arses off," Chloe snapped.

"At least the leprechauns gave us our clothes," Rory said. "Jeans and sweaters are better than your nighties."

Chloe snorted. "To be sure. That was so feckin' nice of them."

Rory's teeth chattered. "I spotted a cave off the south coast. We have our own source of heat. If the place is private, we'll be safe. But as far as coats are concerned, if either of you have a suggestion, let me know."

Chloe withdrew a credit card from her pocket. "I think Molly wants to go shopping."

"You can't!" Shannon said. "That doesn't belong to you."

"These are desperate times, Shannon," Chloe hissed out between her teeth.

"Look," Rory said. "The credit card company will reimburse Molly. I'll take Shannon to the cave I saw, and we'll get a fire going. Then I'll come looking for you. Where do you think you'll be, Chloe?"

Chloe bit out some kind of oath. "Sure. Baby our baby sister some more. That'll really help her get along in the real world."

Rory set his hands on his hips. "If we split the chores, we'll be comfortable that much sooner. We can stand here and freeze to death while we argue, or you can give me a direction so I can come find you in an hour or so."

"Fine," Chloe said. "I'm headin' northwest." She pointed a long, un-manicured finger at a building right off the dock. The place looked like a clothing store with all sorts of outerwear in the window. "What size do you wear?"

Rory rolled his eyes. "Just buy me somethin' extra large and extra warm."

"You can send Molly whatever-her-surname-is a check to cover it later," Shannon said.

Chloe laughed. "Yeah, I'll do that. I'll be sure to give the police our return address too."

Rory grabbed Shannon's wrist before he started swearing and marched off in the opposite direction.

"You don't have to drag me, Brother. I'll come willin'ly."

He sighed and let go. "Thank the gods. At least one of you can be reasoned with."

Although she had to run to keep up with his long-legged strides, she caught him. "Chloe's not really upset. It's just her way."

"Well, I'm glad you're not that way. Otherwise I'd probably be an only child by now."

Shannon laughed.

It was the first smile he'd seen from her since they'd left Ireland. He knew she hadn't accepted their lot. It was just a tiny truce until the next hissy fit. He also knew better than to bring up the name Finn Kelley or she'd begin to weep again.

How had he wound up in these circumstances? They hadn't done a thing. The leprechauns had hidden their castle from humans for centuries, and for the last several years, while the castle crumbled, they'd lived quietly in a cottage on the property far down the dead-end road, away from prying eyes. Suddenly they had been dragged from their beds and marched against their will to the castle, which was no longer hidden but standing—albeit crumbling—on the cliffs in plain sight of the ocean.

When the leprechauns demanded that the Arishes produce the gold that was missing from their coffers, Rory had thought they were daft. Apparently Clancy had discovered the loss and had convinced his cronies that the dragons' love of treasure had finally gotten the better of them.

When Rory and Shannon reached a deserted part of the coast, they found a large cave in which they could make a temporary home. Dragons weren't seafaring creatures, and he was glad to be on solid ground.

Shannon's face screwed up and tears glistened in her eyes.

Oh no. Here we go again.

"What it is, luv?" he asked, dreading the answer.

"Is this what we've come to? Livin' in some hard, dank cave? I miss our peat fire and our lovely flowered sofa. There's not a comfortable spot anywhere."

Rory patted her shoulder. "I need you to make it as homey as you can. Just start a small fire and keep it goin'. I have to fetch Chloe and show her where we are. The three of us will put our heads together and come up with a better plan soon."

Shannon's gaze dropped to her feet. Not long after, he saw shivers rack her body and a fat teardrop fall from her chin. "I hope Chloe gets us some warm boots—I mean Molly."

He thought he'd pull out every last hair on his head if he had to put up with his soggy sister much longer. "Come now. How can you start a fire if you're just goin' to put it out with tears?"

She took a few deep breaths, and he could see her trying to wrestle herself under control.

"That's a good lass. I'm sure you can warm the place a bit while I'm gone. Just don't move so Chloe and I can find you again."

"What am I supposed to keep burnin', Brother? Rock?"

Do I have to think of everything? "We'll bring some newspapers and branches back as fuel and give you a break. For now, just heat the rocks with your breath. That may produce a bit of steam, but it'll warm the air."

Shannon sighed, then took a deep breath and blew out a stream of fire aimed at the cave walls.

"Perfect. Thank you, luv. I'm off to fetch our surly sister." Before Shannon could think of anything else to complain about, he rushed out the cave's entrance and picked his way over the rocks toward town.

When Amber finally reappeared in the airport bathroom, she mumbled, "I need a vacation," and went straight home to her apartment building. She thought she must be losing her mind and just wanted to lie down—after having a much-needed drink. She ignored the sign on the elevator door. It was in small print and official looking. Probably a notice that the landlord would be spraying for bugs or something. She spied the same notice on each tenant's door as she fumbled with her keys. At last she let herself into her apartment and grabbed the notice, intending to look at it later.

Dropping her flight bags outside the kitchen, she took a mini wine bottle out of the fridge. She glanced at the notice on her way to the living room and almost dropped the bottle of Chardonnay. *An eviction notice?*

"Holy mother!"

"I'm right behind you," a woman said.

That caused Amber to whirl around and repeat herself loudly.

"I said, I'm right here!" The white-robed woman

slapped her hands over her ears. She had long, thick, white hair. Her robe was belted with a vine of ivy.

"Hey, aren't you the woman from the bathroom? Brandee's friend?"

"Sheesh. Have a seat, girlie. We need to talk."

Amber hesitated. The woman wasn't carrying a weapon, although something about her seemed ultimately threatening. As if to affirm the feeling, thunder rolled and the sky outside the window darkened. Amber stumbled backward and sat down hard on her beige linen sofa.

"That's better," the woman said. "I'm aware you don't know who I am, so I'll introduce myself. I don't have time for your disbelief, so save me the trouble and just go with it. Okay?"

Amber nodded woodenly.

"Good. The truth is, I'm Mother Nature. Those who know me call me either Goddess or Gaia. That's my title and my name. You should begin by calling me Mother Nature just to drive the point home."

Amber heard herself say, "Okaaay," in a little girl's voice.

"Here's the good news. You won't have to worry about that eviction notice. I have a job for you, and it won't matter where you live. I know you're getting disenchanted with your job as a flight attendant."

"How do you know that?"

The woman smirked. "Really? I'm Mother freakin' Nature. I know just about everything. If people were meant to fly, I'd have given them wings." She cocked her head. "Why did you become a flight attendant anyway?"

"I—uh. I wanted to see the world."

"You mean you wanted to meet a rich businessman and do a little traveling before you settled down. How's that working out for you?"

Her back went up. "He doesn't have to be rich."

"But relationships with men in general aren't working out. Right?"

She sighed. "Not so much. Every guy I get close to assumes I'm cheating when I'm out of the country and eventually finds a 'backup,' or he's just pissed because I'm not around much. And don't even get me started on the pilots."

"So, how much of the world have you actually seen?"

Amber grimaced. "Pretty much the same routes over and over again."

"So…nothing but the same foreign airports and hotels."

"You may have a point."

"Of course I have a point. I always have a point. I don't chat with mortals for my health. Speaking of my health, spreading all that noxious jet fuel so close to my ozone layer is the most harmful thing you can possibly do to me. Did you know that?"

"Um…not really. Is it?"

"Sheesh. How dumb can you be? You blow a hole in my sunscreen, and you think I won't get burned?"

"I…I don't really make those decisions."

Mother Nature—or whoever she was—rolled her eyes and sat down on the chair across from Amber. "Well, you may be able to make those decisions in the future. I want you to be my muse of air travel."

Amber's brows shot up. "Huh? You're offering me a job? As a…what?"

Mother Nature sighed. "I knew you'd have a hard time believing all of this. I gave you a trusting nature but also let you develop some healthy skepticism. Look, I don't have time for a lot of chitchat. I'm in desperate need of some modern muses. You've met one of them. Brandee is my muse of photography."

"I thought muses took care of poetry, dance, and other ancient arts."

The woman let out a groan. "Exactly. The original nine are useless in this modern age. I tried to get them to reeducate themselves in new areas, but it's been a disaster. I can't even get the muse of epic poetry to rap—or the muse of dance to crunk. And forget music videos! Technology is way beyond them, and I can't wait any longer for my muses to catch up. Your world is growing too fast. Therefore, I've begun the task of finding a few modern muses. Any questions so far?"

"Um, yeah. A few hundred…"

"Well, hold your questions for the end. I'll pair you with someone who'll have the patience to answer them. In other words, not me."

Amber wanted to throw her hands in the air and say something sarcastic, but she still wasn't sure how crazy this woman was—or *she* was, so she just waited.

"Good. Let's see now…" Gaia tapped her chin as if deep in thought. "I know. I'll pair you with Brandee since you've already met and she's the one who recommended you. That way if she doesn't answer your questions thoroughly and you screw up, it'll be all her fault."

This insulting woman was trying Amber's patience. How could she get the woman out of her apartment? Playing along with her was getting old.

"Why don't you give me Brandee's phone number? I'll give her a call sometime."

Mother Nature frowned. "You still doubt me, glitter tits?"

"What did you call me?"

"Look down."

Amber was bare to the midriff and indeed her breasts were covered in glitter. She gasped and tried to cover herself with her hands.

"Relax. I've seen them before. Heck, I made them."

Amber was struck dumb. If she protested, who knew what the woman...or goddess would do. "I—I..."

"Mother Nature" waved her hand and Amber was wearing her uniform blouse again. Then the self-proclaimed deity shouted at the ceiling. "Brandee, I need you."

To Amber's shock, the redheaded passenger from her latest flight appeared in her living room.

"Yes, Gaia. How may I be of service?"

"This is the woman you recommended for the muse of air travel, correct?"

Brandee turned to Amber and offered a friendly smile. "Yes. I liked her immediately and thought she'd fit in with the others. As you know, I can sense people's innate goodness and I'm a very good judge of character."

"Well, she needs to talk to someone like you or Bliss. One of my modern muses. She has questions, and I don't have the time or patience to answer them."

"Understood," was all Brandee said.

The woman looked relieved and smiled. "Thank you. As a reward for your help, I'll send an influential customer to visit your gallery tomorrow."

Brandee grinned. "Thanks! We're doing quite well, but I can always use more—"

"Yeah, yeah." Mother Nature disappeared into thin air and Amber let out the breath she'd been holding in a whoosh.

"Where did she go?"

Brandee shrugged. "Who knows? She likes to hang out in her office building on State Street, but she could be creating natural disasters like floods or earthquakes. You just never know with her."

"Is she really…"

"Mother freakin' Nature? Yeah, she is." Brandee chuckled. "You probably pictured someone wearing rainbows as a halo and patting kittens, didn't you?"

"Well, no, but I didn't think…"

Brandee sat next to her and lowered her voice. "You didn't expect a sarcastic crone with the patience of a gnat, am I right?"

Amber chuckled. "Well, no."

"You'll get used to her. You should meet my friend Bliss."

"She mentioned something about a person named Bliss."

"Yeah. She's rather famous among us muses, having been the only one gutsy enough to refuse Mother Nature's generous offer."

"Generous offer? I never received any offer sounding remotely generous."

"Really? Huh. I guess you didn't get that far. Gaia never expects her muses to work for nothing. She rewards us handsomely—usually with our greatest desire. But Bliss…" Brandee shook her head and sighed. "She stood up to Gaia and said no, even with a money tree growing right in the middle of her man's living room."

"Her man, huh?" Amber mumbled.

"Ah!" Brandee said. "Could that be what you want? A boyfriend?"

Amber snorted. "No. I've had plenty of boyfriends. What I'd like is a stable guy who won't cheat on me. I don't seem to be having much luck finding one of those."

Brandee set a sympathetic hand on Amber's shoulder. "We've all had our share of failed romances. If it isn't one thing, it's another, but both Bliss and I are now 'blissfully' happy, if you'll pardon the pun. So, if what you want is a wonderful, faithful man to love, marry, or live with, I'll mention that to the goddess."

"No! Oh no. Don't do that yet. I think I'm leaning more toward Bliss's reaction than yours."

Brandee raised her eyebrows. Then she smiled and seemed to relax. "You know what might be a good idea? If we include Bliss in this conversation."

"Ugh. Please don't. I can't stand any more people popping into my living room. I'm quite convinced I'm losing my mind as it is."

"Oh. Sorry. I forgot what it was like in the beginning. Of course your head is probably spinning. It's natural to doubt your own eyes and sanity. Why don't I give you my address on Beacon Hill? Let the dust settle and meet me there tomorrow. I'll ask Bliss to stop by, *if* you actually show."

"If I say I'll be there, I'll be there. Unlike some people, I can be counted on to keep my word."

Acknowledgments

I'd like to thank the following people for their law enforcement expertise and contributions to this book. (Every one of them shared a rookie prank that went into the story!)

Kristin Fili, for brainstorming the entire plot with me!

Joe Rizzuti, for answering questions pertaining to Massachusetts law enforcement and Boston specifically.

And special thanks to:

Captain Joseph Fay, Nashua, NH, Police Department.

Captain Fay made room in his Friday evening plans to take me on a ride-along and let me watch a booking and fill half a notebook with answers to my nosy questions. I think he was a little disappointed there wasn't more crime on that crisp November evening, but that just attests to the terrific job the Nashua Police are doing, deterring crime in their fair city.

Thank you all for your generosity and kindness.

I would also like to thank my beta reader Peg McChesney, editor Cat Clyne, and agent Nicole Resciniti. To paraphrase John Donne, "No man (or woman) is an island." Thank you all for your feedback, support, and encouragement.

About the Author

Ashlyn Chase describes herself as an Almond Joy bar: a little nutty, a little flaky, but basically sweet, wanting only to give her readers a satisfying story that leaves them smiling.

She holds a degree in behavioral sciences, worked as a psychiatric RN for fifteen years, and spent a few more years working for the American Red Cross. She credits her sense of humor to her former careers, since comedy helped preserve whatever was left of her sanity. She is a multipublished, award-winning author of humorous contemporary and paranormal romances, represented by the Seymour Agency.

Ashlyn lives in beautiful New Hampshire with her true-life hero husband who looks like Hugh Jackman with a salt-and-pepper dye job, and they're owned by two spoiled cats.

Ashlyn loves to hear from readers! Visit ashlynchase .com to sign up for her newsletter. She's also on Facebook (AuthorAshlynChase), Twitter (@GoddessAsh), Instagram (AshlynLaughin), and Yahoo groups (ashlynsnewbestfriends).